CLOSING TIME

A NOVEL BY

Joseph Heller

SIMON & SCHUSTER PAPERBACKS

NEW YORK   LONDON   TORONTO   SYDNEY

SIMON & SCHUSTER PAPERBACKS
ROCKEFELLER CENTER
1230 AVENUE OF THE AMERICAS
NEW YORK, NEW YORK 10020

FIRST SIMON & SCHUSTER PAPERBACKS EDITION 2004
SIMON & SCHUSTER PAPERBACKS AND COLOPHON ARE
REGISTERED TRADEMARKS OF SIMON & SCHUSTER, INC.
FOR INFORMATION REGARDING SPECIAL DISCOUNTS FOR BULK
PURCHASES, PLEASE CONTACT SIMON & SCHUSTER SPECIAL SALES AT
1-800-456-6798 OR BUSINESS@SIMONANDSCHUSTER.COM

DESIGNED BY EVE METZ
MANUFACTURED IN THE UNITED STATES OF AMERICA

13 15 17 19 20 18 16 14 12

LIBRARY OF CONGRESS CATALOGING-IN-PUBLICATION DATA
HELLER, JOSEPH.
CLOSING TIME : THE SEQUEL TO CATCH-22 / JOSEPH HELLER.
P. CM.
I. TITLE.
PS3558.E476C57   1994
813'.54—DC20   94-20604 CIP
ISBN-13: 978-0-684-74604-9
ISBN-10:   0-684-74604-9
ISBN-13: 978-0-684-80450-7 (Pbk.)
ISBN-10:   0-684-80450-6 (Pbk.)

A SIGNED FIRST EDITION OF THIS BOOK
HAS BEEN PRIVATELY PRINTED BY THE FRANKLIN LIBRARY.

BOOK
ONE

BOOK
ONE

1
Sammy

When people our age speak of the war it is not of Vietnam but of the one that broke out more than half a century ago and swept in almost all the world. It was raging more than two years before we even got into it. More than twenty million Russians, they say, had perished by the time we invaded at Normandy. The tide had already been turned at Stalingrad before we set foot on the Continent, and the Battle of Britain had already been won. Yet a million Americans were casualties of battle before it was over—three hundred thousand of us were killed in combat. Some twenty-three hundred alone died at Pearl Harbor on that single day of infamy almost half a century back—more than twenty-five hundred others were wounded—a greater number of military casualties on just that single day than the total in all but the longest, bloodiest engagements in the Pacific, more than on D day in France.

No wonder we finally went in.

Thank God for the atom bomb, I rejoiced with the rest of the civilized Western world, almost half a century ago, when I read the banner newspaper headlines and learned it had exploded. By then I was already back and out, unharmed and, as an ex-GI, much better off than before. I could go to college. I did go and even taught college for two years in Pennsylvania, then returned to New York and in a while found work as an advertising copywriter in the promotion department of *Time* magazine.

In only twenty years from now, certainly not longer, newspapers across the country will be printing photographs of their oldest local living veterans of that war who are taking part in the sparse parades on the patriotic holidays. The parades are sparse already.

I never marched. I don't think my father did either. Way, way back, when I was still a kid, crazy Henry Markowitz, an old janitor of my father's generation in the apartment house across the street, would, on Armistice Day and Memorial Day, dig out and don his antique World War I army uniform, even down to the ragged leggings of the earlier Great War, and all that day strut on the sidewalk back and forth from the Norton's Point trolley tracks on Railroad Avenue to the candy store and soda fountain at the corner of Surf Avenue, which was nearer the ocean. Showing off, old Henry Markowitz—like my father back then, old Henry Markowitz probably was not much past forty—would bark commands out till hoarse to the tired women trudging home on thick legs to their small apartments carrying brown bags from the grocery or butcher, who paid him no mind. His two embarrassed daughters ignored him too, little girls, the younger my own age, the other a year or so older. He was shell-shocked, some said, but I do not think that was true. I do not think we even knew what shell-shocked meant.

There were no elevators then in our brick apartment houses, which were three and four stories high, and for the aging and the elderly, climbing steps, going home, could be hell. In the cellars you'd find coal, delivered by truck and spilled noisily by gravity down a metal chute; you'd find a furnace and boiler, and also a janitor, who might live in the building or not and whom, in intimidation more than honor, we always spoke of respectfully by his surname with the title "Mister," because he kept watch for the landlord, of whom almost all of us then, as some of us now, were always at least a little bit in fear. Just one easy mile away was the celebrated Coney Island amusement area with its gaudy lightbulbs in the hundreds of thousands and the games and rides and food stands. Luna Park was a big and famous attraction then, and so was the Steeplechase ("Steeplechase—the Funny Place") Park of a Mr. George C. Tilyou, who had passed away long before and of whom no one knew much. Bold on every front of Steeplechase was the unforgettable trademark, a striking, garish picture in cartoon form of the grotesque, pink, flat, grinning face of a subtly idiotic man, practically on fire with a satanic hilarity and showing, incredibly, in one artless plane, a mouth sometimes almost a city block wide and an impossible and startling number of immense teeth. The attendants wore red jackets and green jockey caps and many smelled of whiskey. Tilyou had lived on Surf Avenue in his

own private house, a substantial wooden structure with a walkway to the stoop from a short flight of stone steps that descended
right to the margin of the sidewalk and appeared to be sinking. By
the time I was old enough to walk past on my way to the public
library, subway station, or Saturday movie matinee, his family
name, which had been set in concrete on the vertical face of the
lowest step, was already sloping out of kilter and submerged more
than halfway into the ground. In my own neighborhood, the installation of oil burners, with the excavations into the pavement
for pipes and fuel tanks, was unfailingly a neighborhood event, a
sign of progress.

In those twenty more years we will all look pretty bad in the
newspaper pictures and television clips, kind of strange, like people in a different world, ancient and doddering, balding, seeming
perhaps a little bit idiotic, shrunken, with toothless smiles in collapsed, wrinkled cheeks. People I know are already dying and
others I've known are already dead. We don't look that beautiful
now. We wear glasses and are growing hard of hearing, we sometimes talk too much, repeat ourselves, things grow on us, even the
most minor bruises take longer to heal and leave telltale traces.

And soon after that there will be no more of us left.

Only records and mementos for others, and the images they
chance to evoke. Someday one of the children—I adopted them
legally, with their consent, of course—or one of my grown grandchildren may happen upon my gunner's wings or Air Medal, my
shoulder patch of sergeant's stripes, or that boyish snapshot of me
—little Sammy Singer, the best speller of his age in Coney Island
and always near the top of his grade in arithmetic, elementary
algebra, and plane geometry—in my fleecy winter flight jacket and
my parachute harness, taken overseas close to fifty years back on
the island of Pianosa off the western shore of Italy. We are sitting
with smiles for the camera near a plane in early daylight on a low
stack of unfused thousand-pound bombs, waiting for the signal to
start up for another mission, with our bombardier for that day, a
captain, I remember, looking on at us from the background. He
was a rambunctious and impulsive Armenian, often a little bit
frightening, unable to learn how to navigate in the accelerated
course thrown at him unexpectedly in operational training at the
air base in Columbia, South Carolina, where a group of us had
been brought together as a temporary crew to train for combat
and fly a plane overseas into a theater of war. The pilot was a

sober Texan named Appleby, who was very methodical and very good, God bless him, and the two were very quickly not getting along. My feelings lay with Yossarian, who was humorous and quick, a bit wild but, like me, a big-city boy, who would rather die than be killed, he said only half jokingly one time near the end, and had made up his mind to live forever, or at least die trying. I could identify with that. From him I learned to say no. When they offered me another stripe as a promotion and another cluster to my Air Medal to fly ten more missions, I turned them down and they sent me home. I kept all the way out of his disagreements with Appleby, because I was timid, short, an enlisted man, and a Jew. It was my nature then always to make sure of my ground with new people before expressing myself, although in principle at least, if not always with the confidence I longed for, I thought myself the equal of all the others, the officers too, even of that big, outspoken Armenian bombardier who kept joking crazily that he was really an Assyrian and already practically extinct. I was better read than all of them, I saw, and the best speller too, and smart enough, certainly, never to stress those points.

Inevitably, Yossarian got lost on every one of the night missions we flew in our operational training flights over South Carolina and Georgia. It became a joke. From the other enlisted crewmen I met in the barracks and mess hall, I learned that all of their bombardiers turned navigators got lost on all of their night training flights too, and that became another joke. The third officer in our crew was a shy copilot named Kraft, who, promoted to pilot overseas, was shot down by flak on a mission over Ferrara in northern Italy when his flight went over the bridge there in a second pass and was killed. Yossarian, the lead bombardier, who'd failed to drop the first time, got a medal for that one for going round the second time when he saw the others had missed and the bridge there was still undamaged. On those navigational training missions in South Carolina, Appleby would find the way back for us safely with his radio compass. One black night we were lost and had no radio compass for more than an hour. There was electrical interference from storms nearby, and to this day I clearly hear Yossarian's voice on the intercom, saying:

"I see the bank of a river down there. Turn left and cross it and I'll pick up a landmark on the other side."

The bank of that river turned out to be the shore of the Atlantic Ocean, and we were on our way to Africa. Appleby lost patience once more and took over after another half hour, and when he finally pieced together the radio signals to bring us back to our field, there was only enough fuel left to carry us from the landing strip to our plane stand. The engines died before they could be cut.

We had all nearly been killed.

That did not sink in until early middle age, and after that when I related the anecdote, it was not just for the laughs.

In that photograph with me is a buddy, Bill Knight, the top turret gunner that day, who was about two years older than I and already married, with a baby child he had seen but a week, and a skinny kid my own age named Howard Snowden, a waist gunner and radioman from somewhere in Alabama, who would be killed on a mission to Avignon about one month later and died slowly, moaning in pain and whimpering he was cold. We are twenty years old and look like children who are only twenty years old. Howie Snowden was the first dead human I had ever seen and the only dead human I've laid eyes on since outside a mortuary. My wife died at night and was already gone from the room by the time I arrived at the hospital to conclude the paperwork and begin the arrangements for the burial. She went the way the oncologist said she would, almost to the day. There was sickness but seldom much pain, and we like to think she was spared that pain because she was always a very good person, at least to me, and to the children, generally cheerful and bighearted. If angry, it was only with her first husband, and only at times, particularly because he often had not enough money for child support but enough for new girlfriends and enough to marry again a couple more times. I was lucky with dead men, said Lew right after the war, a friend since childhood who was taken prisoner as an infantryman and had seen hundreds of dead people in Europe before he was shipped back home, seen Americans and Germans, and scores of German civilians in Dresden when he was sent back in to help clean up after the British firebombing I learned about first from him, an air raid that had killed just about everyone else in the city but these prisoners of war and their guards and which I did not know about and would not immediately believe.

"Above a hundred thousand? You must be crazy, Lew. That's more than Hiroshima and the atom bomb."

I looked it up and admitted he was right.

But that was almost fifty years ago. No wonder our progeny are not much interested in World War II. Hardly any were born then. They'd be around fifty if they were.

But maybe someday, in a future I can't try to measure, one of the children or grandchildren will happen upon that box or a drawer with my gunner's wings, Air Medal, sergeant's stripes, and wartime photograph inside and perhaps be stimulated to reflect with poignancy on some incidents of a family nature that once took place between us, or which never did and should have. Like me with my father's gas mask from World War I.

I wonder what became of it. I loved that gas mask as a toy when small and I would play with it secretly when he was at work in the city cutting shapes from fabric from patterns for children's dresses. I have his photograph as a soldier too. After I read, while still in elementary school, a biography of the German World War I aerial ace Baron Manfred von Richthofen, I wished for a while to grow up to be a fighter pilot and to duel with him daily in single combat over trenches in France and shoot him down again every time. He was my hero, and I dreamed of shooting him down. Soon after the war, my war, my father died and they called it cancer. He enjoyed cigars. He bought them in the small neighborhood shop around the corner on Surf Avenue, where a contented Mr. Levinson sat with his smile at a worktable with knives and tobacco leaves and marked out and rolled his cigars by hand, while Mrs. Levinson, a tranquil kind of pygmy of a woman with dark hair and freckles, sold bathing caps, earplugs, swimming tubes, and pails and shovels and other small trifles for the sand on the beach just one block away. They were childless.

Everyone worked. As a kid I hawked newspapers for a while through the streets and boardwalk bars. In summer our sisters sold frozen custard at the stands on the boardwalk, root beer. Davey Goldsmith sold hot dogs. On the beach unlicensed peddlers battled like Spartans with dry-ice vapors misting from cumbersome cartons toted in sun-browned arms to dispense for a nickel all of their frozen bars and Dixie cups before they could be nabbed by policemen pursuing them on soft sand through onlookers in bathing suits rooting with all their hearts for them to make good their flight. Many of these fleet-footed older young boys working so perilously were people I knew.

From our apartment we could always hear from the ocean the breaking of waves and the gong from the bell buoy (we called it the "bellboy," and that still sounds right to me). At times of unusual quiet in the early or late afternoon, we could even hear very slightly the indistinct, ghostlike music of our closest merry-go-round, the exotic calliope of the tremendous carousel on the boardwalk with its turning ring of steeds of gold the color of caramels and painted strokes of shiny black and showy tints of blue and pink of other candies, like jelly beans, licorice, and gumdrops—where did those magnificent gliding horses come from? was there a corporation somewhere that manufactured just horses for carousels? was there big money in that?—almost half a mile away. No one was rich.

2

The Little Prick

The new President was coming into office legally with the resignation of his predecessor in a vexation of spiritual fatigue resulting from the need to explain continually why he had chosen such a person as his vice presidential running mate to begin with.

"Why did you pick him?" his closest friend, the secretary of state, felt compelled to keep inquiring. "Tell at least me. Your secret is safe."

"There was no secret!" the nation's chief executive responded pleadingly in his own defense. "There was nothing underhanded, no sneaky reason. I was simply exercising my best judgment. I give you my word, there was no criminal intent."

"That's what's so terrifying."

3

Mr. Yossarian

In the middle of his second week in the hospital, Yossarian dreamed of his mother, and he knew again that he was going to die. The doctors were upset when he gave them the news.

"We can't find anything wrong," they told him.

"Keep looking," he instructed.

"You're in perfect health."

"Just wait," he advised.

Yossarian was back in the hospital for observation, having retreated there once more beneath another neurotic barrage of confusing physical symptoms to which he had become increasingly susceptible since finding himself dwelling alone again for just the second time in his life, and which seemed, one by one, to dissipate like vapor as soon as he described or was tested for each. Just a few months before, he had cured himself of an incurable case of sciatica merely by telephoning one of his physicians to complain of his incurable case of sciatica. He could not learn to live alone. He could not make a bed. He would sooner starve than cook.

This time he had gone bolting back in, so to speak, with a morbid vision of a different morbid vision shortly after hearing that the President, whom he did not like, was going to resign and that the Vice President, whom he did not like even more, would certainly succeed him; and shortly after finding out, inadvertently, that Milo Minderbinder, with whom he too now had been unavoidably and inescapably linked for something like twenty-five years, was expanding beyond surplus stale commodities like old chocolate and vintage Egyptian cotton into military equipment, with plans for a warplane of his own that he intended to sell to

the government: to any government, of course, that could afford
to buy.

There were countries in Europe that could afford to buy, and in
Asia and the Mideast too.

The vision of the morbid vision he had experienced was of a
seizure or a stroke and had set him reminiscing again about dura-
ble old Gustav Aschenbach alone on his mythical strand of Mediterranean beach and his immortal death in Venice, worn out at
fifty in a city with a plague nobody wished to talk about. In Naples
far back, when assembled in line for the troopship sailing him
home after he'd flown seventy missions and survived, he'd found
himself behind an older soldier named Schweik and a man born
Krautheimer who had changed his name to Joseph Kaye to blend
more securely into his culture, and his name, like Schweik's, had
meant not much to him then.

Given a choice, Yossarian still preferred to live. He ate no eggs
and, though he had no headache, swallowed his baby aspirin every
other day.

He had no doubt he had lots to worry about. His parents were
dead, and so were all his uncles and aunts.

A prick in the White House? It would not be the first time.
Another oil tanker had broken up. There was radiation. Garbage.
Pesticides, toxic waste, and free enterprise. There were enemies of
abortion who wished to inflict the death penalty on everyone who
was not pro-life. There was mediocrity in government, and self-
interest too. There was trouble in Israel. These were not mere
delusions. He was not making them up. Soon they would be clon-
ing human embryos for sale, fun, and replacement parts. Men
earned millions producing nothing more substantial than changes
in ownership. The cold war was over and there was still no peace
on earth. Nothing made sense and neither did everything else.
People did things without knowing why and then tried to find out.

When bored in his hospital room, Yossarian played with such
high-minded thoughts like a daydreaming youth with his genitals.

At least once each weekday morning they came barging in
around him, his doctor, Leon Shumacher, and his brisk and serious entourage of burgeoning young physicians, accompanied by
the lively, attractive floor nurse with the pretty face and the magnificent ass who was openly drawn to Yossarian, despite his years,
and whom he was slyly enticing to develop a benign crush on him,
despite her youthfulness. She was a tall woman with impressive
hips who remembered Pearl Bailey but not Pearl Harbor, which

put her age somewhere between thirty-five and sixty, the very best stage, Yossarian believed, for a woman, provided, of course, she still had her health. Yossarian possessed but a hazy idea of what she really was like; yet he unscrupulously exploited every chance to help pass the time enjoyably with her for the several peaceful weeks he was resolved to remain in the hospital to rest up and put his outlook together while the great nations of the world restabilized themselves into another new world order for good and forever once more.

He'd brought his radio and almost always had some Bach or very good chamber, piano, or other choral music on one FM station or another. There were too many disruptions for abiding attention to opera, especially Wagner. It was a good room this time, he was pleased to conclude, with unobjectionable neighbors who were not offensively ill, and it was the attractive floor nurse, in response to his baiting, modestly laughing and with a flounce and a flush of hauteur, who made the defiant boast that the ass she had was magnificent.

Yossarian could see no reason to disagree.

By the middle of the first week he was flirting with her with all his might. Dr. Leon Shumacher did not always look kindly upon this salacious frivolity.

"It's bad enough I let you in here. I suppose we both ought to feel ashamed, you in this room when you aren't sick—"

"Who says I'm not?"

"—and so many people outside on the streets."

"Will you let one in here if I agree to leave?"

"Will you pay the bills?"

Yossarian preferred not to.

A great man with angiograms had confirmed to him soberly that he did not need one, a neurologist reported with equal gloom that there was nothing the matter with his brain. Leon Shumacher again was displaying him pridefully as a rare specimen his pupils would not have opportunity to come upon often in their medical practice, a man of sixty-eight without symptoms of any disease, not even hypochondria.

Late afternoons or sometimes early in the evening, Leon would drop by just to chat awhile in singsong sorrow about his long hours, ghoulish working conditions, and unjustly low earnings in tactless, egocentric fashion to a man they both knew was soon going to die.

He was not considerate.

The name of this nurse was Melissa MacIntosh, and, like all good women to a sophisticated man with a predilection to romanticize, she seemed too good to be true.

By the beginning of his second week she was allowing him to caress with his fingertips the border of lace at the bottom of her slip when she stood or sat beside his bed or chair while she hung around and talked and flirted back by allowing him to advance in his flirting. Pink with discomfort and enlivened by mischief, she neither consented nor prohibited when he toyed with her filmy undergarment, but she was not at ease. She was in terror someone would surprise them in this impermissible intimacy. He was praying somebody would. He concealed from Nurse MacIntosh all the subtle signals of his budding erections. He did not want her to get the idea that his intentions were serious. She was lucky to have him, she agreed when he said so. He was less trouble than the other men and women in the private and semiprivate rooms on the same floor. And he was more intriguing to her, he saw—and therefore more seductive, he understood, and maybe she did not —than all of the few men she was seeing outside the hospital and even the one or two men she had been seeing exclusively, almost exclusively, for a number of years. She had never been married, not even once or twice. Yossarian was so little trouble that he was no trouble at all, and she and the other floor nurses had little more to do for him than look into his room each shift just to make certain he wasn't dead yet and needed nothing done to keep him alive.

"Is everything all right?" each one would inquire.

"Everything but my health," he sighed in response.

"You're in perfect health."

That was the trouble, he took the trouble to explain. It meant he had to get worse.

"It's no joke," he joked when they laughed.

She wore a black slip in one day after he'd begged her to switch, affecting aesthetic longing. Often when he wanted her there he found himself in dire need of something to need. When he pressed his call signal, another nurse might respond.

"Send in my Melissa," he would command.

The others would cooperate. He suffered no nursing shortage. He was in good health, the doctors restated daily, and this time, he was concluding in morose disappointment, with the sense he was being cheated, they appeared to be right.

His appetite and digestion were good. His auditory and spinal apparatus had been CAT-scanned. His sinuses were clear and there was no evidence anywhere of arthritis, bursitis, angina, or neuritis. He was even without a postnasal drip. His blood pressure was the envy of every doctor who saw him. He gave urine and they took it. His cholesterol was low, his hemoglobin was high, his sedimentation rate was a thing of beauty, and his blood nitrogen was ideal. They pronounced him a perfect human being. He thought his first wife and his second, from whom he had now been separated a year, might have some demurrers.

There was a champion cardiologist who found no fault with him, a pathologist for his pathos, who found no cause for concern either, an enterprising gastroenterologist who ran back to the room for a second opinion from Yossarian on some creative investment strategies he was considering in Arizona real estate, and a psychologist for his psyche, in whom Yossarian was left in the last resort to confide.

"And what about these periodic periods of anomie and fatigue and disinterest and depression?" Yossarian rushed on in a whirl-wind of whispers. "I find myself detached from listening to things that other people take seriously. I'm tired of information I can't use. I wish the daily newspapers were smaller and came out weekly. I'm not interested anymore in all that's going on in the world. Comedians don't make me laugh and long stories drive me wild. Is it me or old age? Or is the planet really turning irrelevant? TV news is degenerate. Everyone everywhere is glib. My enthusiasms are exhausted. Do I really feel this healthy now or am I just imagining I do? I even have this full head of hair. Doc, I've got to have the truth. Is my depression mental?"

"It isn't depression and you're not exhausted."

In due course, the psychologist conferred with the chief of psychiatry, who consulted with all the other medical men, and they concluded with one voice that there was nothing psychosomatic about the excellent health he was enjoying and that the hair on his head was genuine too.

"Although," added the chief psychiatrist, with a clearing of throat, "I am honor bound to flag you as a very good candidate for late-life depression."

"Late-life depression?" Yossarian savored the term. "About when would that be?"

"About now. What do you do that you really enjoy?"

"Not much, I'm afraid. I run after women, but not too hard. I make more money than I need."

"Do you enjoy that?"

"No. I've got no ambition, and there's not much left I want to get done."

"No golf, bridge, tennis? Art or antique collecting?"

"That's all out of the question."

"The prognosis is not good."

"I've always known that."

"The way it looks to us now, Mr. Yossarian," said the chief medical director, speaking for the whole institution, with Leon Shumacher's head, three quarters bald, hanging over his shoulder, "you might live forever."

He had nothing to worry about, it seemed, but inflation and deflation, higher interest rates and lower interest rates, the budget deficit, the threat of war and the dangers of peace, the unfavorable balance of trade and a favorable balance of trade, the new President and the old chaplain, and a stronger dollar and a weaker dollar, along with friction, entropy, radiation, and gravity.

But he worried too about his new pal Nurse Melissa MacIntosh, because she had no money saved. Her parents had none either, and if she lived long enough, she would have to live on only her Social Security benefits and a pittance of a retirement pension from the hospital, provided she continued working there for the next twenty or three hundred years, which seemed out of the question, unless she met and married before then some fine gentleman of means who was as appealing to her then as Yossarian was to her now, which seemed to him entirely out of the question also. Few men could talk dirty to her so charmingly. More than once he contemplated her with a pang: she was too innocent to abandon to the heartless dynamics of financial circumstance, too sweet, unsuspecting, and unselfish.

"What you absolutely must do," he said one day, after she had begged him to advise whether she and her roommate should open individual retirement accounts—Yossarian advised that he could not see what fucking practical use an individual retirement account was going to be in the long run to anybody but the banks soliciting them—"is marry someone like me now, a man with some money saved who knows something about insurance policies and legacies and has been married only one time before."

"Would you be too old for me?" she asked in a fright.

"You would be too young for me. Do it soon, do it today. Even a doctor might work. Before you know it you'll be as old as I am and you won't have a thing."

He worried too about the reckless sentimentality of extending concern to a person who needed it.

That was not the American way.

The last thing he needed was another dependent. Or two, for she spoke with pride of an eye-catching, fun-loving roommate in her cramped apartment, a woman named Angela Moore who was taller than she and freer, a natural-blonde Australian with brighter-blonde hair and a larger bosom in stiletto heels and white lipstick and white eye makeup who worked as sales representative for a novelty manufacturer to whom she submitted ribald ideas for new products that rendered tongue-tied and incredulous the two elderly Jewish family men who owned the company as partners and made them blush. She liked the effect she knew she made in the costly midtown bars to which she often went after work to meet the convivial business executives to go dancing with after dinner and then discard without pity at the downstairs doorway of the apartment house when her evening was ended. She hardly ever met any she liked enough to want to stay longer with because she hardly ever let herself drink enough to get drunk. The private phone number she gave out was of the city morgue, Melissa MacIntosh related to him in such joyful praise of her confident and exuberant conduct that Yossarian knew he would fall in love with this woman at very first sight provided he never laid eyes on her, and would remain deeply in love until he saw her the second time. But the tall blonde somewhere near forty with the white makeup and black stockings with climbing serpentine patterns had no rich parents or money saved either, and Yossarian asked himself:

What was wrong with this lousy earth anyway?

It seemed to him reasonable that everyone toward whom he bore no grudge should have enough money assured to face a future without fear, and he hung his head in his noble reverie of compassion and wanted to take this outstanding, full-bosomed waif of a roommate into his arms to dry her tears and assuage all her anxieties and unzip her dress as he stroked her backside.

That would really be something for the private detectives who'd been following him to write home about, wouldn't it? The first private eye—he took for granted the eye was private—had trailed him right into the hospital during visiting hours and come down immediately with a serious staphylococcus infection that confined him to bed with a poisoning of the blood in a different wing of the hospital with three former visitors to other patients in the hospital who had also come down with serious staphylococcus infections and who, for all Yossarian knew, might be private detectives also. Yossarian could have told all four of them that a hospital was a dangerous place. People died there. A man from Belgium checked in one day and had his throat cut. A private detective dispatched to replace the first was laid low in a day by salmonella food poisoning from an egg salad sandwich eaten in the hospital cafeteria and was now bedridden also and recuperating slowly. Yossarian considered sending flowers. Instead, he signed the name Albert T. Tappman on the get-well card he sent to each. Albert T. Tappman was the name of the chaplain of his old army bomber group, and he wrote that calling down too and wondered what the recipients of these get-well cards thought upon receiving them and where the chaplain had been taken and whether he was being intimidated, abused, starved, or tortured. A day after that he sent second get-well cards to both private detectives and signed them with the name Washington Irving. And the day after that he mailed two more cards, and these he signed Irving Washington.

The second private detective was succeeded by two more, who appeared to be strangers to each other, one of whom seemed as mysteriously curious about investigating all the others as in keeping track of Yossarian.

He wondered what they hoped to find out about him that he would not be willing to tell them outright. If they wanted adultery he would give them adultery, and he began to grow so troubled about Melissa MacIntosh's good heart and precarious economic future that he began to worry about his own future as well and decided to demand the oncologist back for some tip-top guarantees about a major killer and to hear him discourse further perhaps on the supremacy of biology in human activities and the tyranny of the genes in regulating societies and history.

"You're crazy," said Leon.

"Then get me the psychiatrist too."

"You don't have cancer. Why do you want him?"

"To do him a good deed, dope. Don't you believe in good deeds? The poor little fuck is just about the gloomiest bastard I've ever laid eyes on. How many patients do you think he sees in a week to whom he can bring good news? That guy's disasters are among the few around me I might be able to avert."

"They aren't mine," said the joyless oncologist, upon whose small features a foreboding aspect seemed to have settled as naturally as the blackness of night and the gray skies of winter. "You'd be surprised, though, how many people come to believe they really are my fault. Even colleagues don't like me. Not many people want to talk to me. It may be the reason I'm quiet. I don't get enough practice."

"I like that spirit," said Yossarian, who could not see that he had much. "Does it buck you up to know that sooner or later you are likely to play an important role in my life?"

"Only a little." His name was Dennis Teemer. "Where would you want me to begin?"

"Wherever you want to that is without pain or discomfort," Yossarian answered cheerily.

"You haven't a symptom anywhere that might suggest closer investigation."

"Why must we wait for symptoms?" queried Yossarian, talking down to his specialist. "Is it not conceivable that since we concluded our last explorations something may have originated that is blooming away hardily even as the two of us sit here procrastinating complacently?"

Dennis Teemer went along, with a shimmer of animation. "I guess I have more fun with you than I do with most of my other patients, don't I?"

"I told Leon that."

"But that may be because you're not really my patient," said Dr. Teemer. "What you conjecture is conceivable, of course, Mr. Yossarian. But it is no more likely to be happening to you than to anybody else."

"And what difference does that make to me?" countered Yossarian. "It is not much solace to know we all are susceptible. Leon thinks I'll feel better knowing I'm no worse off than he is. Let's get started."

"Suppose we begin with another chest X ray?"

"God, no!" cried Yossarian in mock alarm. "That might just get one started! You know how I feel about X rays and asbestos."

"And tobacco too. Should I give you a statistic I think you'll relish? Did you know that more Americans die each year of diseases related to smoking than were killed in all of the years of World War II?"

"Yes."

"Then I suppose we might as well go ahead. Should I hammer your knee to test your reflexes?"

"For what?"

"For free."

"Can't we at least do a biopsy?"

"Of what?"

"Of anything that's accessible and simple."

"If you will find that reassuring."

"I will sleep easier."

"We can scrape another mole or another one of your liver spots. Or should we test the prostate again? The prostate is not uncommon."

"Mine is unique," Yossarian disagreed. "It's the only one that's mine. Let's do the mole. Shumacher has a prostate my age. Let me know when you find something wrong with his."

"I can tell you now," said Yossarian's favorite oncologist, "that it will give me great pleasure to inform you that the results are negative."

"I can tell you now," said Yossarian, "that I will be happy to hear it."

Yossarian yearned to go deeper with this depressed man into the depressing nature of the pathologies in the depressing world of his work and the depressing nature of the universe in which they had each been successful in surviving thus far and which was growing more unreliable daily—there were holes in the ozone, they were running out of room for the disposal of garbage, burn the garbage and you contaminate the air, they were running out of air—but he was afraid the doctor would find that conversation depressing.

All of this cost money, of course.

"Of course," said Yossarian.

"Where is it coming from?" Leon Shumacher wondered out loud, with a palpable snarl of envy.

"I'm old enough for Medicare now."

"Medicare won't cover a fraction of this."

"And the rest is coming from a terrific plan I have."

"I wish I had a plan like that," Leon sulked.

It came, explained Yossarian, from the company for which he

worked, where he was still on the books in a semi-executive capacity as a semi-retired semi-consultant and could remain for a lifetime provided he never tried to get much done.

"I wish I had a job like that. What the hell does it mean?" Leon mimicked in sneering derision: "Yossarian, John. Occupation: semi-retired semi-consultant. What the hell are our epidemiologists supposed to make of that one?"

"It's been another one of my careers. I work part of the time for all of my fee and no one listens to more than half the things I say. I would call that a semi-retired semi-consultant, wouldn't you? The company pays for everything. We are as large as Harold Strangelove Associates and almost as lovable. We are M & M Enterprises & Associates. I am one of the associates. The other people are enterprising. I associate, they enterprise."

"What do they really do?"

"Whatever makes money and isn't dishonestly criminal, I suppose," Yossarian answered.

"Is one word of this true?"

"I have no way of knowing. They can lie to me as well as to everyone else. We keep secrets from each other. I'm not making it up. You can check. Tie me back up to that heart machine and see if it skips a beat when I tell a lie."

"Will it do that?" Leon asked with surprise.

"I don't see why it wouldn't."

"What do you do there?"

"I object."

"Don't get so touchy."

"I'm answering your question," Yossarian informed him pleasantly. "I object to matters that are not up to my ethical standards. Sometimes I work very hard at objecting. Then they go ahead or don't. I am the conscience of the company, a moral presence, and that's another one of the things I've been doing since I dropped by there more than twenty years ago for illegal help in keeping my children out of the Vietnam War. How'd you keep yours out?"

"Medical school. Of course, they both switched to business administration as soon as the danger was past. By the way, my grapevine tells me you still seem to be having a pretty hot time with one of our favorite floor nurses."

"Better than I'm having with you and your associates."

"She's a very nice girl and a very good nurse."

"I think I've noticed."

"Attractive too."

"I've seen that also."

"We have a number of very fine specialists here who tell me frankly they'd like to get into her pants."

"That's crude, Leon, really crude, and you ought to be ashamed," Yossarian rebuked him with disgust. "It's a most obscene way of saying you'd all like to fuck her."

Leon was sheepish and Yossarian manipulated this momentary loss of self-possession into a favor involving a No Visitors sign outside the door, which was in place before the next one came by to disturb him.

The knock was so diffident that Yossarian hoped for an instant the chaplain was back as a free man from wherever it was that he was being lawfully detained unlawfully. Yossarian was out of ideas to aid him and just about helpless there too.

But it was only Michael, his youngest son, the underachiever among four adult children in what used to be a family. In addition to Michael there were his daughter, Gillian, a judge in a very low court; Julian, his eldest, another overachiever; and Adrian, who was average and content and was disregarded by the others because he was only average. Michael, unmarried, unsettled, unemployed, and unobjectionable, had stopped by to see what he was doing in the hospital still again and to confess that he was thinking of dropping out of law school because he found the work there no more stimulating than the medical school, business school, art school, graduate school of architecture, and several other graduate schools of assorted character he had been dropping out of after brief trials for as long now, it seemed, as anyone wanted to remember.

"Oh, shit," mourned Yossarian. "I keep pulling strings to get you in, and you keep dropping out."

"I can't help it," Michael said with discouragement. "The more I find out about the practice of law, the more I'm surprised that it isn't illegal."

"That's one of the reasons I gave that up too. How old are you now?"

"I'm not far from forty."

"You still have time."

"I'm not sure if you're joking or not."

"Neither am I," Yossarian told him. "But if you can delay the decision of what you want to do with your life until you're old enough to retire, you will never have to make it."

"I still can't tell if you're joking."

"I'm still not always sure either," Yossarian answered. "Sometimes I mean what I say and don't mean it at the same time. Tell me, my apple of my eye, do you think in my checkered history I ever really wanted to do any of the work I found myself doing?"

"Not even the film scripts?"

"Not really and not for long. That was make-believe and didn't last, and I wasn't that crazy about the finished products there either. Do you think I *wanted* to go into advertising, or Wall Street, or ever get busy with things like land development or puts and calls? Whoever starts out with a dream to succeed in public relations?"

"Did you really once work for Noodles Cook?"

"Noodles Cook worked for me. Soon after college. Do you think we really *wanted* to write political speeches, Noodles Cook and I? We wanted to write plays and be published in *The New Yorker*. Whoever has much choice? We take the best we can get, Michael, not what enraptures us. Even the Prince of Wales."

"That's a hell of a way to live, Dad, isn't it?"

"It's the way we have to."

Michael was silent a minute. "I got scared when I saw that No Visitors sign on your door," he confessed in a mild tone of injury. "Who the hell put it up? I began to think you might really be sick."

"It's my idea of a joke," mumbled Yossarian, who had added to the sign with a brush-point pen the notice that violators would be shot. "It helps keep people out. They just keep popping in all day long without even telephoning. They don't seem to realize that lying around in a hospital all day can be pretty demanding work."

"You never answer your telephone anyway. I bet you're the only patient here with an answering machine. How much longer are you going to stay?"

"Is the mayor still the mayor? The cardinal still the cardinal? Is that prick still in office?"

"What prick?"

"Whatever prick *is* in office. I want all pricks out."

"You can't stay here that long!" cried Michael. "What the hell are you doing here anyway? You had your annual workup only a couple of months ago. Everyone thinks you're crazy."

"I object. Who does?"

"I do."

"You're crazy."

"We all do."

"I object again. You're all crazy."

"Julian says you could have taken over the whole company a long time ago if you had any ambition and brains."

"He's crazy too. Michael, this time I was scared. I had a vision.

"Of what?"

"It wasn't of taking over M & M. I had an aura, or thought I did, and was afraid I was having a seizure or a tumor, and I wasn't sure if I was imagining it or not. When I'm bored I get anxious. I get things like conjunctivitis and athlete's foot. I don't sleep well. You won't believe this, Michael, but when I'm not in love I'm bored, and I'm not in love."

"I can tell," said Michael. "You're not on a diet."

"Is that how you know?"

"It's one of the ways."

"I thought of epilepsy, you know, and of a TIA, a transient ischemic attack, which you don't know about. Then I was afraid of a stroke—everyone should always be afraid of a stroke. Am I talking too much? I had this feeling I was seeing everything twice."

"You mean double?"

"Not that, not yet. The feeling of suspecting that I had gone through everything before. There was hardly anything new for me in the daily news. Every day there seemed to be another political campaign going on or about to start, another election, and when it wasn't that, it was another tennis tournament, or those fucking Olympic Games again. I thought it might be a good idea to come in here and check. Anyway, my brain is sound, my mind is clear. So is my conscience."

"That's all very good."

"Don't be too sure. Great crimes are committed by people whose conscience is clear. And don't forget, my father died of a stroke."

"At ninety-two?"

"Do you think that made him want to jump with joy? Michael, what will you do with yourself? Disturbing my peace of mind is my not knowing where the hell you're going to fit in."

"Now you *are* talking too much."

"You're the only one in the family I really can talk to, and you won't listen. The others all know this, even your mother, who always wants more alimony. Money does matter, more than almost everything else. Want a sound idea? Get a job now with a company with a good pension plan and a good medical plan, any company and any job, no matter how much you hate it, and stay there until you're too old to continue. That's the only way to live, by preparing to die."

"Oh, shit, Dad, you really believe that?"

"No, I don't, although I think it might be true. But people can't survive on Social Security, and you won't even have that. Even poor Melissa will be better off."

"Who's poor Melissa?"

"That sweetheart of a nurse out there, the one that's attractive and kind of young."

"She's not so attractive and she's older than I am."

"She is?"

"Can't you tell?"

Toward the end of Yossarian's second week in the hospital they hatched the plot that drove him out.

They drove him out with the man from Belgium in the room adjacent to his. The man from Belgium was a financial wise man with the European Economic Community. He was a very sick financial wise man from Belgium and spoke little English, which did not matter much because he had just had part of his throat removed and could not speak at all, and understood hardly any English either, which mattered greatly to the nurses and several doctors, who were unable to address him in ways that had meaning. All day and much of the night he had at his bedside his waxen and diminutive Belgian wife in unpressed fashionable clothes, who smoked cigarettes continually and understood no English either and jabbered away at the nurses ceaselessly and hysterically, flying into alarms of shrieking terror each time he groaned or choked or slept or awoke. He had come to this country to be made well, and the doctors had taken out a hunk of his larynx because he certainly would have died had they left it all in. Now it was not so certain he would live. Christ, thought Yossarian, how can he stand it?

Christ, thought Yossarian, how can I?

The man had no way to make his feelings known but to nod or shake his head in reply to insistent questions fired at him by his wife, who had no serviceable way to relay his responses. He was in more dangers and discomforts than Yossarian could tick off on the fingers of both hands. Yossarian ran out of fingers the first time he counted and did not try again. He had grown no new fingers. There was normally such strident commotion in his vicinity that Yossarian could hardly find the time to think about himself. Yossarian worried about the man from Belgium more than he wanted to. He was moving into stress and knew stress was not healthy. People caught cancer under stress. Worrying about his stress put Yossarian under more stress, and he began to feel sorry for himself too.

The man was in pain that was unimaginable to Yossarian, who received no painkillers for it and felt he would be unable to endure it much longer and pull through. The man from Belgium was drugged. He was suctioned. He was medicated and sterilized. He kept everyone so busy that Nurse MacIntosh hardly could find time for Yossarian to fondle the lace at the bottom of her slip. Business was business, and the sick man from Belgium was serious business. Melissa was rushed and rumpled, distracted and breathless. He did not feel right cajoling her attention with so much that was critical going on right next door and, once spoiled, felt impoverished without her. No one else would do.

The man from Belgium, who could hardly move, kept them all on the run. He was hyperalimentated through a tube stuck in his neck so that he would not starve to death. They fed water intravenously into the poor man so that he would not dehydrate, suctioned fluids from his lungs so he would not drown.

That man was a full-time job. He had a chest tube and a belly tube and required such constant ministration that Yossarian had little time to think about Chaplain Tappman and his problem or Milo and Wintergreen and their squads of invisible bombers or of the tall Australian roommate with the white makeup in stiletto heels with full breasts or anyone else. A few times a day Yossarian would venture into the hallway to look into the other room just to see what was going on. Each time he did he came reeling back to his own bed and collapsed in a woozy faint with an arm pressed over his eyes.

When his vision cleared and he looked up again, the more mysterious of the private detectives would be peering in at him. This secret agent was a dapper man in trimly tailored suits and muted paisley ties, with a foreign complexion and dark eyes in a strong-boned face that looked vaguely Oriental and reminded him of a nut, a shelled almond.

"Who the fuck are you?" Yossarian wanted to shout out at him more than once.

"Hey, who are you?" he did ask one time amiably, forcing a smile.

"Are you talking to me?" was the lordly rejoinder, in a soft voice with perfect enunciation.

"Is there anything I can help you with?"

"Not at all. I was merely wondering about the thickset, balding gentleman with yellow hair who was here in the corridor a good deal up until a few days ago."

"The other private detective?"

"I haven't the faintest idea who you mean!" the man replied, and ducked away.

"Who the fuck *are* you?" Yossarian did shout after him just as the familiar cry went up in the corridor again and the pounding of gum-soled shoes resumed.

"Who speaks French? Who speaks French?" The wounded wail went up a dozen times a day from Nurse MacIntosh, Nurse Cramer, or one of the other nurses, or from one in the myriad of attending physicians, technicians, or Afro-American, Hispanic, or Pacific-rim aides and other kinds of economic refugees attending the Belgian on salary in that bizarre, unnatural hospital civilization that was perfectly natural. Now that there was a cash dispensing machine on every floor alongside the candy and soda dispensing machines, a patient with a credit card and major medical insurance never had to set foot outside again.

The secret agent with the faultless speech and impeccable English tailoring did not once volunteer that he could speak French, although Yossarian would bet he was able to, and could break codes too.

Yossarian spoke a little bit of French very poorly but decided to mind his own business. He was nervous about malpractice. Who could tell? Conceivably, an error in translation might render him liable to a charge of practicing medicine without a license. Yossarian could tell: he could tell about himself that if he ever had to go through all that at his age for four or fourteen days just to be able to go on living with or without a voice box for God knew how little longer, he thought he would object. He would prefer not to. In the end it came down to elementals. He could not stand the Belgian's pain.

He was going to have to leave her.

Yossarian was symptom suggestible and knew it. Within a day his voice turned husky.

"What's the matter with you?" Nurse MacIntosh snapped with concern the very next morning after she had reported for work, put on her makeup, straightened the seams of her seamless stockings, and then come into the room looking her niftiest to make sure he was all right. "You don't sound the same. Why aren't you eating?"

"I know. I'm hoarse. I'm not hungry right now. I don't know why I'm so hoarse."

He had no fever or physical discomfort and there was no visible evidence of inflammation anywhere in his ears, nose, or throat, said the ear, nose, and throat man who was summoned.

The next day his throat felt sore. He felt a lump there too and had difficulty swallowing his food, although there was still not a sign of infection or obstruction, and he knew as surely as he knew anything else that he too would soon lose his larynx to a malignancy if he hung around there any longer and did not get the hell away from that hospital fast.

Nurse Melissa MacIntosh looked heartbroken. It was nothing personal, he assured her. He promised gallantly to take her out soon to dinner at a good restaurant, and to Paris and Florence, and Munich too, perhaps, and window-shop for lacy lingerie with her, if they found they hit it off, and if she did not mind being followed by private detectives whenever they were together. She thought he was joking about the private detectives and said she would miss him. He replied with perfection that he would not give her the chance, wondering, even as he gazed sincerely into her earnest blue eyes and warmly pressed her hand good-bye, whether he would ever even remember to want to see her again.

BOOK
TWO

BOOK
TWO

4
Lew

I was born strong and without fear. To this day I don't think I
know what it is to be afraid of another human being. I didn't get
my muscles and big bones and deep chest from baling old newspapers and doing heavy lifting as a kid in my father's junkshop. If I
didn't have the strength he would not have made me do it. He
would have put me to work keeping count and running errands,
like he did with my sisters and my older brother Ira. We were four
sons in my family and two girls, and of the boys I was the second
from the last. My mother would tell people I was the strongest
baby she ever saw, and also the hungriest. She needed both hands
to pull me away from the breast.

"Like Hercules in his crib," Sammy Singer said once.

"Who?"

"Hercules. The infant Hercules."

"What about him?

"When he was born a couple of big snakes were sent into his
crib to kill him. He strangled one with each hand."

"It was nothing like that, wise guy."

Little Sammy Singer knew things like that even when we were
kids back in public school in the third or fourth grade. Or maybe
it was the sixth or seventh. The rest of us were doing book reports
on *Tom Sawyer* and *Robinson Crusoe* and he was doing them on
the *Iliad*. Sammy was clever, I was smart. He looked things up. I
figured them out. He was good at chess, I was good at pinochle. I
stopped playing chess, he kept losing money to me at pinochle.
Who was the smart one? When we went into the war he wanted
to be a fighter pilot and picked the air corps. I picked the ground

force because I wanted to fight Germans. I hoped to be in a tank and ride right through hundreds of them. He turned out a tail gunner, I wound up in the infantry. He was knocked down into the water once and came home with a medal, I was a prisoner of war and was kept overseas until the end. Maybe he was the smarter one. After the war he went to college with the government paying, I bought a lumberyard outside the city. I bought a building lot and put up a house on spec in partnership with a few of my customers, who knew more about construction than I did. I knew more about business. With the profits from that one I did the next house alone. I discovered credit. We did not know in Coney Island that banks *wanted* to lend money. He went to operas and I went out shooting ducks and Canada geese with local plumbers and Yankee bankers. As a POW in Germany I worried each time I changed hands what would happen when the new guards looked at my dog tags and found out I was a Jew. I worried, but I don't remember that I ever had fear. Each place I moved as they shipped me deeper and deeper into the country toward Dresden, I made sure to find some way to tell them before they found out. I did not want them to get the idea they had someone who was hiding anything. I did not think until Sammy asked later that they might spit in my face or smash my head with the butt of a gun or just lead me away from the others into the bushes with their rifles and bayonets and stab or shoot me to death. We were most of us kids, and I figured they might bully and sneer awhile and that I just might have to bust a few jaws before I taught them to stop. I never had any question I could do that. I was LR, Lewis Rabinowitz from Mermaid Avenue in Coney Island in Brooklyn, New York, and I never had doubts back then that I could not be beaten at anything and could succeed in doing whatever I wanted to.

I always felt that way as a kid. I was big and broad from the start and had a strong voice, and I felt bigger and broader than I was. In public school I could see with my eyes that there were older kids who were bigger than I was, and maybe they were stronger too, but I never felt it. And I was never in dread of the kids in those few Italian families we had in the neighborhood, all those Bartolinis and Palumbos, that all of the others were almost afraid to talk about unless they were home. They carried knives, those guineas, it was rumored in whispers. I never saw any. I left them alone and they didn't bother me. Or anyone else for that matter, as far as I could tell. Except one time one of them did. A skinny older one in the eighth grade came slouching past and stepped on my foot deliberately as I sat on the sidewalk at the front of the line outside the schoolyard after lunch, waiting for the doors to open and the afternoon session to begin. He wore sneakers. We were not supposed to wear sneakers to school except for gym, but all those Bartolinis and Palumbos did whenever they wanted to. "Haaay," I said to myself when I saw it happen. I'd watched him coming. I'd seen him turn in toward me with a mean and innocent look. I did not see my arm shoot out to grab him by the ankle and squeeze there only hard enough to hold him in place when he tried to pull free and continue past me without even moving his eyes, like he had a right, like I wasn't even there. He was surprised, all right, when he saw I wouldn't let him. He tried to look tough. We were under thirteen.

"Hey, what're you doing?" he said with a snarl.

My look was tougher. "You dropped something," I said with a cold smile.

"Yeah? What?"

"Your footsteps."

"Very funny. Let go of my leg."

"And one of them fell on me." With my other hand I tapped at the place he had stepped on.

"Yeah?"

"Yeah."

He pulled harder. I squeezed harder.

"If I did, I didn't mean it."

"I thought you did mean it," I said to him. "If you swear to God and tell me again you didn't mean it, I think I might believe you."

"You a tough guy? You think so?"

"Yeah."

Other kids watched, girls too. I felt good.

"Well, I didn't mean it," he said, and stopped pulling.

"Then I think I believe you."

After that we were friends for a while.

Sammy decided one day to teach me how to fight and to show me while doing it how much better he was at boxing.

"You can't just do it on brawn, Lew."

He had a book of instructions he had read and some boxing gloves he had borrowed. I had to keep smiling at him as we laced each other up. He showed me the stance, the lead, he taught me the jab, the hook, the "uppracut."

"Okay, tiger, you showed me. Now what do we do?"

"We'll go about three minutes, rest for one, and I'll show you what you did wrong, and then we'll go another round. Remember, keep moving. No hitting in the clinches, no wrestling there either. That's not allowed. Put your left hand up, higher, keep it up and stick it out more. Otherwise I'll come right in and bop you. That's good. Let's go."

He struck a pose and danced in and out. I moved straight toward him and with my left hand pushed both his arms down easily. With my right I grabbed his face in my open glove and twisted it playfully from side to side.

"That's a clinch," he yelled. "You're not allowed to hold a face. You have to punch or do nothing. Now we break and start again. Remember, you've got to try to hit me."

He danced around faster this time, popped the side of my head with one of his jabs, and flew right back. I moved right at him again, shoved his arms down easily with one paw, and began patting him on the face lightly with my other paw. I couldn't help laughing as I looked at him. I was grinning, he was panting.

"Let's do something else," he said miserably. "This just isn't working, is it?"

I used to worry sometimes about little Sammy because he couldn't do much and liked to needle people. But he was smart and it turned out he only needled people he could tell would not get angry at him. Like me.

"Hey, Lew, how's your girlfriend with the big tits?" he would say to me during the war when I had started dating Claire and had brought her around.

"You're a clever fellow," I would tell him with a forced smile through gritted teeth. I have a nerve at one side at the back of my jaw and the side of my neck that I used to feel twitch when I was starting to boil. I would feel it in pinochle too when I had bid too high and needed every trick.

"Hey, Lew, give my regards to your wife with the big tits," he used to say after Claire and I got married. Winkler started baiting me that way too, and I couldn't crush him if I didn't crush Sammy, and I couldn't crush Sammy. He would have been my best man, but my folks wanted my brothers, and in my family all of us did what the other ones wanted us to.

They named me Lewis and called me Louie as though my name was Louis, and I never saw that difference until Sammy pointed it out. And even then, I still don't see much difference.

Sammy read newspapers. He liked the colored people and said they should be allowed to vote in the South and be free to live wherever they wanted to. I didn't care where they lived as long as they didn't live near me. I never really liked anyone I didn't know personally. We liked Roosevelt awhile when he became President, but that was mainly because he wasn't Herbert Hoover or another one of those Republicans or one of those hayseed anti-Semites in the South or Midwest or that Father Coughlin in Detroit. But we didn't trust him and we didn't believe him. We didn't trust banks and we didn't trust bank records and we did as much of our business as we could in cash. Even before Adolf Hitler we did not like Germans. And among the Germans who did not stand a chance in our house were German Jews. And that was even after Hitler. I grew up hearing about them.

"I never wished harm on anyone," my mother would repeat. I heard her say that over and over again, and it wasn't true. Her terrific curses fell everywhere, even on all of us. "But if ever a people deserved to be punished it was them. When we came through from Poland to Hamburg they could not make themselves look at us. We were dirt in their eyes. We made them ashamed with our valises and our clothes, and we couldn't talk German. They were all of them ashamed of us and made us know it. Some stole money from us when they could. When there was an empty seat on a train or a bench on the street somewhere they would put down a hat there to make believe somebody was using it so we could not sit down near them. For hours they would make us stand there, even with our children. The people with money all did that. And they even all made believe they could not speak Yiddish."

When Sammy came up to the house for a visit with me not long ago he mentioned he thought that probably German Jews did not speak Yiddish. My mother would have pretended to be hard of hearing if she ever heard that one.

When the war came in Europe we were all of us still a couple of years too young to be drafted right away. I switched from Spanish to German in high school—I began getting ready—and began driving guys like Sammy crazy with my *achtung*s, *wie gehts*, *hallo*s, and *nein*s and *jawohl*s. When they yelled at me to cut it out I threw them a *danke schön* or two. I kept up the German even into the army. By the time I enlisted I knew enough German to bully the POWs I found at Fort Dix and Fort Sill and Fort Riley and Fort Benning. As a POW outside Dresden I could talk to the guards a little and sometimes interpret for the other Americans. Because I could speak German, I was sent into Dresden in charge of a work detail, even though I was a sergeant and didn't have to go.

The junk business boomed while I was still a kid civilian. Sammy's mother saved old newspapers and donated aluminum pots and pans, my father sold them. There was a good living in waste, as the old man found out, and a few small fortunes for the dealers in scrap metal. We went racing for buildings slated for demolition. We followed fire engines. The big Coney Island fires were always a gold mine, for us a copper mine and lead mine, because of the pipes we salvaged. When Luna Park burned down soon after the war we had a bonanza of junk. They paid us to take it away and they paid us again when we sold it to scrap dealers. Everything hot was packed in asbestos and we took the asbestos and baled that too. We were pretty well off after that one and the old man had the ten thousand to lend me to buy the lumberyard, at stiff interest too, because he was always like that, and because he didn't like the idea. He didn't want me to leave the junk business and he didn't want us to move almost three hours away. Old schoolhouses and hospitals were especially good. We bought a second truck and hired neighborhood strongmen who could lift and who could scare other junkmen away. We even hired one big *shvartza*, a strong, quiet black man named Sonny who walked in one day and asked for work. We tore through plaster walls and asbestos insulation with metal claws and hammers to get at the copper and lead pipes with our baling hooks, crowbars, and hacksaws. My pop fired Smokey Rubin.

I passed on the word. News came back from Smokey that he would be out looking for me and that he'd better not find me. At night after that I went to Happy's Luncheonette on Mermaid Avenue and sat down to wait for him. Sammy and Winkler looked weak when they came in and saw me. I thought they would faint.

"What are you doing here?" Winkler said. "Get out, get out."

"Don't you know Smokey is out hunting for you?" said Sammy. "He's got a few of his pals."

"I'm making it easier for him to find me. I'll buy you some sodas and sandwiches if you want to wait here. Or you can sit where you want."

"At least go get your brothers if you want to act crazy," said Sammy. "Should I run to your house?"

"Have a malted instead."

We did not wait long. Smokey spotted me as soon as he walked in—I sat facing the door—and came right up to the booth, backed up by a guy named Red Benny and a weird one known as Willie the Geep.

"I've been looking for you. I've got things to say."

"I'm listening." Our eyes were locked on each other's. "I came to hear them."

"Then come on outside. I want to talk to you alone."

I mulled that one over. They were thirty or over, and we were seventeen and a half. Smokey had been in the ring. He'd been to prison and was cut up badly at least once in a knife fight.

"Okay, Smokey, if that's what you want," I decided. "But have your boys there sit down awhile if you want to talk to me alone outside, and if that's what you want to do."

"You've been saying bad things about me, right? Don't bullshit. Your father too."

"What bad things?"

"That you fired me and I've been stealing. Your father didn't fire me. Let's get that thing straight. I quit. I wouldn't work for any of you anymore."

"Smokey"—I felt that nerve on the side of my cheek and neck start to tick—"the old man wants me to be sure to tell you that if you ever set foot in the shop again he'll break your back."

That made Smokey pause. He knew the old man. If the old man said it, Smokey knew that he meant it. My father was a short man with the biggest, thickest shoulders I ever saw and small blue eyes in a face that reminded people of a torpedo or artillery shell. With his freckles and hard lines and liver spots, he looked like an iron ingot, an anvil five and a half feet tall. He'd been a black-smith. All of us have large heads with big square jaws. We look like Polacks and know we're Yids. In Poland with one blow of his fist to the forehead he'd killed a Cossack who'd raised his voice to my mother, and in Hamburg he came close to doing that again with some kind of immigration warden who'd made that same mistake of being rude to my mother but backed away in time. In my family no one ever got away free with insulting any of us, except, I guess, for Sammy Singer with me and my wife with the big tits.

"How's your dad, Marvin?" Red Benny said to Winkler, while everyone in Happy's Luncheonette watched, and after that Smokey had another reason to be careful.

Winkler drummed the fingers of one hand on the table and kept quiet.

His father was a bookmaker and made more than just about anyone else in the neighborhood. They even had a piano in the house for a while. Red Benny was a runner, a collector, a loan shark, a debtor, and a burglar. One summer he and a gang cleaned out every room in a resort hotel except the one rented by Winkler's folks, making the people upstate start to wonder what Winkler's pop did for a living to let just him be spared.

By then Smokey was already slowing down a little. "You and your father—you're telling people I stole a building from you, right? I didn't steal that house. I found the janitor and made the deal for it all by myself."

"You found it while you were working for us," I told him. "You can work for us or you can go in business for yourself. You can't do both the same hour."

"Now the dealers won't buy anything from me. Your father won't let them."

"They can do what they want. But if they buy from you, they can't buy from him. That's all he said."

"I don't like that. I want to talk to him. I want to talk to him now. I want to straighten him out too."

"Smokey," I said, speaking slowly and feeling suddenly very, very sure of myself, "you ever raise a voice on even one word to my father, and I'll see that you die. You lift a finger to me, and he'll see that you die."

He seemed impressed with that.

"Okay," he gave in, with his face falling. "I'll go back to work for him. But you tell him I'll want sixty a week from now on."

"You don't understand. He might not take you back for even fifty. I'll have to try to talk to him for you."

"And he can have the house I found if he gives me five hundred."

"He might give you the usual two."

"When can I start?"

"Give me tomorrow to try to bring him around." Actually, it did take some talking to remind the old man that Smokey worked hard and that he and our black guy were pretty good together at chasing other junkmen off.

"Loan me fifty now, Louie, will you?" Smokey begged as a

favor. "There's some good smoking stuff from Harlem outside that I want to invest in."

"I can only lend you twenty." I could have given him more. "That's funny," I said when they'd gone out the door. I was flexing my fingers. "Something's wrong with my hand. When I gave him that twenty I could hardly bend it."

"You were holding the sugar bowl," Winkler said. His teeth were shivering.

"What sugar bowl?"

"Didn't you know?" Sammy snapped at me almost angrily. "You were gripping that sugar bowl like you were going to kill him with it. I thought you would squeeze it to pieces."

I leaned back with a laugh and ordered some pie and ice cream for the three of us. No, I hadn't known I was gripping that cylindrical thick sugar shaker while we were talking. My head was cool and collected while I looked him straight in the eye, and my arm was ready for action without my even knowing it. Sammy let out some air and turned white as he lifted his hand from his lap and put back down the table knife he had been holding.

"Tiger, why were you hiding it?" I said with a laugh. "What good would that do me?"

"I didn't want them to see how my hands were shaking," Sammy whispered.

"Would you know how to use it?"

Sammy shook his head. "And I don't ever want to find out. Lew, I've got to tell you right now. If we're ever together and you feel like getting into a fight, I want you to know that you can positively count on me not to stand by you again."

"Me neither," said Winkler. "Red Benny wouldn't do nothing with me around, but I wasn't so sure about the others."

"Gang," I told them, "I wasn't counting on you this time."

"Were you really going to hit him with that sugar shaker?"

"Sammy, I would have hit him with the whole luncheonette if I had to. I would have hit him with you."

I was already past sixty-five, two years to the day, when I nabbed that young purse snatcher, a tall, swift guy in his twenties. It's a cinch to keep track because of my birthday. As a present to me, I had to bring Claire down into the city to one of those shows with songs that she wanted to see and I didn't. We got there early and were standing outside with a bunch of other people under the marquee of a theater that wasn't too far from that Port Authority

Bus Terminal. That bus terminal is a place that still gives me a laugh whenever I remember the time Sammy had his pocket picked coming back from a visit to us and was almost thrown in jail for yelling at the police to try to make them do something about it. By then I'd already made peace with the Germans and drove a Mercedes. Claire had one too, a nifty convertible. All of a sudden a woman let out a *geshrei*. I saw a couple of guys come racing away just in back of me. Without thinking I grabbed hold of one. I spun him around, lifted him up, and slammed him down on his chest on the hood of a car. Only when I had him down did I see he was young, tall, and strong. He was a brown guy.

"If you move a muscle, I'll break your back," I said in his ear. He did not move a muscle.

When I saw how careful the cops were in searching him I kept shaking my head with what should have been fear. They combed through his scalp with their fingers for a blade or some kind of pick. They pinched through his collar and pockets and through all of the seams of his shirt and his pants, feeling him everywhere from top to bottom for a gun or a knife or anything small and sharp. I realized I could have been killed. Only when they got down inside his sneaker tops and finished did they all relax.

"You were very lucky, sir," said the young cop in charge, who was the oldest one there.

People kept smiling at me and I kept smiling back. I felt like a hero.

"Okay, Lew, your show is over," Claire said to me dryly, as I could have bet she was going to. "Let's get inside now for the real show."

"One minute more, Claire," I answered her loudly and swaggered. "There's that nice-looking blonde girl over there who I think might like to get to know me better."

"Lew, will you come inside already, for God sakes," she said, "or do I go in without you?"

We walked in laughing. Just two weeks later my symptoms returned, and I was back in the hospital for chemotherapy.

5

John

Outside the hospital it was still going on. Men went mad and were rewarded with medals. Interior decorators were culture heroes, and fashion designers were the social superiors of their clientele.

"And why wouldn't they be?" Frances Beach had already replied to this observation of Yossarian's, exercising an enunciation so nearly perfect that others often pondered how anyone could pronounce English so flawlessly and escape sounding adenoidal. "Have you forgotten what we look like naked?"

"If a man said that, John," said Patrick Beach, her husband, pleased with her once more, "he'd be flayed alive."

"Men do say that, darling," said Frances Beach, "at their spring and fall collections, and make billions dressing us."

There were still plenty of poor people.

Yossarian looked askance at a bunch sprawled on the sidewalk outside the hospital as he strode out to the curb and the stretch limousine with black windows waiting there to transport him to the luxury high-rise apartment building across town in which he now made his home. He had reserved a sedan; they had sent the limousine again; there would be no additional charge. The high-rise apartment house he lived in was called a luxury building because the costs of living in it were large. The rooms were small. The ceilings were low, there were no windows in his two bathrooms, and no space in the kitchen area for a table or a chair.

Less than ten blocks from this home was the bus terminal of the Port of New York Authority, a structure stacked with landings seven stories high. On ground level was a police desk with three principal holding cells continuously in use, which overflowed with new prisoners several times each day, and into which, a year earlier, Michael Yossarian had been hauled upon emerging from a subway exit and attempting to step back in after realizing he had got off too soon on his way downtown to the architectural firm for which he was doing drawings.

"That was the day," he still recalled, "you saved my life and broke my spirit."

"Did you want to be locked up with all those others?"

"I would have died if that happened. But it wasn't easy, seeing you blow up and bamboozle all those cops and get away with it. And knowing I could never do the same."

"We get angry the way we have to, Michael. I don't think I had much choice."

"I get depressed."

"You had an older brother who bullied you. Maybe that's the difference."

"Why didn't you stop him?"

"We didn't know how. We didn't want to bully him."

Michael responded with a token snicker. "You were really something to watch, weren't you?" he accused with envy. "You had a small crowd. There was even clapping."

Afterward they were both devitalized.

People lived in the bus terminal now, a resident population of men and women and wayward boys and girls, most of them sleeping at night in the darker depths and emerging like commuters for much of each day to conduct in the open what normal business affairs were theirs to attend to.

There was hot and cold running water in the lavatories on the different levels, along with an abundance of whores and homosexuals for every appetite, and plentiful shops close at hand for such basic daily necessities as chewing gum, cigarettes, newspapers, and jelly doughnuts. Toilet tissue was free. Fertile mothers in flight from idealized hometowns arrived regularly with small children and took up lodgings. The terminal was a good home base for streetwalkers, beggars, and young runaways. Thousands of business commuters, along with hundreds of visitors, tried paying them little mind as they passed through each morning on their way to employment and back to their homes at the conclusion of the working day. None were rich, for no one who was rich would travel to work by bus.

From the lofty picture windows in his high-rise apartment, Yossarian commanded an unobstructed view of another luxury apartment building with an even higher rise than his own. Between these structures ran the broad thoroughfare below, which teemed more and more monstrously now with growling clans of bellicose and repulsive panhandlers, prostitutes, addicts, dealers, pimps, robbers, pornographers, perverts, and disoriented psychopaths, all of them plying their criminal specialties outdoors amid multiplying strands of degraded and bedraggled people who now were actually *living* outdoors. Among the homeless were whites now too, and they also pissed against the walls and defecated in the alleyways that others in their circle eventually located as accommodating sites to bed down in.

Even in the better neighborhood of Park Avenue, he knew, women could be seen squatting to relieve themselves in the tended flower beds of the traffic islands in the center.

It was hard not to hate them all.

And this was New York, the Big Apple, the Empire City in the Empire State, the financial heart, brains, and sinews of the country, and the city that was greatest, barring London perhaps, in cultural doings in the whole world.

Nowhere in his lifetime, Yossarian was bound often to remember, not in wartime Rome or Pianosa or even in blasted Naples or Sicily, had he been spectator to such atrocious squalor as he saw mounting up all around him now into an eminent domain of decay. Not even—he had added in his cynicism more than once to Frances Beach, his lady friend from far back—at the sexless fundraising luncheons and black-tie evening events he attended more times than he wanted to as the only presentable official of M & M Enterprises & Associates, an eligible male and a person who could chat with some fluency about something other than business matters to well-informed others who imagined egotistically that they were affecting world events by talking about them.

It was nobody's fault, of course.

"My God, what's that?" cried Frances Beach, as the two rode back in her rented limousine with her rented chauffeur from still another tepid tea-and-wine party for those trustees and friends of the trustees of the New York Public Library who were still in town and had concluded, after long bouts with indecision, that they did want to go there.

"The bus terminal," said Yossarian.

"It's awful, isn't it? What the devil is it for?"

"Buses. What the devil did you think it was for? You know, Frances," Yossarian taunted kindly, "you might consider sponsoring your next fashion show in there, or one of your glittering charity balls. I know McBride."

"What are you talking about? Who's McBride?"

"An ex-cop who works there now. Why not a wedding," he went on, "a really big one? That would really make the news. You've had them—"

"*I* haven't."

"—in the museum and the opera house. The terminal's more picturesque."

"A society wedding in that terminal?" she rejoined with a smirk. "You must be mad. I know you're joking, so let me think. Olivia and Christopher Maxon may be looking for a new place soon. Look at those people!" She sat up suddenly. "Are they men or women? And those others—why must they do those things out there in the street? Why can't they wait till they're home?"

"Many don't have homes, Frances dear," said Yossarian, smiling benignly at her. "And the lines for the toilets at the bus terminal are long. Reservations must be made for the peak hours. No one can be seated without them. The lavatories in the restaurants and hotels, say the signs, are for patrons only. Have you ever noticed, Frances, that men who take leaks in the street usually take very long ones?"

No, she had not noticed, she informed him frostily. "You sound so bitter these days. You used to be funnier."

Years back, before either had married, they had luxuriated together in what would today be termed an affair, although neither then would have conceived of applying a title so decorous to the things they were doing with each other so ardently and incessantly, with never a pledge or serious care of a future together. Then, in little time, he had turned away from his promising work as a beginner in arbitrage and investment banking for a second crack at teaching before going back to the advertising agency and then into public relations and freelance writing, succeeding, in time, as a jack-of-all-trades except any encompassing a product that could be seen, touched, utilized, or consumed, a product that occupied space and for which there was need. While she, with curiosity, drive, and some inborn talent, started finding herself

attractive to theatrical producers and other gentlemen she thought
might prove useful to her in stage, screen, and television.

"And you," he reminded her now, "used to be much more
sympathetic. You've forgotten your past."

"You too."

"And radical."

"So were you. And now you're so negative," she remarked without much feeling. "And always sarcastic, aren't you? No wonder
people are not always comfortable with you. You make light of
everything, and they're never satisfied you really agree with them.
And you're always flirting."

"I am not!"

"Yes, you are," Frances Beach insisted, without even turning
her head to add conviction to her argument. "With just about
everyone but me. You know who flirts and who doesn't. Patrick
and Christopher don't. You do. You always did."

"It's the way that I joke."

"Some of the women imagine you have a mistress."

"Mistress?" Yossarian turned that word into a snorting guffaw.
"Only one would be one too many."

Frances Beach laughed too and her suggestion of strain vanished. They were both past sixty-five. He had known her when her
name was Franny. She remembered when they called him Yo-
Yo. They had not toyed with each other since, not even between
marriages, neither one of them ever possessed by a need to test the
accommodations made by the other.

"There seem to be more and more of these people everywhere,"
she murmured mildly, with a despair she made clear would be
easily controlled, "doing everything imaginable right out in public.
Patrick was mugged just in front of our house, and there are
whores on our corners day and night, unsightly ones in unattrac-
tive outfits, like those at that building."

"Drop me off at that building," said Yossarian. "It's where I
live now."

"There?" When he nodded, she added, "Move."

"I just did. What's wrong? On the top of my magic mountain
we have a couple of health clubs, and one of them is a temple of
love. At the bottom there are nine movie houses, two X-rated and
one gay, and we have stockbrokers, law firms, and advertising
agencies in between. All kinds of doctors. There's a bank with a
cash machine and that great supermarket too. I have suggested a

nursing home. Once we have a nursing home, I can live there a lifetime and practically never set foot outside."

"For God sakes, John, don't always joke. Go to a good neighborhood."

"Where will I find one? Montana?" He laughed again. "Frances, this *is* a good neighborhood. Do you think I'd set foot in a bad one?"

All at once, Frances looked tired and dispirited. "John, you used to know everything," she reflected, dropping the affectation of cultured speech. "What can be done?"

"Nothing," he obliged her helpfully in reply.

For things were good, he reminded her: as measured by official standards, they had not often been better. This time only the poor were very poor, and the need for new prison cells was more urgent than the needs of the homeless. The problems were hopeless: there were too many people who needed food, and there was too much food to be able to feed them profitably. What was wanted was more shortages, he added, with just a small smile. He did not volunteer that by now he was one more in the solid middle class who was not keen to have his taxes raised to ameliorate the miseries of those who paid none. He preferred more prisons.

Yossarian was sixty-eight and somewhat vain, for he looked younger than many men of sixty-seven, and better than all women of his approximate generation. His second wife was still divorcing him. He did not think there would be a third.

All his children had come from his first.

His daughter, Gillian, the judge, was divorcing her husband, who, despite a much better income, was not achieving as much and was unlikely ever to amount to anything more than a reliable husband, father, family man, and provider.

His son Julian, the braggart and oldest of the lot, was a minor major hotshot on Wall Street still with insufficient earnings to move regally into Manhattan. He and his wife now occupied separate quarters of their obsolescent suburban mansion while their respective lawyers made ready to sue and countersue for divorce and attempted, impossibly, to arrive at a division of property and children that would supply entire satisfaction to both. The wife was a good-looking and disagreeable woman of fashionable tastes from a family that spent money recklessly, as loud as Julian and as despotic in certitude, and their boy and girl were bullying too and odiously unsociable.

Yossarian sensed trouble brewing in the marriage of his other son, Adrian, a chemist without a graduate degree who worked for a cosmetics manufacturer in New Jersey and was spending much of his adult working life seeking a formula for dying hair gray; his wife had taken to enrolling in adult education courses.

He fretted most about Michael, who could not seem to make himself want to amount to anything special and was blind to the dangers lurking in that lack of goal. Michael had once joked to Yossarian that he was going to save money for his divorce before starting to save for his marriage, and Yossarian resisted wisecracking back that his joke was not a joke. Michael did not regret that he never had tried hard to succeed as an artist. That role too did not appeal to him.

Women, especially women who had been married one time before, liked Michael and lived with him because he was peaceful, understanding, and undemanding, and then soon tired of living with him, because he was peaceful, understanding, and undemanding. He resolutely refused to quarrel and fell silent and sad in conflict. Yossarian had a respectful suspicion about Michael that in his taciturn way, with women as with work, he knew what he was doing. But not with money.

For money, Michael did freelance artwork for agencies and magazines or for art studios with contract assignments, or, with clear conscience, accepted what he needed from Yossarian, disbelieving a day must dawn when he would no longer find these freelance assignments at hand and that Yossarian might not always choose to safeguard him from eventual financial tragedy.

All in all, Yossarian decided, it was a typically modern, poorly adjusted, new-age family in which no one but the mother truly liked all the others or saw good reason to; and each, he suspected, was, like himself, at least secretly and intermittently sad and regretful.

His family life was perfect, he liked to lament. Like Thomas Mann's Gustav Aschenbach, he had none.

He was still under surveillance. He could not tell by how many. By the end of the week there was even an Orthodox Jew pacing back and forth outside his building on the other side of the avenue, and a call on his answering machine from the nurse Melissa MacIntosh, whom he had all but forgotten, with the information that she'd been rotated to the evening shift for a while, in case he'd been planning to take her to dinner—and to Paris and Florence too for lingerie, she reminded with a caustic snicker—and with the incredible news that the Belgian patient was still alive but in pain and that his temperature was down almost to normal.

Yossarian would have bet his life that the Belgian would already be dead.

Of all those tailing him, he could account for only a few—the ones retained by the lawyer for his estranged wife and those retained by the estranged, impulsive husband of a woman he'd lain with half-drunkenly once not long before, a mother of adolescents, and thought halfheartedly he might wish to lie with some more, if ever he was graced with the urge to lie with a woman again, who had detectives shadow every man she knew in his craze to obtain evidence of fornication to balance the evidence of fornication she had earlier obtained against him.

The idea of the others festered, and after another few spells of aggravated embitterment, Yossarian took the bull by the horns and telephoned the office.

"Anything new?" he began, to Milo's son.

"Not as far as I know."

"Are you telling me the truth?"

"To the best of my ability."

"You're not holding anything back?"

"Not as far as I can tell."

"Would you tell me if you were?"

"I would tell you if I could."

"When your father calls in today, M2," he said to Milo Minderbinder II, "tell him I need the name of a good private detective. It's for something personal."

"He's already phoned," said Milo junior. "He recommends a man named Jerry Gaffney at the Gaffney Agency. Under no circumstances mention that my father suggested him."

"He told you that already?" Yossarian was enchanted. "How did he know I was going to ask?"

"That's impossible for me to say."

"How are you feeling, M2?"

"It's hard to be sure."

"I mean in general. Have you been back to the bus terminal to look at those TV monitors?"

"I need to clock them some more. I want to go again."

"I can arrange that again."

"Will Michael come with me?"

"If you pay him for the day. Are things all right?"

"Wouldn't I want to tell you if they were?"

"But would you tell me?"

"That would depend."

"On what?"

"If I could tell you the truth."

"Would you tell me the truth?"

"Do I know what it is?"

"Could you tell me a lie?"

"Only if I knew the truth."

"You're being honest with me."

"My father wants that."

"Mr. Minderbinder mentioned you were going to call," said the sanguine, soft-spoken voice belonging to the man named Jerry Gaffney when Yossarian telephoned him.

"That's funny," said Yossarian. "Which one?"

"Mr. Minderbinder senior."

"That's very funny then," said Yossarian in a harder manner. "Because Minderbinder senior insisted I not mention his name to you when I phoned."

"It was a test to see if you could keep things secret."

"You gave me no chance to pass it."

"I trust my clients, and I want all of them to know they can always trust Jerry Gaffney. Without trust, what else is there? I put everything out front. I'll give you proof of that now. You should know that this telephone line is tapped."

Yossarian caught his breath. "How the hell did you find that out?"

"It's my telephone line and I want it tapped," Mr. Gaffney explained reasonably. "There, see? You can count on Jerry Gaffney. It's only me who's recording it."

"Is *my* line tapped?" Yossarian thought he should ask. "I make many business calls."

"Let me look it up. Yes, your business is tapping it. Your apartment may be bugged too."

"Mr. Gaffney, how do you know all this?"

"Call me Jerry, Mr. Yossarian."

"How do you know all this, Mr. Gaffney?"

"Because I'm the one who tapped it and I'm one of the parties who may have bugged it, Mr. Yossarian. Let me give you a tip. All walls may have ears. Talk only in the presence of running water if you want to talk privately. Have sex only in the bathroom or kitchen if you want to make love or under the air conditioner with the fan setting turned up to— That's it!" he cheered, after Yossarian had walked into the kitchen with his portable phone and turned on both faucets full pressure to talk secretly. "We're picking up nothing. I can barely hear you."

"I'm not saying anything."

"Learn to read lips."

"Mr. Gaffney—"

"Call me Jerry."

"Mr. Gaffney, you tapped my telephone and you bugged my apartment?"

"I *may* have bugged it. I'll have one of my staff investigators check. I keep nothing back. Mr. Yossarian, you have an intercom system with the staff in the lobby. Can you be sure it's not on now? Are there no video cameras watching you?"

"Who would do that?"

"I would, for one, if I were paid. Now that you know I tell the truth, you see we can become close friends. That's the only way to work. I thought you knew that your telephone was tapped and that your apartment might be bugged and your mail, travel, credit cards, and bank accounts monitored."

"Ho-ly shit, I don't know what I know." Yossarian soaked up the disagreeable intelligence with a prolonged groan.

"Look on the bright side, Mr. Yossarian. Always do that. You'll soon be party to another matrimonial action, I believe. You can pretty much take all that for granted if the principals have the wherewithal to pay us."

"You do that too?"

"I do a lot of that too. But this is only the company. Why should you care what M & M E & A hears if you never say anything you wouldn't want the company to hear? You believe that much, don't you?"

"No."

"No? Keep in mind, Mr. Yossarian, that I'm getting all of this down, although I'll be pleased to erase as much of it as you wish. How can you have reservations about M & M E & A when you share in its progress? Doesn't everybody share?"

"I have never gone on record with that, Mr. Gaffney, and I won't do that now. When can we meet to begin?"

"I've already begun, Mr. Yossarian. Grass doesn't grow under Señor Gaffney's feet. I've sent for your government files under the Freedom of Information Act and I'm getting your record from one of the best consumer credit-rating bureaus. I already have your Social Security number. Like it so far?"

"I am not hiring you to investigate me!"

"I want to find out what these people following you know about you before I find out who all of them are. How many did you say you think there are?"

"I didn't. But I count at least six, but two or four of them may be working in pairs. I notice they drive cheap cars."

"Economy cars," Gaffney corrected punctiliously, "to escape being noticed. That's probably how you noticed them." He seemed to Yossarian to be extremely exact. "Six, you say? Six is a good number."

"For what?"

"For business, of course. There is safety in numbers, Mr. Yossarian. For example, if one or two of them decided to assassinate you, there'd already be witnesses. Yes, six is a very good number," Gaffney continued happily. "It would be nicer to get them up to eight or ten. Forget about meeting me yet. I wouldn't want any of them to figure out I'm working for you unless it turns out that they're working for me. I like to have solutions before I find out the problems. Please turn off that water now if you're not having sex. I'm growing hoarse shouting, and I can hardly hear you. You really don't need it when you're talking to me. Your friends call you Yo-Yo? Some call you John?"

"Only my close ones, Mr. Gaffney."

"Mine call me Jerry."

"I must tell you, Mr. Gaffney, that I find talking to you exasperating."

"I hope that will change. If you'll pardon my saying so, it was heartening to hear that report from your nurse."

"What nurse?" snapped Yossarian. "I have no nurse."

"Her name is Miss Melissa MacIntosh, sir," corrected Gaffney, with a cough that was reproving.

"You heard my answering machine too?"

"Your company did. I'm just a retainer. I wouldn't do it if I didn't get paid. The patient is surviving. There's no sign of infection."

"I think it's phenomenal."

"We're happy you're pleased."

And the chaplain was still out of sight: in detention somewhere for examination and interrogation after tracking Yossarian down in his hospital through the Freedom of Information Act and popping back into his life with the problem he could not grapple with.

Yossarian was lying on his back in his hospital bed when the chaplain had found him there the time before, and he waited with a look of outraged hostility as the door to his room inched open after he'd given no response to the timid tapping he'd heard and saw an equine, bland face with a knobby forehead and thinning strands of hay-colored hair discolored with dull silver come leaning in shyly to peer at him. The eyes were pink-lidded, and they flared with brightness the instant they alighted upon him.

"I knew it!" the man bearing that face burst right out with joy. "I wanted to see you again anyway. I knew I would find you! I knew I would recognize you. How good you look! How happy I am to see we're both still alive! I want to cheer!"

"Who," asked Yossarian austerely, "the fuck are you?"

The reply was instantaneous. "Chaplain, Tappman, Chaplain Tappman, Albert Tappman, Chaplain?" chattered Chaplain Albert Tappman garrulously. "Pianosa? Air force? World War II?"

Yossarian at last allowed himself a beam of recognition. "Well, I'll be damned!" He spoke with some warmth when he at last appreciated that he was again with the army chaplain Albert T. Tappman after more than forty-five years. "Come on in. You look good too," he offered generously to this man who looked peaked, undernourished, harried, and old. "Sit down, for God sakes."

The chaplain sat down submissively. "But, Yossarian. I'm sorry to find you in a hospital. Are you very sick?"

"I'm not sick at all."

"That's good then, isn't it?"

"Yes, that is good. And how are you?"

And all at once the chaplain looked distraught. "Not good, I'm beginning to think, no, maybe not so good."

"That's bad then," said Yossarian, glad that the time to come directly to the point was so soon at hand. "Well, then, tell me, Chaplain, what brings you here? If it's another old air corps reunion, you have come to the wrong man."

"It's not a reunion." The chaplain looked miserable.

"What then?"

"Trouble," he said simply. "I think it may be serious. I don't understand it."

He had been to a psychiatrist, of course, who'd told him he was a very good candidate for late-life depression and already too old to expect any better kind.

"I've got that too."

It was possible, it had been suggested, that the chaplain was imagining it all. The chaplain did not imagine, he imagined, that he was imagining any of it.

But this much was certain.

When none in the continuing stream of intimidating newcomers materializing in Kenosha on official missions to question him about his problem seemed inclined to help him even understand what the problem was, he'd remembered Yossarian and thought of the Freedom of Information Act.

The Freedom of Information Act, the chaplain explained, was a federal regulation obliging government agencies to release all information they had to anyone who made application for it, except information they had that they did not want to release.

And because of this one catch in the Freedom of Information Act, Yossarian had subsequently found out, they were technically not compelled to release any information at all. Hundreds of thousands of pages each week went out regularly to applicants with everything blacked out on them but punctuation marks, prepositions, and conjunctions. It was a good catch, Yossarian judged expertly, because the government did not have to release any information about the information they chose not to release, and it was impossible to know if anyone was complying with the liberalizing federal law called the Freedom of Information Act.

The chaplain was back in Wisconsin no more than one day or two when the detachment of sturdy secret agents descended upon him without notice to spirit him away. They were there, they said, on a matter of such sensitivity and national importance that they could not even say who they were without compromising the secrecy of the agency for which they said they worked. They had no arrest warrant. The law said they did not need one. What law? The same law that said they never had to cite it.

"That's peculiar, isn't it?" mused Yossarian.

"Is it?" said the chaplain's wife with surprise, when they conversed on the telephone. "Why?"

"Please go on."

They read him his rights and said he did not have them. Did he want to make trouble? No, he did not want to make trouble. Then he would have to shut his mouth and go along with them. They had no search warrant either but proceeded to search the house anyway. They and others like them had been back several times since, with crews of technicians with badges and laboratory coats, gloves, Geiger counters, and surgical masks, who took samples of soil, paint, wood, water, and just about everything else in beakers and test tubes and other special containers. They dug up the ground. The neighborhood wondered.

The chaplain's problem was heavy water.

He was passing it.

"I'm afraid it's true," Leon Shumacher had confided to Yossarian, when he had the full urinalysis report. "Where did you get that specimen?"

"From that friend who was here last week when you dropped by. My old chaplain from the army."

"Where did he get it?"

"From his bladder, I guess. Why?"

"Are you sure?"

"How sure can I be?" said Yossarian. "I didn't watch him. Where the hell else would he get it?"

"Grenoble, France. Georgia, Tennessee, or South Carolina, I think. That's where most of it is made."

"Most of what?"

"Heavy water."

"What the hell does all of this mean, Leon?" Yossarian wanted to know. "Are they absolutely sure? There's no mistake?"

"Not from what I'm reading here. They could tell it was heavy almost immediately. It took two people to lift the eyedropper. Of course they're sure. There's an extra neutron in each hydrogen molecule of water. Do you know how many molecules there are in just a few ounces? That friend of yours must weigh fifty pounds more than he looks."

"Listen, Leon," Yossarian said, in a voice lowered warily. "You'll keep this secret, won't you?"

"Of course we will. This is a hospital. We'll tell no one but the federal government."

"The government? They're the ones who've been bothering him! They're the ones he's most afraid of!"

"They have to, John," Leon Shumacher intoned in an automatic bedside manner. "The lab sent it to radiology to make sure it's safe, and radiology had to notify the Nuclear Regulatory Commission and the Department of Energy. John, there's not a country in the world that allows heavy water without a license, and this guy is producing it by the quart several times a day. This deuterium oxide is dynamite, John."

"Is it dangerous?"

"Medically? Who knows? I tell you I never heard of anything like this before. But he ought to find out. He might be turning into a nuclear power plant or an atom bomb. You ought to alert him immediately."

By the time Yossarian did telephone Chaplain Albert T. Tappman, USAF, retired, to warn him, there was only Mrs. Tappman at home, in hysteria and in tears. The chaplain had been disappeared only hours before.

She had not heard from him since, although punctually each week Mrs. Karen Tappman was visited and assured he was well and given cash approximating on the generous side the amount he would have brought in were he still at liberty. The agents glowed with elation upon being told, tearfully, she had not heard from him. It was the confirmation they wanted that he was not getting through to anyone outside.

"I'll keep trying to track him down for you, Mrs. Tappman," Yossarian promised each time they spoke. "Although I don't really know where to turn next."

The lawyers she'd consulted did not believe her. The police in Kenosha were skeptical too. Her children also were dubious, although they could give no currency to the police theory that the chaplain, like many a missing man in their missing-persons book, had run off with another woman.

All that John Yossarian had been able to find out since was that whatever significance the chaplain had for his official captors was only monetary, military, scientific, industrial, diplomatic, and international.

He found this out from Milo.

He went first to good friends in Washington with influence—a lawyer, a fund-raiser, a newspaper columnist, and an image maker —who all said they did not want to go near it and thereafter did not return his calls or want him for a friend anymore. A lobbyist and a public relations counselor both requested large fees and guaranteed they could not guarantee they would do anything to earn them. His senator was useless, his governor helpless. The American Civil Liberties Union backed off too from the Case of the Missing Chaplain: they agreed with the police in Kenosha that he probably had run off with another woman. At last, in frustration, he went to Milo Minderbinder, who chewed his upper and then his lower lip and said:

"Heavy water? How much is heavy water selling for?"

"It fluctuates, Milo. A lot. I've looked it up. There's a gas that comes from it that costs even more. About thirty thousand dollars a gram right now, I'd guess. But that's not the point."

"How much is a gram?"

"About one thirtieth of an ounce. But that's not the point."

"Thirty thousand dollars for one thirtieth of an ounce? That sounds almost as good as drugs." Milo spoke with his disunited eyes fixed on a distance speculatively, each brown iris pointing off in a different direction, as though, in concert, they took in to the horizon the entirety of all that was visible to humankind. The halves of his mustache were palpitating in separate cadences, the individual rusty-gray hairs oscillating skittishly like sensors taking notes electronically. "Is there much of a demand for heavy water?" he inquired.

"Every country wants it. But that's not the point."

"What's it used for?"

"Nuclear energy, mainly. And making atomic warheads."

"That sounds better than drugs," Milo went on in fascination. "Would you say that heavy water is as good a growth industry as illegal drugs?"

"I would not call heavy water a growth industry," Yossarian answered wryly. "But this is not what I'm talking about. Milo, I want to find out where he is."

"Where who is?"

"Tappman. The one I'm talking to you about. He was the chaplain in the army with us."

"I was in the army with a lot of people."

"He gave you a character reference when you nearly got in trouble for bombing our own air base."

"I get a lot of character references. Heavy water? Yes? That's what it's called? What is heavy water?"

"It's heavy water."

"Yes, I see. And what is the gas?"

"Tritium. But that's not the point."

"Who makes heavy water?"

"Chaplain Tappman does, for one. Milo, I want to find him and get him back before anything happens to him."

"And I want to help," promised Milo, "before Harold Strange-love, General Electric, or one of my other competitors does. I can't thank you enough for coming to me with this, Yossarian. You're worth your weight in gold. Tell me, which is worth more, gold or tritium?"

"Tritium."

"Then you're worth your weight in tritium. I'm busy today, but I must find that chaplain and sneak a man inside with the scientists interrogating him to establish ownership."

"How will you manage that?"

"I'll simply say it's in the national interest."

"How will you prove it?"

"By saying it twice," answered Milo, and flew off to Washington for his second presentation of the new secret bomber he had in mind that made no noise and could not be seen.

6
Milo

"You can't hear it and you can't see it. It will go faster than sound and slower than sound."

"Is that why you say your plane is sub-supersonic?"

"Yes, Major Bowes."

"When would you want it to go slower than sound?"

"When it's landing, and perhaps when it's taking off."

"Absolutely, Mr. Wintergreen?"

"Positively, Captain Hook."

"Thank you, Mr. Minderbinder."

They were meeting one level belowground in the basement of MASSPOB, the new Military Affairs Special Secret Projects Office Building, in a circular chamber with Lucite walls of ocean blue illuminated with bowed lines of longitude over warped continents and vivid free-form sculptured panels of fighting fish at war with swooping birds of prey. On the wall behind the barbered heads of the curving row of questioners was a condor with colossal wings and rapacious golden talons. All present were male. No transcript was authorized. These were men of keen intellect and their collective memory was reference enough. Two were already stifling yawns. All took for granted that the room was bugged anyway. Proceedings of such a sort were too secret to remain confidential.

"Will it go faster than light?" inquired a colonel in the half circle of experts flanking the presiding figure in dead center, who sat on a chair higher than the rest.

"It will go almost as fast."

"We can rev it up to go even faster than light."

"There would be some increase in fuel consumption."

"Wait a minute, please wait just one minute, Mr. Minderbinder, let me ask something," slowly cut in a puzzled civilian with a professorial demeanor. "Why would your bomber be noiseless? We have supersonic planes now, and they surely make noise with their sonic booms, don't they?"

"It would be noiseless to the crew."

"Why should that be important to the enemy?"

"It could be important to the crew," emphasized Milo, "and no one is more concerned about those kids than we are. Some of them may be aloft for months."

"Maybe years, with the refueling planes we recommend."

"Will they be invisible too?"

"If you want them to be."

"And make no noise?"

"The crew won't hear them."

"Unless they slow down and allow the noise to catch up."

"I see, Mr. Wintergreen. It's all very clever."

"Thank you, Colonel Pickering."

"How large is your crew?"

"Just two. Two are cheaper to train than four."

"Absolutely, Mr. Minderbinder?"

"Positively, Colonel North."

The officer in the center was a general, and he cleared his throat now as a proclamation of intent. The room fell still. He treasured the suspense.

"Does light move?" he demanded finally.

A leaden silence ensued.

"Light moves, General Bingam," Milo Minderbinder sprang in finally, with relief that he could.

"Faster than anything," ex-PFC Wintergreen added helpfully. "Light is just about the fastest thing there is."

"And one of the brightest too."

Bingam turned dubiously to the men on his left. A few of them nodded. He frowned.

"Are you sure?" he asked, and swiveled his sober mien to the specialists on his right.

A few of these nodded fearfully too. Some glanced away.

"That's funny," Bingam said slowly. "I see that light standing on the corner table and it looks perfectly still."

"That's because," offered Milo, "it's moving so fast."

"It's moving faster than light," said Wintergreen.

"Can light move faster than light?"

"Certainly."

"You can't see light when it's moving, sir."

"Absolutely, Colonel Pickering?"

"Positively, General Bingam."

"You can only see light when it isn't there," said Milo.

"Let me show you," said Wintergreen, surging to his feet impatiently. He snapped off the lamp. "See that?" He switched the lamp back on. "Notice any difference?"

"I see what you mean, Gene," Bingam said. "Yes, I'm beginning to see the light, eh?" General Bingam smiled and inclined himself along the arm of his chair. "Put simply, Milo, what does your plane look like?"

"On radar? It won't be seen by the enemy. Not even when armed with all its nuclear weapons."

"To us. In photographs and drawings."

"That's secret, sir, until you get us some funding."

"It's invisible," added Wintergreen, with a wink.

"I understand, Eugene. Invisible? It's beginning to sound like the old Stealth."

"Well, it is a bit like the old Stealth."

"The B-2 Stealth?" cried Bingam with shock.

"Only a little bit!"

"But better than the Stealth," Milo put in hastily.

"And much prettier."

"No, it's not like the old Stealth."

"Not the least little bit like the old Stealth."

"I'm glad of that." Bingam relaxed again onto his armrest. "Milo, I can say with confidence that all of us here like what I'm hearing from you today. What do you call your wonderful new airplane? We'll have to know that much."

"We call our wonderful new plane the M & M E & A Sub-Supersonic Invisible and Noiseless Defensive Second-Strike Offensive Attack Bomber."

"That's a decent name for a defensive second-strike offensive attack bomber."

"It sort of suggested itself, sir."

"One moment, Mr. Minderbinder," objected a skinny civilian from the National Security Council. "You talk about the enemy as though we have one. We have no enemies anymore."

"We always have enemies," contradicted a contentious geopolitician who also wore rimless spectacles, and considered himself just as smart. "We must have enemies. If we have no enemies, we have to make them."

"But we face no superpower at this time," argued a fat man from the State Department. "Russia is collapsed."

"Then it's time for Germany again," said Wintergreen.

"Yes, there's always Germany. Do we have the money?"

"Borrow," said Milo.

"The Germans will lend," said Wintergreen. "So will Japan. And once we have their money," added Wintergreen triumphantly, "they have to make sure we win any war against them. That's another good secret defensive feature of our wonderful offensive defensive attack bomber."

"I'm glad you pointed that out, Gene," said General Bingam. "Milo, I want to run for the gold with this one and make my recommendation."

"To the little prick?" Milo burst out with hope.

"Oh, no," Bingam replied with a humoring jollity. "It's still too soon for Little Prick. We'll need at least one more meeting with strategists from the other services. And there are always those damned civilians near the President, like Noodles Cook. We'll need leaks to newspapers. I want to start building support. You're not the only one after this, you realize."

"Who are the others?"

"Strangelove is one."

"Strangelove?" said Milo. "He's no good."

"He bullshits," charged Wintergreen.

"He was pushing the Stealth."

"What's *he* up to now?"

"He has this thing called a Strangelove All-Purpose Do-It-Yourself Defensive First Second or Third Strike Indestructible Fantastic State-of-the-Art B-Ware Offensive Attack Bomber."

"It won't work," said Wintergreen. "Ours is better."

"His name is better."

"We're working on our name."

"His Strangelove All-Purpose Do-It-Yourself Defensive First Second or Third Strike Indestructible Fantastic State-of-the-Art B-Ware Offensive Attack Bomber can't compare with our M & M E & A Sub-Supersonic Invisible and Noiseless Defensive Second-Strike Offensive Attack Bomber," said Milo curtly.

"Nothing he does ever works, does it?"

"I'm glad to hear that," said General Bingam, "because you're the buddies I'm backing. Here's his new business card. One of our security agents stole it from one of the security agents in another unit of procurement with which we are just about ready to go to war openly. Your bomber will help."

The business card passed down was emblazoned with the double eagle of the Austro-Hungarian Empire and with engraved lettering in auburn gold that read:

Harold Strangelove Associates
Fine Contacts and Advice
Secondhand Influence Bought and Sold
Bombast on Demand
Note: The information on this business card is restricted

Milo was downcast. The card was better than his.

"Milo, all of us are in the race of the century to come up with the ultimate weapon that could lead to the end of the world and bring everlasting fame to the victor who uses it first. Whoever sponsors that baby could be elevated to the Joint Chiefs of Staff, and I, Bernard Bingam, would like to be that man."

"Hear, hear!" chorused the officers on both sides of General Bingam, who beamed in shy surprise, while the stout civilian and the slim civilian were mum and disconsolate.

"Then you better move quickly, sir," threatened Wintergreen churlishly. "We don't like to sit on our asses with a hot product like this one. If you guys don't want it—"

"Of course, Eugene, of course. Just give me some good sales copy so that we'll know what we are talking about when we talk to people about what you've been talking about to us today. Not much detail, or we might have trouble. Just a few glowing paragraphs of very hard sell, and maybe some drawings in color to give us an idea of what it's going to look like. They don't have to be accurate, just impressive. And we'll all move along as fast as we can. As fast as light, eh? And, Milo, there's one more troubling question I have to ask."

"Me too," said the fat man.

"I have one also," said Skinny.

"It's touchy, so I apologize beforehand. Will your planes work? Will they do the job you say they will? The future of the world may depend on it."

"Would I lie to you?" said Milo Minderbinder.

"When the future of the world may depend on it?" said ex-PFC Wintergreen. "I would sooner lie to my ex-wife."

"You've given me the assurances I need."

"General Bingam," said Wintergreen, with the pained solemnity of a man taking umbrage, "I understand what war is like. In World War II, I dug ditches in Colorado. I served overseas as a PFC. I sorted mail in the Mediterranean during the Normandy invasion. I was right there on D day, in my mailroom, I mean, and it was not much bigger than this room we're in today. I stuck my neck out with stolen Zippo cigarette lighters for our fighting men in Italy."

"I did that with eggs," said Milo.

"We don't have to be reminded of all that's at stake. No one in this room has a stronger awareness of my responsibilities or a deeper commitment to fulfill them."

"I'm sorry, sir," said General Bingam humbly.

"Unless it's you, General, or Mr. Minderbinder here. Or your colleagues at the table with you, sir. Jesus Christ, I knew those fucking bastards were going to want something," Wintergreen complained, when the two of them were out of the conference room.

Together they moved through the convoluted basement complex that teemed with men and women of ebullient demeanor hurrying briskly along on official business in mufti and uniform. The whole fucking bunch of them, Wintergreen noted in a subdued growl, seemed affluent and clean, aseptic, and too fucking self-assured. The women in uniform all seemed petite, except for those who were commissioned officers, and they loomed larger than life. And every fucking one of them, Wintergreen muttered with his eyes down guiltily, looked fishy, fishy.

Continuing toward the elevators, they passed a sign pointing off to the Department of Justice. In the next passageway was another directional arrow, this one black, leading to a shortcut to the new National Military Cemetery. The public area of the new MASS-POB building, with its scintillating shopping center in the soaring atrium, was already the second most popular tourist attraction in the nation's capital; the first most popular was the newest war memorial. One needed special top-secret MASSPOB credentials to go higher and lower than the stacked-up promenades and open mezzanines with their plenitude of nouveau art deco newsstands, food counters, and souvenir shops and their celebrated sideshows, dioramas, and "virtual reality" shooting galleries, which had already excelled in international architectural competitions.

On their right in the basement, an iridescent red arrow like a flaming missile carried their eyes to a directional sign announcing:

Sub-Basements A–Z

The arrow angled downward suddenly to a closed metal door marked:

EMERGENCY ENTRANCE
KEEP OUT
VIOLATORS WILL BE SHOT

This was guarded by two uniformed sentinels, who seemed stationed at the emergency entrance to keep people away. A large yellow letter *S* against a glossy background of black gave comforting reminder that a new old-fashioned bomb shelter had been installed for the convenience and protection of visitors and employees.

At the elevators were other guards, who would not talk even to each other. Inside the elevator was a TV monitor. Milo and Wintergreen did not speak or move, even when back upstairs in the main lobby of the real world, where tour guides were leading tour groups from tour buses parked beyond the revolving doors in the area reserved at the front entrance. They did not converse again until they were outside in a light spring drizzle and walking away from the august special-secret-projects building in which their meeting had just taken place.

"Wintergreen," whispered Milo finally, "will these planes of ours really work?"

"How the fuck should I know?"

"What will they look like?"

"I guess we have to find that out too."

"If the future of the world is going to depend on it," reasoned Milo, "I believe we ought to make this deal while the world is still here. Otherwise we might never get paid."

"We'll need some drawings. That fucking Strangelove."

"And some copy for a leaflet. Who can we get?"

"Yossarian?"

"He might object."

"Then fuck him," said Wintergreen. "Let him object. We'll ignore the fuck again. What the fuck! What the fuck fucking difference does it make if the fuck objects or not? We can ignore the fucking fuck again, can't we? Shit."

"I wish," said Milo, "you wouldn't swear so much in the nation's capital."

"Nobody but you can hear me."

Milo looked hesitant. The gentle sun shower sprinkled raindrops around him through a prismatic haze that circled his brow like a wreath. "Yossarian has been objecting too much again lately. I could murder my son for telling him it was a bomber."

"Don't murder your son."

"I'd like to get some second-rate hack with a good position in government who's not too scrupulous when it comes to making money."

"Noodles Cook?"

"Noodles Cook is who I had in mind."

"Noodles Cook is much too big for that stuff now. And we'd need Yossarian to make the contact."

"I worry about Yossarian." Milo was brooding. "I'm not sure I trust him. I'm afraid he's still honest."

BOOK
THREE

BOOK THREE

7

ACACAMMA

Yossarian went crosstown by taxi to the Metropolitan Museum of Art for the monthly meeting of ACACAMMA, arriving in time for the reading of an anonymous proposal for the creation of a deconstruction fund to reduce the museum from the farcical dimensions to which it had now grown preposterously. He heard the motion ruled out of order, seeing Olivia Maxon turn to fix her glowing black eyes upon him severely while he was turning to gaze with a suppressed smile at Frances Beach, who raised her eyebrows with admiring inquiry at Patrick Beach, who was looking down at his fingernails and paying no attention to Christopher Maxon, who, all jowls and chortles beside him, rolled an imaginary cigar between his fingers, wet its imaginary tip, relished the imagined fragrance he inhaled, inserted the imaginary cigar into a mouth that was real, and puffed himself deeply into a soporific delirium.

ACACAMMA, the select Adjunct Committee for the Advancement of Cultural Activities at the Metropolitan Museum of Art, was an exclusive body of which only thirty or forty of the seventy or eighty members had come that day to deal with the same thorny question: if and how to increase revenues from the utilization of the premises for social events like weddings, bridal showers, bridge classes, fashion shows, and birthday parties, or whether to discontinue those incongruous ceremonies altogether as crass.

The potent need as always was for money.

Introduced and tabled for more comprehensive discussion at future meetings were such topics as the art of fund-raising, the art of the deal, the artistry of publicity, the art of social climbing, the art of fashion designing, the art of the costume, the art of catering, and the art of conducting without dissension and bringing to a close on time a meeting lasting two hours that was pleasant, uneventful, unsurprising, and unnecessary.

What dissonance appeared was managed neatly.

A final anonymous proposal that all anonymous proposals no longer be given even perfunctory consideration was referred to the executive committee for consideration.

At the bar of the hotel nearby to which Yossarian escaped afterward with Patrick and Frances Beach, Frances began a gin and tonic and Patrick Beach looked bored.

"Of course I'm bored," he informed his wife with ill-tempered pride. "By now I hate the paintings as much as I hate hearing them talked about. Oh, Frances"—his sigh was the whimsical plea of a martyr—"why must you keep putting us both into settings like that one?"

"Have we anything better to do?" Frances Beach said sweetly to her husband. "It gets us invited to so many other things that are even worse, doesn't it? And it helps keep our name in the newspapers, so that people know who we are."

"It's so *we* know who we are."

"I think that's divine."

"I have promised to kill her if she uses that word."

"Let's get to the point," said Frances seriously.

"He could not possibly have meant it."

"Yes, he could. Did you mean it, John, when you suggested a wedding in that bus terminal?"

"Of course," lied Yossarian.

"And you think it could be done? A big one?"

"I have no doubt," he lied again.

"Olivia Maxon." Frances made a wry face. "She's giving a wedding for a stepniece or someone and wants fresh ideas for an original venue. That word is her own. The museum isn't good enough since those two Jews had their reception there and those two other Jews were named trustees. Those words are also hers. Poor Olivia just isn't able to remember when talking to me that I might be Jewish."

"Why don't you remind her?" Yossarian said.

"I don't want her to know."

All three chuckled.

"You certainly wanted me to know," chided Patrick affection-
ately. "And everyone in my family."

"I was poor then," said Frances, "and an angry actress who
thrived on dramatic conflict. Now that I'm married to a man of
wealth, I'm loyal to his class."

"With a gift for stilted repartee," said Patrick. "Frances and I
are happiest together when I'm away sailing."

"What I never could trust about high comedy," Yossarian
mused, "is that people say funny things and the others don't laugh.
They don't even know they are part of a comedy."

"Like us," said Patrick.

"Let's get back to our agenda," ruled Frances. "I'd like to see
that wedding at your bus terminal, for Olivia's sake. For mine, I'd
like it to be the disaster of the century."

"I might help with the venue," said Yossarian. "I don't guarantee the disaster."

"Olivia will pitch in. She's sure she can attract our newest President. Christopher gives plenty since he received a suspended sentence and escaped community service."

"That's a good start."

"The mayor would come."

"That would help too."

"And the cardinal will insist."

"We're holding all the cards," said Yossarian. "I'll start casing
the joint if you really want me to."

"Who do you know there?" Frances was eager to learn.

"McMahon and McBride, the cop and a supervisor. McBride
was a detective at the police station there—"

"They have a police station there?" Patrick exclaimed.

"That should be novel," Frances remarked. "We've got our
protection on hand."

"And convenient too," said Yossarian. "They can fingerprint
the guests as we all arrive. McBride should know if it can be done.
We've all gotten pretty close since my son Michael was arrested
there."

"For what?" Patrick demanded.

"For coming out of the subway and stepping back in when he
realized he had mistaken the stop he wanted. They shackled him
to a wall."

"Good God!" Patrick reacted with a look of wrath. "That must
have been horrifying."

"It almost killed both of us," Yossarian said, with a nervous, depressed laugh. "Come there with me, Patrick. I'll be going to look at something new. You'll see more of what modern life is really like. It's not all just the museum."

"I'd rather be sailing."

Patrick Beach, four years older than both, had been born rich and intelligent and was early made indolent by the perception of his own intrinsic uselessness. In Britain, he had remarked to Yossarian, or in Italy or one of the few remaining republican societies with a truly aristocratic tradition, he might have sought to distinguish himself academically as a scholar in some field. But here, where intellectual endeavors generally were rated menial, he was sentenced from birth to be a dilettante or a career diplomat, which he felt was almost always the same thing. After three quick superficial marriages to three superficial women, he had finally settled permanently on Frances Rosenbaum, whose stage name was Frances Rolphe, and who understood easily his recurring attraction for solitude and study. "I inherited my money," he was fond of repeating with overdone amiability to new acquaintances to whom he felt obliged to be civil. "I did not have to work hard to be here with *you*."

He was not disturbed that many did not like him. But that patrician face of his could freeze and his fine lips quiver in powerless frustration with people too obtuse to discern the insult in his condescension, or too brutal to care.

"Olivia Maxon," said Frances in summation, "will agree to anything I want her to, provided I let her think the initiative was hers."

"And Christopher Maxon is always agreeable," Patrick guaranteed, "as long as you give him something to agree with. I have lunch with him frequently when I feel like eating alone."

When he felt like eating with someone, he thought often of Yossarian, who was content to chat disparagingly with him about almost everything current and to reminisce about their respective experiences in World War II, Yossarian as a decorated bombardier on an island near Italy, Patrick with the Office of War Information in Washington. Patrick was still always respectfully enchanted to be talking to a man he liked who knew how to read a newspaper as skeptically as he did and had been wounded in combat once and stabbed in the side by a native prostitute, and who had defied his immediate superiors and compelled them at the last to send him home.

Frances went on with good cheer. "Olivia will be delighted to know you're assisting. She's curious about you, John," she volunteered archly. "Here you've been separated now a whole year, and you're still not attached to another woman. I wonder about that too. You say you're afraid of living alone."

"I'm more afraid of living with someone. I just know the next one too will like movies and television news! And I'm not sure I can ever fall in love again," he observed, pining. "I'm afraid those miracles may be past."

"And how do you think a woman my age feels?"

"But what would you say," Yossarian teased, "if I said I was in love now with a nurse named Melissa MacIntosh?"

Frances welcomed this game. "I would remind you that at our age, love seldom makes it through the second weekend."

"And I'm also attracted to a shapely Australian blonde who shares her apartment, a friend named Angela Moorecock."

"I might fall in love with that one myself," ventured Patrick. "That's really her name? Moorecock?"

"Moore."

"I thought you said Moorecock."

"I said Moore, Peter."

"He did say Moorecock," said Frances, reproachfully. "And I would also accuse you of ruthlessly exploiting innocent young working girls for degenerate sexual purposes."

"She isn't innocent and she isn't so young."

"Then you might as well take up with one of our widows or divorcées. They can be manipulated but never exploited. They have lawyers and financial advisers who won't allow them to be misused by anyone but themselves."

Patrick made a face. "John, how did she talk before she went on the stage?"

"Like I do now. Some people would say you were lucky, Patrick, to be married to a woman who speaks always in epigrams."

"And gets us talking that way too."

"I find that divine."

"Oh, shit, darling," said Patrick.

"That's an obscenity, my sweet, that John would never use with both of us."

"He speaks dirty to me."

"To me too. But never to both of us."

He glanced with surprise at Yossarian. "Is that true?"

"You can bet your sweet ass," said Yossarian, laughing.

"You'll find out what you can? About our wedding at the bus terminal?"

"I'm on my way."

There were no cabs outside the hotel. Down the block was the Frank Campbell Funeral Home, a redoubtable mortuary catering to many of the city's perished notables. Two men out front, one in the sober attire of an employee, the other plebeian in appearance with a knapsack and a hiking pole, were rasping at each other in muted disagreement, but neither gave him a look as he lifted an arm and caught his taxi there.

8
Time

The structure housing the M & M offices, to which Yossarian would be going later that same day, was an edifice of secondary size in the Japanese real estate complex now known as Rockefeller Center. Formerly, it was the old Time-Life Building and the headquarters of the publishing company Time Incorporated, the company for which, in that same building long before, Sammy Singer had gone to work as an advertising-promotion writer shortly after giving up a teaching position in Pennsylvania rather than sign a state loyalty oath to keep a job paying just thirty-two hundred dollars a year, and where he met the woman who five years later would become his wife. Glenda was a year older than Sammy, which would have disqualified her with his mother, had his mother been still alive, and was not Jewish, which might have unsettled her even more.

And she was divorced. Glenda had three young children, one of whom, sadly, was fated to evolve into a borderline schizophrenic of weak will with an attraction to drugs and an incipient bent toward suicide, the other two surviving, it developed eventually, with potential traits marking them especially high risks for neoplastic disorders. Sammy's only regret about the long marriage was its tragic and unexpected termination. Sammy had no strong opinions about loyalty oaths but a passionate dislike for the people advocating them. It was much the same with the Korean War and the Vietnam War: he had no profound convictions either way but developed a hostile revulsion for demagogues in both political parties who demanded threateningly that he believe as they did. He disliked Harry Truman after reveling in his victorious campaign in 1948 and did not care afterward for Eisenhower and Nixon. He cared no more for Kennedy than he had for Eisenhower and ceased voting in presidential elections. Soon he stopped voting altogether and felt smug on election days. Glenda had stopped voting years before he met her and found all campaigning candidates for public office vulgar, boring, and loathsome.

At *Time* magazine his starting salary was nine thousand dollars annually, just about three times more than he would have earned as a college instructor, and he had a four-week summer vacation. And at the end of his third year there he felt blessed to discover himself with a vested interest in a magnanimous company pension and profit-sharing plan. With a university education, paid for and made possible by the federal government under the GI Bill of Rights, and a position with an illustrious, nationally known firm, he was judged already at twenty-five a fabulous success by all his childhood friends from Coney Island. When he moved into Manhattan to a small apartment of his own, he ascended with charisma into the empyrean realm of the elite, and even Lew Rabinowitz eyed him with a kind of savoring envy. Sammy liked his surroundings, he liked his life. After he married, he loved his wife, he loved his stepchildren, and, though Lew refused to believe it, he did not go to bed with another woman for as long as he and Glenda were together.

In his work in the city Sammy found himself among Republicans for the first time in his life. Nothing in his background or higher education had conditioned him to expect that anyone but a bandit, sociopath, or ignoramus would ever want to be a Republican. But these coworkers weren't ignorant, and they were not bandits or sociopaths. He drank martinis at long lunches with other men and women in the company, smoked pot frequently at night for a few years with old friends and new ones, lamented the acquaintances back in Brooklyn now addicted to heroin. It seemed incredible to the Gentile men and women with whom he drank whiskey and smoked marijuana that Jewish youths in Brooklyn, New York, should be drug addicts. He brought friends from Manhattan to Brooklyn to meet them, to eat clams at Sheepshead Bay and hot dogs in Coney Island, to ride on the Parachute Jump and the Wonder Wheel and watch others brave the frightening rollercoasters. He took them to George C. Tilyou's Steeplechase Park. In daylight and darkness he went to bed with young women who used diaphragms and contraceptive vaginal foam, and he had still not gotten over that. Unlike the friends with whom he had grown up, he did not marry immediately upon returning alive from the war, but not until he was almost thirty. He was often lonely in this single life and hardly ever unhappy.

His boss was an articulate man of elegant mannerisms who had contempt for the editors, principally because he was not one of them and because he was better read than all, and he would contend eloquently at meetings that the business and promotion writers in his department were better writers than those on the editorial staff and knew much more. At that time every copywriter there, Sammy too, was writing, or talking about writing, books and articles and stories and scripts; the men and women in the art department did painting and sculpture on weekends and dreamed of exhibitions. The gadfly supervisor, of whom they all were proud, was eventually jostled into early retirement. Not long afterward he died of cancer. Right after he left the company, Sammy, a Coney Island Jew in a Protestant organization dominated by Class A suburbanites, found himself a manager of one of the smaller departments and the stepfather of three children of a Protestant woman from the Midwest of decisive emotional poise, who'd gone off one morning to have her tubes tied to avert bearing more children in a troubled marriage to a philandering husband she saw was certain to break up. She could adjust to the philandering, she'd said—and Sammy had not believed her—but detested his absence of tact. Shortly after the divorce he was stricken with melanoma. He was living still when Sammy moved in with Glenda and was alive when they married.

Sammy stayed on at *Time* contentedly, writing promotion copy to increase the advertising business of a magazine he appreciated only as a superior consumer product and thought little of otherwise. He liked the work, he liked the people he worked with, he enjoyed the increasingly good salary and the comfortable knowledge that he was economically secure. His involvement with the international editions of the magazines *Time* and *Life* gave him opportunities to travel and brought him into lasting friendships with people in other countries. Like others of his generation, he was brought up with the practical ideal that the best work to do was the best work to be found.

He stayed on until he too was nudged into early retirement, at the age of sixty-three, by a thriving company electing to thrive more abundantly by reducing staff and eliminating aging deadwood like himself, and he departed serendipitously with a guaranteed good income for the rest of his life from the organization's liberal pension and profit-sharing plan, plus three thousand shares of company stock valued at more than a hundred dollars each, and with generous hospitalization and medical insurance benefits that took care of just about all the bills incurred by Glenda in her last illness and that would cover him for his lifetime and, had they still been young enough to qualify, the two surviving stepchildren until they reached nineteen or had completed college.

9

PABT

The luggage hustlers at curbside stared through him icily when he alighted without any. Inside the bus terminal things looked normal. Travelers streamed toward goals, those departing descending to buses below that carried them everywhere, or upward to the second, third, and fourth levels to buses that carried them away everywhere else.

"I'll do you for a nickel, mister," a thin boy of about fourteen spoke up to him bashfully.

A nickel was five dollars, and Yossarian did not have the heart to tell the lad that he did not think he was worth it.

"I'll do you for a nickel, mister," said a flat-chested girl immediately beyond, a few years older but lacking the ballooning contours of budding female maturity, while a stout woman with painted lids and rouged cheeks and dimpled faces of fat around the chubby knees exposed by her tight skirt looked on from ahead, laughing to herself.

"I'll lick your balls," the woman proposed while Yossarian walked by, and rolled her eyes coquettishly. "We can do it in the emergency stairwell."

Now he tensed with outrage. I am sixty-eight, he said to himself. What was there about him that gave these people the notion he had come to the terminal to be done or have his balls licked? Where the fuck was McMahon?

Police Captain Thomas McMahon of the Port Authority police force was inside the police station with civilian deputy director Lawrence McBride, watching Michael Yossarian draw with a pencil on the back of a broad sheet of paper, looking on with that special reverence some people of inexperience bestow upon the ordinary skills of the artistic performer which they themselves lack. Yossarian could have told them that Michael probably would stop before finishing his sketch and leave it behind. Michael tended not to finish things and prudently did not start many.

He was busy executing a horrified picture of himself in the wall cuff to which he had still been chained when Yossarian had come charging into the police station the day he was arrested. With looping strokes he had transformed the rectangular modes of the prison cells into a vertical pit of sludge with spinning sides into which one peered slantwise, and in which the stiff human stick figure of himself he had just outlined stood engulfed and forlorn.

"You leave him right where he is!" Yossarian had thundered on the telephone half an hour before to the officer who had called to establish identification because the receptionist at the architectural firm for which Michael was doing elevations did not know he'd been taken on for a freelance assignment. "Don't you dare put him in a cell!"

"One minute, sir, one minute, sir!" broke in the offended cop, in a high-pitched outcry of objection. "I'm calling to establish identity. We have our procedures."

"You go fuck your procedures!" Yossarian commanded. "Do you understand me?" He was mad enough and scared enough and felt helpless enough to kill. "You do what I say or I'll have your ass!" he bellowed roughly, with the belief that he meant it.

"Hey, hey, hey, one minute, buddy, hey, one minute, buddy!" The young cop was screaming now in a frenzy almost hysterical. "Who the fuck do you think *you* are?"

"I am Major John Yossarian of the M & M Pentagon Air Force Project," Yossarian replied in crisp, stern tones. "You insolent cocksucker. Where's your superior?"

"Captain McMahon here," said an older man, with emotionless surprise. "What's your trouble, sir?"

"This is Major John Yossarian of the M & M Pentagon Air Force Project, Captain. You've got my son there. I don't want him touched, I don't want him moved, I don't want him put near anyone who might harm him. And that includes your cops. Do we understand each other?"

"I understand you," McMahon came back coolly. "But I don't think you understand me. Who did you say this is?"

"John Yossarian, Major John Yossarian. And if you tie me up on this any longer it will be your ass too. I'll be there in six minutes."

To the taxi driver he gave a hundred-dollar bill and said respectfully, hearing his heart pound: "Please pass every traffic light you can pass safely. If you're stopped by a cop I'll give you another hundred and go the rest of the way on foot. I've got a child in trouble."

That the child was past thirty-seven did not matter. That he was defenseless did.

But Michael was still safe, handcuffed to the wall on a chain as though he would founder to the floor if he did not have that chain for support, and he was white as a ghost.

The station was in an uproar. People were moving and shouting everywhere. The cages were swarming with arms and sweaty faces and with gleaming eyes and mouths, the hallway too, the air stank of everything, and the officers and prison guards, sweating and swarming all over too, labored powerfully in picking, pulling, shoving, and heaving prisoners to be steered outside into vans and trucked downtown for delivery into other hands. Of all who were there, only Michael and Yossarian showed awareness of anything uncommon. Even the prisoners seemed ideally acclimated to the turbulent environment and vigorous procedures. Many were bored, others were amused and contemptuous, some ranted crazily. Several young women were hooting with laughter and shrieking obscenities brazenly in taunting debauchery, baiting and incensing the frustrated guards, who had to endure and cope with them without retaliating.

McMahon and the desk sergeant were awaiting him with stony faces.

"Captain—you him?" Yossarian began, talking directly into McMahon's light-blue, steely eyes with a hard-boiled stare of his own. "Get used to the idea! You're not going to put him into one of those cells. And I don't want him in a van with those others either. A squad car is all right, but I'll want to go with him. If you like, I'll hire a private car, and you can put some officers in with us."

McMahon listened with folded arms. "Is that right?" he said quietly. He was slim, straight, and more than six feet tall, with a bony face with tiny features, and the crests of his high cheekbones were spotted pink with a faint efflorescence, as though in savoring anticipation of the conflict at hand. "Tell me again, sir. Who did you say you were?"

"Major John Yossarian. I'm at work on the M & M Pentagon Air Force Project."

"And you think that makes your son an exception?"

"He *is* an exception."

"Is he?"

"Are you blind?" Yossarian exploded. "Take a good look, for Christ sakes. He's the only one here with a dry crotch and a dry nose. He's the only one here who's white."

"No, he's not, Captain," meekly corrected the sergeant. "We've got two other Caucasians we're holding in back who beat up a cop by mistake. They were looking for money."

Everyone around was contemplating Yossarian now as though he were something bizarre. And when he finally appreciated why, that he was poised before them with his arms raised in an asinine prizefighter's stance, as though ready to punch, he wanted to whimper in ironic woe. He had forgotten his age. Michael too had been regarding him with astonishment.

And at just that point of unnerving self-discovery, McBride wandered up and, in a gentle manner both firm and conciliatory, asked: "What's up, guys?"

Yossarian saw a sturdy man of middle height with a flushed face and a polyester suit of vapid light gray, with a broad chest that bellied outward and down so that from his neck to his waist he seemed a bulwark.

"Who the fuck are you?" sighed Yossarian in despair.

McBride replied softly, with the fearless confidence of a man competent at riot control. "Hello. I'm Deputy Supervisor Lawrence McBride of the Port Authority Bus Terminal. Hello, Tommy. Something going on?"

"He thinks he's big," said McMahon. "He says he's a major. And he thinks he can tell us what to do."

"Major Yossarian," Yossarian introduced himself. "He's got my son here, Mr. McBride, chained to that wall."

"He's been arrested," said McBride pleasantly. "What would you want them to do with him?"

"I want them to leave him where he is until we decide what we will do. That's all. He has no criminal record." To the police guard nearest Michael, Yossarian barked an order. "Unlock him now. Please do that right now."

McMahon pondered a moment and signaled permission.

Yossarian resumed amicably. "Tell us where you want him to be. We're not running away. I don't want trouble. Should I hire that car? Am I talking too much?"

Michael was aggrieved. "They never even read me my right to be silent."

"They probably didn't ask you to say anything," McBride explained. "Did they?"

"And the handcuffs hurt like hell! Not that one. The real handcuffs, God damn it. That's brutality."

"Tommy, what's he charged with?" asked McBride.

McMahon hung his head. "Beating the subway fare."

"Oh, shit, Tommy," said McBride, entreating.

"Where's Gonzales?" McMahon asked the sergeant.

"That's the guy who grabbed me," Michael called out.

The sergeant blushed. "Back at the subway exit, Captain, making his quota."

"I *thought* they had a fucking quota!" Michael shouted.

"Major, can't you keep your son quiet while we settle this?" asked McMahon, begging a favor.

"Tommy," said McBride, "couldn't you just give him a summons and release him on a DTA? We know he'll appear."

"What did you think we were going to do, Larry?" McMahon replied. He appealed to Yossarian as though they were allies. "You hear that, Major? I'm a captain, he was a sergeant, and now he's telling me how to handle my business. Sir, are you really a major?"

"Retired," admitted Yossarian. He found the business card he wanted of the several he carried. "My card, Captain. And one for you, Mr. McBride—McBride, is it?—in case I can return the favor. You've been a godsend."

"Here's mine, Major," said McBride, and gave a second one to Michael. "And one for you too, in case you're ever in trouble here again."

Michael was moping as they walked out with McBride. "It's a good thing I've still got you to look after me, isn't it?" he accused sullenly. Yossarian shrugged. "I feel like such a fucking weakling now."

McBride intervened. "Hey, you did the right thing, kiddo." He paused for a chuckle, laughed louder. "How could *you* convince us you'd break our backs and legs, when we had you in handcuffs?"

"Is that what I did?" said Yossarian with fright.

McBride laughed again. "Where's the credibility? That right, Major Yossarian?"

"Call me Yo-Yo, for God's sake," said Yossarian jovially. "I must have been forgetting my age."

"You sure were," charged Michael. "I was scared, damn it. And you guys are laughing. You were a champ, Pop," he continued sardonically. "Me, I don't even have a loud voice. Before when I was stopped by that cop, my hands shook so much he was afraid I was having a heart attack and almost let me go."

"It's the way we are, Michael, when we're angry or scared. I get crazy and talk too much."

"I couldn't even give them my right name so they'd believe me. And when the hell were you really ever a major?"

"Want a business card?" Yossarian snickered slyly and turned to McBride. "For about a minute and a half," he explained. "They gave me a temporary boost near the end because they didn't know what else to do with me. Then they shipped me home, brought me back to my permanent grade, and gave me my honorable discharge. I had the medals, I had the points, I even had my Purple Heart."

"You were wounded?" cried McBride.

"Yeah, and crazy too," replied Michael, proudly. "Another time he went walking around naked."

"You walked around naked?" cried McBride.

"And they gave him a medal," boasted Michael, completely at ease now. "A medal for bravery."

"You got a medal for bravery?" cried McBride.

"And couldn't pin it on."

"Because he was naked?"

"Still naked."

"Weren't you embarrassed? Didn't they do anything?"

"He was crazy."

"What'd you get the medal for, Major? How'd you get the Purple Heart? Why'd you walk around naked?"

"Stop calling me Major, Mr. McBride," said Yossarian, who had no wish to talk now about the waist gunner from the South who'd been killed over Avignon and the small tail gunner Sam

Singer from Coney Island who kept fainting away each time he
came to and saw the waist gunner dying and Yossarian throwing
up all over himself as he worked with bandages and tried vainly
to save the dying man. It was sometimes funny to him since in just
those gruesome anecdotal aspects. The wounded waist gunner was
cold and in pain, and Yossarian could find nothing to do that
would warm him up. Every time Singer revived, he opened his
eyes on something else Yossarian was busy with that made him
faint away again: retching, wrapping up dead flesh, wielding scis-
sors. The dying gunner was freezing to death on the floor in a
patch of Mediterranean sunlight, Sam Singer kept fainting, and
Yossarian had taken off all his clothes because the sight of the
vomit and blood on his flight uniform made him want to vomit
some more and to feel with nauseated certitude that he would
never want to have to wear any kind of uniform ever again, not
ever, and by the time they landed, the medics were not sure which
one of the three to take into the ambulance first. "Let's talk about
you."

Yossarian now knew that McBride's wife had left him—transformed almost overnight into a wrathful figure of pure fury by an
inner rage he had never guessed existed—and that he had been
living alone since his daughter had moved to California with a
boyfriend to work as a physical therapist. To McBride, the unexpected breakup of his marriage was one more heartrending cruelty
he could not puzzle out in a world he saw seething barbarously
with multitudes of others. Former detective sergeant Larry
McBride of the Port Authority police force was fifty and had the
boyish, chubby face of an introspective seraph in hard times. As a
cop he had never been able to outgrow the sympathy he suffered
for every type of victim he encountered—even now his knowledge
of the one-legged woman living in the terminal tormented him—
and always after wrapping up a case, to his racking emotional
detriment, he would begin suffering compassion for the criminals
too, no matter how hardened, bestial, or obtuse, no matter how
vicious the crime. He would see them all pityingly, as they'd been
as children. When the opportunity arose to retire on a full pension
and take the executive position at good salary at the bus terminal
—in which, in fact, as one kind of guardian or another, he had by
now spent his entire working life—he seized it joyfully.

The end of a marriage he had thought satisfactory was a blow
from which it seemed at first he did not think he would recover.

Now, while Michael prepared to wait, Yossarian wondered what new thing McBride wanted to show him.

"You tell me," McBride answered mysteriously.

The time before, he had unveiled his plans for a maternity cell, for converting one of the two auxiliary prison cages in the rear, for which there never had been need, into a room for mothers of unwanted babies who most generally disposed of the newborn infants in alleys and hallways or threw them away into wastebaskets, garbage cans, and Dumpsters. He had already moved in at his own expense some pieces of furniture from his apartment for which he no longer had need. Yossarian nodded as he listened, sucking h   odded some more. Nobody v   l him, and nobody cared for   ervice to the community by

For the other jail cell, McBride resumed, he had in mind a sort of pediatric day care center for the several little kids always living in the bus terminal, to afford their mothers a clean, safe place in which to place their offspring while they journeyed outside to panhandle and hustle for drugs and booze and food, and also for the runaway kids who kept showing up in this heart of the city until they made their good connections with a satisfactory drug dealer or pimp.

Yossarian broke in regretfully.

"McBride?"

"You think I'm nuts?" McBride rushed on defensively. "I know Tommy thinks I'm nuts. But we could have mobiles and stuffed toys and coloring books for the little ones. And for the older ones television sets and video games, maybe computers, sure, even word processors, couldn't they learn that?"

"McBride?" repeated Yossarian.

"Yossarian?" McBride had adopted unconsciously a number of Yossarian's speaking traits.

"Mobiles and word processors for kids who want drugs and sex?"

"Just while they're hanging around making their contacts. They'd be safer here than anywhere else, wouldn't they? What's wrong? Yossarian, what's wrong?"

Yossarian sighed wearily, feeling undone. "You're talking about a facility in a police station for aspiring child prostitutes? Larry, the public would scream bloody murder. So would I."

"What would you do that's better? They come here anyway, don't they?"

From the fact that McBride had been silent since on the subject of these humanitarian undertakings, Yossarian surmised they'd been stalled or forbidden.

Today he had some new surprise in store, and Yossarian went outside with him into the capacious structure of the bus terminal, where activities of all varieties had picked up bullishly. People were moving more quickly, and there were many more of them, traveling automatically like spirits who would have chosen a different course than the ones they were following had they found themselves free to decide. So many were eating as they walked, dripping crumbs and wrappers—candy bars, apples, hot dogs, pizzas, sandwiches, potato chips. The hustlers were at work at their assorted specialties, the best of them animated, with sharp eyes fishing around shrewdly for targets of opportunity, others blundering about crudely in search of just about anything, and still others, male and female, white and black, floating in blank-eyed, wistful stupors and looking less like predators than crippled prey.

"Pickpockets," McBride said, with a signal of his chin toward a group of three men and two girls, all of good appearance, and of Latin American countenance. "They're better trained than we are. They even know more law. Look."

A jolly group of transvestites moved up by escalator to the floor above, the faces glistening with a cosmetic sheen, all androgynous and vain in face and attire, the entire bunch as frisky and flirtatious as pubescent girl scouts high on hormones.

With McBride steering him, they passed the empty space below the pillars supporting the mezzanine floor of the observation bubble overhead with its staff of several employees doing drugs while monitoring the five dozen video screens in the Communications Control Center of the terminal. The hundreds of azure-eyed, dumb video cameras poked their flat snouts into every cranny on every level of the rambling, seven-story complex bestriding two city blocks, poking without blushing even into the men's toilets and the notorious emergency stairwells into which most of those living in the terminal crept at night for sleep and friendship and apathetic intercourse. Milo and Wintergreen were already thinking of the Communications Control Center converted into a lucrative enterprise by increasing the number of screens and selling units of time to eager spectators and players, who would replace the Port Authority employees and their salaries and their costly medical plans and vacation and retirement plans. People would flock to watch, to play cop and Peeping Tom. They could call it "The Real Thing." When crime slackened, they would present fakes and that way guarantee enough sex and violence to satisfy even the most bloodthirsty paying crowds.

They could book in Japanese tour groups. Sooner or later they could spin the whole thing off to a Japanese motion picture company.

McBride moved past a newsstand run by Indians, with newspapers and colorful periodicals like *Time, The Weekly Newsmagazine* headlining the collapse of Russian socialism, the grandeur of American capitalism, and the latest business bankruptcy, unemployment figures, and sale of another national mercantile landmark to foreigners, and they came to the entrance of one of the emergency stairwells. Yossarian did not want to take that tour again.

"Just one floor," promised McBride.

"Something awful?"

"I wouldn't do that."

Loafing voices echoed mellifluously from above. The stairway was practically empty, the floor almost tidy. But the odors in this civilization were strong, the air reeking of smoke and unwashed bodies and their waste, a stench of rot and degradation that was violently disgusting and vilely intolerable to all but the mass producing it daily. By midnight there was scarcely a charmed body with enough living space to be free of another body more dissipated and fetid tumbled against it. People squabbled. There were shouts, quarrels, stabbings, burns, sex, drugs, drinking, and breaking glass; by morning there were casualties and an accumulation of filth of all sorts save industrial waste. There was no water or toilet. Garbage was not collected until morning, when the locals roused and took themselves to the sinks and the toilets in the rest rooms in sanitary preparation for the day's work ahead and, despite posted bans, to bathe and do laundry in the washbasins.

By this hour, the maintenance men had been through with their hoses and face masks to clean away the messes of excrement, trash, and garbage left the night before, the charred matchsticks and empty vials from dope, the soda cans, needles, wine bottles, and used condoms and old Band-Aids. The astringent smell of caustic disinfectant hung ineradicably in the air like the carbolic harbinger of a remorseless decay.

McBride took the staircase down past two raffish men of insolent and bored demeanor who were smoking marijuana and drinking wine and fell silent in tacit approbation after sizing him up and acknowledging with a kind of objective acceptance the latent authority and prowess he exuded. Near the bottom of the steps a solitary man slept with his back to the banister.

They passed to the concrete landing without disturbing him and tiptoed carefully around the one-legged woman being raped by a man with scrawny blanched buttocks and a livid scrotum not many yards from a large, brown-skinned woman who had taken off her bloomers and her skirt and was swabbing her backside and her armpits with a few damp towels she had laid out on newspapers with some folded dry ones near two brown shopping bags. She had splotchy freckles about her puffy eyes and bore scarred, tar-colored moles on her neck and back that made him think of melanoma. She stared at each in turn with a separate nod of matter-of-fact amity. Her pendulous breasts in a pink chemise were huge and her armpits were dark and bushy. Yossarian did not want to look down at her exposed vaginal area. He did not know who she was, but he knew he had not one thing he wanted to talk to her about.

On the last flight down to the sub-level outside, there sat only a skinny blonde woman with a bruised eye and a tattered red sweater, dreamily engaged in sewing a rip in a dirty white blouse. At the bottom, where the staircase came to an end facing an exit door to the street, someone had already shit in a corner. They looked away and walked looking down, as though in dire misgiving of a step into something sinful. Instead of heading outside, McBride turned beneath the staircase and proceeded into heavy shadows almost to the end of this lowest landing, until he came to a colorless door that Yossarian would have supposed invisible.

He switched on a light that was weak and yellow. The small room into which they stepped held only a metal closet with rusting doors on broken hinges that stood against a wall. McBride forced these doors apart and stepped inside the wasted relic. It had no back. He located a latch and pushed open an entranceway built into the wall itself.

"An addict found it," he mumbled rapidly. "I let him believe he was imagining it. Go on in."

Yossarian gasped with surprise in a cramped vestibule blocked by a wide fire door a few feet in front of his face. The slick surface was military green and painted at eye level with a warning in bold letters that could not be overlooked by anyone able to read.

EMERGENCY ENTRANCE
KEEP OUT
VIOLATORS WILL BE SHOT

The sturdy door seemed new, the letters fresh on the unmarred surface.

"Go on in. It's what I want to show you."

"I'm not allowed."

"Neither am I."

"Where's the key?"

"Where's the lock?" McBride grinned victoriously, his head cocked. "Go on."

The handle turned and the massive door slid open as though leveraged by counterweights and pivoting on noiseless bearings.

"They make it easy for people to get in, don't they?" said Yossarian softly.

McBride hung back, forcing Yossarian through first. Yossarian recoiled as he discovered himself on a tiny landing of wrought iron near the roof of a tunnel that seemed greatly higher than it was because of the dizzying angle downward of the staircase on which he was standing. Instinctively, he grasped the handrail. Here the flights of steps were small and reversed direction abruptly around an elliptical tiny platform of metal grillwork, where the next flight turned sharply back beneath him and dropped away out of sight at that same precipitous angle of descent. He could not see where the staircase came to an end in that abyss of a basement, whose dark floor seemed newly paved with some kind of rubberized compound. Looking down through the wrought-iron pattern of winding vine leaves that seemed to mock its own heavy composition, he was all at once reminded ridiculously of one of those vertical slides at an old-fashioned amusement park in which one embarked supine into darkness inside a cylindrical pillar with arms folded and went spiraling down with increasing momentum, to be expelled at last into a flat round arena of polished wood with disks rotating in contrary directions that bore him this way and that way for the pleasure of idle watchers until ultimately spilling him aside onto the stationary embankment that ringed the circular area of that particular attraction. The one he remembered best was named the Human Pool Table in the old George C. Tilyou Steeplechase Park in Coney Island. There, an iron handrail circling the viewing enclosure had been rigged electrically to administer stinging shocks of harmless voltage to unwary patrons whenever one of the red-suited attendants in green jockey caps thought the timing appropriate. That sudden onrush of tiny prickling needles bursting into the hands and arms was intolerable and memorable, and all who observed that half second of fright and panicked embarrassment of others laughed; the victims laughed too, afterward. There was laughter bursting from loudspeakers as well. Not many blocks away were freak shows featuring people with small heads.

Yossarian was standing now near the top of something nearly two stories high, a strange subterranean thoroughfare of impressive breadth and no discernible use, with a vaulted ceiling insulated with scored and pitted peach-colored acoustical tiles and outlined with slender borders of apple green. The high, flat walls of stone were of dark-reddish hue. These were tiled in white at the base like those of the underground stations of the subway system. The strange passageway was as wide as a city avenue, without curbs or sidewalks. It could have served as a train station too, except that he saw no rails or platforms. Then he spied near the bottom on the other side a long reflecting arrow in red that reminded him one moment of a fiery penis and the next of a flaming missile that shot vividly to the left and then dipped downward perpendicularly toward words in black that proclaimed:

Sub-Basements A–Z

Above the arrow, where the white tiling ended, and perhaps thirty feet to the right, he recognized a large stenciled letter S of luminescent amber on a square of glossy black. Obviously, they were inside an old bomb shelter, he knew, until he spotted near the ground a door of metal of the same olive-drab shade as on the one behind him, with writing on it in white he could not believe, even after he had donned his trifocals to see into the distance more clearly.

DANGER
NO EXPLOSIVES

"That could mean at least two different things, couldn't it?" he said.

McBride nodded grimly. "That's what I thought too." Unexpectedly, he let out a laugh, as though proud of himself. "Now look at that plaque."

"What plaque?"

"In dark letters. It's set into the wall near the doorway and says that a man named Kilroy was here."

Yossarian gave McBride a searching look. "Kilroy? It says that? Kilroy was here?"

"You know Kilroy?"

"I was in the army with Kilroy," said Yossarian.

"Maybe it's not the same Kilroy."

"He's the one."

"Overseas?"

"Everywhere. Shit, I ought to know him by now. Everywhere I was stationed, he was there too. You always saw it written on a wall. When I was arrested and put in the stockade for a week, he'd been locked up there also. In college after the war, when I went into the library stacks, he'd already been there."

"Could you find him for me?"

"I never met him. I never met anyone who saw him."

"I could find him," said McBride. "Through the Freedom of Information Act. Once I get his Social Security number I can nail him cold. Will you come talk to him with me?"

"Is he still alive?"

"Why wouldn't he be alive?" asked McBride, who was only fifty. "I want to know more about this, I want to know what he was doing here. I want to know what the hell this is."

"How far down does all this go?"

"I don't know. It's not on the plans."

"Why does it bother you?"

"I'm still a detective, I guess. Go down a few steps," McBride instructed next. "Try one more."

Yossarian froze when he heard the noise begin. It was an animal, the heaving ire of something live, the ominous burring of some dangerous beast disturbed, a rumble welling in smoldering stages into an elongated snarling. Next came growling, guttural and deadly, and an agitated shudder of awakened power, and the movement of veering limbs striding about underneath where he could not see. Then a second animal joined in; perhaps there were three.

"Go down," whispered McBride, "one more step."

Yossarian shook his head. McBride nudged. On tiptoe Yossarian touched his foot down one more step and heard the jangling commence, as though of metal scraping on stone and of metal jingling against metal, and those noises were building swiftly toward a demonic climax of some calamitous sort, and all at once, as though without warning, although the warnings had been cumulative and unremitting, there was the blowout, the explosion, the ferocious and petrifying bedlam of piercing barks and deafening roars and a tumultuous charge of forceful paws pounding forward with unleashed savagery and then mercifully brought to a halt in a quaking crash of chains that made him jump with fright and afterward went reverberating like a substance of great ballistic bulk deep into the contracting gloom at both ends of the underground chamber in which they were standing. The fierce rumpus below turned more savage still with the incensed raging of the beasts at the rugged restraints against which they were now tearing and snapping with all their supernatural might. They growled and they roared and they snarled and they howled. And Yossarian kept straining his ears in a frantic irrational desire to hear more. He knew he would never be able to move again. The instant he could move, he stepped up backward in noiseless motion, hardly breathing, until he stood on the landing alongside McBride, where he took McBride's arm and held on. He was icy and he knew he was sweating. He had the giddy fear his heart was going to convulse and stop, that an artery in his head would split. He knew he could think of eight other ways he might die on the spot, if he did not die before he could list them. The raw fury in the fierce passions below seemed gradually to flag. The untamed monsters understood they had missed him, and he listened with relief to the invisible dangers subsiding and to whatever carnivorous forms that drew breath below receding with chains dragging to the dark lairs from which they had sprung. At last there was silence, the last tinkling noises melting away into a tone as delicate as a chime and dissolving into a fading resonance that seemed incongruously to be the pumped, haunting carnival music of some outlying, solitary carousel, and this receded into silence too.

He thought he knew now how it felt to be torn to pieces. He trembled.

"What do you make of it?" McBride asked, in an undertone. His lips were white. "They're always there; that happens every time you touch that step."

"It's recorded," said Yossarian.

For the moment, McBride was speechless. "Are you sure?"

"No," said Yossarian, surprised himself by the spontaneous insight he had just expressed. "But it's just too perfect. Isn't it?"

"What do you mean?"

Yossarian did not want to talk now about Dante, Cerberus, Virgil, or Charon, or the rivers Acheron and Styx. "It might be there just to scare us away."

"It sure scared hell out of that drug addict, I can tell you," said McBride. "He was sure he was hallucinating. I let everyone but Tommy think that he was."

Then they heard the new noise.

"You hear that?" said McBride.

Yossarian heard the wheels turning and looked to the base of the wall opposite. Somewhere beyond it was the muffled rolling of wheels on rails, muted by distance and barriers.

"The subway?"

McBride shook his head. "That's too far. What would you say," he continued speculatively, "to a roller-coaster?"

"Are you crazy?"

"It could be a recording too, couldn't it?" insisted McBride. "Why is that crazy?"

"Because it's not a roller-coaster."

"How do you know?"

"I think I can tell. Stop playing detective."

"When's the last time you rode on one?"

"A million years ago. But it's too steady. There's no acceleration. What more do you want? I'm going to laugh. Let's call it a train," continued Yossarian, as the vehicle came abreast and rolled away to the left. It might have been the Metroliner going down from Boston to Washington, but McBride would know that. And when he considered a roller-coaster, he did start to laugh, for he remembered that he had already lived much longer than he ever thought he would.

He stopped laughing when he saw the catwalk and railing running along the wall about three feet from the bottom and disappearing into the white-misted, golden obscurity of the enclosures on both sides.

"Was that down there all the time?" He was puzzled. "I thought I was hallucinating when I noticed it just now."

"It's been there," said McBride.

"Then I must have been hallucinating when I imagined it wasn't. Let's get the hell out."

"I want to go down there," said McBride.

"I won't go with you," Yossarian told him.

He had never liked surprises.

"Aren't you curious?"

"I'm afraid of the dogs."

"You said," said McBride, "it was only a recording."

"That might scare me more. Go with Tom. That's his business."

"It's not on Tommy's beat. I'm not even supposed to be here," McBride admitted. "I'm supposed to enforce these restrictions, not violate them. Notice anything now?" he added, as they turned back up the stairs.

On the inside of the metal door Yossarian now saw two solid locks, one spring loaded, the other dead bolt. And above the locks, under a rectangle of lacquer, he saw a block of white printing on a scarlet background framed in a thin margin of silver, that read:

EMERGENCY EXIT
NO ADMITTANCE
THIS DOOR MUST BE LOCKED AND BOLTED WHEN IN USE

Yossarian scratched his head. "From this side it looks like they want to keep people out, don't they?"

"Or in?"

He would guess, he guessed, as they proceeded outside, that it was an old bomb shelter that was not on the old plans. He could not explain the signs, he admitted, as McBride closed the fire door quietly and conscientiously switched off the electric light to leave everything the same as when they had come. The dogs, the sound of the killer guard dogs? "To scare people out, I guess, like that addict, and you and me. Why did you want me to see it?"

"To let you know. You seem to know everything."

"I don't know this one."

"And you're someone I trust."

They could tell from voices higher up that the stairwell had crowded considerably. They heard clearly the bawdy laughter, the languorous salutes of greeting and recognition, the obscenities, they could smell the smoke of matches and dope and scorched newspapers, they heard a glass bottle break, they heard the splash one floor up of a man or a woman urinating, and they smelled that too. At the top of the lowest flight, they saw the one-legged woman, who was white, drinking wine with a man and two women who were black. Her expression was blank and she talked in a daze, crushing pink underwear in a hand that lay restfully in her lap. Her wooden crutches, which were old and chipped and splintered and spotted, were lying on the staircase at her hip.

"She gets a wheelchair," McBride had already explained, "and someone steals it. Then friends steal one from someone else. Then someone steals that one."

This time McBride took the exit door, and Yossarian found himself on the sidewalk passing buses on the sub-level driving ramps, where the exploding exhausts and grinding engines were noisier and the air was stinking with diesel fumes and the smell of hot rubber, and they walked past boarding stations with long-distance buses for El Paso and Saint Paul, with connections continuing far up into Canada and down all the way through Mexico into Central America.

McBride took an entrepreneur's gratification in the operational efficiency of the bus terminal: the figures of almost five hundred boarding gates, sixty-eight hundred buses, and nearly two hundred thousand passengers in and out every normal working day tripped from his tongue fluently. The work still went on, he was speedy to assert, the terminal functioned, and that was the point, wasn't it?

Yossarian wasn't sure.

Now they rode by escalator back to the main floor. Passing the Communications Control Center, they glanced uneasily at the flocks of male and female hookers already congregating in the central areas of prostitution, where more and more would continue crowding in crafty and pathetic legions like molecules of matter in human form drawn insensibly to a central mass from which they could not want to free themselves. They strode past a shrunken black woman who stood near a post between state-authorized Lottery and Lotto stands in unlaced sneakers and held out a soiled paper cup while chanting tunelessly, "Fifteen cents? Gimme fifteen cents? Any food? Used food?" A gray-haired bloated woman in a green tam-o'-shanter and green sweater and skirt, with sores on her splotched legs, was singing an Irish song off-key blissfully in a cracked voice near a filthy, sleeping teenager on the floor and a wild-eyed, slender, chocolate-colored tall man who was spotlessly clean and seemed all bones, preaching Christian salvation in a Caribbean accent to a stout black woman who nodded and a skinny white Southerner with closed eyes who kept breaking in with calls of thrilled affirmation. As they drew near the police station, Yossarian remembered with malicious caprice his wish to find out something special from his capable guide.

"McBride?"

"Yossarian?"

"I v   hinking of holding a weddir

McB   ney, that's a good idea. Yeah, Y   pitch in and help. We could make them a nice wedding, I think we could. I've still got that empty cell there for the kids. We could turn that into the chapel. And of course, right next door, ahem, I've still got the bed, for the honeymoon night. We could give them a big wedding breakfast in one of the food shops and maybe buy them some lottery tickets as a good-luck present. What's funny? Why couldn't they use it?"

It took Yossarian a minute to stop laughing. "No, Larry, no," he explained. "I'm talking about a big wedding, gigantic, high society, hundreds of guests, limousines at the bus ramps, newspapermen and cameras, a dance floor with a big band, maybe two dance floors and two bands."

"Are you crazy, Yo-Yo?" Now McBride was the one who was chuckling. "The commissioners would never allow it!"

"These people know the commissioners. They'd be there as guests. And the mayor and the cardinal, maybe even the new President. Secret Service men and a hundred police."

"If you had the President we'd be allowed to go all the way down there to look. The Secret Service would want that."

"Sure, you would like that too. It would be the wedding of the year. Your terminal would be famous."

"You'd have to clear out the people! Stop all the buses!"

"Nah." Yossarian shook his head. "The buses and crowds could be part of the entertainment. It would get in the newspapers. Maybe a picture inside with you and McMahon, if I pose you right."

"Hundreds of guests?" McBride restated shrilly. "A band and a dance floor? Limousines too?"

"Maybe fifteen hundred! They could use your bus ramps and park upstairs in your garages. And caterers and florists, waiters and bartenders. They could go riding on the escalators, in time to the music. I could talk to the orchestras."

"That could not be done!" McBride declared. "Everything would go wrong. It would be a catastrophe."

"Fine," said Yossarian. "Then I'll want to go ahead. Check it out for me, will you, please? Get out of my way!"

He snapped this last out at an oily Hispanic man just ahead who was flashing a stolen American Express credit card at him seductively with a smile of insinuating and insulting familiarity and caroling happily, "Just stolen, just stolen. Don't leave home without it. You can check it out, check it out."

Inside the police station, there were no reports of any new dead babies, the officer at the desk volunteered to McBride with a jocular impertinence.

"And no live ones either."

"I hate that guy," McBride muttered, coloring uncomfortably. "He thinks I'm crazy too."

McMahon was out on an emergency call, and Michael, who was finished with his unfinished drawing, inquired casually:

"Where've you been?"

"Coney Island," Yossarian said jauntily. "And guess what. Kilroy was there."

"Kilroy?"

"Right, Larry?"

"Who's Kilroy?" asked Michael.

"McBride?"

"Yossarian?"

"In Washington once, I went to look for a name on the Vietnam Memorial, with the names of all who'd been killed there. Kilroy was there, one Kilroy."

"The same one?"

"How the fuck should I know?"

"I'll check him out," promised McBride. "And let's talk more about that wedding. Maybe we could do it, I believe we could. I'll check that out too."

"What's this about a wedding?" Michael demanded with truculence, when they were out of the police station and walking away through the terminal.

"Not mine." Yossarian laughed. "I'm too old to marry again."

"You're too old to get married again."

"That's what I said. And are you still too young? Marriage may not be good, but it's not always all bad."

"Now you're talking too much."

Yossarian had his routine for moving through panhandlers, handing one-dollar bills from the folded daily allotment in his pocket to those who were timid and to those who looked threatening. A hulking man with inflamed eyes and a scrap of cloth offered to wipe his eyeglasses for a dollar or smash them to pieces if he declined. Yossarian gave him two dollars and put his eyeglasses away. Nothing surprising seemed unusual anymore in this deregulated era of free enterprise. He was under a death sentence, he knew, but he tried imparting that news to Michael euphemistically. "Michael, I want you to stay in law school," he decided seriously.

Michael stepped away. "Oh, shit, Dad. I don't want that. It's expensive too. Someday," he went on, with a dejected pause, "I'd like to work at something worthwhile."

"Know anything? I'll pay for the law school."

"You won't know what I mean, but I don't want to feel like a parasite."

"Yes, I would. It's why I gave up commodities, currency trading, stock trading, arbitrage, and investment banking. Michael, I'll give you seven more years of good health. That's the most I can promise you."

"What happens then?"

"Ask Arlene."

"Who's Arlene?"

"That woman you're living with. Isn't that her name? The one with the crystals and the tarot cards."

"That's Marlene, and she moved out. What happens to me in seven years?"

"To me, you damned fool. I'll be seventy-five. Michael, I'm already sixty-eight. I'll guarantee you seven more years of my good health in which to learn how to live without me. If you don't, you'll drown. After that I can't promise you anything. You can't live without money. It's addictive once you've tried it. People steal to get it. The most I'll be able to leave each of you, after taxes, will be about half a million."

"Dollars?" Michael brightened brilliantly. "That sounds like a fortune!"

"At eight percent," Yossarian told him flatly, "you'd get forty thousand a year. At least a third will go to taxes, leaving you twenty-seven."

"Hey, that's nothing! I can't live on that!"

"I know that too. That's why I am talking too much to you. Where's your future? Can you see one? Move this way."

They stepped out of the path of a young man in sneakers running for his life from a half-dozen policemen running just as fast and closing in on him from different sides because he had just murdered with a knife someone in another part of the terminal. Pounding among them in heavy black shoes was Tom McMahon, who looked ill from the strain. Cut off in front, the nimble youth left them all in the lurch by swerving sharply and ducking down into the same emergency stairwell Yossarian had taken with McBride and probably, Yossarian mused fancifully, would never be heard of again—or better still, was already back on their level, walking behind them in his sneakers, looking blameless. They passed a man sitting asleep on the floor in a puddle of his own making, and another teenager, out cold, and then found their way blocked by a skinny woman somewhere near forty with stringy blonde hair and a lurid blister on her mouth.

"I'll do you for a nickel, mister," she offered.

"Please," said Yossarian, stepping around her.

"I'll do you both for a nickel each. I'll do you both at the same time for a nickel each. Pop, I'll do you both for the same nickel."

Michael, with a strained smile, skittered around her. She plucked at Yossarian's sleeve and held on.

"I'll lick your balls."

Yossarian stumbled free, mortified. His face burned. And Michael was aghast to see his father so shaken.

10

George C. Tilyou

At a rolltop desk many levels below, Mr. George C. Tilyou, the Coney Island entrepreneur, who'd been dead almost eighty years, counted his money and felt himself sitting on top of the world. His total never decreased. Before his eyes were the starting and finishing stations of the roller-coaster he'd had brought down after him from his Steeplechase amusement park. The tracks had never looked newer as they rose toward the crest of the highest gravity drop at the beginning and climbed out of sight into the cavernous tunnel he occupied. He filled with pride when he gazed at his redoubtable carousel, his El Dorado. Constructed originally in Leipzig for William II, the emperor of Germany, it still was possibly the most magnificent merry-go-round anywhere. Three platforms carrying horses, gondolas, and carved ducks and pigs revolved at individual speeds. Often he would send his El Dorado carousel spinning with no riders aboard, merely to study the reflections of the silver mirrors at the glittering hub and to revel in the stout voice of the calliope, which was, he liked to joke, music to his ears.

He had renamed his roller-coaster the Dragon's Gorge. Elsewhere he had his Cave of the Winds, and at the entrance churned his Barrel of Fun, which brought the unpracticed to their knees right off on the circling bottom and kept them tumbling against each other in tilted disarray until they crawled out the farther end and regained their feet or were assisted by attendants or other customers more experienced. One who knew how could pass through without fuss merely by walking on a mild diagonal contrary to the direction of rotation, but that wasn't fun. Or stride and stride uphill upon the descending floor without getting anywhere and remain forever in the same place, but that was not much fun either. Onlookers of both sexes took special delight in witnessing the unbalanced distress of attractive ladies clutching to hold down their skirts in the days before slacks attained respectability as a befitting mode of female attire.

"If Paris is France," he could remember stating as the playground's foremost spokesman and impresario, "then Coney Island, between June and September, is the world."

The money he sat counting every day would never deteriorate or grow old. His cash was indestructible and would always have value. At his back rose a cast-iron safe that was taller than he was. He had guards and attendants from the old days, costumed in red coats and green jockey caps from the old days. Many were friends from the beginning and had been with him an eternity.

With a genius uncanny and persistent, he had defied and disproved the experts, his lawyers and his bankers, and had succeeded in time in taking it all with him, in holding on to everything he valued particularly and was intent on retaining. His will made adequate provision for his widow and his children. Deeds of ownership, cash instruments, and currency in a large amount were sealed, as directed, in a moistureproof box resistant to decay and interred with him in his sepulcher in Brooklyn's Green-Wood Cemetery, and his tombstone bore the inscription:

MANY HOPES LIE BURIED HERE.

While heirs and executors disputed with each other and with government tax officials, Steeplechase (the "Funny Place") relentlessly disappeared part by part from the face of the earth, except for the phallic, steel-beam, bankrupt skeleton of the Parachute Jump, which came in long after he was gone and was an attraction he would have rejected. It was tame and orderly, and did not frighten or tickle the customers or spectators. Mr. Tilyou relished things that surprised, threw people into confusion, annihilated dignity, blew boy and girl clumsily into each other's arms, and, with luck, flashed a glimpse of calf and petticoat, sometimes even feminine underpants, to a delighted audience just like them who viewed the comedy of their utter, ludicrous helplessness with gaiety and laughter.

Mr. Tilyou always smiled when he recalled the inscription on his tombstone.

He could not now think of anything he lacked. He had a second roller-coaster now, called the Tornado. Overhead he heard continually the stops and starts of the subway trains that had brought crowds in the hundreds of thousands to the beach on summer Sundays, and the sputtering exhausts of automobiles and larger vehicles of transportation traveling to and fro. Hearing the rippling and lapping of a canal of flowing water on a level above, he had brought down his flat-bottomed boats and reinstituted his Tunnel of Love. He had the Whip and the Whirlpool, with which he could lash patrons about and fling them aside, and the Human Pool Table with its vertical slide inside a chamber and spinning disks at the bottom to spin them supine in one direction or another while they screeched with hapless pleasure and prayed all the while it would soon come to an end. He had electric shocks on the railings for the unwary and mirrors for the normal that deformed them into merry and ridiculous monstrosities. And he had his grinning, pink-cheeked trademark, that demonic flat face with a flat head and parted hair and a wide mouth filled with cubes of teeth like white tiles, which people shrank from disbelievingly on first encounter and next time accepted good-humoredly as natural. From some unknown level below he heard repeatedly the passage of smooth-running railroad cars whose turning wheels rolled by day and night, but he was not curious. He was interested only in what he was able to own, and he wished to own only what he was able to see and watch and could control with the simplest action of a switch or a lever. He loved the smell of electricity and the crisp crackle of electrical sparks.

He had more money than he ever could spend. He'd never trusted trusts or seen much foundation to foundations. John D. Rockefeller came to him regularly now to beg for dimes and to cadge free rides, and J. P. Morgan, who'd commended his soul to God with no doubt it would be embraced, sought favors. With little to live on, they had not much to live for. Their children sent nothing. Mr. Tilyou could have told them, he told them often. Without money life could be hell. Mr. Tilyou had an inkling there would always be business as usual everywhere, and he could have told them, he told them.

He was spruce, dapper, alert, and tidy. His bowler hat, his derby of which he was proud, hung spotless on a hook on his coatrack. He dressed daily now in a white shirt with a wing collar, with a dark ascot tied perfectly and tucked neatly into the vest of his suit, and the points of his thin brown mustache were inevitably waxed.

His first major success was a Ferris wheel half the size of the one that had caught his fancy in Chicago, and he boldly proclaimed his own, even in advance of completion, as the largest in the world. He decked it out with dazzling streamers of hundreds of Mr. Edison's new incandescent lightbulbs, and enchanted patrons were diverted and thrilled.

"I have never cheated a soul in anything," he was wont to declare, "and I've never given a sucker an even break."

He liked rides that went round and brought the participants back to the place they had started from. Almost everything in nature, from the smallest to the grandest, seemed to him to move in circles and to return to the point at which it had originated, to perhaps set out again. He found people more fun than a barrel of monkeys, and he liked to manipulate them in this guise with tricks of harmless public embarrassment that would give pleasure to everyone and for which all would pay: the hat whisked away by a jet of air or the skirts gusting upward over the shoulders, the moving floors and collapsing staircases, the lipstick-smeared couple floated back into light from the concealing darkness inside the Tunnel of Love, baffled to know why the onlookers were shaking in laughter at the spectacle they made until ribald jokesters cried out to tell them.

And he still owned his home. On Surf Avenue, across from his Steeplechase amusement park, Mr. Tilyou had lived in a good-sized wooden-frame house with a narrow walk and shallow steps built of masonry, and all seemed to begin sinking into the ground shortly after his burial. On the vertical face of the step at the bottom, the one joined to the sidewalk, he'd paid a stonecutter to chisel the family name, TILYOU. Year-round residents walking by on the way to the movie house or subway station were the first to note from the position of the letters in the name that the step seemed to be settling into the pavement. By the time the whole house was gone, there was not much attention paid to one more empty lot in a dilapidated neighborhood that had passed its prime.

On the north side of the narrow strip of land that made up Coney Island, which was not a true island but a protruding spit about five miles long and half a mile wide, lay a body of water called Gravesend Bay. A dye factory there consumed much sulfur. Boys nearing puberty touched lighted matches to the yellow clumps they found lying on the ground near the building and were intrigued and gratified that they ignited easily and burned with a bluish glare and an odor that was sulfurous. Nearby stood a factory that manufactured ice and once was the scene of a spectacular armed robbery by perpetrators who made good their getaway in a speedboat that raced out to escape into the waters of Gravesend Bay. Thus, there was fire and there was ice before home refrigeration grew practical.

Fire was an ever-present danger, and great Coney Island fires blazed periodically. Within hours after Mr. Tilyou saw his first amusement park destroyed by flames, he posted signs selling his newest attraction, his Coney Island fire, and he kept his ticket takers busy collecting the ten cents admission charge he took from customers eager to enter the devastated area to cast their eyes upon his smoking ruins. Why hadn't he thought of that, mused the Devil. Even Satan called him Mr. Tilyou.

BOOK
FOUR

BOOK FOUR

11

Lew

Sammy and I enlisted the same day. Four of us set out together. All of us went overseas. All four of us came back, although I was captured and Sammy was shot down into the water and crash-landed another time with a forgetful pilot called Hungry Joe, who forgot to try the emergency handle for lowering the landing gear. No one was hurt, Sammy tells me, and that pilot Hungry Joe got a medal. It's a name that sticks. Milo Minderbinder was his mess officer then and not the big war hero he tries to pass himself off as now. Sammy had a squadron commander named Major Major, who was never around when anyone wanted to see him, and a bombardier he thought I would have liked named Yossarian, who took off his uniform after a guy in their plane bled to death, and he even went to the funeral naked, sitting in a tree, Sammy says.

We went up by subway to volunteer at the big army induction center at Grand Central Station in Manhattan. That was a part of the city most of us hardly ever went to. There was the physical examination we'd heard about from the older guys who were already gone. We turned our heads and coughed, we milked down our joints, we bent over and spread the cheeks of our buttocks, and kept wondering what they were looking for. We'd heard of piles from our uncles and aunts, but we didn't really know what they were. A psychiatrist interviewed me alone and asked if I liked girls. I liked them so much I fucked them, I answered.

He looked envious.

Sammy liked them too but didn't know how.

We were past eighteen, and if we'd waited until nineteen, we would have been drafted, said FDR, and that was the reason we gave to our parents, who were not so happy to see us go. We read about the war in the newspapers, heard about it on the radio, saw it done gorgeously in the Hollywood movies, and it looked and sounded better to us than being home in my father's junkshop, like I was, or in a file cage like Sammy in the insurance company he worked for, or, like Winkler, in a cigar store that was a front for the bookmaking operation his father ran in back. And in the long run it *was* better, for me and for most of the rest of us.

When we got back to Coney Island after enlisting, we ate some hot dogs to celebrate and went on the roller-coasters awhile, the Tornado, the Cyclone, and the Thunderbolt. We rode up on the big Wonder Wheel eating caramel popcorn and looked out over the ocean in one direction and out over Gravesend Bay in the other. We sank submarines and shot down planes on the game machines in the penny arcades and dashed into Steeplechase for a while and rolled around in the barrels and spun around on the Whirlpool and the Human Pool Table and caught rings on the big carousel, the biggest carousel in the island. We rode in a flat-bottomed boat in the Tunnel of Love and made loud dirty noises to give laughs to the other people there.

We knew there was anti-Semitism in Germany, but we didn't know what that was. We knew they were doing things to people, but we didn't know what they were.

We didn't know much of Manhattan then. When we went up into the city at all, it was mainly to the Paramount or Roxy theater, to hear the big bands and see the big new movies before they came into the neighborhood six months later, to the Loew's Coney Island or the RKO Tilyou. The big movie houses in Coney Island then were safe and profitable and comfortable. Now they're bankrupt and out of business. Some of the older fellows would sometimes take us along into Manhattan in their cars on Saturday night to the jazz clubs on Fifty-second Street or up into Harlem for the music at the colored ballroom or theater there or to buy marijuana, eat ribs cheap, and get sucked and fucked for a buck if they wanted to, but I didn't go in much for any of that, not even the music. Once the war came, a lot of people started making money, and we did too. Soon after the war you could get that same sucking and the rest right there in the Coney Island neighborhood from Jewish white girls hooked on heroin and married to other local junkies who had no money either, but the price was two bucks now, and they did their biggest business mostly with housepainters and plasterers and other laborers from outside the neighborhood, who hadn't gone to school with those girls and didn't care. Some in my own crowd, like Sammy and Marvelous Marvin Winkler, the bookie's little boy, began smoking marijuana even before the war, and you could find that country smell of pot in the smoking sections of the Coney Island movie houses once you got to recognize what the stuff smelled like. I didn't go for any of that either, and the guys who were my friends never lit up their reefers when I was around, even though I told them they could, if they wanted to.

"What's the use?" Winkler liked to groan, with his eyes red and half closed. "You bring me down."

A guy named Tilyou, who maybe was already dead, became a sort of guy to look up to once I found out about him. When everyone else was poor, he owned a movie house and he owned a big Steeplechase amusement park and a private house across the street from his Steeplechase Park, and I never even connected them all with the same name until Sammy pointed it out to me not long ago on one of his mercy visits up to my house, when all of them were already gone, and George C. Tilyou too. Sammy began coming up a lot to see us after his wife died of cancer of the ovary and he did not know what to do with himself weekends, and especially when I was out of the hospital again and had nothing much to do with myself either but hang around getting my strength back after another session of radiation or more chemotherapy. Between these hospitalizations I could feel like a million and be strong as an ox again. When things got bad here, I'd go into the city to a hospital in Manhattan and an oncologist named Dennis Teemer for treatments they had there. When I felt good, I was terrific.

By now it's out of the bag. And everyone knows I've been sick with something that sometimes puts other people away. We never speak of it by name, or even as something big enough to even have a name. Even with the doctors, Claire and I don't talk about it by name. I don't want to ask Sammy, but I'm not sure we fooled him for a minute in all of the years of my lying about it like I did—*as* I did, *as* he would want to correct me, *like* he does, when I let him. Sometimes I remember, but I talk to him *like* I want to anyway just to heckle him.

"Tiger, I know it," I will tell him with a laugh. "You still think I'm a greenhorn? I'm putting you on, *like* I like to do, and *hopefully*, someday you'll get it."

Sammy is smart and picks up on small things, like the name Tilyou, and the scar on my mouth before I grew my big brush mustache to hide it or let what hair I had left grow long in back to cover the incisions there and the blue burn marks on the glands in the back of my neck. I missed a lot maybe in my lifetime by not going to college, but I never wanted to go, and I don't think I missed anything that would have mattered to me. Except maybe college girls. But I always had girls. They'd never scared me, and I knew how to get them and talk to them and enjoy them, older ones too. I was always priapic, Sammy told me.

"You've got it, tiger," I answered him. "Now tell me what it means."

"You were all prick," he said, like he enjoyed insulting me, "and no conflicts."

"Conflicts?"

"You never had problems."

"I never had problems."

I never had doubt. My first was an older one on the next block named Blossom. My second was an older one we called Squeezy. Another one was a girl I picked up in the insurance office when Sammy was working there, and she was older too, and she knew I was younger, but she wanted more of me anyway and bought me two shirts for Christmas. Back then I think I made it with every girl I really wanted to. With girls, like everywhere else, even in the army, I found out that if you let people know what you want to do and seem sure of yourself about doing it, they're likely to let you. When I was still a corporal, my sergeant overseas was soon letting me do all the deciding for both of us. But I never had college girls, the kind you used to see in the movies. Before the war, nobody we knew went to college or thought about it. After the war, everybody began going. The girls I met through Sammy from his *Time* magazine before he was married, and after too, didn't always find me as popular as I thought they should, so I cut down on the personality with them instead of embarrassing him, and even his wife, Glenda, wasn't really as crazy about me and Claire at first as the people we were used to in Brooklyn and Orange Valley. Claire had the idea Glenda felt like a snob because she wasn't Jewish and was not from Brooklyn, but it turned out it wasn't that. When we began to get sick, first me, then her, we all got close, and even before that, when their boy, Michael, killed himself. We were the married couple they could turn to easiest and Claire was the girl she could confide in most.

In Coney Island, Brighton Beach, and everywhere else, I always had girls, as often as I wanted, and even could get them for others, even for Sammy. Especially in the army, in Georgia, Kansas, and Oklahoma, and married ones too, with husbands away. And that sort of always turned me off a little afterward, but it never stopped me from having the good time when I could. "Don't put it in," they would sometimes try to make me promise before I made us both happier by putting it in. In England before I was shipped into Europe there were lots. In England in the war every American could get laid, even Eisenhower, and sometimes in France in a village or farm, where we were busy moving forward with the fighting, until we had to move back and I was taken prisoner with a whole bunch of others in what I later found out was the Battle of the Bulge. Except in Germany, but even almost in Dresden as a POW working in that liquid vitamin factory making syrups for pregnant women in Germany who needed nourishment and didn't have what to eat. That was late in the war, and I hated the Germans more than ever before, but couldn't show it. Even there I came close to getting laid with my joshing around with the guards and the Polish and other slave-labor women working there, and maybe could really have talked my favorite guards—they were all old men or soldiers who'd been wounded badly on the Russian front—into looking the other way while I slipped off into a room or closet with one or another of them for a while. The women weren't eager but didn't seem to mind me—up until the night of that big firebombing when everything around us came to an end in one day, and all of the women were gone too. The other guys thought I was out of my mind for horsing around that way, but it gave us a little something more to do until the war ended and we could go back home. The Englishmen in the prison detail could make no sense of me. The guards were tired too, and they began to get a kick out of me also. They knew I was Jewish. I made sure of that everywhere.

"*Herr Reichsmarschall,*" I called each one of the German privates as a standing joke whenever I had to speak to them to translate or ask for something. "Fucking Fritz" was what I called each one of them to myself, without joking. Or "Nazi kraut bastard."

"*Herr Rabinowitz,*" they answered with mock respect.

"*Mein Name ist Lew,*" I always kidded back with them heartily. "Please call me that."

"Rabinowitz, you're crazy," said my assistant Vonnegut, from Indiana. "You're going to get yourself killed."

"Don't you want to have fun?" I kept trying to cheer us all up. "How can you stand all this boredom? I bet I can get a dance going here if we can talk them into some music."

"Not me," said the old guy named Schweik. "I'm a good soldier."

Both these guys knew more German than I did, but Vonnegut was modest and shy, and Schweik, who kept complaining he had piles and aching feet, never wanted to get involved.

Then one week we saw the circus was coming to town. We had seen the posters on our march to the food factory from our billets in the reinforced basement that had been the underground room of the slaughterhouse when they still had animals to slaughter. By then the guards were more afraid than we were. At night we could hear the planes from England pass overhead on their way to military targets in the region. And we would sometimes hear with pleasure the bombs exploding in the hundreds not far away. From the east we knew the Russians were coming.

I had a big idea when I saw those carnival posters. "Let's talk to the headman and see if we can't get to go. The women too. We need a break. I'll do the talking." The chance excited me. "Let's go have a try."

"Not me," said that good soldier Schweik. "I can get myself in enough trouble just doing what I'm told."

The women working with us were wan and bedraggled and as dirty as we were, and I don't think there was a sex gland alive in any of us. And I was underweight and had diarrhea most of the time too, but that would have been one screw to tease Claire about later and to boast about now. I could have lied, but I don't like to lie.

Claire and I got married even before I was out of the army, just after my double hernia operation at Fort Dix when I got back from Europe and the prisons in Germany, and I almost went wild with a pair of German POWs there in New Jersey for leering and saying something in German when they saw her waiting for me while we were still engaged.

I saw them first in Oklahoma, those German prisoners of war over here, and I couldn't believe what I was looking at. They were outdoors with shovels and looked better than we did, and happier too on that big army base. This was war? Not in my book. I thought prisoners of war were supposed to be in prison and not outdoors having a good time with each other and making jokes about us. I got angry looking at them. They were guarded by a couple of slouching GIs who looked bored and lazy and carried rifles that looked too heavy. The krauts were supposed to be working at something, but they weren't working hard. There were American stockade prisoners all around who'd gone AWOL and been put to work digging holes in the ground just for punishment and then filling them up, and they were always working harder than any of these. I got even angrier just watching them, and one day, without even knowing what I was doing, I decided to practice my German on them and just walked right up.

"Hey, you're not allowed to do that, soldier," said the guard nearest the two I went to, jumping toward me nervously and speaking in one of those foreign southern accents I was just beginning to get used to. He even started to level his rifle.

"Pal, I've got family in Europe," I told him, "and it's perfectly all right. Just listen, you'll hear." And before he could answer me I began right in with my German, trying it out, but he didn't know that. "*Bitte. Wie ist Ihr Name? Danke schön. Wie alt sind Sie? Danke vielmals. Wo Du kommst hier? Danke.*" By now a few of the others had drawn close, and even a couple of the other guards had come up to listen and were smiling too, like having a good time at one of our USO shows. I didn't like that either. What the hell, I thought, was this war or peace? I kept right on talking. When they couldn't understand me, I kept changing the way I said something until they did, and then there were nods and laughs from all of them, and I made believe I was grinning with happiness when I saw they were giving me good marks. "*Bitte schön, bitte schön,*" they told me when I said "*Danke, danke*" to them in a gush for telling me I was "*Gut, gut.*" But before it was over, I made sure I let them know there was one person there who wasn't having such a good time, and that person was me. "*So, wie geht jetzt?*" I asked them, and pointed my arm around the base. "*Du, gefällt es hier? Schön, ja?*" When they said they did like it there, like we were all practicing our German, I put this question to them. "*Gefällt hier besser wie zuhause mit Krieg? Ja?*" I would have bet they did like it there better than they would have liked being back in Germany at war. "Sure," I said to them in English, and by then they'd stopped smiling and were looking confused. I stared hard into the face of the one I had spoken to first. *"Sprechen Du!"* I drilled my eyes into his until he began to nod weakly, answering. When I saw him fold I wanted to laugh out loud, although I didn't find it funny. *"Dein Name ist Fritz? Dein Name ist Hans? Du bist Heinrich?"* And then I told them about me. *"Und mein Name ist Rabinowitz."* I said it again as a German might. *"Rabinovitz. Ich bin Lew Rabinowitz, LR, von Coney Island in Brooklyn, New York. Du kennst?"* And then I spoke Yiddish. *"Und ich bin ein Yid. Farshstest?"* And then in English. "I am a Jew. Understand?" And then in my fractured German. *"Ich bin Jude. Verstehst?"* Now they didn't know where to look, but they did not want to look at me. I've got blue eyes that can turn into slits of ice, Claire still tells me, and a pale, European skin that can turn red fast when I laugh hard or get mad, and I wasn't sure they believed me. So I opened my fatigues one button more and pulled out my dog tags to show them the letter *J* stamped there on the bottom with my blood type. *"Sehen Du? Ich bin Rabinowitz, Lew Rabinowitz, und ich bin Jude.* Understand? Good. *Danke,"* I said sarcastically, glaring coldly at each of them until I saw the eyes drop. *"Danke schön, danke vielmals, für alles,* and a *bitte* and *bitte schön* too. And on the life of my mother, I swear I will pay you all back. Thanks, buddy boy," I said to the corporal, as I turned to go. "I'm glad you had a good time too."

"What was it all about?"

"Just practicing my German."

In Fort Dix with Claire, I wasn't practicing. I was mad in a second when I saw them snicker and say something about her, and I was ready to wade right in, madder than I'd ever been in combat, as I moved straight toward them. My voice was low and very calm, and that vein in my neck and jaw was already ticking, like the clock of a time bomb just dying to explode.

"Achtung," I said in a soft and slow voice, drawing the word out to make it last as long as I could, until I came to a stop where they were standing on the grass with their shovels near a dirt walkway they were making.

The two of them looked at each other with a hardly hidden smile they must have thought I wouldn't mind.

"Achtung," I said again, with a little more bite on the second part, as though carrying on a polite conversation with someone hard of hearing in the parlor of Claire's mother in her upstate

home in New York. I put my face right into theirs, only inches away. My lips were drawn wide, as they would be if I was going to laugh, but I wasn't even smiling, and I don't think they got that yet. *"Achtung, aufpassen,"* I said for emphasis.

They turned sober when I didn't shout it. They began to see I wasn't kidding. And then they straightened up from their comfortable slouching and began to look a little bit lost, like they couldn't make me out. I didn't know till later that I was clenching my fists, didn't know until I saw blood on my hands from where my nails were digging in.

Now they weren't so sure anymore, and I was. The war in Europe was over, but they were still prisoners of war, and they were here, not there. It was summer and they were healthy and bare-chested and bronzed from the sun, like I used to be on the beach at Coney Island before the war. They looked strong, muscular, not like the hundreds and hundreds more I'd seen taken prisoner overseas. These had been in first, and they had grown healthy as prisoners and strong on American food, while I was away with trench foot from wet socks and shoes, and was covered with bugs I'd never seen before, lice. They were early captures, I guessed, the big bully-boy crack troops from the beginning of the war, that whole generation who by now had been captured, killed, or wounded, and they looked too good and too well-off for my taste, but there were the rules of the Geneva Convention for prisoners, and here they were. The two I faced were older and bigger than me, but I did not doubt I could take them apart if it came to that, weak as I was from the operations and thin from the war, and maybe I was wrong. I wasn't fed as good as they were when I was a prisoner.

"Wie gehts?" I said casually, looking at each in turn in a way that let them know I wasn't being as sociable as I sounded. By now my German was pretty good. *"Was ist Dein Name?"*

One was Gustav, one was Otto. I remember the names.

"Wo kommst Du her?"

One was from Munich. I'd never heard of the other place. I was speaking with authority, and I could see they were anxious. They didn't outrank me. None could be officers if they'd been put to work, not even noncommissioned, not unless they had lied, as I had done, just to get out of the last prison camp and go somewhere to work. *"Warum lachst Du wenn Du siehst Lady hier?* You too." I pointed at the other one. "Why were you laughing just now when you looked at the lady here, and what did you say to him about her that made him laugh some more?"

I forgot to say that in German and spoke in English. They knew what I was talking about, all right, but were not too sure of the words. I didn't mind. This was a hard one to put into another language, but I knew they would get it if I put my mind to it.

"*Warum hast Du gelacht wenn Du siehst mein* girlfriend here?"

Now we all knew they understood, because they did not want to answer. The guard with the gun did not understand what was going on or know what to do about it. He looked more scared of me than of them. I knew that I wasn't even allowed to talk to them. Claire would have wanted me to stop. I wasn't going to. Nothing could have made me. A young officer with campaign ribbons who'd come up quickly halted when he saw my face.

"Better keep back," I heard Claire warn him.

I had campaign ribbons on too, including a Bronze Star I'd won in France for knocking out a Tiger tank with a guy named David Craig. I think that officer was reading my mind and was smart enough to keep out of my way. I seemed official and talked tough as hell. My German threw all of them off, and I made sure to speak it loudly.

"*Antworte!*" I said. "*Du verstehst was ich sage?*"

"*Ich verstehe nicht.*"

"*Wir haben nicht gelacht.*"

"*Keiner hat gelacht.*"

"Otto, you are a liar," I told him in German. "You do understand and you did laugh. *Gustav, sag mir, Gustav, was Du sagen*"—I pointed to Claire—"*über meine Frau hier? Beide lachen, was ist so komisch?*" We weren't married yet, but I didn't mind throwing in that she was my wife, just to tighten the screws a little more. "She is my wife," I repeated, in English, for the officer to hear. "What nasty thing did you say about her?"

"*Ich habe nichts gesagt. Keiner hat gelacht.*"

"*Sag mir!*" I commanded.

"*Ich habe es vergessen. Ich weiss nicht.*"

"*Gustav, Du bist auch ein Lügner, und Du wirst gehen zu Hölle für Deine Lüge.* To hell you will both go for your lie and for your dirty words about this young lady, if I have to put you there myself. Now. *Schaufeln hinlegen!*"

I pointed. They laid down their shovels tamely and waited. I waited too.

"*Schaufeln aufheben!*" I said, with no smile.

They looked about miserably. They picked up the shovels and stood without knowing what to do with them.

"*Dein Name ist Gustav?*" I said after another half a minute. "*Dein Name ist Otto? Jawohl? Du bist von München? Und Du bist von . . . Ach wo!*" I didn't really care where the hell he was from. "*Mein Name ist Rabinowitz.* Lewis Rabinowitz. *Ich bin Lewis Rabinowitz,* from Coney Island, on West Twenty-fifth Street, between Railroad Avenue and Mermaid Avenue, *bei Karussell,* the merry-go-round on the boardwalk." I could feel the pulses in my thumbs beating too when I took out my dog tags to make them look at that letter *J*, to make extra sure that they knew what I was saying when I told them next in Yiddish: "*Und ich bin ein Yid.*" And then in German: "*Ich bin Jude, jüdisch. Verstehst Du jetzt?*" They weren't so bronze anymore, and didn't look so powerful. I felt peaceful as can be, and never more sure of myself as LR, Louie Rabinowitz from Coney Island. There was no more need to fight with them. I spoke with my hateful smile that Claire says looks worse than a skeleton's and like a deadly grimace. "*Jetzt . . . noch einmal.*" They put down the shovels when I told them to and picked them back up as though I had trained them perfectly. I indicated Claire. "*Hast Du schlecht gesagt wie als er hat gesagt wie Du gesehen Dame hier?*"

"*Nein, mein Herr.*"

"*Hast Du mitgelacht als er hat gesagt schlecht?*"

"*Nein, mein Herr.*"

"You are lying again, both of you, and it's lucky that you are, because I might break both your backs if you told me you did laugh at her or said something bad. *Geh zur Arbeit.*" I turned away from them with disgust. "Corporal, they're yours again. Thanks for the chance."

"Lew, that wasn't nice," Claire said first.

Then the officer spoke. "Sergeant, you're not allowed that. You're not allowed to talk to them that way."

I saluted respectfully. "I know the rules of the Geneva Convention, Captain. I was a prisoner of war there, sir."

"What was it all about?"

"They looked at my fiancée, sir, and said something dirty. I'm only just back. I'm not right in the head yet."

"Lew, you're *not* right in the head." Claire started in the minute we were alone. "Suppose they didn't do what you told them to?"

"Calm down, little girl. They did do what I told them. They had to."

"Why? Suppose the guard made you stop? Or that officer?"

"They couldn't."

"How did you know?"

"Just understand."

"Why couldn't they?"

"I tell you and you must believe me. Certain things happen the way I say they will. Don't ask me why. To me it's simple. They insulted you, and they insulted me by doing that, and I had to let them know they couldn't do that. They're not allowed to do that." We were already engaged. "You're my fiancée, n'est-ce pas? My Fräulein. I would get mad at anyone who looked at you and made a smutty remark, and so would my father and my brothers, if they saw any other guy ever snicker at you like that, or at one of my sisters. Enough chitchat, my dear. Let's go back to the hospital now. Let's go say good-bye to Herman the German."

"Lew, it's enough with Herman already. I'll wait downstairs and have a soda if you feel you have to go through that with him again. I don't find it funny."

"You still won't believe it, baby, but I don't find it funny either. That's not why I do it to him."

The problem with Claire then, as Sammy and Winkler saw and let me know, was that she did have big tits. And the trouble with me was that I got jealous fast and felt ready to just about kill any other guy who noticed them, Sammy and Winkler too.

So four of us went down to enlist that day and all four of us came back. But Irving Kaiser from the apartment house next door was killed by artillery fire in Italy and I never saw him again, and Sonny Ball was killed the same way there too. Freddy Rosenbaum lost a leg, and Manny Schwartz still walks around with hooks on an artificial hand and is not so good-humored about it anymore, and Solly Moss was shot in the head and hasn't been able to hear or see too clearly since, and as Sammy mentioned once when looking back, that seems to have been a lot of casualties for just a couple of blocks in a pretty small section of a pretty small neighborhood, so a lot of others everywhere must have been killed or wounded also. I thought so too. But the day the four of us went off we didn't think there'd really be danger or casualties.

We were going to war and we didn't know what it was.

Most of us married young. And none of us knew from divorce

then. That was for the Gentiles, for the rich people we used to read about in the newspapers who went to Reno, Nevada, for six weeks because it was easier there. And for someone like Sammy's Glenda and her roving first husband who liked to play around a lot and just didn't seem to give a shit who knew it. Now even one of my own daughters has got her divorce. When I first heard about that marriage breaking up I wanted to set right out after my ex-son-in-law and work out the property settlement with my bare hands. Claire shut me up and took me back to the Caribbean to cool off instead. Sammy Singer was the only one I know of who waited, and then he married his *shiksa* with three children and the light-brown hair that was almost blonde. But Sammy Singer was always a little bit different, short and different, quiet, thinking a lot. He was strange and went to college. I was smart enough and also had the GI Bill of Rights to pay for it, but was already married, and I had better things to do than go to school some more, and I was in a bigger hurry to get somewhere. That's another reason I never liked John Kennedy or anyone around him when he jumped into the limelight and began to act like an actor having too good a time. I could recognize a man in a hurry. I blinked once when he was shot, said too bad, and went back to work the same day, and got ready to begin disliking Lyndon Johnson, when I wanted to take the time. I don't like bullshitters and people who talk a lot, and that's what Presidents do. I hardly read newspapers anymore. Even back then I couldn't figure out why a guy with brains like Sammy Singer would want to go to college just to study things like English literature, which he could read in his spare time.

When I was thirteen and ready for high school, I got into Brooklyn Technical High School, which was not so easy to do back then, and did well in things like math, mechanical drawing, and some of the science courses, as I did not doubt I would. And then I forgot just about everything but the arithmetic when I got out and went to work for my father in the junkshop with my brother and one of my brothers-in-law, who lived with my oldest sister in the basement flat of the four-family brick house with a porch the family already owned. I used the arithmetic most in pinochle, I guess, in the bidding and playing, where I could pretty much hold my own in the boardwalk and beach games with almost the best of the old-world Jews from Russia and Hungary and Poland and Romania, who talked and talked and talked even while they played, about cards and the Jewish newspapers, and about Hitler, whom I hated early, as early as they did, and Stalin, Trotsky, Mussolini, and Franklin Delano Roosevelt, whom they liked, so I liked him too. In Coney Island I'll bet there was never a single Jewish voter for any Republican except maybe my brother-in-law Phil, who was always against everything everyone else around him was for, and still is.

My father did not think much of my genius at cards. When I asked him what else I should do with my time when we weren't working, he didn't know. When he didn't know something, he didn't want to talk about it. In the army there was no real pinochle, so I made my money at blackjack, poker, and craps. I almost always won because I always knew I would. If I didn't feel I would win I hardly ever played. When I lost, it wasn't much. I could tell in a minute if there were players at work who were just as good as I was and on a streak, and I knew enough to wait. Now I use my math to calculate discounts, costs, tax breaks, and profit margins, and I can do my figuring without even feeling I'm thinking, like my bookkeeper or counter girls could with their computers, and just about as fast. I'm not always right, but I'm almost never wrong. With the idea for metered home heating oil for builders and developers, even after I found the meter that would do it, I never felt sure. With metered oil there'd be no need for a fuel tank for each house in a development, and the company that owned the meter would sell the oil there. But I had the feeling I'd have trouble getting the people at the big oil companies to take me seriously, and I did and they wouldn't. When we met I was not myself. I wore a suit with a vest and had a different personality, because I had the feeling they would not like mine. They didn't care much for the one I used either. I was out of my league and knew it the minute I tried to step into theirs. There were limits, and I had guessed from the start that the sky was not one of mine.

The war was a big help, even to me, with the building boom and the shortages of materials to build with. We made money on the demolitions and on the first Luna Park fire right after the war when my hernias were fixed and I was back in the junkshop and strong as a bull again. I found I still loved the hard and heavy work with my brothers and brother-in-law and the old man. Smokey Rubin and the black guy were gone, but we had others when we needed them, and two trucks and another one we rented by the week. But I hated the dirt, hated the grease and the filth, and the stink from the rot from the ocean in the newspapers from the trash cans on the beach the scavenging ragpickers brought in to sell on the carts they pushed and pulled. I was afraid of the dirt and the air we breathed. I'm afraid of bugs. The old newspapers sometimes came with dead crabs and clumps of mussels with sand and seaweed and with orange peel and other kinds of garbage, and we put those in the middle of the big bales of papers we still wired up with our hands with pliers. There were machines now to bale newspapers, Winkler let us know like the voice of experience on one of those days when he had nothing better to do and came by to watch us working our asses off and hang around until I finished up. Winkler could find machines for anything, second-hand ones too. State-of-the-art machines, he liked to call them. I wasn't sure what that meant.

Winkler had found his state-of-the-art machines to slice up surplus army aerial film into sizes for consumer cameras and planned to make his first millions doing that before Eastman Kodak caught wise and tooled up again for the whole population and took back the market. People were getting married and having babies, and they wanted baby pictures.

"Never mind the machines, I don't want your machines," the old man grumbled at Winkler, grinding his dental plates and speaking in the thick Polish-Jewish accent Claire had hardly ever heard before she started going out with me and sleeping over in my other sister's room. No one would let us get together under that roof. She was upstate Jewish, where things were different than in Coney Island, and both her parents had been born in this country, which was different also. We met when they rented in Sea Gate one summer, for the beach and the ocean—we had one of the best beaches and ocean for swimming when it wasn't filthy with condoms and other things from the toilets on the big ocean liners steaming past into the harbor almost every day, and from sewers. We called the condoms "Coney Island whitefish." We called the garbage and the other floating stuff "Watch-out!" We had another name for the condoms. We called them scumbags. Now we call those pricks in Washington that. Like Noodles Cook, and maybe that new one now in the White House too.

"I got my own machines, two right here," the old man said, and flexed his muscles and smiled. He meant his shoulders and arms. "And three more machines right there." He meant me and my brother and my brother-in-law. "And my machines are alive and don't cost so much. Pull, pull," he called out. "Don't stand there, don't listen to him. We got pipes to cut and boilers to get later."

And he and his three live machines went back to work with our baling claws and long pliers and thin steel baling rods to be pulled and twisted into knots, keeping our eyes and nuts out of the way in case a wire snapped. We tumbled one bale down on top of the other, where they both shook and quivered, in a way Claire thought was sexual, she told me, like a big guy like me tumbling himself down on top of a girl like her.

The old man took to Claire right off, from the time she started showing up at the junkshop to watch and help so I could finish up earlier when we had a date, and because she spent good time talking to my mother, who was not always easy to talk to anymore. And she gift-wrapped the small presents she brought for birthdays and holidays. Gift-wrapped? Claire was the first we knew of to gift-wrap. Before Claire showed up, who in the whole large family, in the whole world of Coney Island, knew about gift-wrapping? Or "stemware"? None in the family was sure what stemware was, but I knew I wanted it once Claire did, and I talked about our "stemware" to a higher-level Italian guy named Rocky I bought things from. Rocky liked me and liked Claire's way of talking straight with him, and after we both moved away and went separately into buying lots and building houses, we sometimes did things for each other. Rocky liked girls, blondes and redheads with lots of makeup and high heels and big bosoms, and was very respectful of wives, like Claire and his own.

Her father was dead, and my father put his foot down at the beginning about me ever sleeping over at her house, even with her mother home.

"Listen, Louie," my father, Morris, told me, "listen to me good. The girl is an orphan. She has no father. Marry her or leave her alone. I'm not making a joke."

I decided to marry her, and I found out, when I thought about it, that I wanted my wife to be a virgin. I was surprised, but that was the kind of a guy I turned out to be. I had to admit that every time I talked a girl into coming across, I thought at least a little bit less of her afterward, even though I usually wanted to do it with them again. And even six years later, when Sammy got married to Glenda with her three children, I still could not make myself understand how any man like him or me could get married to a girl who'd been fucked by someone else, especially by someone who was still alive, and more than once, and by more than one guy. I know it's funny, but that's the kind of a guy I turned out to be.

And still am, because there are things about my two daughters that Claire and I no longer even try to argue about. They wouldn't believe me when I let them know their mother was a virgin until we got married. And Claire made me swear I would never tell that to anyone again.

I usually backed away from Claire's temper, but never from fear. I was not afraid in the army or the prison camps, not even in the firefights and scattered artillery barrages when we were pushing forward through the rest of France and Luxembourg and in toward the German border, not even when I looked up from the snow after the big December surprise and saw those German soldiers with clean guns and nice new white uniforms and the bunch of us were captured.

But I was afraid of the rats in our junkshop. And I hated the filth, especially when I was back after the war. Even a mouse at a baseboard would be enough to make me nauseous and set me shivering for a whole minute, like I do now when I get the taste of my mother's green apples or even remember it. And when I finally set up in business for myself in the town over two and half hours from our place in Brooklyn, the best location I could find was the building of a bankrupt mousetrap factory near the freight siding of the railroad station, and now there were plenty of mice there too.

One day after another I was disgusted by the dirt under my fingernails, and I was ashamed. All of us were. We scrubbed ourselves clean when we finished up, with cold water from the hose, which was all we had there. It took maybe an hour. Even in the winter we soaped and hosed ourselves down with stiff industrial brushes and lye soap. We didn't want to walk out and come home with all that muck on us. I hated the black beneath the fingernails. In Atlanta in the army I discovered the manicure—along with the shrimp cocktail and the filet mignon beefsteak—and in England I found the manicure again, and in France, moving through, I had my manicure whenever I could. And back in Coney Island I never wanted to be without it. And I never have been. Even in the hospital, at times when I'm feeling the lousiest, I still care about my cleanliness, and a manicure is one of the things I always make sure of getting. Claire already knew about manicures. After our marriage it was part of our foreplay. She liked pedicures too, and having her back scratched and her feet massaged, and I liked holding her toes.

I drove a good car as soon as I had money for one and bought another good one for Claire when I had money for that, and we didn't have to go out on dates in the company pickup anymore, and once I discovered hand-tailored suits I never wanted to dress myself up in anything else. When Kennedy became President it turned out we both had our suits made by the same shop in New York, but I had to admit I never looked as good in mine as he did in his. Sammy always said I didn't know how to dress, and Claire used to say so too, and maybe they're right, because I never did pay much attention to things like colors and style and left that to the tailors to choose for me. But I knew enough to know I always felt just grand walking around in a handmade suit that cost over three hundred dollars with the sales tax and might have cost as much as five hundred. Now they're over fifteen hundred and go up to two thousand, but I still don't care, and I have more of them now than I'll ever have time to wear out, because my weight keeps changing a lot between remissions, and I always like to look my tidiest in a suit and manicure whenever I dress up and go out.

I wore cotton shirts, only cotton. No nylon, no polyester, no creaseproof, never any wash-and-wear. But no Egyptian cotton, not ever, not after Israel and the war of 1948. When Milo Minderbinder and his M & M Enterprises went big into Egyptian cotton, I stopped carrying their M & M toilet bowls and sinks in my plumbing business and their building materials in my lumberyard. Winkler knows I don't like the idea, but he still buys Minderbinder cocoa beans for the chocolate Easter bunnies he's into, but we throw them out when he sends them as gifts.

I discovered cheese when I discovered the Caribbean, French cheese. I loved French cheeses from the day I found them. And Martinique and Guadeloupe and later Saint Barts became our favorite vacation spots in the Caribbean in winter. Because of the cheeses. I was not hot for Europe. I went once to France and once to Spain and Italy and never cared to go back to any place that didn't speak my language and couldn't get a good idea of the kind of person I thought I was. And then one day on Saint Barts, while having just a grand time with Claire after picking up two neat parcels of land in Saint Maarten at what I just knew would turn out to be a very good price, I ate a piece of cheese I always liked on a piece of bread I liked too, a Saint André cheese, I think I remember it was, and then a little while later felt coming up that taste of green apples I'd never forgotten, a burning, sour taste that I remembered from very far back when being sick as a kid, and I was scared that something not right might be going on inside me. And my neck felt stiff, like it was swelling up. Sammy would say that it *had* to swell *up,* because it couldn't swell down. I can smile at that now. It was something more than just indigestion. Till then I almost never felt nauseous, no matter how much I ate and drank, and I don't think I'd ever felt anything but good as a grown-up. In the army I was cold and dirty a lot and wanted more sleep and better food, but I don't think I ever felt anything but safe and healthy, or that anything that was bad and unusual was ever going to happen to me. Even when that sniper got that corporal named Hammer in the head when we were standing near that recon jeep and talking to each other just a foot apart. The town looked clear, that's what he was reporting back to me, and he was sure we could move on in. It didn't surprise me that it was him, not me. I didn't feel it was just good luck. I felt it had to happen that way.

"Honey, let's go back tomorrow," I said to Claire, when I felt that old, sick taste of green apples bubble up, and later gave her some baloney after we were back in our room and had balled each other again. "I thought of something I might do in Newburgh that might turn out pretty good for us."

I was feeling fine after the sex together and even after we were home. But just to make sure I dropped in at the doctor's. Emil looked and found nothing. I still don't know if he should have looked harder, or if it would have made any difference. Emil could easily believe that what I had on the island was not what I have now.

I'm not afraid of people but I'm getting more afraid of green apples. The first time in my life I remember getting sick, my mother told me I was sick because I had eaten some green apples she was keeping in a bowl to bake or cook something with. I don't know if I'd even really eaten them. But every time I got sick that way again and felt nauseous and threw up, from mumps, from chicken pox, from a strep throat one time, she put the blame on those same green apples, and after a while I began to believe her, even though I'd eaten no green apples, because that taste of throwing up was always the same. And I believe it still. Because each time I get sick to my stomach, before the radiation or chemotherapy and during the radiation or chemotherapy and after the radiation or chemotherapy, I taste green apples. I tasted my green apples with the surgery for the double hernia. And when I got really sick that first time driving back from a weekend at Sammy's house on Fire Island with a couple of some of Sammy's lively friends from *Time* and felt my neck swell so that I couldn't turn my head to keep driving and then went faint over the steering wheel and threw up just outside the car and began to babble to myself a little deliriously, it was about green apples I was babbling, Claire told me. And the kids in the back of the station wagon, we had just three then, said so too. We told people who wondered why we weren't home till late that it was only an upset stomach, because that's what we thought it was. Later we said it was angina. Then mononucleosis. Then tuberculosis of the glands. When I had my first real collapse seven years later and was in a hospital in the city and Claire told Glenda what it really was, it turned out she and Sammy both already knew or guessed. Glenda had some experience with an ex-husband with a different kind of cancer, and Sammy, as we knew, was smart, from reading *Time* magazine every week.

Claire had never met a family like ours, with Brooklyn accents and Jewish accents from my mom and pop, or gone out with a guy like me, who had picked her away from someone else on a double blind date and was able to do whatever he wanted to do, and whose future was in junk. I didn't like that last idea, but never showed it until we were already married.

"There's no future in junk, because there's too much of it," Winkler would say to us before his first business failure. "Louie, a surplus is always bad. The economy needs shortages. That's what's so good about monopolies—they keep down the supply of what people want. I buy Eastman Kodak surplus army aviation film for practically nothing that nobody wants because there's too much, and I turn it into regular color camera film that nobody has. Everybody's getting married and having babies, even me, and everybody wants pictures in color and can't get enough film. Eastman Kodak is helpless. It's their film, so they can't knock the quality. I use the Kodak name, and they can't come near me for price. The first order I got when I mailed out my postcards was from Eastman Kodak for four rolls of film, so they could find out what I was doing."

He and Eastman Kodak soon found out that army aviation film, which was good at ten thousand feet, left grainy splotches on babies and brides, and then he was back driving a truck for us on days we needed him before he began making honey-glaze and chocolate-covered doughnuts for the first of the bakeries he went into next before he moved to California and bought the first of his chocolate-candy factories that didn't work out either. For twenty years I slipped him money now and then and never told Claire. For twenty years, Claire sent them money when they needed it and never told me.

Before I got out of the army, Claire, still just a kid, talked seriously to me about reenlisting because she liked the opportunities to travel.

"You must be joshing," I told her, back from Dresden and flat on my back in the hospital after my operations. "My name is Louie, not screwy. Travel where? Georgia? Kansas? Fort Sill, Oklahoma? You've got no chance."

Claire helped at the junkshop with the telephone and business records when my big sister Ida had to be home with my mother. And she helped with my mother when Ida was in the shop. She could make her smile more than we could. The old lady was getting stranger and stranger with what the doctor told us was hardening of the arteries of the head, which was natural with age, he said, and which we now think was probably Alzheimer's disease, which maybe we now think of as natural too, like Dennis Teemer does with cancer.

Claire is still not much good at math, and that worries me now. She can add and subtract all right, especially after you give her a hand calculator, and even divide and multiply a little bit, but she is lost with fractions, decimals, and percentages and doesn't understand the arithmetic of markups, markdowns, and interest rates. She was good enough for the bookkeeping then, though, and that's about all the old man wanted her to do after the time she began throwing pieces of brass and copper into the last paper bale of the day to help us finish up sooner. The old man couldn't believe it, and his groan shook the walls and probably drove all our rats and mice and cockroaches jumping out in a panic onto McDonald Avenue.

"I'm trying to help," she gave as an excuse. "I thought you wanted the bales to be heavier."

I laughed out loud. "Not with brass."

"With copper?" asked my brother, and laughed also.

"*Tchotchkeleh,* where did you go to get educated?" the old man asked her, scraping his dental plates, with the different noise they made when he was feeling jolly. "Copper, brass too, sells for fourteen cents a pound. Newspapers sell for *bubkes,* for nothing by the pound. Which is worth more? You don't have to go to Harvard to figure that out. Here, *tchotchkeleh,* sit here, little darling, and write numbers and say who must pay us money and who we got to pay. Don't worry, you'll go dancing yet. Louie, come here. Where did you find such a little toy?" He took my arm into that grip of his and pulled me into a corner to talk to me alone, his face red, his freckles big. "Louie, listen good. If you were not my own son, and if instead she was my daughter, I would not let her go out with a *tummler* like you. You must not hurt her, not even a little."

She wasn't as easy to fool as he thought, although I probably could have done everything I wanted with her. She'd heard from a cousin nearby about the Coney Island boys and their social clubs, that they would dance you into the back room with the door and the couches and get some clothes off you fast so you couldn't go back out without feeling ashamed, until you gave them at least some of what they wanted. When she said she wouldn't go back there with me the first time, I just picked her up off her feet while we still were dancing and danced her around down the hall into our back room just to show her it wasn't always true, not with me, not then. What I didn't let her know was that I had already been there with a different girl about an hour before.

She was weak at arithmetic for sure, but I soon found out I was better off leaving business things in her hands than leaving them with any of my brothers or my partners, and I always trusted my brothers and partners. None of them ever cheated me that I know of, and I don't think that any of them would have wanted to, because I always picked men who were generous and liked to laugh and drink as much as I did.

Claire had good legs and that beautiful bust, and she still does. She spotted before I did that nearly all the Italian builders we did business with always showed up for appointments on the site with flashy blondes and redheads for girlfriends, and she would pitch in by tinting her own hair back closer to blonde when I brought her along to something maybe more important than normal. She would load on the costume jewelry, and she could talk to them all, men and girls alike, in their own language. "I always wear this when I'm with him," she would say with a bit of a tired sneer about the wedding ring she was sporting, and about the low V neck of the dress or suit she had chosen to wear, and all of us would laugh. "I don't have the license with me to prove it," she'd answer, whenever any of them asked if we were really married. I'd leave those answers to her and enjoy them, and sometimes if the deal was good and the lunch went long, we would sign into the local motel also for the rest of the afternoon and always leave before evening. "He has to get home," was the way she would put it. "He can't stay out all night here either." In restaurants, nightclubs, and vacation spots she was always great at starting up conversations in the ladies' room and scoring chicks for any of the guys with us who didn't have any and wanted one. And she spotted before I did what I was beginning to have in mind for one knockout of a tall Australian blonde girlfriend of one of the Italian builders, a lively, swinging thing in white makeup with high heels and another great pair of boobs who couldn't stand still for wanting to dance, even though there was no music, and who kept making broad wisecracks about the naughty toys she had in mind for the toy manufacturers she worked for.

"She's got a roommate," the guy said to me without moving his lips. "She's a nurse and a knockout. They both put out. We could go out together."

"I'll want this cookie," I said for her to hear.

"That's okay too. I'll take my chances with the nurse," he said, and I knew I would not want to pal around with him. He couldn't see my fun was in charming her, not in getting her as a gift.

Claire guessed it all. "No, Lew, not that," she let me know for all time, as soon as we were in the car. "Not ever, no, not when I see it happening."

I took the message, and she never saw that happening again, as far as I know.

And in the hospital at Fort Dix, she faced me down over Herman the German. I knew then she was right for me, after I cooled off and stopped simmering.

"Who takes care of you here?" she wanted to know, on one of her weekend visits from the city. "What do you do when you need something? Who comes?"

I'd be enchanted to demonstrate, I assured her. And then I bellowed, "Herman!" I heard the frightened footsteps of the orderly before I could roar out a second time, and then Herman my Ger-

man was standing there, slight, timid, panting, nervous, in his
fifties, no Aryan superman hero he, no *Übermensch,* not that one.

"*Mein Herr Rabinowitz?*" he began immediately, as I'd taught
him I wanted him to. "*Wie kann ich Ihnen dienen?*"

"*Achtung,* Herman," I ordered casually. And after he clicked
his heels and snapped to attention, I gave the order he understood.
"*Anfangen!*" He began to tell me about himself. And I turned to
Claire. "So, honey, how was the trip down? And where are you
staying? Same hotel?"

Her eyes boggled as the man recited, and she couldn't believe it
when she caught on. And she didn't look pleased. I almost had to
laugh at her comical expression. Herman reported his name, rank,
and serial number, and then his date and place of birth, education,
work experience, family background and situation, and everything
else I'd told him I wanted from him each time I stood him at
attention and asked him to begin telling me about himself again.
And I continued chatting with Claire as though I didn't see him
and certainly didn't care.

"So I'll tell you what I've been thinking. I'm not going to reen-
list, so forget about that one. The old man might need me back in
the junkshop for a while."

Claire couldn't figure out which of us to pay attention to. I kept
a straight face. The room went quiet. Herman had finished and
stood there blinking and sweating.

"Oh, yes," I said, without turning, as though I had just remembered him. "*Noch einmal.*"

And he began again. "*Mein Name ist Hermann Vogeler. Ich bin
ein Soldat der deutschen Armee. Ich bin Bäcker. Ich wurde am
dritten September 1892 geboren und ich bin dreiundfünfzig Jahre
alt.*"

"Lew, stop—it's enough already," Claire broke in finally, and
she was angry. "Stop! Stop it!"

I didn't like her talking to me that way, in front of Herman or
anyone else. That vein in my neck and jaw started ticking. "So I
think I'll begin with the old man again," I said right past her. "Just
to have some kind of income while I try to decide what we want
to do with ourselves."

"Lew, let him go," she ordered. "I mean it!"

"My father raised cows and sold milk," Herman was reciting in
German. "I went to school. After school I applied for college, but
I was not accepted. I was not smart."

"It's okay," I told her innocently, while Herman went on as obediently as the first time. "It's what he's trained to do. They trained him to bake. I trained him to do this. When he's finished I'll have him do it a few more times, so that none of us will ever forget. We can live with the folks for a while in the top-floor apartment. We're the youngest, so they'll make us climb stairs. I don't think I want to take time to go to college, not if we're married. You want to be married?"

"Lew, I want you to let him go! That's what I want! I warn you."

"Make me."

"I will. Don't push me."

"How?"

"I'll take my clothes off," she decided, and I could see she meant it. "Right here. I'll undress. It's enough! I'll take everything off and get on the bed on top of you, right now, if you don't let him stop. I'll sit on top of you, even with your stitches, even if they open. I'll let him see everything you've seen, I'll show it to him, I swear I will. Send him away."

She knew how I felt, that slick one. When bikini bathing suits came in, I didn't have to tell her not to wear one, and I finally gave up trying to talk to my daughters about them and just did not want to go to the beach when they were there.

She began unbuttoning. She kept unbuttoning, and she unbuttoned some more. And when I saw the white slip with the low neck and lace and the swell underneath of those really big tits that I never wanted any other man in the world ever even to take notice of, I had to back down. I could picture her unzipping and stepping out of her skirt with him still in the room, and then raising her slip, and I was afraid of that and just couldn't stand the thought, and I had to stop Herman, and I did it as though I were angry with him instead of her, like it was all his fault, not hers, or mine, and I had to send him away.

"Okay, enough, button up." I was in a rage with her too. "Okay, Herman. *Genug. Fertig. Danke schön.* Go out now! *Schnell! Mach schnell!* Get the hell out."

"*Danke schön, Herr Rabinowitz. Danke vielmals.*" He was quivering, which embarrassed me, and backed out bowing.

"That wasn't funny, Lew, not to me," she was letting me know as she buttoned up.

"I wasn't doing it to be funny." I felt nasty too.

"Then why?"

I didn't know why.

By the time he left, I actually had a soft spot for the poor old guy, and I went out of my way to wish him luck before they shipped him off for what they called repatriation.

By then I felt pity for him. He was weak. Even by other Germans he would be considered weak, and at his age he would never be strong. He'd reminded me already in certain ways of Sammy's father, a sweet old quiet man with silver hair who all summer went off for a long dip in the ocean as soon as he came home from work. Sammy or his brother or sister would be sent out by Sammy's mother to keep an eye on him and remind him to come home in time for supper. Sammy and I were both lucky. We each had an older sister to take care of the parents at the end. Sammy's father read all the Jewish newspapers, and in his house they all liked to listen to classical music on the radio. At the Coney Island library, Sammy would put in reservations for books for him that had been translated into Yiddish, novels mostly, and mostly by Russians. He was friendly. My father was not. My folks hardly read at all. I never could find the time. At the beginning when Sammy tried writing short stories and funny articles to sell to magazines, he tried them out on me. I never knew what to say, and I'm glad he stopped using me.

Sammy had that old picture of his father in uniform from the First World War. He was a funny-looking young guy, like all those soldiers then, in a helmet that looked too big for his small head, and with a gas mask and a canteen on his belt. Old Jacob Singer had come to this country to get away from the armies over there, and here he was back in one. His eyes were kind and smiling and they looked into yours. Sammy doesn't always meet your eye. When we were younger and started with the kissing games, we had to tell him to look right at the girl he was holding and hugging, instead of off to the side. Sammy at sixty-eight is already older than his father was when he died. I already know I'm not going to live as long as mine did.

Sammy and I lived on different blocks and our parents never met. Except for relatives who lived somewhere else and came on summer weekends for a day at the beach, none of us ever invited other families in for dinner or lunch.

My old man was not especially friendly to anyone outside the family, and friends like Sammy and Winkler were not all that

comfortable when they came to my house and he was home. I was
the favorite he had in mind to run the business when he grew too
old and see to it that there was always a livelihood for him and
for all of the brothers and sisters and their children who needed it
and couldn't find anything else. The Rabinowitzes were close.
Always I was the best outside man there too, the talker, the
schmeichler, the salesman, the *schmoozer*, the easygoing guy who
would go to one old building after another to butter up some poor
wretch of a janitor who was shoveling coal into a cellar furnace
or rolling out garbage cans and ask him politely if he was the
"superintendent" or the "manager." I wanted to talk to the "gentleman" who was in charge and would hint at all the ways we
could help each other. I would leave him a business card Winkler
had made up for me cheap through a printer he knew, and try to
establish a contact with him that could lead to our getting the old
pipes and the old plumbing fixtures like sinks and toilet bowls and
bathtubs and the broken steam and hot-water boilers in the house,
sometimes even before they were broken. We knew people who
could fix anything. If it couldn't be fixed, we could sell it for junk.
There would always be junk, my father would promise us like an
optimist, while Claire and I would try not to smile, and always
someone to pay you to take it and pay you to sell it. He made sure
to talk to both of us when he talked about money after I was back.
Now that I was not a child, he would raise me to sixty dollars a
week, almost double. And to sixty-five a week after we were married. And of course we could have the top-floor apartment until
we could afford something of our own.

"Listen, Morris, listen to me good," I told him when he finished.
I had almost four thousand in the bank from my gambling and
army pay. "I will do better for you. And sometime you will do
better for me. I will give you a year free. But after one year, I will
decide my salary. And I will be the one to say where, when, and
how I want to work."

"Free?"

That was okay with him. From that came the move after a while
into the old mousetrap factory in Orange Valley, New York, and
the idea of selling used building materials and plumbing fixtures
and boilers and hot-water heaters in a place that didn't have much
and needed things in a hurry.

Claire was a better driver than any of us—she'd come from
upstate and had a license at sixteen—and she drove the truck back

and forth into Brooklyn when I was too busy. She was tough and she was smart and could talk fresh when she had to, and she knew how to use her good looks with cops and filling station garages to get help when anything went wrong, without promising anything or putting herself in trouble. I remember the first ad for the local newspaper Sammy helped write that we still laugh over. WE CUT PIPE TO SKETCH.

"What's it mean?" he asked.

"What it says," I told him.

That line brought in more business of all kinds up here than anybody but me would have thought.

From that came the lumberyard and then the plumbing supply company, with the ten-thousand-dollar loan from my father, at good interest. He was worried about his old age, he said. He had a shaking in his head from a small stroke he'd already been through that nobody ever talked about but him.

"Louie, talk to me, tell me good," he would ask me. "Does it look like my head shakes a little, and the hand?"

"No, Pop, no more than mine."

I remember that when my mother's mind was all but gone, she still wanted her hair combed and whitened with rinse and the hairs tweezed from her face. I know that feeling now of wanting to look your best. And for almost thirty years now I try to keep out of sight until I look fine and healthy again.

"You're a good boy, Louie," he said with a kidding disgust. "You're a liar, like always, but I like you anyway."

We rented a house in our new community and had two kids, then bought a house and had a third, and then I built a house to sell and built some more, one at a time, with partners on the first few, and they did sell, for profit. Profit was always the motive. I found myself lunching and drinking with people who hunted and voted Republican, mainly, and who flew the flag on national holidays and felt they were serving the country by doing that. They put out yellow ribbons each time the White House went to war and acted like military heroes who were fighting it. Why yellow, I would jolly them, the national color of cowardice? But they had a volunteer fire department that was always on the spot and an emergency ambulance service I had to use the second time I got nauseous suddenly and lost all my strength and Claire panicked and rushed me into the hospital. That time they transferred me back to the hospital in Manhattan with Dennis Teemer, who fixed me up again and sent me home when I was back to normal. I joined the American Legion when we first moved up here, to make some friends and have a place to go. They taught me to hunt, and I liked doing that and liked the people I went with, felt beautiful when I hit. They cheered me whenever I brought down a goose and one time a deer. They had to gut it for me. I couldn't even watch. "It's the Christian thing to do," I'd say, and we'd all laugh. When I took my first son out, it was always with other people so there'd be someone to do that for us. He wasn't crazy about hunting and soon I stopped going too.

Next we got the golf club in a town nearby. I made more friends, a lot from the city who moved up out here to the distant suburbs, and we had different places to go and ate and drank with other married couples.

I learned more about banks, and bankers too. At the beginning they let us know, even the women who were tellers, that they didn't much like having to serve customers with names like Rabinowitz. That changed, I admit. But I didn't. They got used to me and a lot of others, as the area kept growing. They thought more of me when I borrowed than when I put money in. When I put money in I was only another hardworking guy struggling with a small business. When I was big enough to borrow, I turned into *Mr.* Rabinowitz, then Lew to the officers, to Mr. Clinton and Mr. Hardy—a *client,* of means and net worth—and I would bring them as guests to my golf club as soon as I got in and introduce them as Ed Clinton and Harry Hardy, my bankers, and they were so tickled they blushed. I found out about bankruptcies. I couldn't believe those laws the first time I found myself being screwed by them.

I found out about Chapter 11 from a builder named Hanson and his lawyer, and they found out about me. When they left his house at the start of a business day, I was out of my car while they were still on the porch.

"Lew?" Hanson was so surprised he actually smiled, until he saw I didn't. He was a tall man and he had his hair cut close to the ears in the kind of haircut we had to wear in the army, and I didn't like it even then. The one with him was a stranger. "How are you?"

"Hanson, you owe me forty-two hundred dollars," I said right off. "For lumber and shingles and toilet and kitchen fixtures and pipes. I've sent you bills and talked to you on the telephone, and now I'm telling you to your face I want it today, this morning. Now. I'm here to collect."

"Lew, this is my new lawyer. This one is Rabinowitz."

"Ah, yes," said the new lawyer, with the kind of a smile you always see on lawyers that makes them look like hypocrites you want to strangle on the spot. "My client is in Chapter 11, Mr. Rabinowitz. I think you know that."

"Tell your client—sir, what is your name? I don't think he gave it."

"Brewster. Leonard Brewster."

"Please advise your client, Brewster, that Chapter 11 is for him and his lawyers, and for the court and maybe for the other people he owes. It's not for me. It's not for Rabinowitz. Hanson, we made a bargain, you and me. You took my material, you used it, you didn't complain about the delivery or quality. Now you must pay for it. That's the way I work. Listen to me good. I want my money."

"You can't collect it, Mr. Rabinowitz," said Brewster, "except through the court. Let me explain."

"Hanson, I can collect it."

"Lew—" Hanson began.

"Explain to your lawyer that I can collect it. I don't have time for court. I can collect it through the pores of your skin if I have to, one drop at a time, if you make me. You're keeping your house? Not with my forty-two hundred. It will go out from under you brick by brick. Are you listening good?"

"Lenny, let me talk to you inside."

When they came out, Brewster spoke with his eyes down.

"You'll have to take it in cash," he told me under his breath. "We can't leave a record."

"I think I can do that."

I trusted banks a little better now, but not that much, and I put the money in a safe-deposit box, because I didn't ever want to have to trust my accountant either. Claire looked faint when I said where I'd been.

"You didn't know they would pay."

"If I didn't know, I would not have gone. I don't waste time. Don't ask me how I know. People do what I want them to. Haven't you noticed? Didn't you? Next—what about Mehlman, that *gonif*, as long as this is pay-up day?"

"The same story."

"Call him. I'll talk to him too."

"How much should I ask him for?"

"How much is six times seven?"

"Don't confuse me. Does he still get the discount?"

"Would you know how to figure it?"

"Does he pay interest or not? That's all I want from you! Don't put me back in school again."

Claire didn't care for deadbeats and chiselers either, no matter what their religion, any more than I did back in the days when we were working very hard and she would help out on the phone when the lumberyard was still small and she wasn't busy getting the kids off to school or rushing home to be there when they got back. Later on, when she had more time and we had more money, she had a piece of an art gallery up here that wasn't supposed to make money and didn't, and after that even a half share of an art school in Lucca in Italy I bought her to help give her something else to think about when there wasn't always that much good anymore to think about here. When Mehlman called back, I grabbed the phone from her. She was too polite, like we were the ones who were supposed to apologize.

"Mehlman, you are a liar," I began right in, without even knowing what he'd been saying. "Listen to me good. If you force me to prove it you will hang yourself, because you'll have nowhere left to turn and no lies left to tell, and I will make you ashamed. Mehlman, I know you are a very religious man, so I'll put the matter to you in religious terms. If I don't have the money in my hands by Thursday noon, this *shabbos* you will crawl to *shul* on your knees, and everyone in the temple will know that Rabinowitz broke your legs because he says you are a liar and a cheat."

I didn't know if Mehlman was lying or not. But the money was mine, and I got it.

Of course, later on I had a much more lenient view of Chapter 11 when I finally had to go into bankruptcy myself, but none of the creditors were people. They were only corporations. People were proud of me and clapped me on the back.

By then I was older and had this ailment slowing me down. I had less pep and not much reason for keeping up with newcomers who were younger and hungrier and willing to work as hard as we used to want to. I would have liked to hold on to the lumberyard and the plumbing business to pass on to the children if they wanted to keep it or sell if they didn't. We both felt the cost was too high and it was not worth the risk.

By then the cat was out of the bag. My disease was an open

secret in the family. The children knew but didn't know what to make of it, and three of them weren't so small anymore. For a while they must have thought I didn't know. It was a couple of days before even Claire could look me in the eye and tell me what I already knew and did not want her to find out, that I had this disease called Hodgkin's disease, and that it was serious. I didn't know how she would take it. I didn't know how I could take it, having her see me ailing and weak.

I've lasted longer than anyone thought I would. I count. I divide my life into seven-year stretches since.

"You listen to me now," I told her that first week in the hospital up here. "I don't want anyone to know."

"You think I do?"

"We'll make something up."

By the time we let the business go and stuck only to our land and building, it was out of the bag everywhere and we could finally stop pretending to everyone that I had angina pectoris, which often laid me up and made me want to vomit, or relapsing mononucleosis, which did the same, or a nuisance of a minor inflammation I thought up and decided to call tuberculosis of the small glands that left those small scars and blue burn marks on the neck and lips and chest when treated. My muscles came back fast, and so did my appetite. Between spells I kept myself overweight just in case, and I still looked large.

"Okay, Emil, no more kid stuff," I'd said to my doctor in the hospital after the tests, when I saw his laugh was false. He was swallowing a lot and clearing his throat. If I shook his hand I knew it would be limp. "Listen to me good, Emil. It wasn't green apples like I told you, because I don't eat green apples, and I don't even know what they taste like anymore. My neck is swollen and hurts. If it's not an allergy, and you won't say it was food poisoning, then it's got to be something else, doesn't it?"

"Hodgkin's disease," said Emil, and that's the last time in twenty-eight years anyone spoke of it to me by name. "It's what it's called," Emil added.

"Cancer?" It was hard for me to speak that word too. "It's what we're all afraid of."

"It's a form of that."

"I was afraid it was leukemia."

"No, it's not leukemia."

"I don't know the symptoms, but I was afraid it was that. Emil,

I don't want to hear it, but I guess I have to. How much time do I have? No lies, Emil, not yet."

Emil looked more relaxed. "Maybe a lot. I don't want to guess. A lot depends on the biology of the individual."

"I don't know what that means," I told him.

"They're your cells, Lew. We can't always tell how they're going to behave. A lot depends on you. How much can you take? How strong is your resistance?"

I'd been holding him by the forearm without realizing it, and I squeezed good-naturedly until he turned a little pale. I laughed a little when I set him free. I was still very strong. "The best you'll ever meet, Emil."

"Then, Lew, you might be okay for a long, long while yet. And feel good most of the time."

"I think that's what I'm going to do," I informed him, as though making a business decision. "Now, don't tell Claire. I don't want her to know what it is."

"She knows, Lew. You're both adults. She didn't want you to know."

"Then don't tell her you told me. I want to watch how she lies."

"Lew, will you grow up? This thing is no joke."

"Don't I know it?"

Emil took off his glasses. "Lew, there's a man in New York I want you to see. His name is Teemer, Dennis Teemer. You'll go into his hospital there. He knows more about this than anybody here."

"I won't want an ambulance."

We went down by limo, in a pearl-gray stretch limousine with black windows that allowed us to see out but nobody to see in, with me stretched out in back in a space big enough to hold a coffin, maybe two.

"We sometimes use it for that," said the driver, who'd told us he was from Venice and the brother of a gondolier there. "The seats go flat and the back opens."

Claire left him a very big tip. We always tip big, but this time it was for luck.

Teemer had his office on Fifth Avenue across from the Metropolitan Museum and a waiting room of quiet patients. Down the block on the way uptown to his hospital was the Frank Campbell Funeral Home—a "home," they called it—and I made jokes to myself about the convenient location. Now when I hear about those big society parties they have at the museum and places like that, I get the feeling I'm upside down in a world that's turned topsy-turvy. There are big new buildings in the city that I don't even recognize. There are new multimillionaires where there used to be Rockefellers and J. P. Morgans, and I don't know where they came from or what they're doing.

After that first time in Dr. Teemer's office, I never let Claire walk inside there with me again. She would cross into the museum and I would meet her when I was finished and we'd look at pictures if she still wanted to and then go off for lunch somewhere and go home. In that waiting room there is no one ever laughing, and I am never in a mood myself to try to get anything jolly going there. Teemer himself is still a skinny little guy with a gloomy manner, and when he does cheer me up, he does it in a way that always leaves me cranky.

"You might be interested to know, Mr. Rabinowitz," he began when we met, "that we no longer think of it as incurable."

All at once I felt very much better. "I'll strangle Emil. He didn't tell me that."

"He doesn't always know."

"So there is a cure? Huh?"

Teemer shook his head, and my breath caught. "No, I wouldn't put it that way. We don't think of it as a cure."

Now I felt I might sock him. "I'm listening good, Dr. Teemer. The disease is now curable, but you don't have a cure?"

"It's a matter of vocabulary," he went on. "We have treatments." He was trying his hardest, maybe too hard, to be nice. "And the treatments usually work. They will work with you, but we don't know how well. Or how long. We can't really cure it. We can suppress it. That's not the same as a cure. We never feel sure we've gotten rid of it for good, because the genesis of the disease, the origin, is always in yourself."

"For how long can you suppress it?"

"For very long when the treatments are effective. There are problems, but we'll handle them. In the periods of remission you should feel perfectly normal. When the symptoms come back, we will treat it some more."

"You're sure they'll come back?"

"They mostly seem to."

It was not the asbestos I'd worked with that brought it on. He could almost be positive about that, if anyone could be sure of anything when it came to one's genes, which were always selfish, he said, and oblivious too.

"They won't do what I want?" I almost laughed, nervously. "They're mine and they don't care about me?"

"They don't know about you, Mr. Rabinowitz." He smiled just a bit. "It might be triggered by any number of things. Tobacco, radiation."

"From what?"

"Radium, electricity, uranium, maybe even tritium."

"What's tritium?"

"A radioactive gas that comes from heavy water. You may even have some on your wristwatch or bedroom clock."

"Radiation causes it and radiation cures it—excuse me, suppresses it?" I said, making my joke.

"And chemicals too," he said. "Or—I almost hate to say this, some people don't like hearing it—it might be your natural biological destiny, nothing more sinister than that."

"Natural? You'd call that natural?"

"In the world of nature, Mr. Rabinowitz, all diseases are natural." It made sense to me at the time, but I didn't like hearing it. "I've depressed you enough. Now let me help. You will be going into the hospital. You've got transportation? Has your wife made plans to stay?"

She stayed at a hotel that first time, the next, seven years later, when we both thought she was losing me, with Sammy and Glenda, because she needed someone to talk to. This last time there was no Glenda, so she stayed at a hotel again with my older daughter, but they ate with Sammy and he came every day. Teemer had been Glenda's doctor too.

I was better in three days and home in five. But the day I knew I'd survive I felt very bad too, because then I knew I was going to die.

I'd always known I was going to die. But then I *knew* I was going to die. The night that sank in, I woke up in the morning with my eyes wet, and one of the night nurses noticed but didn't say anything, and I never told anyone but Claire. We were going home after my breakfast.

"Last night I shed a tear," I admitted.

"You think I didn't?"

. . .

That was just over twenty-eight years ago, and for most of the first seven I felt as good as I had ever felt before. I couldn't believe how fine I felt and I would come to believe it was gone forever. When I didn't feel fine I went into the city for Teemer once a week for half a day. When I did feel good, I played golf or cards with Emil maybe once a week and kept in touch with him that way. When the diaphragm slipped and Claire found herself pregnant again, we decided against the abortion without even saying so and had our little Michael, I felt so good. It's a way we showed confidence. We named him after my father. Mikey, we called him, and still do when we're kidding around. I felt so vibrant I could have had a hundred more. His Jewish name is Moishe, which was the Jewish name of my father. By then the old man had passed away too, and we could use his name without seeming to wish to put a curse on him while he was still alive. We Jews from the east don't name kids after parents who are still alive. But now I worry about Michael, little Mikey, because apart from money, I don't know what else I'm leaving him in the way of genes and his "natural biological destiny," and the other kids too, and maybe even my grandchildren. Those fucking genes. They're mine and won't listen to me? I can't believe that.

I don't really take to Teemer, but I'm not afraid of him or his diseases anymore, and when Sammy needed a specialist like him for Glenda, I recommended him over the one they already had, and he's the one they stuck with for the little time it took. It's those green apples I'm more afraid of now, all the time, those green apples in my mother's loony theory that green apples were what made people sick. Because more than anything else now, I'm afraid of nausea. I am sick of feeling nauseous.

"That's a good one, Lew," Sammy complimented me, when he was up here the last time.

Then I got the joke.

Sammy wears his hair combed back and parted on the side, and it's silver and thinning too, like I remember his father's. Sammy doesn't have much to do since his wife died, and then later he was forced out of his work at his *Time* magazine and into retirement, so he comes up here a lot. I don't want him in the hospital up here, but he comes in anyway sometimes, with Claire, and we bullshit until he sees I've had enough. We talk about the good old days in Coney Island, and now they do seem good, about Luna Park and Steeplechase and the big old RKO Tilyou movie theater, and how they've all gone away, disappeared, in *d'rerd,* as my father and mother used to say, in the earth, underground. He comes up by bus and, when he doesn't sleep over, goes back at night by bus to the bus terminal, that unreal city, he calls it, and then into the modern high-rise apartment he took in a building with everything, including some knockout models and call girls, when he found himself living alone in empty space he no longer wanted. Sammy still doesn't know what to do with himself, and we don't know what to do to help. He doesn't seem interested yet in settling in with someone else, although he talks about wanting to. My oldest daughter has introduced him to some of her unmarried lady friends and so has Glenda's oldest daughter, but nothing happened. They always find each other only "nice" and that's all. Claire's unattached women friends are too old. We decide that without even having to say it. He still likes to get laid now and then, and does, he tries to hint, when I kid about it. Sammy and I can chuckle now when he tells of the times he came in his pants— I never had to—and the first few times he finally got up the nerve to get girls to jerk him off: girls went for him, but he didn't know what to do with them. And the night his pocket was picked in the bus terminal and he found himself with no money and no wallet, not even carfare to get home, and was arrested and locked up in the police station there. I was the person he telephoned. I told off the cop after I vouched for Sammy and demanded the sergeant, I told off the sergeant and asked for the man in charge, and I told off the captain, McMahon, and said I would bring the wrath of the American Legion and National Guard and Pentagon down upon him, and the full force of me, former Sergeant Lewis Rabinowitz of the famed Army First Division, if he didn't show some sense and give him the cab fare to get him home. Sammy still can't get over how good I could be at things like that.

"He was lying down, that Captain McMahon," Sammy swore, "on a bed in a cell in the back of that police station that was furnished like a bedroom, and he looked sick. And the cell next to that one was set up with desks and toys like a little classroom, a kindergarten, but cops with ashtrays were playing cards with each other. There were children's mobiles hanging over them in a prison cell, and one was a mobile of a black-and-white cow jumping over the moon, and they were luminescent, like they reflected light and would shine in the dark," Sammy explained, "like those old radium watches we all used to wear before we found out they were dangerous. There was another man there, named McBride, who was dusting and moving things around, and he's the one who lent me the money to get home. When I mailed him a check to pay him back, he even sent me a thank-you note. How's that one?"

When the kid, their Michael, flipped out with his drugs and disappeared upstate about a year before he hanged himself, I did the same thing on the telephone, although I would have driven right up to Albany if I had to, but I didn't have to. I called the governor's office, the head of the National Guard, and the headquarters of the state police. It was personal, I knew, but this was Sergeant Rabinowitz, formerly of the famed First Division in Europe, the Big Red 1, and it was a matter of life and death. They found him in a hospital in Binghamton and had him transferred in a government car to a hospital in the city at state expense. Sammy never got over how good I could be at something like that one too.

"I've made jokes that were funnier," I told him this time, when he pointed out the one I'd just made about getting sick of feeling nauseous. "I wasn't trying to be funny."

"And the word is *nauseated*," he said to me.

"What?" I had no idea what he was talking about.

"The word is *nauseated*, not *nauseous*," he explained. "People don't get nauseous. They get nauseated."

I liked it better my way.

"Sammy, don't you be a prick," I told him. "You can get nauseated. I'll get nauseous, if I want to. Just think, Sammy. It wasn't so long ago that I nabbed that kid in the city with the stolen pocketbook. I picked him right up, turned him around in my hands in midair, and slammed him down on the hood of a car just hard enough to let him know I was Lew Rabinowitz. 'Move and I'll break your back,' I warned him, and held him there until the cops came. Who would believe it, looking at me now? Now I feel like I couldn't lift a pound of butter."

My weight is not coming back fast enough, and Teemer and Emil are thinking of trying something new. My appetite isn't back to normal either. Mostly I have none, and I'm beginning to wonder if maybe this time there's something new going on I don't know about yet. Sammy may be ahead of all of us, because he looks worried about me, but he doesn't say. What he does say, with his small smile, is this:

"If you're that weak, Lew, I might be willing to take you on at arm wrestling now."

"I'd still beat you," I came back at him. That made me laugh. "And I'd beat you at boxing too, in case you ever want to try that one with me again."

He laughs too and we eat the rest of our tuna sandwiches. But I know I look thin. My appetite has just not come rushing back like after the other times, and now I seem to be beginning to know—this has not happened to me before—this time I seem to be beginning to know that this time, I may be getting ready to die.

I don't tell Claire.

I say nothing to Sammy.

I'm well into my sixties and we're into the nineties, and this time I'm beginning to feel, like my father felt when he got old, and his brother too, that this time things are beginning to come to an end.

12
Noodles Cook

The ascent to the throne room of the White House by the man with the code name Little Prick was not without its ceremonial falterings and sundry spiteful amusements, as G. Noodles Cook could have documented in detail were it not for a lifelong propensity to be guarded, self-serving, calculating, mendacious, and mercenary—all qualities commending him as a soul singularly qualified for his exalted post as the tenth of nine senior tutors to the man who had eventually become the country's newest President. Yossarian had informed the FBI that his old friend and business colleague G. Noodles Cook was a sneak and a snake and that the administration was not going to find a much better person to fill whatever position he was being considered for. Noodles Cook was a man who could always be trusted to lie.

He got the job.

As far back as seminars in graduate school, where they had met, Noodles had unmasked himself as a person with a tendency to display his gifts only in the presence of a designated mentor, who could note that anything original emerging had originated precociously with him. Noodles, who'd done well at a less-than-elegant preparatory school while Yossarian was away at war, labored on to obtain his doctoral degree and soon found out there was not much for him to do with it but teach.

By that time, Yossarian, who had dropped out of graduate school with just a master's degree, was already in a position to hire Noodles for his group in the public relations agency where he was at work when Noodles wisely decided to give that kind of business a shot. He had good family connections, and the public relations agency seemed to him a good launching pad for something bigger and better.

Coworkers soon smelled out that Noodles never proposed an idea save when Yossarian was close enough to hear and, more frequently, would postpone suggesting anything even to Yossarian until both were in the presence of the client or with a superior official of the company. Too often when they were collaborating on their screenplays and television scripts, Noodles would supply the pregnant line in a way that aroused suspicion that the key to the problem had been lying in his grasp the day before. Telling him to change, Yossarian would tell himself, would be like telling a hunchback to stand up straight. A noodle was a noodle. In his way he was loyal to Yossarian, who did not like him but did not mind him, and they persisted as friends.

Departing graduate school with the matter-of-fact discovery that he did not want his higher education to go any higher, Yossarian had done some teaching and then moved into advertising. He did well, enjoyed his annual raises and small promotions, liked the people there better than those at the university, received a small raise again at the end of his third year, and decided to go out exploring for a better-paying job doing work of a different kind. He found a new better-paying job quickly with a different agency that handled accounts pretty much the same as the one he had just left. He remained until he received his annual raise and then went looking for another new job, and another quicker increase in salary.

Each time he took leave of one place for another, it was with the discouraging resolution that he did not want to spend the balance of his life exercising his intelligence, ingenuity, and good looks furthering the progress of products he did not himself use and of publications he would not normally read. On the other hand, he could not think of a product or cause with which he did wish to become involved that paid enough for the things he had learned to want for himself and his wife and children. The dilemma was not agonizing.

There was no need to rationalize.

He worked because he had to.

In Wall Street, of course, lay the exotic attraction in quantities unimaginable of a distilled product denuded of all complicating attributes. It was called money, and mountains of it could be manufactured out of nothing, as magically, almost, and as naturally, as a simple tree manufactures tons of wood out of thin air, sunlight, and rainwater. Money might be shit, as every college student with some knowledge of Freud might point out perversely at parties and family gatherings; but it was shit that could buy things: friends of rank and means; a coat of arms in the furriers' and jewelers' and in the fashion hubs of the world; baronial estates in Connecticut, Virginia, Mexico, East Hampton, and Colorado; and titles of knowing distinction that admitted the truncating of first names into the mere initial and the graceful relocation of accent onto the middle name, as in G. Noodles Cook and C. Porter Lovejoy, that most gray of graying eminences in the Washington Cosa Loro.

The forbearing Noodles Cook was tireless in repeating that his mother had been a daughter of the Goodman Noodles family of Goodman Noodles fame and his father a collateral descendant of the British Cooks of Cook's Tours, and that he himself was something of a scion of the Noodles and the Cooks, with some means and property devolving upon him through the normal processes of heritage. Noodles Cook had been Goody in college, Goodman in business, and Noodles in newspaper gossip coverage of such social doings as are reported regularly. And today he was G. Noodles Cook in *Who's Who* and on official White House stationery.

Noodles, beginning in government as the tenth of nine senior tutors to the freshman Vice President, never failed to respond on the rare occasions Yossarian had need to telephone him, and Yossarian had found that this access still obtained, even in his present post as one of the more trusted confidants of the new man recently installed in the White House.

"How's the divorce going?" one or the other of them was certain to inquire each time they spoke.

"Fine. How's yours?"

"Pretty good. Mine's having me followed anyway."

"So is mine."

"And how are you getting along with that guy you're working for?" Yossarian never failed to ask.

"Better and better—I know you're surprised."

"No, I'm not surprised."

"I don't know what to make of that. You ought to join us here in Washington if I can find some way to worm you aboard. Here at last is a real chance to do some good."

"For whom?"

The answer always was a self-effacing laugh. Between these two it was not necessary to put more into words.

Neither back then at the public relations agency was troubled ethically by the work they were doing for corporate clients who never had the public interest in mind and political candidates they would not vote for, and for a large cigarette company owned mainly by New Yorkers who did not have to grow tobacco to scratch a livelihood from the earth. They made money, met people of substance, and generally enjoyed succeeding. Writing speeches for others to deliver, even people they abhorred, seemed but a different form of creative writing.

But time passed, and the work—like all work to a man of open intellect—turned tiresome. When there was no longer doubt that tobacco caused cancer, their children looked daggers at them, and their roles took a subtle turn toward the unsavory. They separately began thinking of doing something else. Neither had ever tried pretending that the advertising, public relations, and political work they were accomplishing was ever anything but trivial, inconsequential, and duplicitous. Noodles revealed himself first.

"If I'm going to be trivial, inconsequential, and deceitful," announced Noodles, "then I might as well be in government."

And off he moved to Washington, D.C., with letters of recommendation, including one from Yossarian, to utilize his family connections in an aspiring endeavor to slither his way into the Cosa Loro there.

While Yossarian had a second crack at high-finance easy money with an insider on Wall Street who sold sure things at a time when there were sure things. He continued writing short stories and small articles of trenchant satirical genius just right for publication in the prestigious *New Yorker* magazine; each time his pieces were rejected, and each time he applied and was turned down for an editorial post there, his respect for the magazine escalated. He was successful with two screenplays and half successful with another, and he outlined ideas for an acerbic stage play that he was never able to finish and a complex comic novel that he was not able to start.

He made money also by consulting with clients profitably on a personal freelance basis for fees, percentages, and commissions and by participating on a modest scale in several advantageous real estate syndication ventures, which he never understood. When national affairs again took a turn toward the menacing, he found himself going as a father in anguished consternation to his old wartime acquaintance Milo Minderbinder. Milo was elated to see him.

"I was never even sure you always really liked me," he revealed almost gratefully.

"We've always been friends," said Yossarian evasively, "and what are friends for?"

Milo showed caution instantaneously with a native grasp that never seemed to fail him. "Yossarian, if you've come to me for help in keeping your sons out of the war in Vietnam—"

"It's the only reason I have come."

"There is nothing I can do." By which Yossarian understood him to mean he had already used up his quota of illegal legal draft exemptions. "We all have our share to shoulder. I've seen my duties and I've done them."

"We all have our jobs to do," added Wintergreen. "It's the luck of the draw."

Yossarian remembered that Wintergreen's jobs in the last big war had consisted mainly of digging holes as a stockade prisoner and filling them back up for having gone AWOL one time after another to delay going overseas into danger; selling stolen Zippo cigarette lighters once there; and serving in a managerial capacity in military mailrooms, where he countermanded orders from high places that fell short of his standards, simply by throwing them away.

"I'm talking about one kid, damn it," pleaded Yossarian. "I don't want him to go."

"I know what you're suffering," said Milo. "I have a son of my own I worry about. But we've used up our contacts."

Yossarian perceived dismally that he was getting nowhere and that if Michael had bad luck in the draw, he would probably have to run off with him to Sweden. He sighed. "Then there's nothing you can do to help me? Absolutely nothing?"

"Yes, there *is* something you can do to help me," Milo responded, and for the moment, Yossarian feared he had been misunderstood. "You know people that we don't. We would like," Milo continued, and here his voice grew softer, in a manner sacramental, "to hire a very good law firm in Washington."

"Don't you have a good firm there?"

"We want to hire *every* good law firm, so that none of them can ever take part in an action against us."

"We want the influence," explained Wintergreen, "not the fucking law work. If we had the fucking influence we'd never need the fucking law work or the fucking lawyers. Yossarian, where could we begin if we wanted to get all the best legal connections in Washington?"

"Have you thought of Porter Lovejoy?"

"C. Porter Lovejoy?" At this, even Wintergreen succumbed to a state of momentary awe.

"Could *you* get to C. Porter Lovejoy?"

"I can get to Lovejoy," casually answered Yossarian, who'd never met Lovejoy but got to him simply with a phone call to his law office as the representative of a cash-rich corporate client seeking the services of someone experienced in Washington for an appropriate retainer.

Milo said he was a wizard. Wintergreen said he was fucking okay.

"And Eugene and I agree," said Milo, "that we want to retain you too, as a consultant and a representative, on a part-time basis, of course. Only when we need you."

"For special occasions."

"We will give you an office. And a business card."

"You'll give more than that." Yossarian turned suave. "Are you sure you can afford me? It will cost a lot."

"We have a lot. And with an old friend like you, we're prepared to be generous. How much will you want, if we try it for a year?"

Yossarian pretended to ponder. The figure he would name had jumped instantly to mind. "Fifteen thousand a month," he finally said, very distinctly.

"Fifteen dollars a month?" Milo repeated, more distinctly, as though to make sure.

"Fifteen *thousand* a month."

"I thought you said hundred."

"Eugene, tell him."

"He said thousand, Milo," Wintergreen sadly obliged.

"I have trouble hearing." Milo pulled violently at an earlobe, as though remonstrating with a naughty child. "I thought fifteen dollars sounded low."

"It's thousand, Milo. And I'll want it on a twelve-month basis, even though I might be available for only ten. I take two-month summer vacations."

He was delighted with that whopper. But it would be nice to have summers free, maybe to return to those two literary projects of yore, his play and comic novel.

His idea for the stage play, reflecting *A Christmas Carol*, would portray Charles Dickens and his fecund household at Christmas dinner when that family was at its most dysfunctional, shortly before that splenetic literary architect of sentimental good feeling erected the brick wall indoors to close his own quarters off from his wife's. His lighthearted comic novel was derived from the *Doctor Faustus* novel of Thomas Mann and centered on a legal dispute over the rights to the fictitious and horrifying Adrian Leverkühn choral masterpiece in those pages called *Apocalypse*, which, stated Mann, had been presented just once, in Germany in 1926, anticipating Hitler, and possibly never would be performed again. On one side of the lawsuit were the heirs of the musical genius Leverkühn, who had created that colossal composition; on the other would be the beneficiaries to the estate of Thomas Mann, who had invented Leverkühn and defined and orchestrated that prophetic, awesome, and unforgettable unique opus of progress and annihilation, with Nazi Germany as both the symbol and the substance. The attraction to Yossarian of both these ideas lay in their arresting unsuitability.

"Fifteen a month," Milo finally tabulated aloud, "for twelve months a year, will come to . . ."

"A hundred and eighty," Wintergreen told him curtly.

Milo nodded, with an expression that revealed nothing.

"Then we agree. You will work for us for one year for one hundred and eighty dollars."

"*Thousand*, Milo. A hundred and eighty *thousand* dollars a year, plus expenses. Tell him again, Eugene. And write out a check for three months in advance. That's the way I'm always paid, quarterly. I've already gotten you C. Porter Lovejoy."

Milo's look of pain was habit. But from that date on, Yossarian knew, but did not care to admit, he had not been in serious want of ready cash, except in those uncommon times of divorce and the successive collapse of his tax shelters a dozen years after each had been erected by infallible specialists.

"And by the way"—Wintergreen took him aside at the end— "about your son. Establish a legal residence in a black neighborhood where the draft boards don't have trouble meeting their quotas. Then, lower back pain and a letter from a doctor should do the rest. I have one son technically living in Harlem now, and a couple of nephews who officially reside in Newark."

Yossarian had the feeling about Michael, and himself, that they would sooner flee to Sweden.

C. Porter Lovejoy and G. Noodles Cook took to each other symbiotically from the day Yossarian brought them together, with a reciprocating warmth Yossarian had never felt toward Noodles or for Porter Lovejoy either the few times they had met.

"That's one I owe you," Noodles had said afterward.

"There's more than one," Yossarian took the precaution of reminding him.

C. Porter Lovejoy, silver-haired, bipartisan, and clearheaded, as the friendly press chose consistently to describe him, was a man still very much at ease with life. He had been a Washington insider and a made member of the Cosa Loro there for almost half a century and by now had earned the right, he liked to ruminate to listeners, to start slowing down.

Publicly, he served often on governmental commissions to exonerate and as coauthor of reports to vindicate.

Privately, he was the major partner and counsel-at-large to the Cosa Loro Washington law firm of Atwater, Fitzwater, Dishwater, Brown, Jordan, Quack, and Capone. In that capacity, because of his aristocratic prestige and reputation for probity, he could freely represent whatever clients he liked, even those with adversarial interests. From a border state, he professed legitimate home ties in all directions and could speak in the soothing accents of the well-bred southern gentleman when talking to Northerners and with the phonetics of the cultivated true Ivy Leaguer when talking to Southerners. His partner Capone was dark and balding and looked down-to-earth and rather tough.

"If you are coming to me for influence," Porter Lovejoy would stress to each hopeful prospect seeking him out, "you have come to the wrong man. However, if you wish to retain the services of experienced people who know their way blindfolded through the corridors of power here, who are on close terms with the people you will want to see and can tell you who they are and can arrange for them to see you, who can accompany you to meetings and do much of the talking for you, who can find out what is happening about you at meetings you don't attend, and who can go over heads directly to superiors if the decisions are not those you like, I may be able to help."

It was C. Porter Lovejoy who did most to foster the aspirations of G. Noodles Cook and to increase their range. He astutely calibrated the parameters of the younger man's initiative and moved with openhanded celerity to place him with other celebrities in the Cosa Loro family who could best utilize his ingenious insights into the mechanics of political public relations and image building: his knack for the rabble-rousing motto, the snide insinuation, the smooth and sophisticated insult, the tricky prestidigitation in logic that was quicker than the eye and could glide by invisibly, and the insidious lie. Once given the chance, Noodles had never disappointed anyone who, like C. Porter Lovejoy, expected the worst from him.

Between Yossarian and a Cosa Loro hit man like Noodles Cook a breach of peaceable distaste had taken shape which neither saw any necessity to repair. Yet Yossarian had no hesitation in calling now about the ridiculous possibility of inducing the new President to pretend to take seriously an invitation from Christopher Maxon to the wedding of a stepniece or something at the Port Authority Bus Terminal.

"He raises millions for your party, Noodles."

"Why not?" said Noodles merrily. "It sounds like a lark. Tell them he says he'll think seriously about coming."

"You don't have to ask him?"

"No." Noodles sounded surprised. "John, the brain has not yet come into being that is large enough to deal with all of the matters any President has to pretend he understands. I'm still riding high since I helped him through the inauguration."

As the tenth and newest of the nine senior tutors with eleven doctoral degrees in the brain trust surrounding the man who had since become President, G. Noodles Cook was still unstained by that particular contempt which familiarity is often said to breed.

It was C. Porter Lovejoy, observing the dimming luster of the original nine tutors, who had proposed the appointment of G. Noodles Cook as a tenth to rekindle an illusion of brilliance in high office, a choice, he maintained with disinterested authority, that had to be beneficial to this Vice President, the administration, the country, to Noodles Cook himself, and, unsaid but understood, to C. Porter Lovejoy and his partnership interest in the

Cosa Loro lawyer-lobbying firm of Atwater, Fitzwater, Dishwater, Brown, Jordan, Quack, and Capone. Capone, like Lovejoy a founding partner, played golf at good clubs with business leaders and high government officials, and was rarely permitted to lose.

The impediments in the formalities of the inauguration arose from the natural preference of the Vice President to be inducted into the higher office with an oath administered by the chief justice of the U.S. Supreme Court. The honorable gentleman occupying the post, a steely, rather domineering personality with eyeglasses and a high-domed forehead, resigned abruptly rather than collaborate in an act he felt was outside the spirit of the law, if not the letter.

The unexpected action left the new chief executive little choice but to call on one of the other celebrities on the court with party affiliations akin to his own.

The woman then on the court resigned voluntarily fourteen minutes after she was sounded out. She put forth as her explanation an overwhelming yearning to return to the field she loved most: housework. All her life, she stated, she had aspired only to be a housewife.

And the other star of magnitude in that revered constellation of honorable justices to which people had formerly been prone to look up, an honorable gentleman commended frequently by friendly newspapermen for what they called his wit and his showman's preening flair for tendentious and self-amusing hair-splitting, went fishing.

The Afro-American was of course out of the question. White America would not tolerate a President whose legitimacy in office had been validated by a black man, and especially by a black man like that one, who was not much of a lawyer and not much of a judge and had seemed at his confirmation hearings to be composed entirely out of equal measures of bile and bullshit.

The other orthodox party members on the court were spurned as simply not colorful enough and insufficiently well known. Their rejection became all the more final when from their chambers the constitutional doubt filtered out through unnamed sources and unidentified background officials as to whether any honorable member of any court in the land truly possessed the right to swear a man like him into the office of the highest government official in the land. In rare unanimous decision, they hailed the chief justice for resigning, the woman for her housework, and the witty one for going fishing.

That left only the Democrat, who'd been appointed by the putative liberal John Kennedy long back, and had voted conservative ever since.

Could a President take office without taking the oath of office? There was not enough court left to decide. But then Noodles Cook, and Noodles alone of the senior tutors, came up with the enterprising suggestion he'd had in mind from the start but had kept to himself until the climactic time, which at length brought a satisfactory resolution to the embarrassing impasse.

"I still don't get it," said the Vice President once more, when the two of them were again conferring alone. By then the other nine of his senior tutors with eleven doctoral degrees had steadily lost face with him. "Please explain it again."

"I don't think I can," Noodles Cook said, grimly. He liked the position he held but was no longer sure about the work, or his employer.

"Try. Who appoints the new chief justice of the Supreme Court?"

"You do," said Noodles, gloomily.

"Right," said the Vice President, who, with the resignation of his predecessor, was technically already the President. "But I can't appoint him until I've been sworn in?"

"That's right too," said Noodles Cook, glumly.

"Who swears me in?"

"Whoever you want to."

"I want the chief justice."

"We have no chief justice," said Noodles, grouchily.

"And we will have no chief justice until I appoint one? And I can't appoint one until—"

"You've got it now, I think."

In silence, and with an expression of surly disappointment, Noodles was regretting once more that he and his third wife, Carmen, with whom he was in the throes of a bitter divorce, were no longer on speaking terms. He hankered for someone trustworthy with whom he could burlesque such conversations safely. He thought of Yossarian, who by this time, he feared, probably thought of him as a shit. Noodles was intelligent enough to understand that he himself probably would not think much of himself either if he were somebody other than himself. Noodles was honest enough to know he was dishonest and had just enough integrity left to know he had none.

"Yes, I think I have got it," said the Vice President, with a glimmer of hope. "I think I'm beginning to click again on all cylinders."

"That would not surprise me." Noodles sounded less affirmative than he meant to.

"Well, why can't we do them both together? Couldn't I be swearing him in as chief justice at the same time that he is swearing me in as President?"

"No," said Noodles.

"Why not?"

"He'll have to be confirmed by the Senate. You would have to appoint him first."

"Well, then," said the Vice President, sitting up straight with that very broad smile of nifty achievement he usually wore when at the controls of one of his video games, "couldn't the Senate be confirming him while I am appointing him at the same time that he is swearing me in?"

"No," Noodles told him firmly. "And please don't ask me why. It's not possible. Please take my word for it, sir."

"Well, I really do think that's a crying shame! It seems to me the President should have the right to be sworn into office by the chief justice of the Supreme Court."

"No one I know of would disagree."

"But I can't be, can I? Oh, no! Because we have no chief justice! How did something like this ever come about?"

"I don't know, sir." Noodles warned himself reprovingly that he must not sound sarcastic. "It could be another oversight by our Founding Fathers."

"What the hell are you talking about?" Here the Vice President leaped to his feet, as though propelled into a choleric rage by some inconceivable blasphemy. "There were no oversights, were there? Our Constitution was always perfect. Wasn't it?"

"We have twenty-seven amendments, sir."

"We do? I didn't know that."

"It's not a secret."

"How was I supposed to know? Is that what an amendment is? A change?"

"Yeah."

"Well, how was I supposed to know?" His mood was again one

of morose despair. "So that's where we still stand, right? I can't appoint a—"

"Yes." Noodles deemed it better to cut him off rather than to have them both subjected to the litany once more.

"Then it's just like Catch-22, isn't it?" the Vice President blurted out unexpectedly, and then brightened at this evidence of his own inspiration. "I can't appoint a chief justice until I'm the President, and he can't swear me in until I appoint him. Isn't that a Catch-22?"

Noodles Cook stared fiercely at the wall and made up his mind sooner to forfeit his position of prestige with the incoming administration than deal with a person like this one with a conjecture like that one.

He was staring, he saw, at a large, simplified chart, hanging as art, of the disposition of forces at the battle of Gettysburg. Noodles began brooding on the historical past. Possibly it had always been thus, he was thinking, between sovereign and adviser, that the subordinate was in all ways but rank the superior. It was then that Noodles, in exhausted desperation, snapped out in command the solution that in the end saved the day:

Use the Democrat!

What?

"Yes, use the fucking Democrat." He swept objections aside by anticipating them. "He was a Kennedy Democrat, so what does that mean? That guy is as bad as the rest of us. You'll get better press coverage for being bipartisan. And when you turn unpopular, you can blame him for swearing you in."

Porter Lovejoy's vision was vindicated again. In briefing Noodles he had stressed the good use the Vice President could make of him. The need was immediate, the opportunities unlimited. There would be an interview. "How much should I tell him?" Noodles had wanted to know. Porter Lovejoy beamed owlishly. "As much as he lets you. Actually, you will be interviewing him to see if you want the job, although he won't know it." And how, Noodles wondered, amused, would he manage that? Porter Lovejoy merely beamed again. The code name?

"Don't bring that up now," Porter Lovejoy cautioned. "He chose it himself, you know. You will have no trouble."

"Come in, come in, come in," said the Vice President jovially to Noodles Cook, after convivial salutations in the anteroom that Noodles found bewilderingly informal.

It surprised him that the younger man of distinguished title had come bounding out to welcome him warmly. Noodles barely had time to note the high school and college pennants on the walls of the reception room. He could not take count of the large number of television screens, all of them tuned to different channels. "Waiting for old clips and sound bites," the girls there explained, giggling, and Noodles could not tell whether that was serious or not.

"I've been looking forward to meeting you," the Vice President went on convincingly. "Varoom, varoom, varoom," he said confidentially when they were alone, with the door closed. "That's from a video game I'm undefeated at called *Indianapolis Speedway*. Do you know it? You will. Are you good at video games? I'll bet I can beat you. Well, now, please tell me all about yourself. I'm dying to know more."

For Noodles, this was child's play. "Well, sir, what is there about me you'd like to find out? Where should I begin?"

"The thing about me," answered the Vice President, "is that when I've set my mind to do something, I've always been able to accomplish it. I'm not going to cry over spilt milk, and what's past is past. Once I set a goal, I pursue that goal with a vengeance."

"I see," said Noodles, after a minute's surprise, when he guessed that a chance was being offered to comment. "And are you saying that you had the goal of becoming Vice President?"

"Oh, yes, definitely, definitely. And I pursued that goal with a vengeance."

"What did you do?"

"I said yes when they asked me to accept it. You see, Mr. Cook —may I call you Noodles? Thank you. It's a privilege—to me the word that best describes the office of Vice President is be prepared. Or is that two words?"

"I believe it's two."

"Thank you. I don't think I could get an answer that clear from any of my other tutors. And that's what I want to continue to pursue with a vengeance. Being prepared. Obviously, the more days you have as Vice President, the better prepared you are to be President. Don't you agree?"

Noodles dodged that question adroitly. "And is that the goal you want to pursue with a vengeance next?"

"It's the main job of the Vice President, isn't it? My other tutors agree."

"Does the President know?"

"I would not pursue it with a vengeance now unless he gave his full approval. Is there anything more you wish to know about me that will help me decide if you're good enough for the job? Porter Lovejoy says you are."

"Well, sir," said Noodles Cook, and went ahead gingerly. "Is there anything you're taking on now that you feel you might not be perfectly equipped to do entirely on your own?"

"No. I can't think of a thing."

"Then why do you feel you need another tutor?"

"To help me with questions like that one. You see, I made a mistake in college of not really applying myself to my studies, and I regret that."

"You got passing grades anyway, didn't you?"

"As good as those I got when I did apply myself. You've been to college, Mr. Cook? You're an educated man?"

"Yes, I have, sir. I have my graduate degrees."

"Good. I went to college too, you know. We have much in common and should get along—better, I hope"—and here a sound of the querulous crept in—"than I am getting along with those others. I have a feeling they make jokes about me behind my back. Looking back, I should have pursued philosophy and history and economics and things of that sort in college more. I'm making up for that now."

"How—" Noodles started to ask, and changed his mind. "Sir, my experience has been—"

"I'm not going to cry over spilt milk, and that's past."

"My experience has been," Noodles threaded his way onward obsequiously, "as a student, and even when teaching a bit, that people do what they are. A person interested in athletics, golf, and parties will spend time at athletic events, golf, and parties. It is very difficult in later life to grow interested in subjects like philosophy and history and economics if one was not attracted to them earlier."

"Yes. And it's never too late either," said the Vice President, and Noodles did not know whether they were in agreement or not. "Lately I have been studying the Napoleonic Wars, to sort of round out my education."

For a second or two Noodles sat motionless. "Which ones?" was all he could think to reply.

"Was there more than one?"

"That was not my field," answered Noodles Cook, and began to give up hope.

"And I'm doing the battle of Antietam too," he heard the man who was next in line for the presidency continue. "And after that I'm going to have a crack at Bull Run. That was really a great war, that Civil War. We've not had one like it since, have we? You'd be very surprised, but Bull Run is only a short car ride from here, with a police escort."

"Are you preparing for war?"

"I'm broadening myself. And I believe in being prepared. All of the rest of the work of a President is pretty hard, it seems to me, and sort of dull. I'm having all of these battles put onto videocassettes and turned into games where either side can win. Varoom, varoom, varoom! Gettysburg too. Do you like video games? Which is your favorite?"

"I don't have a favorite," Noodles muttered, downcast.

"Soon you will. Come look at these."

On a cabinet beneath a video screen—there was a video screen with game controls in many recesses in the office—to which the Vice President walked him lay the game called *Indianapolis Speedway*. Noodles saw others, called *Bombs Away* and *Beat the Draft*.

And one more, called *Die Laughing*.

His host gave a chuckle. "I have nine college men on my staff with eleven doctoral degrees, and not one has been able to beat me at any of these a single time. Doesn't that tell you a lot about higher education in this country today?"

"Yes," said Noodles.

"What does it tell you?"

"A lot," said Noodles.

"I feel that way too. There's a new one coming out just for me, called *Triage*. Do you know it?"

"No."

"*Triage* is a word that comes from the French, and in case there's a big war and we have to decide which few should survive in our underground shelters—"

"I know what the word means, Mr. Vice President!" Noodles interrupted, with more asperity than he had intended. "I just don't know the game," he explained, forcing a smile.

"Soon you will. I'll break you in on it first. It's fun and challenging. You would have your favorites and I would have mine, and only one of us could win and decide who would live and who would die. We'll enjoy it. I think I'll want you to specialize in *Triage* because you never can tell when we really might have to put it into play, and I don't think those others are up to it. Okay?"

"Yes, Mr. Vice President."

"And don't be so formal, Noodles. Call me Prick."

Noodles was appalled. "I could not do that!" he retorted emphatically in a reflex of spontaneous defiance.

"Try."

"No, I won't."

"Not even if it means your job?"

"No, not even then, Mr. Prick—I mean Mr. Vice President."

"See? You'll soon be doing it easily. Take a look at these other things Porter Lovejoy says you can handle. How much do you know about heavy water?"

"Almost nothing at all," said Noodles, feeling himself on firmer ground. "It's got something to do with nuclear reactions, doesn't it?"

"Don't ask me. It says something like that here. I don't know much about it either, so already we've got a good meeting of the minds."

"What's the problem?"

"Well, they've got this man in custody who's producing it without a license. A retired chaplain from the old army air corps, it says, back in World War II."

"Why don't you make him stop?"

"He can't stop. He's producing it sort of, if you know what I mean, biologically."

"No. I don't know what you mean."

"Well, that's what it says here on this synopsis of a summary of this classified folder, code name Tap Water. He eats and drinks like the rest of us, but what comes out of him, I guess, is this heavy water. He was researched and developed by a private corporation, M & M E & A, that now has an option on him and a patent pending."

"Where have they got him?"

"Underground somewhere, in case he decides to turn radioactive. He was in contact with some kind of associate just before they nabbed him, and his wife and this other guy talk on the telephone in code regularly and pretend to know nothing about anything. Nothing dirty between them yet. He talks on the telephone to a nurse also, and a lot that's dirty may be starting between those two. It's as though they never heard of AIDS. And there may be a Belgian spy connection with the new European Economic Community. 'The Belgian is swallowing again,' she reported to him, the last time they spoke."

"Well, what do you want to do about him?"

"Oh, we could easily have him killed by one of our antiterrorist units, if it comes to that. But we may need him, because we're having a problem with a shortage of tritium too. How much do you know about tritium, Noodles?"

"Tritium? I've never heard of it."

"Good. You can be objective. I think it's a radioactive gas of some kind that we need for our hydrogen bombs and other things. They can get it from heavy water, and this chaplain could be very valuable if he can train others to start passing heavy water too. The President hasn't got much patience for this and wants me to handle it. I don't have the patience for it either, so I'll give it to you."

"Me?" exclaimed Noodles, with surprise. "You mean I'm hired?"

"We've been talking, haven't we? Let me know what you think I should recommend."

He handed Noodles a red folder of some bulk with a top sheet with a one-sentence précis of an abstract of a digest of a synopsis of a status report of a summary of a condensation about a retired military chaplain of seventy-one who was manufacturing heavy water internally without a license and was now secretly in custody for examination and interrogation. Noodles knew little about heavy water and nothing about tritium, but he knew enough to betray no flicker of recognition when he read the names John Yossarian and Milo Minderbinder, although he pondered somberly over the nurse Melissa MacIntosh, of whom he had never heard, and a roommate named Angela Moore or Angela Moorecock, and about a mysterious Belgian agent in a New York hospital with throat cancer, about whom the nurse regularly transmitted coded messages by telephone, and a suave, well-dressed mystery man who appeared to be keeping the others under surveillance, either to snoop or as bodyguard. As a connoisseur of expository writing, Noodles was impressed by the genius of an author to abridge so much into a single sentence.

"You want me to decide?" Noodles murmured finally with puzzlement.

"Why not you? And then here's this other thing, about someone with a perfect warplane he wants us to buy and someone else with a better perfect warplane that he wants us to buy, and we can only buy one."

"What does Porter Lovejoy say?"

"He's busy preparing for his trial. I want you to judge."

"I believe I'm not qualified."

"I believe in the flood," the Vice President replied.

"I don't think I heard that."

"I believe in the flood."

"What flood?" Noodles was befuddled again.

"Noah's flood, of course. The one in the Bible. So does my wife. Don't you know about it?"

Through narrowed eyes Noodles searched the guileless countenance for some twinkle of play. "I'm not sure I know what you mean. You believe it was wet?"

"I believe that it's true. In every detail."

"That he took the male and the female of every animal species?"

"That's what it says."

"Sir," said Noodles, with civility. "We have by now catalogued more kinds of animal and insect life than anyone could possibly collect in a lifetime and put onto a ship that size. How would he get them, where would he put them, to say nothing of room for himself and the families of his children, and the problems of the storage of food and the removal of waste in those forty days and nights of rain?"

"You do know about it!"

"I've heard. And for a hundred and fifty days and nights afterward, when the rain stopped."

"You know about that too!" The Vice President regarded him approvingly. "Then you probably also know that evolution is bunk. I hate evolution."

"Where did all this animal life we know about now come from? There are three or four hundred thousand different species of beetles alone."

"Oh, they probably just evolved."

"In only seven thousand years? That's about all it was, as biblical time is measured."

"You can look it up, Noodles. Everything we need to know about the creation of the world is right there in the Bible, put down in plain English." The Vice President regarded him placidly.

"I know there are skeptics. They are all of them Reds. They are all of them wrong."

"There's the case of Mark Twain," Noodles could not restrain himself from arguing.

"Oh, I know that name!" the Vice President cried, with great vanity and joy. "Mark Twain is that great American humorist from my neighboring state of Missouri, isn't he?"

"Missouri is not a neighboring state of Indiana, sir. And your great American humorist Mark Twain ridiculed the Bible, despised Christianity, detested our imperialistic foreign policy, and heaped piles of scorn on every particular in the story of Noah and his ark, especially for the housefly."

"Obviously," the Vice President replied, with no loss of equanimity, "we are talking about different Mark Twains."

Noodles was enraged. "There was only one, sir," he said softly, and smiled. "If you like, I'll prepare a summary of his statements and leave it with one of your secretaries."

"No, I hate written things. Put it on a video, and maybe we can turn it into a game. I really can't see why some people who read have so much trouble coming to grips with the simple truths that are put down there so clearly. And please don't call me sir, Noodles. You're so much older than I am. Won't you call me Prick?"

"No, sir, I won't call you prick."

"Everyone else does. You have a right to. I have taken an oath to support that constitutional right."

"Look, you prick—" Noodles had jumped to his feet and was glancing around frantically, for a blackboard, for chalk and a pointer, for anything! "Water seeks its own level."

"Yes, I've heard that."

"Mount Everest is close to five miles high. For the earth to be covered with water, there would have to be water everywhere on the globe that was close to five miles deep."

His future employer nodded, pleased that he finally seemed to be getting through. "There was that much water then."

"Then the waters receded. Where could they recede to?"

"Into the oceans, of course."

"Where were the oceans, if the world was under water?"

"Underneath the flood, of course," was the unhesitating reply, and the genial man rose. "If you look at a map, Noodles, you will see where the oceans are. And you will also see that Missouri *does* border on my state of Indiana."

"He believes in the flood!" Noodles Cook, still stewing, and speaking almost in a shout, reported immediately to Porter Lovejoy. It was the first time in the relationship that he had presented himself to his sponsor with anything other than a conspiratorial contentment.

Porter Lovejoy was unruffled. "So does his wife."

"I'll want more money!"

"The job doesn't call for it."

"Change the job!"

"I'll talk to Capone."

His health was good, he was not on welfare, and it was understood now by all involved that as the secretary in charge of health, education and welfare in the new cabinet, Noodles would focus his energies entirely on the education of the President.

BOOK
FIVE

BOOK
FIVE

13

Tritium

Heavy water was up another two points, read the fax in the M & M office in Rockefeller Center in New York, on the same floor, and in much the same spot, in which Sammy Singer had spent almost all his adult working life with *Time* magazine, an office that, as Michael Yossarian again saw, had windows overlooking the fabled skating rink far below, the glittering, frozen centerpiece of the venerable Japanese real estate complex obtained for money earlier from the vanishing Rockefeller financial dynasty. The rink was the same site on which Sammy years before had, with Glenda, gone ice skating for the first time in his life, and didn't fall, and had gone again with her on more than one long lunch hour after they commenced seeing each other regularly, while she was still pressing him to come live with her in her West Side apartment, together with her three children and her remarkable frontier mother from Wisconsin, who approved of Sammy and departed gladly to live again with a sister on a small family farm after he did—none of the New York parents he knew, not even his own, were ever so gracefully self-sacrificing—and tritium, the gas derived from heavy water, had gained an additional *two hundred and sixteen points* on the international radioactive commodity exchanges in Geneva, Tokyo, Bonn, Iraq, Iran, Nigeria, China, Pakistan, London, and New York. The rise in tritium was buoyed optimistically by the natural property of that hydrogen isotope to degenerate at a predictable rate in atomic weapons, necessitating periodic replenishment, and the enticing disposition of the gas to lessen in quantity between the time it was sealed by the shipper and the hour it was received by the purchaser, who, more commonly than not, was a manufacturer of novelties or marking devices with outer surfaces intrinsically luminous or an assembler and supplier of nuclear warheads.

Customers frequently reported receiving as much as forty percent less of the tritium than they had paid for and forty percent less than had been packed and shipped, with no indications of theft, diversion, or leakage.

The tritium simply was not there when delivered.

Not long before, a test shipment from merely one building to another to comprehend this loss resulted in no new information and the disappearance of three quarters of the tritium packed for the test. It was inaccurate to say, said a sheepish spokesman, that it disappeared into thin air. They were monitoring the air. The air was not thin and the tritium wasn't in it.

Despite the radiation and consequent potential as a galvanizer of cancer, tritium was still the material of choice for illuminated guides and dial faces, for gun sights for nighttime marksmanship, for icons like swastikas, crosses, Stars of David, and halos that glowed in the dark, and for the stupendous enhancement in the explosive yield of nuclear weapons.

Melissa MacIntosh's ravishing roommate, Angela Moore, whom Yossarian could no longer resist thinking of by any other name than Angela Moorecock, had by now already put forth to her elderly, gentlemanly employers the idea of luminescent items highlighting the more protuberant organs of copulation phosphorescently and had tested on buyers at the toy fair, men and women, her notion for a bedroom clock with a radiating face of tritium in a compound of paint in which the hour and minute hands were circumcised male members and the numbers were not numbers but a succession of nude female figures unfolding sensually and progressively with the hours in systematic stages of erotic trance until satiation was attained at the terminal hour of twelve. Yossarian got hot hearing her discourse on this inspiration for a consumer product in the cocktail lounge a day or two before she sucked him off the first time and sent him home because he was older than the men she was accustomed to and she was not sure she cared to know him more intimately than that, and afterward, because of Melissa's growing affection for him, along with a growing apprehension of AIDS, declined to suck him off a second time or oblige him in any equivalent way; and listening observantly to her rave that first time, he'd found himself with almost half a semi-hard-on, and he took her hand as they sat beside each other on the red velvet banquette at the plush cocktail lounge and rubbed it over the fly of his pants to let her feel for herself.

The great jump in explosive yield induced by the action of tritium in atomic warheads made possible an aesthetic reduction in the size and weight of the bombs, missiles, and shells devised, allowing a greater number to be carried by smaller implements of delivery like Milo's projected bombers, and Strangelove's too, with no notable sacrifice in nuclear destructive capability.

The chaplain was up in value and completely safe.

14

Michael Yossarian

"When can I see him?" Michael Yossarian heard his father demand. His father's hair was thicker than his own and curly white, a color for which his brother Adrian was assiduously seeking a chemical formula for tinting to a youthful, natural gray that would not be youthful on any man Yossarian's age and would not look natural.

"As soon as he's safe," answered M2, in a clean white shirt that was not yet rumpled, wet, or in need of ironing.

"Michael, didn't he just say the chaplain was safe?"

"It's what I thought I heard."

Michael smiled to himself. He pressed his brow against the pane of the glass window in order to gaze down intently at the ice rink below and its colorful kaleidoscope of leisurely skaters, wondering, with a downhearted presentiment of already having missed out on much, if there could possibly be abiding in that pastime rewards he might find diverting if ever he could bring himself to take the trouble to seek them. The reflecting oval of ice was ringed these days with drifting tides of panhandlers and vagrants, with working strollers on lunch and coffee breaks, with mounted policemen on daunting horses. Michael Yossarian would not dance; he could not get into the rhythm. He would not play golf, ski, or play tennis, and he knew already he would never ice-skate.

"I mean safe for us." He heard M2 defend himself plaintively and turned to watch. M2 appeared triumphantly prepared for the question he'd been asked. "He is safe for M & M Enterprises and cannot be appropriated by even Mercedes-Benz or the N & N Division of Nippon & Nippon Enterprises. Even Strangelove is barred. We will patent the chaplain as soon as we find out how he works, and we are looking for a trademark. We are thinking of a halo. Because he is a chaplain, of course, a Day-Glo halo. Maybe one that lights up in the dark, all night long."

"Why not tritium?"

"Tritium is expensive and radioactive. Michael, can you draw a halo?"

"It shouldn't be hard."

"We would want something cheerful but serious."

"I would try," said Michael, smiling again, "to make it serious, and it's hard to picture one that isn't cheerful."

"Where have they got him?" Yossarian wanted to know.

"In the same place, I would guess. I really don't know."

"Does your father know?"

"Do I know if he knows?"

"If you did would you tell me?"

"If he said that I could."

"If he said that you couldn't?"

"I would say I don't know."

"As you're saying right now. At least you're truthful."

"I try."

"Even when you lie. There's a paradox here. We are talking in circles."

"I went to divinity school."

"And what," said Yossarian, "do I tell the chaplain's wife? I'll be seeing her soon. If there's anyone else I can advise her to complain to, I will certainly tell her."

"Who could she find? The police are helpless."

"Strangelove?"

"Oh, no," said M2, turning whiter than customary. "I will have to find out. What you can tell Karen Tappman now—"

"Karen?"

"It's what it says on my prompt sheet. What you can tell Karen Tappman truthfully—"

"I don't think I would lie to her."

"We never choose to be anything but truthful. It's right there in our manual, under Lies. What you must tell Karen Tappman," M2 recited dutifully, "is that he is well and misses her. He looks forward to rejoining her as soon as he is not a danger to himself or the community and his presence in the family and the conjugal bed would not be injurious to her health."

"That's a new fucking wrinkle, isn't it?"

"Please." M2 flinched. "This one happens to be true."

"You would say that even if it weren't?"

"That is perfectly true," admitted M2. "But if tritium starts showing up inside him from that heavy water, he could be radioactive, and we'd all have to keep clear of him anyway."

"M2," said Yossarian harshly, "I'm going to want to talk to the chaplain soon. Has your father seen him? I know what you'll say. You have to find out."

"First, I'll have to find out if I can find out."

"Find out if you can find out if he can arrange it. Strangelove could."

M2 paled again. "You'd go to Strangelove?"

"Strangelove will come to me. And the chaplain won't produce if I tell him not to."

"I must tell my father."

"I've already told him, but he doesn't always hear."

M2 was shaken. "I just thought of something else. Should we be talking about all this in front of Michael? The chaplain is secret now, and I'm not sure I'm authorized to let anyone else hear about him."

"About who?" asked Michael mischievously.

"The chaplain," responded M2.

"What chaplain?"

"Chaplain Albert T. Tappman," said M2. "That friend of your father's from the army who's producing heavy water inside himself without a license and is now secretly in custody while they investigate and examine him while we try to patent him and register a trademark. Do you know about him?"

Michael spoke with a grin. "You mean that friend of my father's from the army who began producing heavy water inside himself illegally and is now—"

"That's the one!" M2 cried, and gaped as though confronted by a specter. "How'd you find out?"

"You just told me," laughed Michael.

"I did it again, didn't I?" blubbered M2, and collapsed with a thump into the chair at his desk in a grieving paroxysm of repentant lamentation. Now his shiny white shirt, which was of synthetic fabric, was rumpled, wet, and in need of ironing, and sopping adumbrations of a fidgety, sweltering anxiety were already darkening the fabric below the armholes of a sleeveless white undershirt he never failed to wear as well. "I just can't keep a secret, can I? My father is still angry with me for telling you about the bomber. He says he could kill me. So is my mother. So are my sisters. But it's your fault too, you know. It's his job to restrain me from telling him secrets like that."

"Like what?" asked Michael.

"Like that one about the bomber."

"What bomber?"

"Our M & M E & A Sub-Supersonic Invisible and Noiseless Defensive Second-Strike Offensive Attack Bomber. I hope you don't know about it."

"I know about it now."

"How'd you find out?"

"I have my ways," said Michael, and turned to his father with a glower. "Are we in munitions now too?"

Yossarian answered testily. "Somebody is going to have to be in munitions whether we like it or not, they tell me, so it might as well be them, and somebody is going to work with them on this, whether I say yes or no, so it might as well be you and me, and that's the perfect truth."

"Even though it's a lie?"

"They told me it was a cruise ship."

"It does cruise," M2 explained to Michael.

"With two people?" Yossarian contradicted him. "And here's another way out, to put your conscience at rest," Yossarian added to Michael. "It won't work. Right, M2?"

"We guarantee it."

"And besides," said Yossarian, with resentment surfacing, "you're only being asked to draw a picture of the plane, not to fly the fucking thing or launch an attack. This plane is for the new century. These things take forever, and we both may be dead before they get one into the air, even if they do get the contract. They don't care now if it works or not. All they want is the money. Right, M2?"

"And we'll pay you, of course," offered M2, coming back to his feet and fidgeting. He was slender, spare, with formless shoulders and prominent collarbones.

"How much will you pay?" asked Michael awkwardly.

"As much as you want," answered M2.

"He means it," said Yossarian, when Michael looked clownishly at him for interpretation.

Michael tittered. "How about," he ventured extravagantly, watching his father for the reaction, "enough for another year in law school?"

"If that's what you want," M2 immediately agreed.

"And my living expenses too?"

"Sure."

"He means that also," said Yossarian reassuringly to his incredulous son. "Michael, you won't believe this—I don't really believe it either—but sometimes there is more money in this world than anybody ever thought the planet could hold without sinking away into somewhere else."

"Where does it all come from?"

"Nobody knows," said Yossarian.

"Where does it go when it isn't here?"

"That's another scientific mystery. It just disappears. Like those particles of tritium. Right now there's a lot."

"Are you trying to corrupt me?"

"I think I'm trying to save you."

"Okay, I'll believe you. What do you want me to do?"

"A few loose drawings," said M2. "Can you read engineering blueprints?"

"Let's have a try."

The five blueprints required for an artist's rendering of the external appearance of the plane had already been selected and laid out on a conference table in an adjoining outer inner conference room just outside the rear false front of the second fireproof stand-up vault of thick steel and concrete, with alarm buttons and radioactive dials of tritium.

It took a minute for Michael to assemble coherence in the mechanical drawings of white lines on royal blue, which looked at first like an occult shambles ornamented with scribbled cryptic notations in alphabets that were indecipherable.

"It's kind of ugly, I think." Michael felt stimulated to be at work on something different that was well within his capabilities. "It's starting to look like a flying wing."

"Are there wings that don't fly?" teased Yossarian.

"The wings of a wing collar," Michael answered, without lifting his analytical gaze. "The wings of a theater stage, the wings of a political party."

"You do read, don't you?"

"Sometimes."

"What does a flying wing look like?" M2 was a moist man, and his brow and chin were beaded with shiny droplets.

"Like a plane without a fuselage, Milo. I've got a feeling I've seen this before."

"I hope you haven't. Our plane is new."

"What's this?" Yossarian pointed. In the lower left corner of all five sheets the identifying legends had been masked before copying by a patch of black tape on which was printed a white letter *S* without loops. "I've seen that letter."

"And so has everyone else," Michael answered lightly. "It's the standard stencil. You've seen it on old bomb shelters. But what the hell are these?"

"I meant those too."

To the right of the letter *S* was a trail of minuscule characters that looked like flattened squiggles, and while Yossarian was donning his glasses, Michael peered through a magnifying glass there and found the small letter *h* repeated in script, with an exclamation point too.

"So that," he remarked, still in very good humor, "is what you're going to call your plane, eh? The M & M Shhhhh!"

"You know what we call it." M2 was offended. "It's the M & M E & A Sub-Supersonic Invisible and Noiseless Defensive Second-Strike Offensive Attack Bomber."

"We'd save time calling it Shhhhh! Tell me again what you want."

M2 talked diffidently. What was wanted were nice-looking pictures of the plane in flight from above, below, and the side, and at least one of the plane on the ground. "They don't have to be accurate. But make them realistic, like the planes in a comic strip or science movie. Leave out details. My father doesn't want them to see any until we get the contract. He doesn't really trust our government anymore. They'd also like a picture of what the plane will really look like in case they ever have to build it."

"Why don't you ask your engineers?" mused Michael.

"We don't really trust our engineers."

"When Ivan the Terrible," reflected Yossarian, "finished building the Kremlin, he had all the architects executed, so that no one alive would ever duplicate it."

"What was so terrible about him?" M2 wondered. "I must tell my father that."

"Leave me alone now," said Michael, rubbing his chin and

concentrating. He was slipping off his corduroy jacket, whistling a Mozart melody to himself. "If you close the door, remember I'm locked in and don't forget to get me out one day." To himself, he observed aloud, "It's looking cute."

At the turn into the next century, he was cynically sure, there would be months of senseless ceremonies, tied in with political campaigns too, and the M & M warplane could be an exalted highlight. And no doubt, the first baby born in the new century would be born in the east, but much farther east this time than Eden.

He looked down again at the plans of this weapon for the close of the century and saw a design that seemed to him aesthetically incomplete. Much was lacking in anticipated form, much was missing. And when he looked at the blueprints and into the future in which that plane would fly, he could spy no place staked out anywhere into which he, in the stale words of his father, could fit, in which he could flourish with any more security and satisfaction than he presently enjoyed. He had room for improvement but saw not much chance of any. He remembered Marlene and her astrological charts and tarot cards, and he felt himself missing her again, even though uncertain he had ever cared for her more than any of the others in his sequence of monogamous romances. It was beginning to scare him that he might have no future, that he was already in it; like his father, about whom he'd always harbored mixed feelings, he was already there. He must risk a call to Marlene.

Even his brother Julian was having trouble these days making as much money as he had insolently projected he was destined to make. And his sister too would have to delay her divorce while testing the waters discreetly for a job in private practice with one of the law firms with whose partners she occasionally had contact.

His father would be dead. Papa John had made clear more than once that he did not expect to go deeply into that twenty-first century. For much of his life Michael had confidently presumed his father would always be alive. He felt that way still, although he knew it was untrue. That never happened with real human beings.

And who else would be there for him? There was no one to esteem, no figure to look up to whose merit persisted without blemish for more than fifteen minutes. There were people with power to confer great benefits upon others, like movie directors and the President, but that was all.

The half-million dollars his father had hopes to bequeath him no longer seemed an everlasting fortune. He would not be able to live on the income, though nine tenths of the country lived on less. In time he would have nothing, and no one, have *no one,* his father had underlined, to aid him. His father always had struck him as somewhat peculiar, rationally irrational and illogically logical, and did not always make consistent sense.

"It's easy to win debates as a nihilist," he'd said, "because so many people who ought to know better absurdly take positions."

He spoke slickly of things like Ewing's tumor, Hodgkin's disease, amyotrophic lateral sclerosis, TIAs, and osteogenic sarcomas, and talked freely about his dying with an objectivity so matter-of-fact that Michael had to wonder if he was kidding himself, or faking it. Michael did not always know when he was serious and when he was not, and when he was right and when he was mistaken, and when he was right and wrong at the same time. And Yossarian would profess that he did not always know that about himself either.

"A problem I have," his father had admitted penitently, but with a hint of pride, "is that I'm almost always able to see both sides of almost every question."

And he was almost always too eager to be friendly with one woman or another, obsessed still with the dream to find work that he wished to do and the need to be what he called "in love." Michael had never found work that he wished to do—the law was no worse to him than anything else, and art was no better. He was writing a screenplay but did not want his father to know that yet. But with one thing central, Yossarian seemed right on the button.

"Before you know it, you damned fool," he'd snapped at him irascibly in a tender bad temper, "you'll be as old as I am now, and you won't have a thing."

Not even children, Michael could add ruefully. As far as he could see, that was not in the cards for him either, not in Marlene's tarot cards or any others. Michael again looked down narrowly at the blueprints before him, pulled his pad closer, and took up a pencil. He did not envy people who wished to work much harder to get much more, but had to wonder afresh why he was not like them.

15

M2

"Y̲ou like Michael, don't you?"

"Yes, I like Michael," said M2.

"Give him work when you can."

"I do that. I will want to work more with him on those video screens at the bus terminal. I'll pay him for another year in law school."

"I'm not sure he'll want that. But go ahead and try."

All the parents he knew with grown children had at least one about whose doubtful prospects they were constantly troubled, and many had two. Milo had this one, and he had Michael.

Irritation mingled with puzzlement as he studied the new messages from Jerry Gaffney of the Gaffney Agency. The first advised him to call his answering machine at home for good news from his nurse and bad news from his son about his first wife. The good news from his nurse was that she was free for dinner that evening to go to a movie with him and that the Belgian patient in the hospital was making a good recovery from the bad dysentery generated by the good antibiotics administered for the bad pneumonia provoked by the salutary removal of a vocal cord in the invasive effort, successful thus far, to save his life. The second fax reported that he had now qualified for the mortgage. Yossarian had no idea what that meant. "How did he even know I was here?" he heard himself thinking out loud.

"Mr. Gaffney knows everything, I think," M2 answered, with faith. "He monitors our fax lines too."

"You pay him for that?"

"Somebody does, I think."

"Who?"

"I've no idea."

"Don't you care?"

"Should I?"

"Can't you find out?"

"I'll have to find out if I can find out."

"I'm surprised you don't want to know."

"Should I want to?"

"M2, Michael calls you Milo. Which name do you prefer?"

Milo's only son turned ill at ease. "I would rather," he said, breathing noisily, "be called Milo, even though that's my father's name. It's my name too, you know. He gave it to me."

"Why haven't you said so?" asked Yossarian, resenting the implication imposed upon him to feel at fault.

"I'm timid, you know. My mother says I'm rabbity. So do my sisters. They keep asking me to change my personality to be strong enough to take over when I have to."

"To be more like your father?"

"They don't think much of my father."

"Who then? Wintergreen?"

"They hate Wintergreen."

"Me?"

"They don't like you either."

"Then who?"

"They can't think of any man who's good enough."

"Let me ask you," said Yossarian, "if you still have your catering company."

"I think we do. It's your company too, you know. Everybody has a share."

The M & M Commercial Catering Company was the oldest continuous catering service in the history of the country, having origins in Milo's labors as a mess officer for his squadron in World War II, wherein he contrived the fruitful and abstruse financial strategies for buying fresh Italian eggs from Sicily in Malta for seven cents apiece and selling them to his mess hall in Pianosa for five cents apiece at a handsome profit that increased the squadron's capital supply, in which everybody had a share, he said, and bettered the quality of life and the standard of living of everyone there, and for buying Scotch whisky for Malta at the source in Sicily, eliminating middlemen.

"M2," said Yossarian, and remembered he had forgotten. He

had no wish to hurt him. "What will you want me to call you when you're here with your father? Two Milos may prove one too many, maybe two."

"I'll have to find out."

"You really don't know, not even that?"

"I can't decide." M2 was writhing. His hands turned red as he wrung them together. The rims of his eyes reddened too. "I can't make a decision. You remember the last time I tried."

One time far back, just before Yossarian went begging to Milo for help in keeping Michael out of the Vietnam War, a much younger M2 had attempted to make up his mind independently on a subject of transcendent importance. He thought his idea a fine one: to answer the call of what he'd been told was his country and enlist in the army to kill Asian communists in Asia.

"You'll do no such thing!" determined his mother.

"The way to serve your government more," responded his father, in a manner more deliberative, "is to find out who the draft boards are *not* drafting, and then you'll see who's really needed. We'll look into that for you."

The two and a half years M2 spent in divinity school had scarred him for life and instilled in him a traumatic aversion to all things spiritual and a fear and distrust of men and women who did not smoke or drink, swear, wear makeup, walk around anywhere even partly disrobed, did not make sex jokes, smiled an awful lot, even when nothing humorous was said, and smiled when alone, and manifested a shared, beatific faith in a hygienic virtue and self-esteem they thought exclusively their own and which he found malicious and repulsive.

He had never married, and the women he'd kept company with were invariably ladies approximately his own age who dressed plainly in pleated skirts and prim blouses, wore very little makeup daintily, were shy, colorless, and quickly gone.

Make effort as he might, Yossarian could not put to rest the low surmise that M2 belonged to that class of solitary and vindictive men that largely comprised the less boisterous of the two main classes of resolute patrons of prostitutes to be seen in his high-rise apartment building, riding up the elevators for the sex cures in the opulent temple of love on top or downward into the bowels of the structure to the three or four massage parlors of secondary dignity in the sub-basements underlying the several general cinema houses on the first sub-level down from the public sidewalk.

Michael had remarked lightly already to Yossarian that M2

seemed to him to possess all the typical attributes of the serial sex killer: he was white.

"When we went to the terminal," he confided, "he was only interested in looking at the women. I don't think he could recognize the transvestites. Is his father that way?"

"Milo knows what a prostitute is and didn't like us going after them. He's always been chaste. I doubt he knows what a transvestite is or would see much difference if he found out."

"Why did you ask me," M2 asked Yossarian now, "if we still have our catering service?"

"I might have some business. There's this wedding—"

"I'm glad you mentioned that. I might have forgotten. My mother wants me to talk to you about our wedding."

"This is not your wedding," corrected Yossarian.

"My sister's wedding. My mother wants my sister married, and she wants it done at the Metropolitan Museum of Art. She expects you to arrange it. She knows you're in ACACAMMA."

Yossarian was genially amazed. "The ceremony too?"

"It's been done before?"

"The actual ceremony? Not that I know of."

"You know trustees?"

"I'm with ACACAMMA. But it might be impossible."

"My mother won't accept that. She says—I'm reading now, from her fax—that if you can't manage that, she doesn't know what else you're good for."

Yossarian shook his head benignly. He was anything but insulted. "It will take money, and time. You would have to begin, I would say, with a donation to the museum of ten million dollars."

"Two dollars?" asked M2, as though repeating.

"Ten *million* dollars."

"I thought I heard two."

"I did say ten," said Yossarian. "For the construction of another new wing."

"We can handle that."

"With no strings attached."

"There'll be strings attached?"

"I said no strings attached, although of course there will be strings. Your father specializes in string. You're practically out-of-towners, and they just don't take ten million from every Tom, Dick, and Harry who wants to give it."

"Couldn't you persuade them to take it?"

"I think I could do that. And then there's no guarantee."

"There's a good guarantee?"

"There is no guarantee," Yossarian corrected again. "You and your father seem to have the same selective hearing impairment, don't you?"

"Collective hearing impairment?"

"Yes. And it will have to be wasteful."

"Tasteful?"

"Yes. Wasteful. It will have to be lavish and crude enough to get into the newspapers and high-fashion magazines."

"I think it's what they want."

"There might just be an opening they don't know about yet," Yossarian finally judged. "The wedding I mentioned will be in the bus terminal."

M2 reacted with a start, just as Yossarian had expected. "What's good about that?" he wanted to know.

"Innovation, Milo," Yossarian answered. "The museum isn't good enough for some people anymore. The bus terminal is just right for the Maxons."

"The Maxons?"

"Olivia and Christopher."

"The big industrialist?"

"Who never set foot in a factory and never laid eyes on a product any company of his ever manufactured, except maybe his Cuban cigars. I'm helping Maxon out with the logistics," he embroidered nonchalantly. "All the media will cover it, naturally. Will you take the bus terminal if we can't get the museum?"

"I'll have to ask my mother. Offhand—"

"If it's good enough for the Maxons," tempted Yossarian, "with the mayor, the cardinal, maybe even the White House . . ."

"That might make a difference."

"Of course, you could not be the first."

"We could be first?"

"You could not be first, unless your sister marries the Maxon girl or you want to make it a double wedding. I can talk to the Maxons for you, if your mother wants me to."

"What would you do," M2 asked, with a gaze that seemed circumspect, "with the whores at the bus terminal?"

The white light in M2's gray eyes as he said the word *whores* invested him instantaneously with the face of a ravenous man blistering with acquisitive desire.

Yossarian gave the answer he thought most fit.

"Use them or lose them," he answered carelessly. "As much as

you want. The police will oblige. The opportunities are boundless.
I'm being realistic about the museum. Your father *sells* things,
Milo, and that's not elegant."

"My mother hates him for that."

"And she lives in Cleveland. When is your sister getting married?"

"Whenever you want her to."

"That gives us latitude. Who is she marrying?"

"Whoever she has to."

"That might open it up."

"My mother will want you to make up the guest list. We don't
know anyone here. Our dearest friends all live in Cleveland, and
many can't come."

"Why not do it at the museum in Cleveland? And your dearest
friends could come."

"We would rather have your strangers." M2 seated himself
gently in front of his computer. "I'll fax my mother."

"Can't you phone her?"

"She won't take my calls."

"Find out," said Yossarian, with more mischief in mind, "if
she'll take a Maxon. They might just have an extra one."

"Would they take a Minderbinder?"

"Would you marry a Maxon, if all they have is a girl?"

"Would they take me? I have this Adam's apple."

"There's a good chance they might, even with the Adam's apple,
once you fork over that ten million for another new wing."

"What would they name it?"

"The Milo Minderbinder Wing, of course. Or maybe the Temple of Milo, if you'd rather have that."

"I believe they would choose that," guessed M2. "And that
would be appropriate. My father was a caliph of Baghdad, you
know, one time in the war."

"I know," said Yossarian. "And the imam of Damascus. I was
with him, and everywhere we went he was hailed."

"What would they put in the wing at the museum?"

"Whatever you give them, or stuff from the storeroom. They
need more space for a bigger kitchen. They would certainly put in
a few of those wonderful statues of your father at those stone
altars red with human blood. Let me know soon."

And as M2 beat a bit faster on his keyboard, Yossarian walked
away to his own office, to cope on the telephone with some matters of his own.

16

Gaffney

"She wants more money," Julian told him right off in his no-nonsense manner.

"She isn't getting it." Yossarian was equally brusque.

"For how much?" challenged his son.

"Julian, I don't want to bet with you."

"I'll advise her to sue," said his daughter, the judge.

"She'll lose. She'd have money enough if she called off those private detectives."

"She swears she isn't employing any," said his other son Adrian, the cosmetics chemist without the graduate degree, whose wife had concluded, through an adult education course in assertiveness training, that she wasn't really as happy as she'd all along thought herself.

"But her lawyer might be, Mr. Yossarian," said Mr. Gaffney, when Yossarian phoned and brought him up-to-date.

"Her lawyer says he's not."

"Lawyers, Mr. Yossarian, have been known to lie. Of the eight people following you, Yo-Yo—"

"My name is Yossarian, *Mr.* Gaffney. *Mr.* Yossarian."

"I expect that will change, sir," said Gaffney, with no decrease in friendliness, "once we have met and become fast friends. In the meanwhile, Mr. Yossarian"—there was no insinuating emphasis —"I have good news for you, very good news, from both the credit checking services. You have been coming through splendidly, apart from one late alimony check to your first wife and an occasional late separate maintenance check to your second wife, but there is an overdue bill for eighty-seven dollars and sixty-nine cents from a defunct retail establishment formerly known as The Tailored Woman that is, or has been, in Chapter 11."

"I owe eighty-seven dollars to a store called The Tailored Woman?"

"And sixty-nine cents," said Mr. Gaffney, with his flair for the exact. "You might be held responsible for that charge by your wife Marian when the dispute is finally adjudicated."

"My wife wasn't Marian," Yossarian advised him, after cogitating several moments to make sure. "I had no wife named Marian. Neither of them."

Mr. Gaffney replied in a coddling tone. "I'm afraid you're mistaken, Mr. Yossarian. People frequently grow befuddled in matrimonial recollections."

"I am not befuddled, Mr. Gaffney," Yossarian retorted, with his hackles up. "There has been no wife of mine named Marian Yossarian. You can look that one up if you don't believe me. I'm in *Who's Who*."

"I find the Freedom of Information Act consistently a much better source, and I certainly will look it up, if only to clear the air between us. But in the meanwhile . . ." There was a pause. "May I call you John yet?"

"No, Mr. Gaffney."

"All the other reports are in mint condition, and you can obtain the mortgage anytime you want it."

"What mortgage? Mr. Gaffney, I intend no disrespect when I tell you categorically I have no idea what the fuck you are talking about when you mention a mortgage!"

"We live in encumbering times, Mr. Yossarian, and sometimes things befall us too rapidly."

"You are talking like a mortician."

"The real estate mortgage, of course. For a house in the country or at the seashore, or perhaps for a much better apartment right here in the city."

"I'm not buying a house, Mr. Gaffney," replied Yossarian. "And I'm not thinking of an apartment."

"Then perhaps you should begin thinking about it, Mr. Yossarian. Sometimes Señor Gaffney knows best. Real estate values can only go up. There is only so much land on the planet, my father used to say, and he did well in the long run. All we'll need with your application is a specimen of your DNA."

"My DNA?" Yossarian repeated, with a brain bewildered. "I confess I'm baffled."

"That's your deoxyribonucleic acid, Mr. Yossarian, and contains your entire genetic coding."

"I know it's my deoxyribonucleic acid, God damn it! And I know what it does."

"No one else can fake it. It will prove you are you."

"Who the hell else could I be?"

"Lending institutions are careful now."

"Mr. Gaffney, where will I get that sample of my DNA to submit with my mortgage application for a house I don't know about that I will never want to buy?"

"Not even in East Hampton?" tempted Gaffney.

"Not even East Hampton."

"There are excellent values there now. I can handle the DNA for you."

"How will you get it?"

"Under the Freedom of Information Act. It's on file in your sperm with your Social Security number. I can get a certified photocopy—"

"Of my sperm?"

"Of your deoxyribonucleic acid. The sperm cell is just a medium of transportation. It's the genes that count. I can get the photocopy of your DNA when you're ready with your application. Leave the driving to me. And indeed, I have more good news. One of the gentlemen who is following you isn't."

"I will resist the wisecrack."

"I don't see the wisecrack."

"Do you mean that he isn't a gentleman or that he isn't following me?"

"I still don't see it. Isn't following you. He is following one or more of the others who are following you."

"Why?"

"We will have to guess. That was blacked out on the Freedom of Information report. Perhaps to protect you from abduction, torture, or murder, or maybe merely to find out about you what the others find out. There are a thousand reasons. And the Orthodox Jew—excuse me, are you Jewish, Mr. Yossarian?"

"I am Assyrian, Mr. Gaffney."

"Yes. And the Orthodox Jewish gentleman parading in front of your building really is an Orthodox Jewish gentleman and does live in your neighborhood. But he is also an FBI man and he is sharp as a tack. So be discreet."

"What does he want from me?"

"Ask him if you wish. Maybe he's just walking, if he's not there on assignment. You know how those people are. It may not be you. You have a CIA front in your building masquerading as a CIA front and a Social Security Administration office there too, not to mention all those sex parlors, prostitutes, and other business establishments. Try to hold on to your Social Security number. It always pays to be discreet. Discretion is the better part of valor, Señor Gaffney tells his friends. Have no fear. He will keep you posted. Service is his middle name."

Yossarian felt the need to take a stand. "Mr. Gaffney," he said, "how soon can I see you? I'm afraid I insist."

There was a moment of chortling, a systematic bubbling suffused with overtones of self-satisfaction. "You already have seen me, Mr. Yossarian, and you didn't notice, did you?"

"Where?"

"At the bus terminal, when you went below with Mr. McBride. You looked right at me. I was wearing a fawn-colored single-breasted herringbone woolen jacket with a thin purple cross-pattern, brown trousers, a light-blue Swiss chambray shirt of finest Egyptian cotton, and a complementing tie of solid rust, with matching socks. I have a smooth tan complexion and am bald on top, with black hair trimmed very close at the sides and very dark brows and eyes. I have noble temples and fine cheekbones. You didn't recognize me, did you?"

"How could I, Mr. Gaffney? I'd never seen you before."

The quiet laughter returned. "Yes, you did, Mr. Yossarian, more than once. Outside the hotel restaurant after you stopped in there that day with Mr. and Mrs. Beach following the ACACAMMA meeting at the Metropolitan Museum of Art. In front of the Frank Campbell Funeral Home across the street. Do you remember the red-haired man with a walking stick and green rucksack on his back who was with the uniformed guard at the entrance?"

"You were the redheaded man with the rucksack?"

"I was the uniformed guard."

"You were in disguise?"

"I'm in disguise now."

"I'm not sure I get that one, Mr. Gaffney."

"Perhaps it's a joke, Mr. Yossarian. It's told very widely in my profession. Maybe my next sally will be better. And I really believe you ought to call your nurse. She's back on the day shift and free for dinner tonight. She can bring that friend."

"Her roommate?"

"No, not Miss Moorecock."

"Her name is Miss Moore." Yossarian reproved him coldly.

"You call her Miss Moorecock."

"You will call her Miss Moore, if you wish to keep working for me. Mr. Gaffney, keep out of my private life."

"No life is private anymore, I'm sad to say."

"Mr. Gaffney, when do we meet?" Yossarian demanded. "I want to look you in the eye and see who the hell I'm dealing with. I'm not easy with you, Mr. Gaffney."

"I'm sure that will change."

"I'm not sure it will. I don't think I like you."

"That will change also, after we talk in Chicago."

"Chicago?"

"When we meet in the airport and you see that I'm trustworthy, loyal, helpful, courteous, and kind. Better?"

"No. I'm not going to Chicago."

"I believe you will be, Mr. Yossarian. You could make reservations now."

"What will I be doing in Chicago?"

"Changing planes."

"For where?"

"To come back, Mr. Yossarian. From Kenosha, Wisconsin, after your visit to Mrs. Tappman. Probably, you will want to continue to Washington directly for your meetings with Mr. Minderbinder and Mr. Wintergreen, and perhaps Noodles Cook too."

Yossarian sighed. "You know all that about me now?"

"I hear things in my work, Mr. Yossarian."

"Who else do you work for when you hear things about me?"

"For whoever will pay me, Mr. Yossarian. I don't discriminate. We have laws now against discrimination. And I don't play favorites. I'm always objective and don't make distinctions. Distinctions are odious. And invidious too."

"Mr. Gaffney, I haven't paid you yet. You haven't sent me a bill or discussed the fees."

"Your credit is good, Mr. Yossarian, if the credit rating companies can be believed, and you can get that mortgage anytime you want. There are excellent lakefront properties available now in New York, Connecticut, and New Jersey, and good seashore values too in Santa Barbara, San Diego, and Long Island. I can help you with the mortgage forms, if you like, as well as with your DNA. This is a good time for a mortgage and a very good time to buy."

"I don't want a mortgage and I don't want to buy. And who was that friend you mentioned before?"

"Of your nurse?"

"I have no nurse, damn it. I'm in excellent health, if you're still keeping track, and by now she's a friend. Melissa."

"Nurse MacIntosh," Mr. Gaffney disagreed formally. "I am reading from the records, Mr. Yossarian, and the records never lie. They may be mistaken or out-of-date, but they never lie. They are inanimate, Mr. Y."

"Don't dare call me that!"

"They are not able to lie, and they are always official and authoritative, even when they are in error and contradict each other. Her friend is the nurse in the postoperative surgical recovery room you expressed a desire to meet. Her given name is Wilma but people are prone to call her angel, or honey, particularly patients as they emerge from anesthesia after surgery, and two or three physicians there, who now and then entertain ambitions of, as they put it, not I, getting into her pants. That may be a medical term. You may be joined by Miss Moore."

"Miss Moore?" Yossarian, with senses awhirl, was finding it still harder to keep up. "Who the hell is Miss Moore?"

"You call her Moorecock," reminded Gaffney, in a dropped tone of admonition. "Forgive me for inquiring, Mr. Yossarian. But our listeners have not picked up sounds of sexual activity in your apartment in some time. Are you all right?"

"I've been doing it on the floor, Mr. Gaffney," answered Yossarian steadily, "below the air conditioner, as you advised me to, and in the bathtub with the water running."

"I'm relieved. I was concerned. And you really should call Miss MacIntosh now. Her telephone is free at this moment. She has troubling news about the Belgian's blood chemistry, but she seems eager to see you. I would predict that despite the differences in your respective ages—"

"Mr. Gaffney?"

"Forgive me. And Michael is just about finishing up and making ready to return, and you might forget."

"You see that too?"

"I see things too, Mr. Yossarian. That's also essential to my work. He's putting on his jacket and will soon be back with his first sketches of this new Milo Minderbinder wing. You'll permit Señor Gaffney that little wisecrack? I thought you might find it funnier than my first one."

"I'm grateful . . . Jerry," said Yossarian, with no doubt left that he was finding Mr. Gaffney a jumbo pain in the ass. He kept to himself his temper of hostile sarcasm.

"Thank you . . . John. I'm pleased we are friends now. You'll phone Nurse MacIntosh?"

"No fancy lingerie yet?" Melissa taunted when he did. "No Paris, or Florence?"

"Use your own for tonight," Yossarian bantered back. "We ought to keep seeing how we get along before we take off on a trip. And bring your roommate, if she wants to come."

"You can call her Angela," Melissa told him tartly. "I know what you did with her. She told me all about you."

"That's too bad, I think," Yossarian said, taken somewhat aback. With these two, he saw, he must keep on his mettle. "For that matter," he charged, "she told me all about you. It must be a nightmare. You could enter a convent. Your antiseptic terrors are almost unbelievable."

"I don't care," Melissa said with a hint of fanatical resolution. "I work in a hospital and I see sick people. I'm not going to take chances anymore with herpes or AIDS or even chlamydia, or vaginitis or strep throat or any of those other things you men like to pass around. I know about diseases."

"Do what you want. But bring that other friend of yours. The one that works in the surgical recovery room. I might as well start getting friendly with her now."

"Wilma?"

"They call her angel, don't they, and honey?"

"Only when they're recovering."

"Then I will too. I want to look ahead."

BOOK

SIX

17
Sammy

K nee-action wheels.

I doubt I know more than a dozen people from the old days who might remember those automobile ads with the knee-action wheels, because I don't think there's more than a dozen of us left I could find. None live in Coney Island now, or even in Brooklyn. All that is gone, closed, except for the boardwalk and the beach and the ocean. We live in high-rise apartment houses like the one I'm in now, or in suburbs in traveling distance of Manhattan, like Lew and Claire, or in retirement villages in condominiums in West Palm Beach, Florida, like my brother and sister, or, if they have more money, in Boca Raton or Scottsdale, Arizona. Most of us have done much better than we ever thought we would or our parents dreamed we could.

Lifebuoy soap.
Halitosis.
Fleischmann's Yeast, for acne.
Ipana toothpaste for the smile of beauty, and Sal Hepatica for the smile of health.
When nature forgets, remember Ex-Lax.

Pepsi-Cola hits the spot
(When I drink it, how I fot).
Twice as much for a nickel too.
Pepsi-Cola is the drink for you.

None of us wise guys in Coney Island then believed this new drink Pepsi-Cola, notwithstanding the "Twelve full ounces, that's

a lot" in the original ditty of that musical radio commercial, stood
a chance in competition against the Coca-Cola drink we knew and
loved, in the icy, smaller, sweating, somewhat greenish glass bottle
with the willowy ripples on the surface that fit like balm into
hands of every size and was by far the prevailing favorite. Today
they taste to me identically the same. Both companies have grown
mightier than any business enterprise ever ought to be allowed to
do, and the six-ounce bottle is just about another extinct delight
of the past. Nobody wants to sell a popular soft drink of just six
ounces for only a nickel today, and nobody but me, perhaps,
wants to buy one.

There was a two-cent "deposit" charged on every small soda
bottle, a nickel on sodas of larger size that sold for ten cents, and
none of the members in all of the families on that West Thirty-
first Street block in Coney Island were inattentive to the value of
those empty soda bottles. You could buy things of value for two
pennies then. Sometimes as kids we'd go treasure hunting for deposit bottles in likely places on the beach. We would turn them in
for cash at the Steinberg candy store right on my street at the
corner of Surf Avenue and use the coins to play poker or twenty-
one for pennies once we knew how, or spend them at once on
things to eat. For two cents you could buy a nice-sized block of
Nestlé's or Hershey's chocolate, a couple of pretzels or frozen
twists, or, in the fall, a good piece of the halvah we all went crazy
about for a while. For a nickel you could get a Milky Way or
Coca-Cola, a Melorol or Eskimo Pie, a hot dog in Rosenberg's
delicatessen store on Mermaid Avenue or at Nathan's about a
mile down in the amusement area, or a ride on the carousel. For
two cents you could buy a newspaper. When Robby Kleinline's
father worked at Tilyou's Steeplechase we got free passes and with
a few cents could usually win a coconut at the penny pitch game
there. We learned how. Prices were lower then and so was income.
Girls skipped rope and played jacks and potsy. We played punch-
ball, stoopball, stickball, and harmonicas and kazoos. In the early
evening after dinner—we called it supper—we might play blind-
man's bluff on the sidewalk with our parents looking on, and all
of us knew, and the parents saw, that we not-so-blind boys were
using the game mainly as a chance to fumble with the titties of
the girls for a few seconds every time we caught one and felt
around pretending we were not yet set to identify her. That was
before we boys began to masturbate and before they began to
menstruate.

Early every weekday morning, all of the fathers on the block, and all of the brothers and sisters already out of school, would begin materializing soundlessly from their buildings and turn toward the stop of the Norton's Point trolley cars on Railroad Avenue that would take them to the elevated Stillwell Avenue terminus of the four separate subway lines, following different routes, that ended in Coney Island, to the subway cars that would then transport them into the city to their various places of work or, as with me when I was just seventeen and a half with my high school diploma, to the succession of employment agencies in Manhattan in timorous search of a job. Several would walk the mile to the train station for the exercise or the nickel saved. At night, in the rush hour, they would plod back home. In winter it would already be dark. And on most evenings from late spring into early fall, my father would walk by himself to the beach with his ever-present smile, in a fluffy bathrobe with a towel draped over his shoulders, to go for his relaxing dip or swim, sometimes staying until darkness was falling and the rest of us were contracting the fear from my mother that this time he would really drown if someone did not fetch him in a hurry.

"Go get him," she would instruct the one of us nearest her. "Tell him to come eat."

It probably was the one hour in the day he could enjoy being alone and contemplate whatever hopeful thoughts gave to him that pleasant demeanor and brought that tranquil smile to his tan face. We were all in excellent health then, and that good fact was certainly one of them. He had his job. He had his Jewish newspaper, and both parents had the music they loved from the radio: Puccini especially; *The Bell Telephone Hour;* the NBC Symphony of the Air; WQXR, the radio station of the *New York Times;* and WNYC, the radio station, said the announcer, "of the City of New York, where seven million people live in peace and harmony and enjoy the benefits of democracy."

I went beyond them in music, from Count Basie, Duke Ellington, and Benny Goodman into Beethoven and Bach, chamber music and piano sonatas, and now Wagner and Mahler again.

And Hitler and his brave legionnaires would have murdered us all.

The forty-hour workweek was a watershed in social reform I was just barely in time to appreciate and a step into a better way of life that my children and grandchildren take for granted. They are stepchildren, for Glenda had already had her tubes tied by the time I met her. Suddenly we all had jobs in places that closed Saturdays. We could stay up late Friday nights. Whole families could have whole weekends off. The minimum wage and the child labor laws were other blessings flowing from FDR and his New Deal, although the latter seemed obscure. Not until college did I learn that children twelve and under *everywhere* in the industrialized Western world had *always* been putting in workdays twelve hours and longer in coal mines and factories; and not until I got into the army and began associating with people from outside Coney Island did I find out that a Coney Island "fot" was really a fart.

The minimum wage then was twenty-five cents an hour. When Joey Heller in the apartment house across the street turned old enough to get his working papers at age sixteen and found a job with Western Union delivering telegrams in the city four hours a day after high school, he brought home five dollars a week every Friday. And out of that, he almost never failed to buy a new secondhand phonograph record for the social club on Surf Avenue we already had in which we learned to dance the lindy hop, smoke cigarettes, and muzzle girls in the back room if we were lucky enough to trick or induce any into going back there with us. While my friend Lew Rabinowitz and his other friend Leo Weiner and a couple of the other bolder guys were already screwing them on the couches and in other places too. Joey Heller's father was dead and his older brother and sister worked too whenever they could, mainly part time in Woolworth's or in summer on the boardwalk at the frozen custard and hot dog stands. His mother, a seamstress when a girl, now did work for my mother, taking in and letting out dresses, and raising and lowering hems, and turning the frayed collars on shirts for the local laundry, for two or three cents apiece, I think, maybe a nickel.

They got by. Joey wanted to be a writer too. It was from Joey I first heard that variation on the Pepsi-Cola radio commercial. I remember the first verse of another parody he did on a popular song that was up near the top of the Lucky Strike Hit Parade, one you can still hear today on records by some of the better singers we had at the time:

> If there's a gleam in her eye
> Each time she unzips your fly,
> You know the lady's in love with you.

I wish I could remember the rest. He wanted to write comedy sketches for the radio, movies, and theater. I wanted to do these with him and also to write short stories someday good enough to be published in *The New Yorker* magazine, or anywhere else. Together we collaborated on skits for our Boy Scout troop, Troop 148, and later, older, for dance-night entertainments at our social club, when we charged ten cents or a quarter admission for people from a dozen of the other social clubs in Coney Island and Brighton Beach, girls free. One of our longer Boy Scout skits, "The Trials and Tribulations of Toby Tenderfoot," was so comical, I remember, that we were asked to put it on again at one of the regular assemblies that were conducted every Friday at our elementary public school, P.S. 188. Joey went into the air corps too and became an officer and a bombardier, and he also taught college in Pennsylvania. By then he was no longer "Joey" and I was no longer "Sammy." He was Joe and I was Sam. We were younger than we thought we were, but we were no longer kids. But Marvin Winkler still talks of him as Joey when he looks back, and thinks of me as Sammy.

"They laughed when I sat down at the piano."

That ad became the most successful direct-mail advertising campaign ever run, and possibly it still is. You filled out a coupon and received a packet of instructions that taught you, they said, to play the piano in ten or so easy lessons. It helped, of course, if, like Winkler, you had a piano, although he never cared to study it.

We had a Ford in our future, the manufacturer told us, and there was no-knock gasoline at Gulf or at the sign of the flying red horse at the filling stations for the automobiles with knee-action wheels we could not yet afford to buy. Lucky Strike meant fine tobacco in those days of the knee-action wheels, and people called for Philip Morris and would walk a mile for a Camel and for the other cigarettes and cigars that gave my father the lung cancer that spread to his liver and his brain and then very quickly killed him. He was on in years when he passed away, but Glenda was not old when stricken with her ovarian cancer and died exactly thirty days after the diagnosis. She began feeling ill with different things after Michael did away with himself and today we might guess her

affliction resulted from stress. She was the one who found him.
There was one stunted tree in the backyard of the house we'd
rented for the summer on Fire Island, and he'd managed to hang
himself from that. I cut him down, aware I ought not to, rather
than leave him dangling to be stared at by us and the women and
children from neighboring houses for the two hours it might take
for the police and the medical examiner to come in their beach
buggies.

A dollar an hour . . . a mile a minute . . . a hundred a week . . . *a
hundred miles an hour, wow!*

These were all possible. We knew there were cars that sped that
fast, and all of us there in Coney Island had relatives living elsewhere who were better off than we were and had those cars that
might go a mile a minute or more. Ours lived for the most part in
New Jersey, in Paterson and Newark, and came in their automobiles on summer Sundays, to walk the boardwalk to the carousel
or as far as Steeplechase, to use the beach or wade in the ocean.
They would stay for the dinner that my mother liked to cook, my
sister helping, to serve them the breaded veal cutlets with roasted
fried potatoes she made deliciously, to "give them good eat." Civil
service jobs were coveted, for the pay, the steady, white-collar
work, and the vacation and pension benefits, and because they
went to Jews too, and those who obtained them were looked up
to as professionals. You could start as an apprentice in the U.S.
Government Printing Office, my older brother read to me from a
civil service newspaper, and then work as a printer at a starting
salary of sixty dollars a week—there was that dollar an hour,
almost in reach, and more—once the apprenticeship was over. But
I would have to live and work in Washington, and none of us was
sure I ought to leave home for that. A shorter stint at the Norfolk
Navy Yard in Portsmouth, Virginia, as a blacksmith's helper, with
a bunch of the other guys from Coney Island working in the navy
yard too, seemed a more inspiring idea, while we waited to see if
the war would be over before I reached nineteen and whether or
not I was going to be drafted into the army or navy. At 30 Bank
Street in the city of Norfolk, we'd been told, a ferry ride across
from Portsmouth, was a cathouse, a brothel, but I never had nerve
enough to go, and lacked the time. I lasted at hard physical labor

there close to two months, working fifty-six consecutive days for the time and a half on Saturdays and Sundays, before I gave up in total exhaustion and came back home, and finally found a job as a file clerk with an automobile casualty insurance company for much less money, in the same building in Manhattan, coincidentally, the old General Motors building at 1775 Broadway, in which Joey Heller had worked in his uniform as a Western Union messenger, delivering and picking up telegram messages.

Where were you?

When you heard about Pearl Harbor. When the atom bomb went off. When Kennedy was killed.

I know where I was when the radio gunner Snowden was killed on the second mission to Avignon, and that meant more to me then than the Kennedy assassination did later, and still does. I was in the tail section of my B-25 medium bomber in a dead faint, after coming around from the crack on the head that knocked me out for a while when the copilot lost control of himself and put the plane into a sheer drop and then wailed on the intercom for everyone in the plane to help everyone else in the plane who wasn't answering him. Each time I came to and heard Snowden moaning and saw Yossarian doing something else in his vain struggle to help him, I fainted again.

Before that mission, I had crash-landed once with a pilot we all called Hungry Joe, who had loud nightmares when he was not on combat duty, and I had ditched once with a pilot named Orr, who they said later wound up safe in Sweden somehow; but I was not injured either time, and I still could not make myself believe it was not honestly only like the movies. But then I saw Snowden with his insides out, and after that saw a skinny man frolicking on a raft at the beach cut in half by a propeller, and I believe now that if I'd thought earlier that either one of those things could occur in my presence, I might not have been able to make myself want to go. My mother and father both knew that war was a more dreadful thing than any of us kids in the neighborhood could picture. They were appalled later when I told them I had been accepted for flying duty as an aerial gunner. Neither had ever been up in a plane. Nor had I, or anyone else I knew.

Both walked with me to the trolley stop on Railroad Avenue,

near the second candy store we had on our street. From there I would ride to Stillwell Avenue and, with the three others, take the Sea Beach subway line into Manhattan to Pennsylvania Station to report for duty on my first day in. I learned years later that after my mother hugged me good-bye with a gentle smile and a straight face and I'd gone away on the trolley, she collapsed in tears right there and wept inconsolably, and it was nearly a half hour before my father and my sister could get her back down the street into our apartment.

The day I went into the army my standard of living practically doubled. I was making sixty dollars a month as a file clerk in the insurance company and had to pay my carfare and buy my lunches, or bring them. In the army I was paid seventy-five dollars a month as a buck private from day one, and food and clothes and rent and doctors and dentists were all free. And before I was out, as a sergeant with flight pay, overseas pay, and combat pay, I was making more a month than a government printer and was already closer as a young man to that hundred dollars a week than I'd believed I ever would be able to get.

Where did all that money come from?

As my mother might say, in Yiddish: On Monday one third of the nation was ill-housed, ill-clothed, and ill-fed. And on Thursday there were ten million people in the military making more than most had been able to earn before, and two million civilian employees, and tanks, airplanes, ships, aircraft carriers, and hundreds of thousands of jeeps and trucks and other vehicles pouring out of the factories almost too rapidly to count. Suddenly there was enough for everything. Does all the credit belong to Hitler? Capitalism, my father probably would answer with a smile of resignation, as though for this humane socialist all of the evils of inequality could be clarified in that sinful single word. "For war there is always enough. It's peace that's too expensive."

From that first train ride out from Pennsylvania Station to the reception center on Long Island, I experienced in the army a loss of personal importance and individual identity that I found, to my amazement, I welcomed. I was part of a directed herd, and I found myself relieved to have everything mapped out for me, to be told what to do, and to be doing the same things as the rest. I felt unburdened, more free than as a civilian. I had more free time too, a sense of greater liberty, once the orientation phases were over.

The four of us who'd enlisted together came back unharmed,

although I had a pretty bad time of it on both missions to Avignon, and Lew was taken prisoner and kept in a prison camp in Germany for half a year before he was set free by the Russians. He knows what a long shot it was that he survived at all after Dresden was bombed while he was there. But Irving Kaiser, who had been our Toby Tenderfoot in the skit by Joey Heller and me, was blown apart in Italy by artillery fire and I never saw him again, and Sonny Ball was killed there too.

By the time of Vietnam I did know what war was like, and White House wickedness, and I swore to Glenda I would do everything conceivable, legal and illegal, to keep the boy Michael from going if he came even close to passing his physical and being called up. I had doubts that could happen. Even before he was old enough to be on drugs or medication he showed signs of behaving like someone who was. He was good at facts and figures but was lost with things like maps and floor plans. His memory for things statistical was phenomenal. But he was not much good at algebra or geometry, at anything abstract. I let Glenda continue to think he'd been affected that way by the divorce. I outlined heroic plans to move to Canada if the draft board called him. I would even go to Sweden with him if that looked safer. I gave her my word but did not have to keep it.

Lew wanted the paratroops or a tank with a cannon in front to roll over Germans who were persecuting Jews, but wound up in the infantry after training in the field artillery. Overseas, he made it to sergeant when his own sergeant was killed. Even earlier, in Holland, he had taken that position of command when his sergeant grew unsure of himself and began relying on Lew for orders to give. I wanted to be a fighter pilot and fly the P-38, because it looked so fast and flashy. But I had no depth perception, so I became an aerial gunner instead. I saw the posters stressing the need for gunners and volunteered. It was the most dangerous game of all, rumor had it, and it was going to be a cinch. And for me, as it turned out, it pretty much was.

I was small enough to be a ball-turret gunner on a Flying Fortress in England, but luckily nobody noticed, and I wound up as a tail gunner in the sunnier Mediterranean on the easier, safer B-25 instead.

In training, I always liked very much the feel of the grip on the .50 caliber machine gun. I liked being aloft and firing away with real live bullets at tow targets in the air and at stationary targets on the ground, walking the tracer bullets with their white streamers up to them from in front. I learned quickly about inertia and relative movement, that a bomb or bullet from a plane going three hundred miles an hour starts out moving in that same direction at that identical speed, and that gravity is at work from the first instant, and I was put to work at a blackboard occasionally by our first gunnery officer, helping some with difficulties try to understand. I learned electrifying things about Isaac Newton's laws of motion: if you were in motion or the target was, you would never hit it by aiming right at it. I have one that still surprises me: if a bullet is fired from a horizontal weapon at the same moment an identical bullet is dropped at the spot from the same height, they will strike the ground at the same time, even though the first one may land half a mile away. I liked the combat-simulation trainers less, because the guns were not real, although they were almost as diverting as the gun games in the boardwalk penny arcades. You sat in an enclosed contraption and fighter planes of different makes flew at you on a screen from different directions and heights for a fraction of a second, and it was realistically impossible to distinguish friend from foe that quickly and bring your sights to bear and depress the trigger. No one scored impressively on these; on the other hand, no one washed out. Two guys I knew of were reassigned because of fear. From these trainers I grew skeptical: if that was the way it was going to be, the only thing to do was to let go in a general direction as quickly as possible with as many rounds as you could in the few seconds you had. And that is the way it turned out to be, just about everywhere. The side that could bring the most firepower into play was the side that always won.

People don't want to know that the ancient battle of Thermopylae and the heroic Spartan stand to the last man there was not a Greek triumph but a crushing defeat. All that valor was wasted. It's the kind of fact I like to throw out at people to shake them up a little and get them going.

I had faith in my machine gun, but it never crossed my mind that I would always be firing away at someone who would be flying in to fire at me.

I liked the horsing around and I found myself friendly with more people I enjoyed than I'd had even in Coney Island. In the army I had personality advantages. I had read more and knew more. I found it practical to let people learn right off that I indeed was as Jewish as they might have guessed, and I would find some way of working that in and adding as well that I was from Coney Island in Brooklyn, New York. I had uncomplicated and close relationships with people with names like Bruce Suggs from High Point, North Carolina, and Hall A. Moody from Mississippi, with Jay Matthews and Bruce J. Palmer from different places in Georgia, who did not exactly like each other, with Art Schroeder, and with Tom Sloane from Philadelphia. In a barracks at Lowry Field, Colorado, where I was shipped for power-turret training, I saw hostility and threat from Bob Bowers, who also was from Brooklyn, from a rougher neighborhood of Norwegians and Irishmen that was known to us for its anti-Semites, and John Rupini, from somewhere upstate, and we were notably careful to keep out of each other's way. I knew how they felt and they knew that I knew, and they were almost equally unfriendly with just about everyone else. Lew would have had it out with them right off the bat, I suppose. In a poker game the second or third day on the troop train carrying me from Arizona to Colorado, I thought I heard one of the other players say something about a Jew, but wasn't sure. Then the one opposite me, who had already said he was from a small place down south, smirked and remarked, "We've got some too, that own a clothing store. You ought to see how they look." Now I *was* sure and knew I had to speak up.

"Just one moment, please, if you don't mind," I told him abruptly and somewhat pompously. Inwardly, I was rattled. It was not my voice. "But I happen to be Jewish and don't like to hear you talking that way. I'll leave the game right now if you want me to. But if you want me to keep playing, you have to stop saying things that hurt my feelings and make me feel bad. I don't know why you want to do that to me anyway."

The game had come to a stop, and we swayed and listened to the sound of the train. If I left the game, Lesko would leave with me, and if it came near anything violent, they knew that Lesko would be on my side. But the one I'd spoken to, Cooper, was stricken with guilt and mumbled his apology. "I'm sorry, Singer. I didn't know you were."

Lew would have broken his back, I guess, and gone to jail. I had made a temporary friend of someone who always wanted to atone. Lew is Lew, and I am not.

My name is Samuel Singer, no middle initial—Sammy NMI Singer—and I was born short and grew up smaller than most and physically unimpressive. Not like another good neighborhood friend, Ike Solomon, who was no taller but had burly biceps and a deeper chest and could lift weights and enjoy himself on a chinning bar. All my life I've been wary of fistfights, so I've done what I could not to get into any. I could be witty and sympathetic, and I have always managed to make friends. I've always been good at getting things going with needling questions and keeping a conversation lively with the clever revelations of iconoclasm.

"Do you think the country would have been better off if we'd *lost* the Revolutionary War against the British?" I would inquire searchingly, as though really mystified, and was ready with critical questions for whatever answer came.

"If Lincoln was so smart, why didn't he let the South secede? How would it hurt as much as the war did?"

"Is the Constitution constitutional?"

"Can democracy ever be created democratically?"

"Wasn't the Virgin Mary Jewish?"

I knew things other people didn't. I knew that if we walked into a floor of any barracks with no fewer than forty people, there would almost always be two with the same birthday, and half the time another two who shared a different birthday. I could make bets even with people from Nevada and California that Reno, Nevada, was farther west than Los Angeles, and almost make bets with them a second time after we'd looked it up, so determined were they to cling to an old concept. I've got one ready for the cardinal should I ever find myself sitting next to him and feel like fooling around.

"Whose genes did Jesus have?" And with a look of innocence I would remind, when given whatever response the poor figure could find, that he was born as a baby and grew to a man, and was circumcised on the eighth day.

In class in gunnery school I did come close to trouble with the decorated warrant officer instructing us when he remarked that the average life of an aerial gunner in combat was three minutes and later invited questions. He had completed his tour of duty in a B-17 with the battered Eighth Air Force in England, and I wasn't baiting him—I was curious.

"How could they tell, sir?" I asked, and I've never trusted surveys and estimates since.

"What do you mean?"

"How could they measure something like that? Sir, you must have been in combat for at least an hour."

"Much more than one hour."

"Then for every hour you lasted, nineteen others had to die in even less than the first second to average out to three minutes. And why is it more dangerous for gunners than for pilots and bombardiers? Sir, they're shooting at the whole plane, aren't they?"

"Singer, you're a wiseass, aren't you? You hang on a bit when the others go."

He let me know that I must never contradict him in the classroom again and introduced me to what I later came, with Yossarian, to call the Korn Laws, after Lieutenant Colonel Korn in Pianosa: under Korn's laws, the only ones ever permitted to question anything were those who never did. But he put me to work tutoring others with simple examples from algebra and geometry in the reasons one must always shoot well ahead of a target moving in relation to you—and in order to shoot ahead of a plane you had to shoot behind. If a plane is so many yards away and a cartridge travels at so many yards a second, how many seconds will it take for your cartridge to reach it? If the plane is traveling at so many feet per second, how many feet will it travel by the time the bullet reaches it? They saw it in practice in the hours we spent skeet shooting and firing on the gunnery range from a moving truck. But though I taught it and knew it, even I had trouble with the principle that you fired ahead of a plane coming in on attack by always aiming behind it, between the target and your tail, because of the forward airspeed of the bullets from your own plane and the swerving path that plane would have to follow to fire in front of you.

The friends I've made have always been of a generous nature. And somehow or other, a bigger, tougher guy was always around as a buddy in case things went wrong, like Lew Rabinowitz and Sonny Bartolini, one of the bolder Italians in a family in Coney Island. And Lesko, the young coal miner from Pennsylvania, whom I'd met in gunnery school. And Yossarian in operational training in Carolina and later in Pianosa in combat, after the five of us, Yossarian, Appleby, Kraft, Schroeder, and I, had flown overseas as a crew.

The fear of being beaten up had always been with me, looming larger in my meditations than the fear of being shot down. In South Carolina one night, it began to come to pass. This was after another training flight into darkness in which Yossarian could not find his way around to places like Athens, Georgia, and Raleigh,

North Carolina, and Appleby from Texas again had to bring us back with his radio compass. We had gone to our enlisted men's mess hall for a midnight meal, Schroeder and I and Yossarian. The officers' club was closed. Yossarian was always hungry. He had taken off his insignia to pose as an enlisted man, with a right to be there. People were always milling around outside at night. As we moved through them, I was jostled suddenly by a big, drunken lout, a private, bumped so hard as to leave no doubt the act had been deliberate. I whirled around with instinctive surprise. Before I could speak, he was at me, he shoved me furiously backward into a group of soldiers who had already turned to watch. It was happening almost too fast to understand. While I was still dumbfounded, staggering, he came charging after me with his arms raised and a fist cocked back to punch. He was taller than I and broad and heavier too, and there was no way I could fend him off. It was like that time I had tried to teach Lew how to box. I could not even run. I don't know why he picked me out and can only guess. But then, before he could strike, Yossarian was there between us to break it up, with his arms extended and his palms open, urging him to hold it, attempting to cajole him into calming down. And before he could even complete his first sentence, the man let go and hit him squarely on the side of the head and then hit him hard again with a punch from his other fist, and Yossarian went falling back in a helpless daze as the man followed up, hitting him about the head with both hands while Yossarian reeled with each blow, and before I knew what I was doing, I had flung myself forward to grab one of the man's thick arms and hang on. When that didn't work, I slid down to grasp him about the waist and dug my feet into the ground to strain with all my might to shove him off balance if I could. By that time Schroeder had also pounced on him, from the other side, and I heard Schroeder talking away. "You dumb fuck, he's an officer, you dumb fuck!" I could hear him rasping into the man's ear. "He's an officer!" Then Yossarian, who was pretty strong himself, was at him from in front and managed to tie up both his arms and propel him backward until he lost his footing and had to hold on. I felt all the fight go out of him as Schroeder's words sank in. He looked sick by the time we turned him loose.

"Better put your bars back on, Lieutenant," I reminded Yossarian softly, panting, and added as I saw him feeling his face:

"There's no blood. You'd better get away and put your bars back on, before somebody comes. We can pass up the meal."

From then on I was always on Yossarian's side in his frictions with Appleby, even at the time of what we both came to call the Splendid Atabrine Insurrection, although I would conscientiously take the antimalarial tablets as we flew through the equatorial climates when we traveled overseas, and he would not. The Atabrine would temper the effects of malaria, we'd been briefed before our first stop in Puerto Rico, while having no effect upon the disease itself. Regulations or not, Yossarian saw no sensible need for treating the symptoms before he suffered any. The disagreement between them crystallized into a controversy to save face. Kraft, the copilot, was as usual neutral. Kraft spoke little, smiled a lot, seemed unaware often of much that was going on. When he was killed in action over Ferrara not long afterward, I still thought of him as neutral.

"I'm the captain of this ship," Appleby made the mistake of telling Yossarian in front of us in Puerto Rico, our first stop after jumping off from Florida for the fourteen-day flight overseas. "And you'll have to follow my orders."

"Shit," said Yossarian. "It's a plane, Appleby, not a boat." They were of equal height and equal rank, second lieutenant then. "And we're on the ground, not at sea."

"I'm still the captain." Appleby spoke slowly. "As soon as we start flying again, I'm going to order you to take them."

"And I'm going to refuse."

"Then I'm going to report you," said Appleby. "I won't like doing it, but I'm going to report you to our commanding officer, as soon as we have one."

"Go ahead," Yossarian resisted stubbornly. "It's my body and my health, and I can do what I want with it."

"Not according to regulations."

"They're unconstitutional."

We were introduced to the aerosol bomb, the first time I saw one, now the spray can, and instructed to use it in the interior of the plane as soon as we climbed in, as a defense against mosquitoes and the diseases they might transmit as we headed down through the Caribbean into South America. On each leg of the trip to Natal in Brazil, we were asked to keep our eyes peeled for signs of the wreckage of a plane or two that had disappeared from the skies into the seas or jungle a day or so before. This should have been more sobering than it was. The same was true on the eight-hour flights over ocean from Brazil to Ascension Island in a plane designed to go no more than four, and from there, two days later, into Liberia in Africa and then up to Dakar in Senegal. All through these boring long flights over water we kept our eyes peeled for debris and yellow rafts, when we remembered to. In Florida we had time and evenings free, and there were dance floors there in saloons and cafés.

I wanted to start getting laid. Older guys from Coney Island like Chicky Ehrenman and Mel Mandlebaum, who had gone into the army sooner, would come back on leave from far-off places like Kansas and Alabama with similar reports of women who were all too willing to lie down for our brave boys in the service, and now that I was a boy in the service, I wanted to get laid too.

But I still didn't know how. I was shy. I could make jokes, but I was bashful. I was too easily entranced by some quality in a face or figure I found pretty. I was too quickly aroused, and inhibited by the concern it might show. I could be premature, I knew, but that was better than nothing for most of us then. When I danced close with a girl, just about any girl, I always grew an erection almost immediately and, with great embarrassment, would back myself away. Now I know I should have pressed it in against them harder to leave no doubt it was there and begin making suggestive jokes about what I wanted and was going to get, and I would have made out better. When I moved into the back room with a girl to begin muzzling her or joined them in some apartment when they were baby-sitting, I usually got what I wanted quickly enough and felt pretty good about myself until I was forced to remember there was a lot more. I was short, I knew, and always thought I had a little cock and that most of the others had pretty big ones, until one summer day in the locker room of the Steeplechase swimming pool, I looked in the mirror intrepidly while standing alongside Lew as we were washing up and saw that mine was just as good.

But he was using his. And I was always coming too quickly, or not at all. The first time that Lew and his other friend Leo Weiner set me up with a girl they'd found who had come to the Island for the summer to work in a soda fountain and was not unwilling to put out for anyone who asked her to—they were both very good at talking that way to girls—I came in the rubber before I even got in. The first time I fixed myself up, with a girl in the clubroom who'd let me know while I was still using my hand that she wanted to go all the way, I lost my erection as soon as we bared ourselves, although I'd certainly been hard enough and ready before we both took down our pants. Glenda loved those stories.

I can't be positive, but I don't think I finally did get laid until I was already overseas. There, it was effortless, as one in a body of guys all doing the same things with youthful self-assurance and a general taste for rowdy good times, near bunches of local girls in the main city of Bastia close by who did not speak our language and then especially in Rome, where the women we met on the streets smiled to let us know what they were doing there and expected us to approach with solicitations and cash and cigarettes and chocolate bars and with careless gaiety and our flies already half open. We could not think of them as prostitutes or whores, only as streetwalkers. I can't be positive I'd not really done it before because of that incident with a sweet southern girl in the dance hall in West Palm Beach, Florida, where we'd been flown to check out the plane given us for the flight overseas and to calibrate the various instruments for faults and deviations.

I still don't know if that one counted or not. She was perky as could be, with very black hair and eyes almost lavender, an inch shorter than I, with dimples too, and very much dazzled by my sharp New York lindy hop routines, which she had never beheld and wanted to learn. Schroeder had not seen them either, or Lieutenant Kraft, who had requisitioned from the motor pool the jeep in which we had gone there. After a while we went outside for some air. I walked with my arm still around her waist and we drifted without talking about it to one of the darker areas of the parking lot. We passed couples embracing in different sheltered places. I gave her a helping hand up to a seat on the fender of a low sports car.

"Oh, no, Sammy honey, we are not going to do that thing tonight, not here, not now," she let me know very strictly, holding me off with her hands on my chest, and placed a quick friendly kiss on my nose.

I had eased myself in between her legs, close enough to keep kissing, and I had just slid my hands up under her dress along her thighs to the elastic band of her panties, with my thumbs rubbing on the insides. Until she spoke, that was almost as far as I hoped to get in that parking lot.

Staring into her eyes, I confessed with a smile, "I wouldn't even know how, I think. I've never done it before." We were leaving the following day for the hop to Puerto Rico, and I could risk being truthful.

She laughed at that one as though I were still making wisecracks. She could hardly believe that a sharpie like me was still a virgin.

"Oh, you poor boy," she commiserated with me mellifluously. "You've been greatly deprived, haven't you?"

"I taught you to dance," I hinted.

"Then I'll show you how we do it," she agreed. "But you mustn't put it in. You must promise me that. Now stand back a minute and let me twist myself a little. That's better. See? Oh, that's a very nice one you have, isn't it? And all ready to go like the best little boy, ain't he?"

"I was circumcised by a sculptor."

"Now, not so fast, Sammy honey. And not so quick. Not there, baby, not there. That's almost my belly button. You've got to learn to give me a chance to put my thing up there where you can get at it. That's why we call it putting out, honey, see? Now, I'm not going to do that for you tonight. Understood? Come back a little closer. That's more like it, right? But you mustn't put it in! *Don't* put it in! *You're putting it in!*"

This last was a cry that could have shaken the neighborhood. She bounced about under me wildly for about fifteen seconds or so, trying frantically to wriggle free, and all I was trying to do was raise my weight to help, and then the next thing I knew I was up and watching myself shoot in midair across the hood of the car. The stuff spurted a mile. Shoot is just the right word for a boy of nineteen or twenty. When a man is past sixty-eight, he comes. When he can. If he wants to.

I never thought I'd be this old, wake with stiff joints, and have nothing really to occupy myself with most days but my volunteer fund-raising work for cancer relief. I read late at night, as the poet said, and many mornings too, and go south in the winter with a lady friend with a house in Naples, Florida, to be near the ocean, and sometimes to a daughter who lives in Atlanta and sometimes to Houston, Texas, to visit my other daughter, who lives there with her husband. I play bridge and meet people that way. I have a small summer house in East Hampton, near the ocean, with one guest room with a private bathroom. Each time Lew goes back into treatment, I travel to see him at least once a week by bus from the bus terminal. It takes all day. I never thought I'd live longer than he would, and maybe I won't, because in the long remissions he's enjoyed in the more than twenty years I've known about his Hodgkin's disease, he is hardier than I am and does much more. This time, though, he seems thinner longer, downhearted, fatalistic, but Claire, who talks to Teemer, is more concerned about his mental attitude than his illness.

"I'm sick of feeling nauseous," he told me last time, when we were talking alone, as though getting ready to give up, and I could not tell if he was intending a joke.

So I tried one of my own. "The word is *nauseated*."

"What?"

"The correct word is *nauseated*, Lew. Not *nauseous*."

"Sammy, don't be a prick again. Not now."

He made me feel foolish.

It's not in the cards for me to live with my children when old, so I've put money away for my nursing home. I am waiting for my prostate cancer. I might marry again soon if my well-off widowed lady friend ever overcomes her pecuniary mistrusts and tells me we ought to. But for how long? Seven more years? I do miss family life.

Glenda decided the one outside the dance hall didn't count. "Cheese!" she said with a laugh, shaking her head in disbelief, whenever we recalled that experience. "You didn't know anything, did you?"

"No, I didn't."

"And don't try that come-help-me act now."

It was not always solely an act. Just about all the women I've ever been with seemed always to have had more experience than I did. There are two kinds of men, I think, and I belong to the second kind.

She herself had done it first in college her first time away from home, with the man she married soon after graduation, who came down with cancer before she did, with his melanoma, and then married two more times, and even fathered another child. I didn't get my chance to go to college until after the war, and by then it was hardly much trouble getting a girl to go to bed, because I was less inexperienced, and most girls were doing it too.

Appleby made it to Ascension Island from Natal in Brazil, navigating all the way by radio compass, with an auxiliary fuel tank installed in the bomb bay for the extended journey. He had no faith left in Yossarian's compass directions. Yossarian had none either and was offended only slightly. Appleby was the one with the growing grudge. The gamble in relying only on the radio compass, I found out from Yossarian, who'd learned at least that much, was that we approached the island eight hours away on a circular path instead of straight on and consumed more gasoline.

I learned more about war and capitalism and Western society in Marrakech in Morocco when I saw affluent Frenchmen drinking aperitifs on the terraces of luxurious hotels with their children and well-turned-out wives while they bided their time complacently until others invaded at Normandy and later in southern France to recapture their country and enable them to return and regain their estates. At the immense American replacement center in Constantine in Algeria, where we waited two weeks for our final assignment to a bomber group, I first learned a little bit specific about Sigmund Freud. There, I shared a tent with a medical assistant, older than I, also waiting assignment, who also wished to write short stories like William Saroyan and was also positive he could. Neither of us understood that there was no need for more than one Saroyan. Today we might conclude from the insignificance of Saroyan that there had not been great need for even one. We exchanged books we had finished.

"Do you ever have dreams your teeth are falling out?" he inquired of me slyly one day apropos of nothing else we were discussing. We had nothing to do while we sat around waiting. We could play softball or volleyball if we chose. We'd been cautioned against going into Constantine to roam about carelessly for whiskey or women, cautioned by the tale of a murdered GI who'd been found castrated, with his scrotum sewn into his mouth, which we thought probably apocryphal. We ate from mess kits.

His question hit home. I reacted with a start, as though discovering myself with some magical mind reader. "Yeah, I do dream that!" I admitted gullibly. "I had one last night."

He nodded smugly. "You jerked off yesterday," he alleged, with no hesitation.

"You're full of shit!" I answered right back heatedly, and wondered guiltily how he had found out.

"It's no crime," he defended himself reassuringly. "It isn't even a sin. Women do it too."

I put no trust in that last part then. I would be surprised, he guaranteed.

After landing at Pianosa we looked around with enchantment at the mountains and woods so near to the sea as we waited for the vehicles that would drive us with our bags to the orderly room of our squadron to report with our orders and receive our tent assignments. It was May and sunny, and in all ways beautiful. Not much was stirring. We were relieved to find ourselves safely there.

"Good job, Appleby." Yossarian commended him humbly, speaking for all of us. "We would never have made it if you'd had to rely on me."

"I don't much care about that part," Appleby told him unforgivingly, in his moderate Texas accent. "You broke regulations, and I said I would report you."

In the orderly room, where we were welcomed by the obliging first sergeant, Sergeant Towser, Appleby could hardly restrain himself until the formalities were completed. Then, through tightened lips in a face just about quivering with insulted fury, he asked, demanded, to see the squadron commander about the daily insubordination of a crew member who'd refused to take his Atabrine tablets and had disobeyed direct orders to do so. Towser repressed his surprise.

"Is he in?"

"Yes, sir. But you will have to wait a bit."

"And I would like to speak with him while all of us are still here together, so the others can bear witness."

"Yes, I understand. You can all sit down if you wish."

The commanding officer of the squadron was a major, and his surname was Major too, I saw, and was amused by the oddity.

"Yes, I think I will sit down," said Appleby. The rest of us kept silent. "Sergeant, about how long will I have to wait? I've still got a lot to get done today so that I can be fully prepared bright and early tomorrow morning to go into combat the minute they want me to."

To me it seemed that Towser could not believe his ears.

"Sir?"

"What's that, Sergeant?"

"What was your question?"

"About how long will I have to wait before I can go in to see the major?"

"Just until he goes out to lunch," Sergeant Towser replied. "Then you can go right in."

"But he won't be there then. Will he?"

"No, sir. Major Major won't be back in his office until after lunch."

"I see," Appleby decided uncertainly. "I think I'd better come back after lunch, then."

Schroeder and I stood mute, as we always did when the officers were settling things. Yossarian was listening with an appearance of incisive inquiry.

Appleby walked first out the door. He stopped abruptly as soon as I stepped out behind him and drew back against me with a gasp. My gaze followed his, and I was sure I saw a tall, dark officer wearing the gold leaf of a major come jumping out the window of the orderly room and go scooting out of sight around the corner. Appleby was squeezing his eyes closed and shaking his head as though in fear he was ill.

"Did you—" he began, and then Sergeant Towser was tapping him on the shoulder and telling him he could now go in to see Major Major if he still wished to do that, since Major Major had just gone out. Appleby regained his good military posture.

"Thank you, Sergeant," he replied very formally. "Will he be back soon?"

"He'll be back after lunch. Then you'll have to go right out and wait for him in front till he leaves for dinner. Major Major never sees anyone in his office when he's in his office."

"Sergeant, what did you just say?"

"I said that Major Major never sees anyone in his office while he's in his office."

Appleby stared at Sergeant Towser intently a few moments and then adopted a stern tone of rebuking formality. "Sergeant," he said, and paused, as though waiting until certain he was commanding his undivided attention, "are you trying to make a fool out of me just because I'm new in the squadron and you've been overseas a long time?"

"Oh, no, sir," answered Towser. "Those are my orders. You can ask Major Major when you see him."

"That's just what I intend to do, Sergeant. When *can* I see him?"

"Never."

But Appleby could make his report in writing, if he chose. In two or three weeks we were practically veterans, and the matter was no longer of consequence even to Appleby.

Appleby was soon a lead pilot and was paired with a bombardier of longer experience named Havermeyer. Yossarian was good enough at first to be lead bombardier and was matched with a sweet-tempered pilot named McWatt. Later I preferred Yossarian for his quicker bomb runs.

We had everything, it seemed to me. The tents were comfortable and there was no hostility that I could see toward anyone. We were at peace with each other in a way we would not find feasible anywhere else. Where Lew was, with the infantry in Europe, there was death, terror, blame. We were all of us fun-loving for the most part and did not grieve deeply over our occasional losses. The officer in charge of both our mess halls then was Milo Minderbinder, the industrialist and big export-import man now, and he did an excellent job, the best in the whole Mediterranean Theater of Operations, everyone knew. We had fresh eggs every morning. The workers in the kitchen under Corporal Snark were Italian laborers recruited by Milo Minderbinder, and he found local families nearby who were pleased to do our laundry for practically nothing. All we had to do to eat was follow orders. We had ice cream sodas every weekend, the officers had them every day. Only after I ditched off France with Orr did we find out that the carbonation for the ice cream sodas from Milo was coming from the carbon dioxide cylinders that were supposed to be in our Mae West life jackets to inflate them. When Snowden died, we found out Milo had taken the Syrettes of morphine from the first-aid kits too.

As I was moving into my tent that first day, I stopped at the sound of many planes and, looking up, watched three flights of six returning from a mission in perfect formation against the clear blue backdrop of the windless sky. They had gone that morning to bomb a railroad bridge on the near side of Italy outside a town called Pietrasanta, and they were back in time for lunch. There had been no flak. There were no enemy planes. There were never enemy planes in all the time I was there. This war looked just right to me, dangerous and safe, exactly as I'd hoped. I had an occupation I enjoyed that was respectable too.

Two days later I flew my first mission, to a bridge at a place called Piambino. I regretted there was no flak.

Not until I saw a kid my own age, Snowden, bleed and die just a few yards away from me in the back of a plane did the truth finally dawn that they were trying to kill *me* too, really trying to kill me. People I did not know were shooting cannons at me almost every time I went up on a mission to drop bombs on them, and it was not funny anymore. After that I wanted to go home. There were other things that weren't funny either, because the number of missions I had to complete had gone up first from fifty to fifty-five and then to sixty and sixty-five, and might go up even further before I could get there, with the ghastly chance I might not survive that far. I had thirty-seven missions then, and twenty-three more to fly, then twenty-eight. They had gotten rougher too, and after Snowden, I prayed on every one as soon as we were aloft and I had taken my place on my bicycle seat in the tail, facing backward, before I prepared to load and test-fire my machine gun when we were in formation and setting out over the water. I remember my prayer: "Dear God, please get me home safe, and I swear I will never go into an airplane again." Later on I broke that promise for a sales conference without a second thought. I never told Glenda or anyone else I ever prayed.

My second week there I found myself riding to Bastia in a jeep with a lieutenant named Pinkard I'd already made friends with on a mission, who had the car from the motor pool and invited me along to see the place. When we weren't on missions our time was our own. Not long after that, Pinkard went down over Ferrara in the plane with Kraft and was presumed dead with the rest. Along the straight road heading north on the level terrain near the beaches we came upon two grinning girls hitchhiking, and he screeched to a stop to take them aboard. A few minutes later he turned off the road into a flat patch of ground shielded by bushes, where he brought the car to another skidding stop, pointing out and downward and talking gibberish.

"Ficky-fick?" the elder of the two inquired, when she guessed she understood.

"Ficky-fick," Pinkard answered.

The girls glanced at each other and agreed, and we dismounted and paired off in different directions. I had the older one and we walked with our arms around each other. Mine went to the ground near the rusting pair of railroad tracks that ran down that coast of the island and were no longer in use. Between the tracks lay the metal pipeline that brought us our gasoline from the docks in Bastia. She knew what to do. She prepared herself quickly and put me inside. I did not feel as much contact as I had expected would be there, but I had no doubt I was at last doing it. I even reared up once and enjoyed looking down to make sure. I finished before Pinkard did, but I was ready for a second one sooner. By then we were back in the jeep and none of the others wanted to stop again.

A week or so after that the Germans pulled out of Rome and the Americans came in, by coincidence on D day in France. Within hours, it seemed, the executive officer in our squadron—I still don't know what an executive officer is, but ours was a major named de Coverley—rented two apartments there for us to use on short leaves, the one for the officers an elegant establishment of four bedrooms for four men, appointed with marble, mirrors, curtains, and sparkling bathroom fixtures on a broad thoroughfare called Via Nomentana, which was out of the way and a fairly long walk. Ours lay on two entire floors at the top of a building with a creeping elevator just off the Via Veneto in the center of the city, and because of the convenience of location, the officers on leave at the same time were there a lot, even to eat and occasionally to make time with the girls who were always around. We came in larger groups with supplies of food rations, and thanks to Milo and Major de Coverley, there were women to cook for us all day long. We had maids to clean who had a good time working there and being with us, and friends of theirs would come to visit and stay the evening, often the night, for the food and the fun. Any unplanned urge could be appeased simply. Once I walked into Snowden's room and came upon Yossarian in bed on top of a maid still holding her broom, whose green panties were on the mattress beside them.

I'd never had so good a time as those I had in that apartment; I doubt I've had many better ones since.

On the second day of my first leave there I returned from a short stroll alone and came back just as the pilot called Hungry Joe was getting down from a horse-drawn cab with two girls who looked lively and lighthearted. He had a camera.

"Hey, Singer, Singer, come along," he yelled out at me in the excited, high-pitched voice with which he always seemed to say everything. "We'll need two rooms up there. I'll pay, I'll treat you. They said they'd pose."

He let me start out with the pretty one—black hair, plump, round face with dimples, good-sized breasts—and it was very good, as Hemingway might say, thrilling, relaxing, fulfilling. We liked each other. When we switched and I was with the wiry one, it was even better. I saw it was true that women could enjoy doing it too. And after that it has always been pretty easy for me, especially after I'd moved into New York in my own small apartment and was cheerily at work in the promotion department at *Time* magazine. I could talk, I could flirt, I could spend, I could seduce women into deciding to seduce me, which is how I lured Glenda into luring me into moving in with her after many weekends away together and then marrying.

Back at the squadron after that, I felt secure and adventurous, a ladies' man, almost a swashbuckler. I had a decent role in a pretty good film. We called them movies then. Everything ran very well, it seemed to me, with no effort on my part. We had our fresh eggs every morning, the bombs had already been loaded each time we came to our plane. Everything necessary was seen to by others, and none of the logistical work that went into it was mine. I was living with Gentiles and getting along.

Among us when I arrived were a number of aerial gunners and officers who had already completed their combat tours. They had flown their fifty missions and many had been wheedled into going on one or two more when personnel for some reason or another was short for a day or so, and they were waiting for the orders to come that would ship them back to the States. Before the transfer of the bomb group from the mainland to the island, they had been on missions to Monte Cassino and Anzio while the Germans still had fighter planes in the region to attack them, and more recently, with most of the others there before me, to hot targets they talked about like Perugia and Arezzo. Ferrara, Bologna, and Avignon still lay ahead, in my future. When the number of missions constituting a tour of duty was raised from fifty to fifty-five, those who'd not yet shipped out to Naples for the trip home to the States were ordered back to combat duty to fly the additional missions now designated. And they went, I noted, these veteran combat fliers with more knowledge than I had, without dread or outrage, with some irritation at inconvenience, but with no panic or protest. I found that encouraging. They survived without harm and in time went home. Most were not much older than I was. They had come through untouched. I would too. I felt my life as a grown-up was about to begin. I stopped masturbating.

18
Dante

"In what language?"

"In translation, of course. I know you don't read Italian."

"Three or four times," Yossarian remembered about Dante's *Divine Comedy*, as they waited for the elevator after Michael had dropped off the finished artwork. "Once as a kid—I used to read more than you ever wanted to. One time in a course in Renaissance literature, with Noodles Cook. Maybe a couple of times since, just the *Inferno* part. I never did get as much satisfaction out of it as I should have. Why?"

"It reminds me of it," said Michael, alluding to the PABT building, to which they both now were scheduled separately to go, Michael with M2 to clock the actions on the video monitors, Yossarian with McBride, with cops in flak jackets, if needed, armed with tranquilizer guns for the dogs at the bottom of the first staircase. "Even that name. Port, authority, terminal. I know what terminal means. I never tried," he went on in a tone of truculent braggadocio. "But each time I think of that bus terminal, I imagine it's what Dante's *Inferno* might represent."

"That's a fresh concept," Yossarian observed wryly. They were the sole passengers.

"Except," amended Michael, as they descended, "the PABT building is out in the open. Like something normal."

"That makes it worse, doesn't it?" said Yossarian.

"Than hell?" Michael shook his head.

"Sartre says hell is other people. You should read him."

"I don't want to read him. That's silly, if he was serious. It sounds like something said just for people like you to quote him."

"You're smart."

"We get used to this one," said Michael.

"Doesn't that make it worse? Do you think in hell they don't get used to it?" Yossarian added with a laugh. "In Dante they answer questions, pause in their tortures to tell long stories about themselves. Nothing God did ever came out right, did it? Not hell. Not even evolution."

Michael was an educated man who had not found magic in *The Magic Mountain*. He had not read *Schweik*, although he harbored favorable notions about him. He'd found Kafka and Joseph K. amusing but clumsy and unexciting, Faulkner passé, and *Ulysses* a novelty that had seen its time, but Yossarian had elected to like him anyway.

Starting out as a young father, with children amounting in time to four, Yossarian had never considered, not once, that in his declining years he might still be related to them.

"And I'm beginning to feel the same way about this office building of yours," said Michael, when they were out of the elevator and leaving the lobby.

"Ours," corrected Yossarian.

Michael had a spring in his step and an M & M paycheck in his pocket, and his animated spirit was in striking disharmony with his sulky observations.

"And all the rest of the buildings here in Rockefeller Center. They used to be taller, like real skyscrapers. Now they seem to be going to hell too, shrinking."

Michael might indeed be on to something, Yossarian reflected, as they came out on a sunlit street clogged with vehicles and astir with pedestrians. In fact, the slender edifices of rigid line and uniform silver stone constituting the original, true Rockefeller Center were overshadowed throughout the city now by taller structures of more extravagant style and more daring design. Old buildings had made way for new ones. These no longer meant much. The rooftops did indeed look lower, and Yossarian wondered impractically if all could indeed be sinking slowly into the mysterious muddy depths of some unreal sea of obsolescence somewhere.

Down the block toward Sixth Avenue, their job interviews for executive positions over, the line of well-dressed beggars in three-piece business suits had already taken up station, some soliciting alms with outstretched paper drinking cups from McDonald's, others looking almost too insensible to beg, their staring faces sunk to the neck into their bodies below. Across the street was the skating rink, reflecting the brilliant space of its own presence with a marvelous clarity. The rising, boxed structures of the office buildings around it climbed in slabs of windowed stone like flat, dull monoliths carved by a single mason. One pausing to listen could easily distinguish the resonance of trains traveling beneath the ground and feel the vibrations issued by their frictions. On street level, in letters cut in stone or in mosaics on small round escutcheons of gold and blue, appeared the epigraph of the principal corporate tenant in each of the buildings. Soon, when the existing lease was renegotiated, the old Time-Life headquarters would be renamed as the new M & M Building.

On the loftiest construction of all in that complex architectural exploit, at number 30 Rockefeller Center, a transformation of notable significance had already taken place. The institutional name of the original corporate tenant, the Radio Corporation of America, a famed organization pioneering in radio and television broadcasting and the production of popular, vulgar entertainments for grateful international multitudes, had been expunged without trace and replaced by the epigraph of the grander business entity that had bought it, the General Electric Company, a leading producer of military wares, locomotives, jet airplane engines, river pollutants, and electric toasters, blankets, and lightbulbs suitable for home use.

The synthetic gold used in the lettering of the newer name was of a longer-lasting glisten than real gold and, though poorer, of better value. Overlooking the skating rink was an airy metal sculpture of a male figure in polished lemon-yellow gilt, alleged to be a representation of the mythical Prometheus, an incongruous choice overlooking ice for the demigod who had brought fire to man.

"Come cross," said Yossarian prudently, to get out of the way of youths in sneakers and high spirits bearing down toward them fearlessly through black and white pedestrians hastily clearing an opening.

At the rink itself, on the oval of ice below street level, a cleansing intermission between sessions was in progress, performed by grinning Japanese attendants on ice skates with red jackets and green jockey caps and conspicuous button badges on lapels, with a cartoon drawing of a grinning pink face with too many teeth on a glossy white background. Moisture sparkled in drops like frozen tears atop the prominent cheekbones of the Asiatic workers in red and green. In gentle coordination these uniformed attendants of subservient mien now sporting the Tilyou Steeplechase insignia on snow-white buttons glided their machines smoothly over the blade-scarred surface of the ice, applying a fresh coat of water for a new frigid glaze for the next bunch of newcomers. The earliest among them were already on line; almost all were eating something, raw fish and rice, salt-covered bagels, or a southern pork barbecue sandwich, with nothing more to do until the hour struck.

Recalling Dante, Yossarian was unable to name what lay beneath that lake of ice in hell, if not the domain of shaggy, hideous Satan himself. He knew what underlay the skating rink and the buildings around it: refrigeration tubes for the ice, water mains, electric cables, telephone lines, pipes of steam to bring heat in winter to the offices. And also below street level were the pedestrian passageways fanning out on different courses with shops that were no longer smart, and at least one subway line from another borough with transfer points to other lines in other directions. It took ages, perhaps, but a rider with time could make connections to just about anywhere he had to go.

"Cross back," said Yossarian again, rather than brush by the middle-class mendicants, whose stupefied faces always discombobulated him. He had not thought American free-market capitalism had undone so many of its disciples.

A chorus of chittering laughter behind him caused him to look back toward one of the liver-spotted marble planters on the observation level. He saw a redheaded man with a walking stick and a loose green rucksack obligingly taking snapshots of a merry pack of subdued, dark-haired, Oriental tourists. Yossarian had the idea he had seen him before. The man had thin lips, orange lashes, a straight, sharp nose, and his face was of the fragile, milk-white complexion not uncommon among people with hair that color. As he gave back the camera, he turned Yossarian's way with an arrogant air that implied he knew perfectly well precisely the person he was going to find. Their eyes locked, and all at once Yossarian thought he had met him before, at the North Cemetery in Munich at the entrance to the mortuary chapel at the start of the famous Mann novella, the mysterious red-haired man whose presence and swift disappearance had been unsettling to Gustav Aschenbach—one glimpse and he was out of sight, gone from the story. This

man flaunted a fuming cigarette recklessly, as though equally contemptuous of him and cancer. And while Yossarian stared back at
him in defiant and indignant scrutiny, the man grinned brazenly,
and Yossarian suffered an inner shudder just as a long, pearl-white
limousine with smoked windows eased to a stop between them,
although there were no cars in front. The car was longer than a
hearse, with a swarthy driver. When the limousine drove forward
again, he saw wide streaks of red on the ground disfigured by tire
treads, like blood dripping from the wheels, and the man with red
hair and green rucksack was gone. The Asians remained with
faces turned upward, as though straining to read some inscrutable
message in the blank walls and vitreous mirrors of the windows.

Walking westward to Eighth Avenue, he knew, would bring
them to the sex parlors and cramped adult theaters on the asphalt
boulevard linking the PABT building on the left to his high-rise
luxury apartment building to the right, which was already in
bankruptcy but functioning no less well than before.

The days were growing shorter again, and he did not want
Michael to know that he would be dating Melissa MacIntosh a
third time and taking her to dinner and another movie, where he
would tease with his fingertips her neck and ear again, which had
caused her to stiffen and smile grimly to herself the first time,
blushing up to her eyes, which were small and blue, and fondle
her knees, which she'd kept pressed together all through the film
and in the taxi to her apartment, where, she had already made
clear, she did not want him to enter that night, and where he did
not truly want to go, and had not, even by indirection, asked to
be admitted. She liked movies more than he did. Two of the men
following him did not seem to like movies at all but had followed
him in anyway, and a woman in a red Toyota went distraught
finding a parking space in which to wait and was getting fat from
bags of candies and pastries she ate from gluttonously. His second
time with Melissa, she had relaxed her knees as though accustomed to his touch and sat enjoying the film thoroughly, but with
her back straight and her hands clasped firmly across her lower
thighs, the forearms determined. He prized the resistance. He'd
learned enough from her now, and even more from Angela, to
know that Melissa, when younger, thinner, lighter, swifter, and
more nimble, had found sex bawdy fun in dexterous ways.

"I had to tell her how," laughed Angela. "Most men are stupid
and don't know anything. Do you?"

"I get complaints," he answered.

"You're tricky." Angela eyed him doubtfully. "Ain't you?" she added with a smirk.

Yossarian shrugged. Melissa herself refused to speak of specifics and would put on airs of staunch decorum when he hinted of past and prospective licentious escapades.

Looking ahead in pleasurable inventions, Yossarian had to bring into solemn contemplation the handicaps of his own weight, years, joints, agility, and virility. What he did not doubt was his eventual success in seducing her back into that same playful state of salacious enthusiasm and ready acquiescence that reputedly was hers formerly. She was not buxom above the waist, and that helped keep his ardor temperate. He calculated the risks and cost: he might even have to take her dancing once or twice and perhaps go to rock concerts and musical comedies, maybe even watch television together, news broadcasts. He was confident he could overwhelm her fear of germs with red roses by the dozens and his evocative promises of lingerie in Paris, Florence, and Munich, and that he could win her heart with the magical romantic vow in his inventory of bantering tricks, uttered tenderly at exactly the correct moment: "If you were my girl, Melissa, I know I would want to fuck you every day."

He also knew it would be a lie.

But he could think of few pleasures more satisfying than the silly bliss of new sexual triumph shared by parties who knew, liked, and laughed with each other. And at least he had a goal now more enticing than most.

He lied a little more and swore his divorce was final.

On the corner ahead a crowd was collecting before a policeman on a horse. Yossarian gave a dollar to a black man with a hand with cracked skin and a dollar to a white one with a hand like a skeleton's. He was amazed it was alive.

"This must be," despaired Michael, "the worst fucking city in the world."

Yossarian withheld agreement dubiously. "It's the *only* city we have," he decided finally, "and one of the few real cities in the world. It's as bad as the worst and better than the rest."

Michael looked wan as they wove their way with others of reputable pursuit through more idle bums, beggars, and prostitutes counting abstractly on windfalls. Many of the women and girls wore nothing down below beneath their black, pink, and white vinyl raincoats, and several of the enticing harpies were fleet to flash themselves hairy and bare, with shaving rashes at the joints, when police were not observing alertly.

"I would hate to be poor," Michael murmured. "I wouldn't know how."

"And we wouldn't be smart enough to learn," said Yossarian. He was sardonically glad he'd soon be out of it all. It was another consolation of age. "Come this way, cross back now—that one looks mad enough to stab. Let him get someone else. What *is* that on the corner? Have we seen it before?"

They had seen it before. Hardened onlookers were watching with smiles a spindly, shabby man at work with a razor blade, cutting away the rear trouser pocket of a drunk on the sidewalk to gain nonviolent possession of the wallet inside, while two neatly uniformed policemen stood waiting patiently for him to finish before taking him into custody, with the ill-gotten fruits of his labor already on his person. Contemplating the scene was a third policeman, the one on a large chestnut horse, supervising like a doge or a demi-deity. He was armed with a revolver in a leather holster and looking, with his glistening belt of cartridges, as though armed with arrows too. The man with the razor glanced up every few seconds to stick his tongue out at him. Everything was in order, no peace was disturbed. All played their roles out jointly, like conspirators in a tapestry of symbolic collaboration overripe with meaning that defied explanation. It was as peaceful as heaven and as disciplined as hell.

Yossarian and Michael turned away uptown, stepping around an elderly lady snoozing soundly on the sidewalk against a wall, more soundly than Yossarian was accustomed to sleeping since the breakup—and the beginning, and the middle—of his second marriage. She was snoring contentedly and had no pocketbook, Yossarian noted as he was seized by a brown man in a gray military doublet with black stitching and a maroon turban who jabbered unintelligibly while steering each into the revolving door of the uncrowded Indian restaurant in which Yossarian had made a reservation for lunch that now proved unnecessary. In a roomy booth, Yossarian ordered Indian beer for both and knew he would drink Michael's too.

"How can you eat all this now?" Michael inquired.

"With relish," said Yossarian, and spooned more of the tangy condiments onto his plate. For Michael, Yossarian ordered a salad and tandoori chicken, for himself a lamb vindaloo, after a spicy soup. Michael feigned disgust.

"If I ate that I'd be nauseous."

"Nauseated."

"Don't be a pedant."

"That's what I said the first time I was corrected."

"In school?"

"In Columbia, South Carolina," said Yossarian. "By that smart little wiseass tail gunner I've told you about, Sam Singer, from Coney Island. He was Jewish."

Michael smiled in a patronizing way. "Why do you point that out?"

"At that time it was important. And I'm going back to that time. What about me, with this name Yossarian? It wasn't always that easy, with rednecked Southerners and bigots from Chicago who hated Roosevelt, Jews, blacks, and everyone else except bigots from Chicago. You'd think with the war over, everything ugly would change for the better. Not much did. In the army everyone asked me, sooner or later, about the name Yossarian, and everyone was satisfied when I told them I was Assyrian. Sam Singer knew I was extinct. He'd read a short story by a writer named Saroyan that's probably no longer in print anywhere. That's extinct too, like Saroyan. And me."

"We're not Assyrian," Michael reminded. "We're Armenian. I'm only half Armenian."

"I said Assyrian to be funny, jerk. They took it as fact." Yossarian looked fondly at him. "Only Sam Singer caught on why. 'I bet I could be Assyrian too,' he said to me once, and I knew just what he meant. I think I was an inspiration to him. When the showdown came, he and I were the only ones who declined to fly any more than the seventy missions we had. Shit, the war was practically over. 'Fuck my superiors,' I decided, when I saw that most of my superiors were not superior. Years later I read where Camus said that the only freedom we have is the freedom to say no. You ever read Camus?"

"I don't want to read Camus."

"You don't want to read anything?"

"Only when I'm really bored. It takes time. Or when I feel all alone."

"That's a good time. In the army I never felt all alone. Singer was a bookish little prick and began to act like a comic smartass with me once he saw I would let him. 'Wouldn't it be better if the country had lost the Revolutionary War?' he asked me once. That was before I'd found out they were slamming people into prison for criticizing the new political party. Michael, which is farther west—Reno, Nevada, or Los Angeles?"

"Los Angeles, of course. Why?"

"Wrong. That's another thing I learned from him. In South Carolina one night a big drunken bully from somewhere began to knock him around for no reason. It was no contest. I was the officer, although I had taken my bars off to get a midnight meal in the enlisted men's mess hall. I felt I had to protect him, and as soon as I stepped between them to try to break it up, the guy began beating the shit out of me." Yossarian broke into hearty laughter.

"Oh, God," moaned Michael.

Yossarian laughed again, softly, when he saw Michael's dismay. "The funny part is—and it was funny: I almost laughed even when he was hitting me, I was filled with such surprise—that none of it hurt. He was punching me in the head and face, and I didn't feel pain. In a little while I tied up his arms, and then people pulled us apart. Sam Singer had jumped on him from the side and this other gunner with us, Art Schroeder, had jumped on his back. When they quieted him down and told him I was an officer, he sobered up fast and nearly died. The next morning, even before breakfast, he showed up at my room in the officers' barracks to beg forgiveness and got down on his knees. I mean that. I never saw anyone cringe like that. And he just about started to pray to me. I mean that too. And he wouldn't stop, even after I told him to go away and forget it. I think I might have gotten into trouble too for taking off my lieutenant's bars just to eat in the enlisted men's mess hall, but he didn't think of that. I didn't tell him how much it disgusted me to see him cowering that way. *That's* when I hated him, that's when I got angry and ordered him away. I never want to see anybody so abject again, I like to tell myself."

Michael was through eating after that story. Yossarian changed plates with him and finished his chicken and mopped up the leftover rice and bread. "My digestion is still good too, thank God."

"What isn't good?" said Michael.

"My sex drive."

"Oh, fuck that. What else?"

"My memory, for names and telephone numbers, I can't always

find the words I know I know, I can't always remember what I meant to remember. I talk a lot and say things twice. I talk a lot and say things twice. My bladder a little, and my hair," added Yossarian. "It's white now, and Adrian tells me I shouldn't be satisfied with that. He's still trying to find a dye to turn it gray. When he finds it I won't use it. I'm going to tell him to try genes."

"What's in a gene? It's in your talk a lot."

"That's because of my genes, I guess. Blame that on Teemer. My God, that fistfight was forty years ago and seems like only yesterday. Everybody I meet now from way back then has back problems or prostate cancer. Little Sammy Singer, they called him. I wonder now what ever became of him."

"After forty years?"

"Almost fifty, Michael."

"You just said forty."

"See how fast a decade passes? That's true, Michael. You were born a week ago—I remember it like it was only yesterday—and I was born a week before that. You've no idea, Michael, you can't imagine—*yet*—how laughable it is, how disorienting, to walk into a room for something and forget what you came for, to look into a refrigerator and not remember what you wanted, and to be talking to so many people like you who have never even heard of Kilroy."

"I've heard of him now," Michael argued. "But I still don't know a thing about him."

"Except that he was probably here in this restaurant too," said Yossarian. "Kilroy was everywhere you went in World War II— you saw it written on a wall. We don't know anything about him either. That's the only reason we still like him. The more you find out about anyone, the less you're able to respect him. After that fight, Sam Singer thought I was the best person in the world. And after that, I wasn't ever afraid to get into a real fistfight again. Today I would be."

"Were there others?"

"No, almost one, with a pilot named Appleby, the one I flew overseas with. We never got along. I couldn't navigate and I don't know why they expected me to. One time I got lost on a training mission and gave him a compass heading that would have taken us out over the Atlantic Ocean toward Africa. We would have died right then if he hadn't been better at his job than I was at mine. What a schmuck I was, as a navigator. No wonder he was sore. Am I talking too much? I know I talk a lot now, don't I?"

"You're not talking too much."

"Sometimes I do talk too much, because I find I'm more interesting than the people I'm talking to, and even they know that. You can talk too. No, I never had to actually get in a fistfight again. I used to look pretty strong."

"I wouldn't do it," Michael said, almost proudly.

"I wouldn't do it either, now. Today people kill. I think you might anyway, if you saw brutality and you didn't take time to think about it. The way that little Sammy Singer jumped at that big guy when he saw him beating me up. If we took the time, we'd think of calling 911 or look the other way. Your big brother Julian sneers at me because I won't get into an argument with anyone over a parking space and because I'll always give the right of way to any driver that wants to take it from me."

"I wouldn't fight over that either."

"You won't even learn to drive."

"I'd be afraid."

"I'd take that chance. What else are you afraid of?"

"You don't want to know."

"One thing I can guess," said Yossarian, ruthlessly. "You're afraid for me. You're afraid I will die. You're afraid I'll get sick. And it's a fucking good thing you are, Michael. Because it's all going to happen, even though I pretend it won't. I've promised you seven more years of my good health, and now it's more like six. When I reach seventy-five, kiddo, you're on your own. And I'm not going to live forever, you know, even though I'm going to die trying."

"Do you want to?"

"Why not? Even when sad. What else is there?"

"When are you sad?"

"When I remember I'm not going to live forever," Yossarian joked. "And in the mornings, if I wake up alone. That happens to people, especially those like me with a predisposition to late-life depression."

"Late-life depression?"

"You'll find that out too, if you're lucky enough to last. You'll find it in the Bible. You'll see it in Freud. I'm pretty much out of interests. I wish I knew what to wish. There's this girl I'm after."

"I don't want to hear about it."

"But I'm not sure I can ever really fall in love again," Yossarian went on, despite him, knowing he was talking too much. "I'm afraid that might be gone too. There's this vile habit I've gotten into lately. No, I'm going to tell you anyway. I think of women I've known far back and try to picture what they look like now. Then I wonder why I ever went crazy over them. I've got another one I can't control, one that's even worse. When a woman turns, I always, every time now, have to look down at her backside before I can decide if she's attractive or not. I never used to do that. I don't know why I have to do it now. And they all of them almost always get too broad there. I don't think I'd ever want my friend Frances Beach to know I do that. Desire is starting to fail me, and that joy that cometh in the morning, as you'll read in the Bible—"

"I don't like the Bible," Michael interrupted.

"Nobody does. Try *King Lear* instead. But you don't like to read anything."

"It's why I decided to become an artist."

"You never really tried, did you?"

"I never really wanted to. It's much easier to want to succeed at nothing at all, isn't it?"

"No. It's good to want something. I'm finding that out. I used to wake up each day with a brain full of plans I couldn't wait to get started on. Now I wake up listless and wonder what I can find to keep me entertained. It happened overnight. One day I was old, just like that. I've run out of youth, and I'm barely sixty-nine."

Michael gazed at him with love. "Dye your hair. Dye it black if you can't get it gray. Don't wait for Adrian."

"Like Aschenbach?"

"Aschenbach?"

"Gustav Aschenbach."

"From *Death in Venice* again? I never liked that story much and can't see why you do. I bet I can tell you a few things wrong with it."

"So can I. But it remains unforgettable."

"To you."

"To you too someday, maybe."

Aschenbach too had run out of interests, although he distracted himself with his ridiculous obsession and the conceit that there was still much left for him to do. He was an artist of the intellect, who had tired of working on projects that would no longer yield to even his most patient effort, and knew he now was faking it. But he did not know that his true creative life was over and that he and his era were coming to a close, whether he liked it or not. And he was only just past fifty. Yossarian had the advantage over him there. He had never had much that he had allowed himself to enjoy. A strange nature for Yossarian to empathize with now, this man who lived like a tightened fist and began each day with the same cold shower, who worked in the morning and wished nothing more than to be able to continue his work in the evening.

"He dyed his hair black," Yossarian related, like a lecturer, "easily allowed a barber to persuade him to do that, to put makeup around his eyes for the illusion of a glisten, to color his cheeks with a touch of red, to plump up his eyebrows, to erase the age from his skin with a face cream and round out his lips with tints and with shadows, and he gave up the ghost anyway, right on the dot. And got nothing in return for his trouble but the tormenting delusion that he had fallen in love with a boy with crooked teeth and a sandy nose. Our Aschenbach could not even bring himself to die dramatically, not even of the plague. He simply bowed his head and gave up the ghost."

"I think," said Michael, "you might be trying to make it sound better than it really is."

"Maybe," said Yossarian, who felt qualms it might be so, "but that's where I stand. Here's what Mann wrote then: that a menace had hung over Europe for months."

"World War II?" Michael guessed, indulging him.

"World War I!" Yossarian corrected emphatically. "Even back then, Mann could see where this ungovernable machine we call our civilization was heading. And here's what's been my fate in this latter half of my life. I make money from Milo, whom I don't care for and condemn. And I find myself identifying in self-pity with a fictional German with no humor or any other likable trait. Soon I'll be going down deeper into PABT with McBride to find out what's there. Is that my Venice? I met a man in Paris once, a cultured book publisher, who could not bring himself ever to go to Venice, because of that story. I met another man who could not vacation for as long as a week at any resort in the mountains because of *The Magic Mountain*. He'd have the hideous dream that he was dying there and would never get away alive if he stayed, and he'd get the hell out the next day."

"Is a Minderbinder going to marry a Maxon?"

"They both have brides to offer. I've suggested M2."

"When are you going back there with McBride?"

"Soon as the President says he might come and we get permission to examine the place. When are you going with M2?"

"As soon as he's hot to look at dirty pictures again. I draw my pay from M & M too."

"If you want to live under water, Michael, you must learn to breathe like a fish."

"How do you feel about that?"

"That we never had a choice. I don't feel good about it, but I won't feel bad. It's our natural destiny, as Teemer might say. Biologically, we are a new species and haven't learned to fit into nature yet. He thinks we're cancers."

"Cancers?"

"But he likes us anyway, and he doesn't like cancer."

"I think he's crazy," Michael protested.

"He thinks so too," Yossarian replied, "and has moved into the psychiatric ward of the hospital for treatment while he continues work as an oncologist. Does that seem crazy?"

"It doesn't seem sane."

"That doesn't mean he's mistaken. We can see the social pathology. What else worries you, Michael?"

"I'm pretty much alone, I told you," said Michael. "And I'm starting to get scared. About money too. You've managed to get me worried about that."

"I'm glad I've been useful."

"I wouldn't know where to get it if I didn't have any. I couldn't even mug anybody. I don't know how."

"And would probably get mugged trying to learn."

"I can't even learn how to drive a car."

"You would do what I would do if I had no money."

"What's that, Dad?"

"Kill myself, son."

"You're a barrel of laughs, Dad."

"It's what I would do. It's no worse than dying. I couldn't learn to be poor either, and I'd sooner give up."

"What will happen to those drawings I did?"

"They'll be printed in brochures and taken to Washington for the next meeting on the plane. I may have to go there too. You made money on that one, that flying wing."

"Finishing something I never even wanted to start."

"If you want to live like a fish . . . Michael, there are things you and I won't do for money, but there are some things we have to,

or we won't have any. You've got those few more years to find
out how to take care of yourself. For Christ sakes, learn how to
drive! You can't live anywhere else if you can't do that."

"Where would I go?"

"To whoever you want to see."

"There's no one I want to see."

"To drive away from people you don't want to be with."

"I just know I'll kill somebody."

"Let's take that chance."

"You said that before. Is there really going to be a wedding at
the bus terminal? I'd like to go."

"I'll get you an invitation."

"Make it two?" Michael moved his eyes away sheepishly.
"Marlene is back in the city and needed a place for a while. She'll
probably like that."

"Arlene?"

"Marlene, the one who just left. Maybe this time she'll stay. She
says she doesn't think she'd mind if I have to work as a lawyer.
My God, a wedding in that bus terminal. What kind of people
would hold a wedding in a place like that just to get their name in
the newspapers?"

"Their kind."

"And what kind of asshole came up with a crazy notion like
that one?"

"My kind," said Yossarian, roaring. "It was your dad's idea."

19

MASSPOB

"And what does a flying wing look like?"

"Other flying wings," Wintergreen interposed adroitly, with Milo struck dumb by a query he had not anticipated.

"And what do other flying wings look like?"

"Our flying wing," answered Milo, his composure restored.

"Will it look," asked a major, "like the old Stealth?"

"No. Only in appearance."

"Absolutely, Colonel Pickering?"

"Positively, Major Bowes."

Since the first session on the M & M defensive second-strike offensive attack bomber, Colonel Pickering had elected early retirement with full pension benefits to capitalize on the opportunity for a more remunerative, if less showy, position with the Airborne Division of M & M Enterprises & Associates, where his opening yearly income was precisely half a hundred times richer than his earnings in federal employ. General Bernard Bingam, at Milo's request, was delaying a similar move in hopes of promotion and eventual elevation to the Joint Chiefs of Staff and after that, given half a break with a good war, perhaps the White House itself.

It was fortunate Pickering was there to help, for this newest session on the Minderbinder bomber was proving more prickly than the others. A hint of difficulties in store had come with the unexpected attendance of the fat man from the State Department and the skinny one from the National Security Council. It was now no secret they were partisans of the competitive Strangelove entry, and they had placed themselves on opposite ends of the curved table to project the impression they were speaking separately with independent voices.

Both were career diplomats who regularly spent time away as Strangelove Associates, replenishing with newly acquired supplies the secondhand influence and fine contacts that, with bombast, were the stock-in-trade of the Strangelove empire. Another cause of consternation for Milo was the absence of an ally he'd counted on, C. Porter Lovejoy, who was otherwise occupied, perhaps, Milo feared, at a similar meeting in MASSPOB on the Strangelove B-Ware, as an ally of that one.

General Bingam was obviously delighted to be parading his aptitudes before officers from other branches who outranked him and masters in atomic matters and related abstruse scientific areas. Bingam knew a feather in his cap when he had one. There were thirty-two others in this elite enclave, and all were eager to speak, even though there were no television cameras.

"Tell them about the technology, Milo," General Bingam suggested, to move things along advantageously.

"Let me distribute these pictures first," answered Milo, as rehearsed, "so we can see what our planes look like."

"These are lovely," said a bespectacled lieutenant colonel with experience in design. "Who drew them?"

"An artist named Yossarian."

"Yossarian?"

"Michael Yossarian. He is a specialist in military art and works exclusively for us."

Coming down as instructed from the MASSPOB basement through the door to Sub-Basement A, Milo and Wintergreen had been met by three armed MASSPOB guards in uniforms they had not seen before: red battle jackets, green pants, and black leather combat boots, with name tags in cerise letters against a lustrous fabric of silken mother-of-pearl. They were checked against a roster and replied correctly when asked the password: Bingam's Baby. They were handed round pasteboard passes with numbers in a border of blue, to be worn around the neck on a skimpy white string, and instructed to proceed directly to the Bingam's Baby conference room in Sub-Basement A, the circular chamber in which Michael's pictures were now making so auspicious an impression.

All present were reminded that the plane was a second-strike weapon designed to slip through remaining defenses and destroy weapons and command posts surviving the first strike.

"Now, everything you see in these pictures is absolutely right," continued Milo, "except those that are wrong. We don't want to show anything that will allow others to counter the technology or copy it. That make sense, General Bingam?"

"Absolutely, Milo."

"But how will any of us here know," objected the fat man from the State Department, "what it will really look like?"

"Why the fuck must you know?" countered Wintergreen.

"It's invisible," added Milo. "Why must you see it?"

"I guess we don't have to know, do we?" conceded a lieutenant general, and looked toward an admiral.

"Why do we have to know?" wondered the other.

"Sooner or later," fumed the skinny Strangelove partisan, "the press will want to know."

"Fuck the press," said Wintergreen. "Show them these."

"Are they true?"

"What the fuck difference does it fucking make if they're fucking true or not?" asked Wintergreen. "It gives them another fucking story when they find out we lied."

"Now you're talking my fucking language, sir," said the adjutant to the commandant of marines.

"And I applaud your fucking honesty," admitted a colonel. "Admiral?"

"I can live with that. Where's the fucking cockpit?"

"Inside the fucking wing, sir, with everything else."

"Will a crew of two," asked someone, "be as effective as a fucking crew of four?"

"More," said Milo.

"And what the fuck fucking difference does it fucking make if they're fucking effective or not?" asked Wintergreen.

"I get your fucking point, sir," said Major Bowes.

"I don't."

"I can live with that fucking point."

"I'm not sure I get that fucking point."

"Milo, what's your angle?"

There were no angles. The flying wing allowed the aircraft to be fabricated with rounded edges in material deflecting radar. What was being fucking offered, explained Wintergreen, was a fucking long-range airplane to roam over fucking enemy territory with only two fucking fliers. Even without midair refueling, the plane could go from there to San Francisco with a full load of bombs.

"Does this mean we could bomb San Francisco from here and get back without more gas?"

"We could bomb New York too on the way back."

"Guys, get serious," commanded the major general there. "This is war, not social planning. How many refuelings to China or the Soviet Union?"

"Two or three on the way in, maybe none coming back, if you don't get sentimental."

And just one M & M bomber could carry the same bomb load as *all thirteen* fighter-bombers used in the Ronald Reagan air raid in Libya in—in—April 1986.

"It seems like only yesterday," mused an elderly air force man dreamily.

"We can give you a plane," promised Wintergreen, "that *will* do it yesterday."

"Shhhhh!" Milo said.

"The Shhhhh!?" said the expert on military nomenclature. "That's a perfect name for a noiseless bomber."

"Then the Shhhhh! is the name of our plane. It goes faster than sound."

"It goes faster than light."

"You can bomb someone before you even decide to do it. Decide it today, it's done—yesterday!"

"I don't really think," said someone, "we have need for a plane that can bomb someone yesterday."

"But think of the potential," argued Wintergreen. "They attack Pearl Harbor. You shoot them down the day before."

"I could live with that one. How much more—"

"Wait a minute, wait a minute," begged someone else among the several now stirring rebelliously. "How can that be? Artie, can anything go faster than light?"

"Sure, Marty. Light can go faster than light."

"Read your fucking Einstein!" yelled Wintergreen.

"And our first operational plane can go on alert in the year 2000 and give you something really to celebrate."

"What happens if we get in a nuclear war before then?"

"You won't have our product. You have to wait."

"Your bomber, then, is an instrument for peace?"

"Yes. And we also have a man we'll throw in," confided Milo, "who can produce heavy water for you internally."

"I want that man! At any price!"

"Absolutely, Dr. Teller?"

"Positively, Admiral Rickover."

"And our instrument for peace can be used to dump heavy bomb loads on cities too."

"We don't like to bomb civilians."

"Yes, we do. It's cost-effective. You can also arm our Shhhhh! with conventional bombs, for surprise attacks too. The big surprise will come when there's no nuclear explosion. You can use these against friendly nations, with no lasting radiation after-effects. Will Strangelove do that?"

"What does Porter Lovejoy say?"

"Not guilty."

"I mean before his indictment."

"Buy both planes."

"Is there money for both?"

"It doesn't matter."

"I wouldn't want to tell the President that."

"We have a man who will talk to the President," volunteered Milo. "His name is Yossarian."

"Yossarian? I've heard that name."

"He's a very famous artist, Bernie."

"Sure, I know his work," said General Bingam.

"This is a different Yossarian."

"Isn't it time for another recess?"

"I may need Yossarian," muttered Milo, with his palm sheltering his mouth, "to talk to Noodles Cook. And where the fuck is that chaplain?"

"They keep moving him around, sir," whispered Colonel Pickering. "We don't know where the fuck he is."

This ten-minute recess turned out to be a five-minute recess in which six MASSPOB guards paraded in with a mulberry birthday cake for General Bernard Bingam and the papers promoting him from a brigadier general to a major general. Bingam blew out the candles on his first try and asked jovially:

"Is there anything more?"

"Yes! Definitely yes!" cried the stout man from the State Department.

"I'll say there is!" cried just as loudly the slim one from National Security.

Fat and Skinny had a race to make the most of the fact that a number of features in the M & M Shhhhh! were identical to those of the old Stealth.

"Sir, your fucking ejection seats were originally in plans for the fucking old Stealth. Our reports show these fucking seats were shredding dummies in tests."

"We can supply you," said Milo, "with all the replacement dummies you need."

Fat fell down and broke his face.

"He was concerned, I believe," interposed the Dean of Humanities and Social Work at the War College, "about the men, not the fucking dummies."

"We can supply as many men as you need too."

Skinny was muddled, and Fat was struck dumb.

"We are inquiring as to their safety, sir. Your machines, you say, can stay aloft for long periods, even years. Our machines with men aboard must be able to come back."

"Why?"

"Why?"

"Yeah, what for?"

"Why the fuck do they have to come back?"

"What the fuck is wrong with all you fucking idiots anyway?" demanded Wintergreen, with a disbelieving shake of his head. "Our plane is a second-strike weapon. Colonel Pickering, will you talk to these fucking shitheads and explain?"

"Certainly, Mr. Wintergreen. Gentlemen, what the fuck difference does it make if the fucking planes come back or not?"

"None, Colonel Pickering."

"Thank you, Major Bowes, you fuck."

"Not at all, you bastard."

"Gentlemen," said Skinny, "I want the record to show I have never in my life been called a shithead, not since I was a young boy."

"We're not keeping a record."

"Shithead."

"Asshole."

"Prick, where would they escape to?" asked Wintergreen. "Most of everything here is gone then too."

"Permit me," snarled Skinny, leaving no doubt he was bitter. "Your fucking bombers, you say, carry nuclear bombs that will penetrate the fucking earth before exploding?"

"Your fucking missiles can't do that."

"Please tell us why the fuck we would want them to."

"Well, you fucking people, in your fucking assessments, always emphasize enemy underground bunkers for their fucking political and military leaders."

"Do we fucking emphasize that?"

"Does the President play *Triage?*"

"You should read what you write."

"We don't like to read."

"We hate to read."

"We can't read what we write."

"We have bombs that will go down a hundred miles before they explode. Your present depth of planning is to live forty-two miles underground. We can fuse our bombs to detonate so far past forty-two that they won't damage anybody on our side or theirs. You can wage a nuclear war that causes no damage to life or property on earth. That's humane, isn't it? That's fucking humane, I'd say."

"I'd call that fucking humane."

"Let me get one fucking thing straight. Please, Skinny, let me get a word in. These fucking units are for a second strike by us?"

"They will go after surviving enemy units that have not been used in their first strike."

"Why would they not use them in their first strike?"

"How the fuck should I know?"

"You guarantee your planes will work?"

"They've been working more than two years now. We've had models flying back and forth that long. You must tell us now if you want to go ahead. Otherwise we'll take our fucking Shhhhh! somewhere else."

"You could not do that," said Fat. "Excuse me, Skinny, let me continue."

"It's my turn, Fat. That would be against the law."

Milo's laugh was benign. "How would you know? The planes are invisible and make no noise."

"Oh, shit, I can't believe these questions," said Wintergreen. "What the fuck difference does it make if it works or not? Its chief value is to deter. By the time it goes into action it has already failed."

"I still have a question. Let me proceed, Fat."

"It's my turn, you skinny prick."

"No, it isn't, you fat fuck."

"Don't listen to that shithead," persisted Fat. "If it's invisible and noiseless, what's to stop you from selling it to the enemy anyway?"

"Our patriotism."

And after that one, Bingam called a final recess.

"Wintergreen," whispered Milo, in the pause before they concluded, "do we really have a bomb that will go down a hundred miles before exploding?"

"We'll have to look. What about the old Stealth? Do you think they'll catch on?"

"They're not really the same. The Stealth was never built. So our Shhhhh! is newer."

"I'd say so too."

There were those on the panel who wanted more time, and others like Fat and Skinny who were insisting on a comparison check with the Strangelove B-Ware. They would need Yossarian, Milo grunted dejectedly, while the three senior military officers conferred in whispers. Bingam waited tensely. Wintergreen fumed visibly. Milo advised him to stop, since no one was watching. Finally, the rear admiral looked up.

"Gentlemen." His manner of speaking was unhurried. "We are after a weapon for the new century that will render all other armaments subsidiary and inconsequential."

"You need look no further," Milo advised hopefully.

"I myself," continued the admiral, as though he had heard nothing, "am inclined to put myself in the camp of General Bingam. Bernie, that's another feather in your cap. I want to recommend your Shhhhh! But before I put myself on record, there's a question of substance." He bent closer toward them, with his elbows on the table and his chin on clasped hands. "Your plane, Mr. Minderbinder. You must tell me honestly. If deployed in sufficient numbers, can it destroy the world?"

Milo exchanged a frantic look with Wintergreen. They chose to come clean. Wintergreen lowered his eyes while Milo responded sheepishly.

"I'm afraid not, sir," confessed Milo, with a blush. "We can make it uninhabitable, but we can't destroy it."

"I can live with that!"

"Absotively, Admiral Dewey?"

"Posilutely, General Grant."

"I'm sorry I called you a skinny prick," humbly apologized the diplomat from the Department of State.

"That's okay, you fat fuck."

BOOK
SEVEN

20

Chaplain

Each time Chaplain Albert Taylor Tappman was transferred to a new location, he felt himself still in the same place, and with good reason. The lead-lined living space to which he was confined was a railroad car, and neither before nor after each journey was he permitted to leave at will. His surroundings were no different.

The several laboratories, equipment cars, and medical examination rooms were also on wheels, as were, just past his kitchen, the carriages containing the offices and domiciles of the executive officers currently in charge of what by now had come to be called, in official parlance, the Wisconsin Project. His doors were locked and guarded by men in uniform bearing automatic assault weapons with short barrels and large ammunition clips. He had learned this about his train: there generally was no place to go but to another part of the train.

He was not permitted to dismount, except for infrequent invitations for restricted forms of recreation, which he now invariably declined. He was free to say no to that. He had never enjoyed exercise particularly and was not tempted now. While he sat in his leather easy chair, his muscle tone was improved through painless procedures of electrical stimulation. The advantages of vigorous aerobic exertions were as well obtained without effort from specialized machinery boosting his pulse beat and respiration and enlarging his blood flow. He was in hardier physical condition than before and, he noticed each morning when he shaved, looked better too.

Sometimes the travel from one place to another used up several days, and he quickly understood he was on a train with smoothly turning, quiet, tranquilizing wheels, a noiseless engine, and rails and a roadbed that were as close to perfection as anything conceived and engineered in this world could ever hope to come. He had all conveniences. His car was a pullman apartment with a walk-through bedroom and living room with gray wall-to-wall carpeting. He had a combination study–recreation room with a dark Mexican rug patterned in pink rose blossoms and white and yellow meadow flowers, on a knotty-pine floor bleached to a cream color with a patina of polyurethane. At the far end was a pullman kitchen with enough space for a table and two chairs, and there he took his meals and supplementary nourishment, always scrutinized intently as he chewed and swallowed by at least one sullen observer in a white laboratory coat, always making notes. He knew of nothing that was kept hidden from him. Everything he ate and drank was measured, sampled, analyzed, and inspected beforehand for radiation and mineral content. Somewhere nearby, he'd been informed, perhaps in another railroad car for the convenience of proximity, was at least one control group comprising individuals who consumed just what he did at the very same time, in the same portions and combinations, who did exactly as he did from morning to night. As yet there were no signs of an abnormality like his own. There were built-in Geiger counters in all his rooms, for *his* protection too, and these were tested twice daily. All the people who came near him—the chemists, physicists, medical doctors, technicians, and military officials, even the guards with their guns and the waiters who served him and cleared his table and the women who showed up to clean and help cook—wore name tags of mother-of-pearl and badges to register the stigmata of radioactivity immediately. He was still safe. They gave him everything he could ask for except the freedom to go home.

"Although?"

Although life at home, he admitted, had ceased being as pleasing as in the past, and he and his wife, overfull with television dramas, newscasts, and situation comedies, had speculated often about ways to bring back into the untroubled lives of their long marriage a greater amount of voluntary activities and pleasurable surprises. Trips abroad with tour groups had lost their flavor. They had fewer friends than before, a scarcity of energy and motivation, and their excitements and diversions resided almost wholly now in watching television and in contacts with their children and grandchildren, all of whom—they gave thanks daily for this—

continued to reside in easy traveling distance of their home in Kenosha.

The malady of mind he outlined was not uncommon among Americans of his generation, said the understanding psychiatrist in uniform sent every other day to do what he could to ameliorate the stress of the chaplain's imprisonment and at the same time, as he admitted, pry out any knowledge germane to his remarkable condition that he was not yet consciously willing to bare.

"And at age seventy-two, Chaplain, you are probably a very likely candidate for what we label late-life depression," said the qualified medical man. "Shall I tell you what I mean?"

"I've been told that before," said the chaplain.

"I'm half your age, and I'm a good candidate too, if that brings you any solace."

He missed his wife, he confided, and knew that she missed him. She was well, he was assured at least three times weekly. They were not permitted to communicate directly, not even in writing. The youngest of his three children, a mere toddler when he was overseas, was now near fifty. The children were fine, the grandchildren too.

Nevertheless, the chaplain worried about all in his family inordinately ("Pathologically?" guessed the psychiatrist discreetly. "But of course, that would be normal too") and reverted in torment obsessively to other dreads he sensed were imminent yet could not name.

That was normal too.

In spite of himself, he regressed habitually to the same insistent fantasies of disaster with which he had tortured himself in the past in the desolating shock of loneliness and loss attending his first separation from his wife and children, during his tour of duty in the army.

There were accidents again to worry about and diseases like Ewing's tumor, leukemia, Hodgkin's disease, and other cancers. He saw himself young again on Pianosa and he saw his smallest son, an infant again, die two or three times every week because his wife still had not been taught how to stop arterial bleeding; watched again in tearful, paralyzed silence his whole family electrocuted, one after the other, at a baseboard socket because he had never told her that a human body would conduct electricity; all four still went up in flames almost every night when the water heater exploded and set the two-story wooden house afire; in ghastly, heartless, revolting detail he saw his poor wife's trim and fragile younger body again crushed to a viscous pulp against the brick wall of a market building by a half-witted drunken automobile driver and watched his hysterical daughter, now again about five, six, seven, ten, or eleven, being led away from the grisly scene by a kindly middle-aged gentleman with snow-white hair who raped and murdered her time and time again as soon as he had driven her off to a deserted sandpit, while his two younger children starved to death slowly in the house after his wife's mother, who had been baby-sitting then and had long since passed away peacefully in old age from natural causes, dropped dead from a heart attack when news of his dear wife's accident was given her over the telephone.

His memories of these illusions were merciless. Nostalgic and abject, he regressed repetitiously and helplessly with a certain disappointed yearning to these earlier times of young fatherhood nearly half a century back, when he was never without misery, and never without hope.

"That's another commonplace feature of late-life depression," advised the psychiatrist, with tender appreciation. "When you get older, you might find yourself regressing to times when you were even younger. I do that already."

He wondered where his memory would end. He did not want to speak about his extraordinary vision, perhaps a miracle, of that naked man in a tree, just outside the military cemetery in Pianosa at the sad burial of a young boy named Snowden, who'd been killed in his airplane on a mission bombing bridges over Avignon in southern France. Standing at the open grave with Major Danby to the left of him and Major Major to the right, across the gaping hole in the red earth from a short enlisted man named Samuel Singer, who had been on the mission in the same plane with the deceased, he could recall again with mortifying clarity how he had faltered with a shiver in his eulogy when he lifted his eyes toward the heavens and they fell instead on the figure in the tree, halted in midsentence as though stricken speechless for the moment with all breath sucked out of him. The possibility that there really had been a naked man in a tree had still never entered his mind. He kept this memory to himself. He would not want the sensitive psychiatrist with whom he was on fine terms to conclude he was crazy.

No sign of similar divine immanence had been granted him since, although he begged for one now. Secretly, in shame, he prayed. He was not ashamed that he prayed but ashamed that someone should find out he prayed and challenge him about it. He prayed also for Yossarian to come swooping into the scene like a superman in another miracle—he could think of no one else to wish for—and set him free from the unfathomable crisis in which he was now helplessly enmeshed, so that he could go back home. Always in his lifetime he had wanted only to be home.

It was not his fault that he was passing heavy water.

At various times when not in transit he was led down the few steps from his carriage to walk briskly around it for twenty, thirty, then forty minutes, observed by armed guards positioned some distance away. Always someone paced alongside—a medical specialist, a scientist, an intelligence agent, an officer, or the general himself—and periodically there was a medical cuff on his arm to record his pressure and his pulse, and a mask with a canister covering his nose and his mouth in which his exhalations were recovered. From these sessions of exercise and exertion he perceived that he was underground at least much of the time.

Indoors in his quarters he could approach any of the windows on either side in all his rooms and see Paris, if he chose, Montmartre from the prominent rampart of the Arc de Triomphe, or a view from Montmartre enveloping the Louvre, the same triumphal arch, the Eiffel Tower, and the serpentine Seine. The receding spectacle of the rooftops was monumental too. Or he could look out a window and see, if he preferred, the Spanish city of Toledo from a choice of perspectives, the university city of Salamanca, the Alhambra, or move to Big Ben and the Houses of Parliament, or Saint Catherine's College at Oxford University. The controls on the consoles at each of the windows were simple to master. Each window was a video screen offering a virtually unlimited selection of locations.

In New York the default perspective was from a picture window on an upper floor of a high-rise apartment building. He could move about the city as expeditiously as he could move about the world. Across the avenue from the Port Authority Bus Terminal one day soon after he was taken into custody he was so positive he saw Yossarian dismounting from a taxicab that he nearly cried out his name. In Washington, D.C., he was enabled to pass indoors and window-shop in leisure in the lobby of MASSPOB and at any of the fabulous displays on the retail mezzanines. In all of his places the lighting and various colorations altered with the hours to match his own time of day. His favorite views in darkness were of the casinos in Las Vegas and of the city of Los Angeles at night from the Sunset Strip. He was free to look outside at almost any place he wanted from his windows except at what really was there. In Kenosha, Wisconsin, he had the sight of his city from the covered veranda at the front of his house and the equally reassuring picture at the back from the small patio bordering his small garden, where he was wont to sit with his wife on the swing at dusk on temperate moonlit nights and, while watching fireflies, wonder together in tristful reminiscence where all the time had gone, how fast the century had passed. His green thumb had lost its expert touch. He still loved weeding but tired quickly and was frequently discouraged by the aches in his legs and lower back from what his doctor called lumbago. Looking out the window of his train from the front of his house one time, he saw a neighbor across the street he was certain had passed away a few years before, and he was momentarily disoriented. He was stunned to think that beneath the surface of his familiar city, in which he had spent nearly his whole life, there might be this hidden, subterranean railway on which he was now an unwilling passenger.

By this time, everything and, though most did not know it, everyone in a broad vicinity surrounding the chaplain's home in Kenosha had been looked at, inspected, examined, and investigated by the most discerning and discriminating of advanced instruments and techniques: the food, the drinking water from wells and the reservoir, the air they breathed, the sewage, the garbage. Every flush of a toilet was logged for analysis, and every disposal by a home garbage disposal unit. There was no evidence yet of a contamination related however remotely to the one of which he himself was still uniquely the possessor. Nowhere in Kenosha was a molecule to be found of deuterium oxide, or, in plainer language, heavy water.

"It began as a urinary problem," Chaplain Albert Taylor Tappman repeated still one more time.

"I've had those too," revealed the psychiatrist, and emitted a sigh. "But not, of course, like yours. If I had, I suppose I would be in quarantine here with you. You really don't know how you do it, or what you did to start it?"

The chaplain said so again with an apologetic stammer. He sat with his soft fists resting on his thighs, and this doctor seemed to believe him. His doctor at home had sensed something not normal right away and had taken a second specimen.

"I don't know, Albert. It still feels funny to me, sort of heavy."

"What's it mean, Hector?"

"I'm not sure, but I don't think you're allowed to do what you're doing without a government license. Let's see what the laboratory says. They might have to report it."

In no time at all the government agents moved into his house and swarmed all through it; then came the chemists, the physicists, the radiologists and urologists, the endocrinologists and gastroenterologists. In short order he was plumbed medically by every conceivable kind of specialist and environmentalist in a determined and comprehensive effort to find out where that extra hydrogen neutron was coming from in every molecule of water he passed. It was not in his perspiration. That was clean, as were the fluids everywhere else inside him.

Then came the interrogations, mannerly at first, then abusive and filled with connotations of brutality. Had he been drinking liquid hydrogen? Not to his knowledge. Oh, he would know it if he had been. He'd be dead.

"Then why are you asking me?"

It was a trick question, they crowed, cackling. They all smoked cigarettes and their hands were yellow. Liquid oxygen? He wouldn't even know where to get it.

He would have to know in order to drink it.

He didn't even know what it was.

Then how could he be sure he had not been drinking it?

They put that one down for the record too. It was another trick question.

"And you fell for it, Chaplain. That was good, Ace. Right, Butch?"

"You said it, Slugger."

There were three, and they insisted on knowing whether he had friends, wives, or children in any of the countries formerly behind the iron curtain or had any now in the CIA.

"I don't have any in the CIA either," said the psychiatrist. "I don't know how I'd defend myself if I did."

Right off, they had confiscated his passport and tapped his telephone. His mail was intercepted, his bank accounts were frozen. His safe-deposit box was padlocked. Worst of all, they had taken away his Social Security number.

"No checks?" exclaimed the psychiatrist in horror.

The checks were continuing, but the Social Security number was gone. Without it, he had no identity.

The psychiatrist went ashen and trembled. "I can guess how you must feel," he commiserated. "I couldn't live without mine. And you really can't tell them how you do it?"

The chemical physicists and physical chemists ruled out an insect bite. The entomologists agreed.

At the beginning, people on the whole tended to be kind and patronizing and to handle him considerately. The medical men approached him amiably as both a curiosity and opportunity. In short order, however, the sociability of all but the psychiatrist and the general grew strained and thinner. Accumulating frustration shortened tolerance. Tempers turned raw and the consultations turned adversarial. This was especially true with the intelligence agents. They were not from the FBI and not from the CIA but from someplace deeper under cover. His inability to illuminate insulted, and he was censured for an obstinate refusal to yield explanations that he did not possess.

"You are being willful," said the biggest of the bullying interrogators.

"The reports all agree," said the thin, mean-looking, swarthy one with a sharp, crooked nose, manic eyes that seemed ignited by hilarity, small, irregular teeth stained brown with nicotine, and almost no lips.

"Chaplain," said the chubby one, who smiled and winked a lot with no hint of merriment and always smelled sourly of beer. "About radiation. Have you been, before we brought you here—and we want the truth, buddy boy, we'd rather have nothing if we can't have the truth, got that?—had you been absorbing radiation illegally?"

"How would I know, sir? What is illegal radiation?"

"Radiation that you don't know about and we do."

"As opposed to what?"

"Radiation that you don't know about and we do."

"I'm confused. I don't hear a difference."

"It's implied, in the way we say it."

"And you missed it. Add that one to the list."

"You got him on that one. By the balls, I'd say."

"That's enough, Ace. We'll continue tomorrow."

"Sure, General."

There was palpable insolence in the manner in which Ace spoke to the general, and the chaplain was embarrassed.

The officer in overall charge of the Wisconsin Project was General Leslie R. Groves, of the earlier Manhattan Project, which had developed the first atom bombs in 1945, and he gave every indication of being genuinely solicitous, warmhearted, and shielding. By now the chaplain was comfortable with him. He had learned much from General Groves about the rationale warranting his despotic incarceration and ceaseless surveillance, as well as the differences between fission and fusion and the three states of hydrogen with which he appeared to be meddling, or which were meddling with him. After hydrogen 1, there was deuterium, with an extra neutron in each atom, which combined with oxygen to form heavy water. And then came tritium, the radioactive gas with two extra neutrons, which was used as paint in self-illuminating gauges and clock faces, including those of the new line of novelty pornographic bedroom clocks that overnight had captured the lustful fancy of the nation, and to boost the detonating process in thermonuclear devices like hydrogen bombs containing lithium deuteride, a deuterium compound. The earliest of these bombs, set off in 1952, had produced a destructive force one thousand times greater—*one thousand times* greater, emphasized General Groves—than the bombs dropped on Japan. And where did that deuterium come from? Heavy water.

And he'd been flushing his away.

"What have you been doing with mine?"

"Sending it out to be turned into tritium," answered General Groves.

"See what you've been pissing away, Chaplain?"

"That will do now, Ace."

With General Groves at his side, the chaplain had stepped down once from his pullman apartment onto a small playground with squares of white concrete in back of a blank-faced pebblestone building with a cross on top that looked like an ancient Italian church. There was a basketball hoop and backboard raised on a wooden beam whose dark varnish looked recent and the pattern of a shuffleboard court on the ground in paint of flat green. A soccer ball in black and white stitched sections that gave it the look of a large molecular model primed to explode lay in the center as though waiting to be kicked. In a corner was a sun-browned vendor at a souvenir stand featuring picture postcards, newspapers, and sailors' hats of ocean blue with white piping and white letters spelling the word VENEZIA, and the chaplain wondered aloud if they really were in Venice. The general said they were not but that it made a nice change to think so. Despite the illusion of sky and fresh air, they were still indoors, underground.

The chaplain did not want to play basketball or shuffleboard or to kick the soccer ball and wanted no souvenirs. The two walked around the railroad car for forty minutes, with General Groves setting a fairly energetic pace.

Another time, after they had dismounted near a small underpass going off on a course perpendicular to their tracks, he heard dim, tiny gunpowder reports, like those of small firecrackers, sounding somewhere from a hollow distance inside. It was a shooting gallery. The chaplain did not choose to try his luck and perhaps win a stuffed teddy bear. He did not want to pitch pennies on the chance of winning a coconut. He heard also from inside that space the music of a carousel and then the alternating roaring rise and fall of the squealing steel wheels and wrenching cars of a roller-coaster in motion. No, the chaplain had never been to Coney Island or heard of George C. Tilyou's Steeplechase Amusement Park, and he had no wish to go there now. He had no desire either to meet Mr. Tilyou himself or to visit his resplendent carousel.

General Groves shrugged. "You seem sunk in apathy," he offered with some pity. "Nothing seems to interest you, not television comedy, news, or sports events."

"I know."

"Me neither," said the psychiatrist.

It was on the third trip back to his home in Kenosha that the first of the food packages from Milo Minderbinder was delivered to him. After that these parcels came every week on the same day. The gift card never changed:

> WHAT'S GOOD FOR MILO MINDERBINDER
> IS GOOD FOR THE COUNTRY.

The contents did not alter either. Neatly placed in a bed of excelsior were a new Zippo cigarette lighter, a packet of sterile swabs on sticks of pure Egyptian cotton, a fancy candy box containing one pound of M & M's premium chocolate-covered Egyptian cotton candy, a dozen eggs from Malta, a bottle of Scotch whisky from a distiller in Sicily, all made in Japan, and souvenir quantities of pork from York, ham from Siam, and tangerines from New Orleans, which also originated in the Orient. The chaplain gave consent when General Groves suggested he donate the package to people above who still had nowhere to live. The chaplain was surprised the first time.

"Are there homeless in Kenosha now?"

"We are not in Kenosha now," answered General Groves, and moved to the window to press the location button.

They were in New York again, looking out past the bootblacks and the sidewalk carts of the food vendors with their smoking charcoal fires lining the streets near the front entrance to the bus terminal, looking past the PABT building to the two barren architectural towers of the World Trade Center, still possibly the tallest commercial structures in the universe.

Another time, while certain he was in MASSPOB in Washington, the chaplain saw by default mode that he was inside PABT, parked somewhere below while they switched engines and laboratory cars. He was able to gaze out through his window even into the Operations Control Center of the terminal and tie into any of the video screens there, to watch the buses arrive and depart, the diurnal tides of people, the undercover policemen who dressed like drug dealers and drug dealers who dressed like undercover policemen, the prostitutes, addicts, and runaways, the sordid, torpid couplings and other squalid acts of community life in the emergency stairwells, and even to peek inside the different washrooms to see humans peeing and doing laundry and, if he wanted to, inside the toilet cubicles themselves to observe the narcotic injections, oral sex, and defecations. He did not want to. He had television sets that could bring in programs with excellent reception on three hundred and twenty-two channels, but he found it was not fun to watch anything without his wife watching with him. Television was not much fun when they were together either, but they could at least fix their faces on the common point of the set while they fished around for something new to talk about that might lighten the lethargy. This was old age. He was still merely just past seventy-two.

Another time in New York he looked through his window at the Metropolitan Museum of Art at an hour when a meeting of ACACAMMA was disbanding, and he was certain again that he saw Yossarian leaving in the company of an elderly woman in fashionable dress and a man taller than both, and he wanted to cry out again, for this time he observed a man with red hair and a green rucksack eyeing the three craftily and falling in behind them, and then two other men, with brighter orange hair, following also, and behind them came still another man, who unmistakably was following them all. He distrusted his eyes. He felt he must be seeing things again, like that time of the vision of the man in the tree.

"And what is that other noise I continue to hear?" the chaplain finally inquired of General Groves, when they were rolling again and moving out of the city.

"You mean of water? That stream or river?"

"I hear it often. Maybe all the time."

"I can't say."

"You don't know?"

"My orders are to tell you everything I do know. That one is out of my jurisdiction. It's more secret and lower down. We know from our sonar that it's a fairly narrow, slow-moving body of water and that small boats without power, maybe rowboats, come by on it regularly, moving always in one direction. There's music too. The pieces have been identified as the prelude and wedding march from the third act of the opera *Lohengrin*." And faintly underlying that music, from someplace deeper, was an unrelated children's chorus of anguish that the government musicologists had not yet been able to identify. Germany was consulted and was in anguish also over the existence in performance of a choral piece of advanced musical complexity, perhaps genius, of which they knew nothing. "The water is on my papers as the river Rhine. That's all I know."

"The Rhine River?" The chaplain was awed.

"No. The river Rhine. We are not in Germany now."

They were back in the nation's capital.

There was no good reason to doubt General Groves, who made a noticeable point of being present at all the sessions with Ace, Butch, and Slugger. The chaplain understood that even the general's friendship might be no more than a calculated tactic in a larger strategy involving a clandestine plot with the three intelligence men, of whom he was most in fear. There was no way of knowing anything, he knew, not even that there was no way of knowing anything.

"I often feel that same way," the general was quick to agree, when he voiced his misgivings.

"Me too," admitted the psychiatrist.

Was the sympathizing psychiatrist also a trick?

"You've no right to do this to me," the chaplain protested to General Groves when they were again alone. "I think I know that much."

"You're mistaken, I'm afraid," answered the general. "I think you'll find that we have a right to do to you anything you can't stop us from doing. In this case, it's both legal and regular. You were a member of the army reserves. They've simply called you back into service."

"But I was discharged from the reserves," responded the chaplain with triumph. "I have the letter to prove it."

"I don't think you do anymore, Chaplain. And it doesn't show in our records."

"Oh, yes it does," said the chaplain, gloating. "You can find it in my Freedom of Information file. I saw it there with my own eyes."

"Chaplain, when you look again, you'll find it's been blacked out. You're not completely innocent, you know."

"Of what am I guilty?"

"Of offenses the intelligence agents don't know about yet. Why won't you say that you're guilty?"

"How can I say if they won't tell me what they are?"

"How can they tell you if they don't know? To begin with," General Groves went on, in a more instructive tone, "there's this thing with the heavy water you're producing naturally and won't say how."

"I don't know how," protested the chaplain.

"It's not I who don't believe you. Then there's this second thing, with a man named Yossarian, John Yossarian. You paid him a mysterious visit in New York as soon as we found out about this. That's one of the reasons they picked you up."

"There was nothing mysterious about it. I went to see him when all of this started to happen. He was in a hospital."

"What was wrong with him?"

"Nothing. He wasn't sick."

"Yet in a hospital? Try to imagine, Albert, how most of this sounds. He was in that hospital at the same time a Belgian agent with throat cancer was there. That man is from Brussels, and Brussels is the center of the EEC. Is that coincidence too? He has cancer of the throat but doesn't get better and doesn't die. How come? In addition, there are these coded messages about him to your friend Yossarian. They go out to him four or five times a day from this woman who pretends she just likes to talk to him on the telephone. I've not met a woman like that. Have you? Now his kidney is failing again, she says, just yesterday. Why should his kidney be failing and not yours? You're the one with the heavy water. I have no opinion. I don't know any more about these

things than I do about the prelude to Act III of *Lohengrin* or a
chorus of children singing in anguish. I'm giving you the questions
raised by others. There's even a deep suspicion the Belgian is with
the CIA. There's even some belief that *you're* CIA."

"I'm not! I swear I've never been with the CIA!"

"I'm not the one you have to convince. These messages go out
from the hospital through Yossarian's nurse."

"Nurse?" cried the chaplain. "Is Yossarian ill?"

"He is fit as a fiddle, Albert, and in better shape than you or I."

"Then why does he have a nurse?"

"For carnal gratification. They have been indulging themselves
in sexual congress one way or another now four or five times a
week"—the general looked down punctiliously at a line graph on
his lap to make absolutely sure—"in his office, in her apartment,
and in his apartment, often on the floor of the kitchen with the
water running or on the floor of one of the other rooms, beneath
the air conditioner. Although I see on this chart that the frequency
of libidinous contact is diminishing sharply. The honeymoon may
be ending. He no longer sends her long-stemmed red roses often
or talks as much about lingerie, according to this latest Gaffney
Report."

The chaplain was squirming beneath these accumulating personal details. "Please."

"I'm merely trying to fill you in." The general turned to another
page. "And then there's this secret arrangement you seem to have
with Mr. Milo Minderbinder that you have not seen fit to mention."

"Milo Minderbinder?" The chaplain's reaction was one of in-
credulity. "I know him, of course. He sends these packages. I don't
know why. I was in the war with him, but I haven't seen or spoken
to him in almost fifty years."

"Come, Chaplain, come." Now the general feigned a look of
exaggerated disappointment. "Albert, Milo Minderbinder claims
ownership of you, has a patent pending on you, has registered a
trademark for your brand of heavy water, with a halo, no less. He
has offered you to the government in conjunction with a contract
for a military airplane for which he is vying, and he receives
weekly a very, very hefty payment for every pint of heavy water
we extract from you. You're amazed?"

"I've never heard any of this before!"

"Albert, he'd have no right to do that on his own."

"Leslie, now I'm sure I've got you." The chaplain came near to smiling. "You said just a while ago that people have a right to do whatever we can't stop them from doing."

"That's true, Albert. But in practice, it's an argument we can use and you cannot. We can go through all of this again at the weekly review tomorrow afternoon."

At the weekly assembly conducted every Friday, it was the general himself who got wind first of the newest development.

"Who farted?" he asked.

"Yeah, what is that smell?"

"I know it," said the chemical physicist on duty that week. "It's tritium."

"Tritium?"

The Geiger counters in the room were clicking. The chaplain dropped his eyes. An appalling transformation had just come to pass. There was tritium in his flatulence.

"That changes the game, Chaplain," the general reproved him gravely. Every test and procedure would have to be repeated and new ones initiated. "And immediately check everyone in all the other groups."

None of the people in any of the control groups were blowing anything out their asses but the usual methane and hydrogen sulfide.

"I almost hate to send this news on," said the general with gloom. "From now on, Chaplain, no more farting around."

"And no more pissing against the wall."

"That will do, Ace. Does it not strike you as odd," General Groves inquired philosophically one week later at the freewheeling brainstorming symposium, "that it should be a man of God who might be developing within himself the thermonuclear capability for the destruction of life on this planet?"

"No, of course not."

"Why should it?"

"Are you crazy?"

"What's wrong with you?"

"Who else would it be?"

"They molest altar boys, don't they?"

"Shouldn't the force that created the world be the one to end it?"

"It would be even odder," concurred the general, after weighing these contemplations, "if it were anyone else."

21
Lew

It's this feeling nauseous I don't like anymore. By now I can tell the difference. If I think it's nothing, it goes away. If I think it's something, the remission is over and the relapse is back. I'll soon be scratching myself in different places and sweating at night and running a fever. I can tell before anyone if I'm losing weight. The wedding ring gets loose on my finger. I like a few drinks every night before dinner, that same old kid's blend people laugh at now of Carstairs whiskey and Coke, a C & C. If I feel pain after drinking alcohol, in my neck again or shoulders or in my abdomen now, I know it's time to phone the doctor and start hoping it's not into the city again for another round with Teemer and maybe into his hospital for another session with one of his radiation sharpshooters. I always let Claire know when I feel something is up. I don't give her false scares. Heartburn is easy. That comes from eating too much. The nausea I'm tired of comes with the sickness and comes with the cure. There's no mistaking it. When I think of the nausea I think of my mother and her green apples. To my mind they taste like what I taste when I'm nauseous. One time as a kid I had an abscessed ear that was lanced at home by a specialist who came to the house with Dr. Abe Levine, and she told us, me and the doctors and anyone else around, that I must have been eating her green apples again. Because that's what you got when you ate green apples. I have to smile when I think of the old girl. She was cute, even toward the end, when she was not always all there. She would remember my name. She had trouble recognizing the others, even the old man, with his watery eyes, but not me. "Louie," she would call quietly. "Boychik. Loualeh. *Kim aher to der momma.*"

By now I've grown sick of feeling sick.

Sammy gets a kick out of hearing me put it that way, so I always make sure to say it every time I see him, just to give him a laugh, when he's up here on another visit or in the city sometimes when we come in to go out. We go into the city for an evening now and then just to prove we still can. We don't know anyone who lives there anymore but him and one of my daughters. I'll go to plays with Claire and try hard not to sleep while I pretend to keep interested in what's happening on the stage. Or I'll sit with Sammy and eat or drink while she goes to museums or art galleries with my daughter Linda or alone. Sometimes Sammy brings along a nice woman with a good personality, but it's easy to see there's nothing hot going on. Winkler calls from California every few weeks just to see how things are and to tell me who died out there we know and to get the latest on people we're still in touch with here. He's selling shoes now, real leather shoes, he tells me, to stores in big chains with shoe departments, and using the cash flow from the shoes to tide him over the slow seasons with his chocolate eggs and Easter bunnies. He's doing something else I don't want to know more about, with overstocks of frozen foods, mainly meats. Sammy still gets a smile out of Marvelous Marvie's business enterprises too. Sammy doesn't seem to have much to enjoy himself with since he's been living alone in that new high-rise apartment building of his. He still doesn't know what to do with his time, except for that work raising money for cancer relief. He's got a good pension from his *Time* magazine, he says, and had money put away, so that's not a problem. I give him ideas. He doesn't move.

"Go to Las Vegas and play with some hookers awhile."

Claire even approves of that one. I'm still crazy about her. Her breasts are still big and look as good as new since she had them prettied up again. Or he could go to Bermuda or the Caribbean and find a nice secretary on vacation to treat like a princess. Or to Boca Raton for a nifty middle-aged widow or divorced woman past fifty who really wants to remarry.

"Sammy, you really ought to think about getting married again. You're not the kind who can live alone."

"I used to."

"Now you're too old," Claire tells him. "You really can't cook a thing, can you?"

We forget that Sammy is still shy with women until the ice is broken and doesn't know how to pick up a girl. I tell him I'll go with him when I'm better and help him find some we like.

"I'll come too," says Claire, who's always ready to go off anywhere. "I can sound them out and spot the cuckoos."

"Sammy," I press him, "get up off your ass and take a trip around the world. We ain't kids anymore, you and me, and the time might be short to start doing things we always thought we wanted to. Don't you want to go to Australia again and see that friend of yours there?"

Sammy got to go everywhere when he was moved into the international division of that Time Incorporated job he used to have and still knows people in different places.

I'm even thinking myself I might be willing to take a trip around the world once I get my weight back this time, because Claire would like that. Lately, I enjoy seeing all of them get the things they want.

Maybe it's my age too, along with the Hodgkin's, but I feel better knowing they'll all be left okay when I'm gone. At least for a start. Now that Michael is a CPA in a place he likes, they all seem set. Claire still has her face and her figure, thanks to the trips to the health farms and the secret nips and tucks she sneaks away for every now and then. Along with all else, I've got a good piece of beach property in Saint Maarten just right for development that's in her name too, and another piece in California she doesn't know about yet, even though that's in her name also. I've got more than one safe-deposit box, with things inside she's not been taught to handle yet. I wish she were better at arithmetic, but Michael's there now to help her with that part, and Andy in Arizona has got some business sense too. Michael seems to know his stuff, along with a number of things he learned from me I know they didn't teach him in accounting school. I trust my lawyer and my other people as long as I'm around to make sure they know what I want and see they do it right away, but after that I wouldn't bet. They get lazy. Emil Adler has gotten lazy with age too and is quick to pass you on to another kind of specialist. The kids have all given him up for new doctors of their own. I'm training Claire to be tougher with lawyers than I am, to be independent.

"Bring in anyone else you want to anytime you like. You can handle it all for me from now on. Don't let them brush you off for a second. We don't owe them anything. They're sure to ask for it anytime we do."

None in my family gamble, not even on the stock market. And only Andy has a taste for extravagant things, but he married well, a nice-looking girl with good personality, and seems to be solidly settled in partnership with his father-in-law in a couple of lively automobile dealerships in Tempe and Scottsdale in Arizona. But he'll never be able to afford a divorce, which might be good, and she will. I own a piece of his share, but that's already been made over to him. Susan has children nearby and is married to a well-mannered carpenter I helped put into building houses, and so far that seems to be working out okay too. Linda is set for life in a teaching job that gives her long vacations and a good pension. She knows how to attract men and maybe she'll marry again. I sometimes wish that Michael was more like me, bolder, had more force of character, asserted himself more loudly and more often, but that could be my doing, and Claire thinks that maybe it is.

"Lew, what else?" she says, when I ask. "You're not an easy act to follow."

"I wouldn't be happy if I thought I was."

Claire won't cooperate when I want to talk about my estate plans and refuses to listen for long.

"Sooner or later—" I tell her.

"Make it later. Change the subject."

"I don't enjoy it either. Okay, I'll change the subject. Eight percent interest on a hundred-thousand-dollar investment will bring you how much a year?"

"Not enough for the new house I want to buy! Lew, for God sakes, will you stop? Have a drink instead. I'll fix it."

She's got more confidence in Teemer now than I have and than he seems to have in himself. Dennis Teemer has moved into the nut ward of his hospital, he tells me, for treatment, although he keeps the same office hours and hospital practice. That sounds crazy to me. So maybe he does know what he's doing, as Sammy says in a wisecrack. When Emil can't help me in the hospital up here, I start going back into the city to Teemer, to be MOPPed up again with those injections that give me that nausea I hate, at least one time a week, at best. MOPP is the name of the mixture in the chemotherapy they give me now, and Teemer lets me think the "mopped up" joke I made is original with me and that he's still never heard it from anyone else.

By now I hate going back to him. I'm in dread and I'm weary. I have to, Emil tells me, and I know that too. By now I think I hate

Teemer also. But not enough to break his back. He's become the disease. There's always gloom in his waiting room. When Claire doesn't bring me, I go down and back in the black or pearl-gray limousine from the car service with the same driver, this guy Frank, from Venice, and going in is a drag too. From Teemer's office, to get back uptown to go home or the hospital, you have to ride past that funeral parlor near the corner, and I don't like that part either. There's almost always at least one attendant waiting outside, looking too tidy to be normal, and usually a guy with a knapsack and a walking stick, who must work there, he looks like a hiker, and they eye each car that slows down for the intersection. They eye me too.

By now I'm scared of going back inside Teemer's hospital, but I'll never let it show. With Sammy's Glenda gone and Winkler and his wife living in California, Claire has to stay in a hotel, alone or with one of the girls, and that's not much fun for her. It's the nausea that's going to put me away. I remember what it feels like, and that makes me nauseous too. I'm tired a lot, tired from age, I guess, and tired from the ailment, and by now, I think, I really *am* sick of . . . *it!* I worry about that time coming up when I go into the hospital and can't make it out on my own feet.

No one has to tell me I've lived longer than any of us thought I would. And nobody does. If anyone tried to, I think I would jump right up like the Lew Rabinowitz from Coney Island of old and really break a back. Teemer thinks I'm setting some kind of record. I tell him *he* is. The last time I was in to see him he had a bone man look at a CAT scan of my leg that turned out to be all right. They're starting to think it could have come from a virus. That's okay with me. It makes no difference to Teemer, who would have to deal with it the same way, but it cheers me to know I might not be passing it along as something hereditary. My kids get symptoms when I do. I can tell by their faces when they talk to me. They look nauseous. And they think of running right off to a doctor every time they feel queasy or wake up with a stiff neck. I'm not the unluckiest person who ever lived, but I don't think that makes any difference now.

I'm not young anymore. I have to remember that. I keep forgetting, because between spells I feel as good as ever and can find more ways to have fun than most people I know. But when Marty Kapp died on a golf course in New Jersey and then Stanley Levy did from a heart attack too, and David Goodman almost did at only thirty-eight, and Betty Abrams died of cancer in Los Angeles and Lila Gross from cancer here, and Mario Puzo had a triple bypass and Casey Lee too, and Joey Heller got that paralysis from that crazy Guillain-Barré syndrome no one ever heard of and has to consider now how much his weakened muscles will weaken as he gets older, I had to start getting used to the idea that time was closing in on Lew Rabinowitz too, that I had reached the age where even healthy people got sick and died, and I was not going to live forever either. I picked up a taste for French wines along with my appetite for cheeses on our Caribbean vacations in Martinique and Guadeloupe, and Claire hasn't noticed that I've begun opening all our better ones. I'm emptying my wine cellar. It's harder for me to score a lot of money now than it used to be, and maybe that's another sign I've gotten older. Each time we go someplace now we both take more bottles of different medicines with us. It was easy to see that things like my personal plumbing were going to just stop working right and that sooner or later the serious ailments were going to start piling in. I already had one of mine.

Way back, I never felt that way, that life for me ever could be short, not even in the army in my infantry combat in Europe. I knew there was danger, I saw it right off the bat, but I never thought it could touch me. Coming through in August as a replacement into a French town called Falaise after the big battle there, I saw enough dead Germans rotting in stacks on the ground to last me a lifetime. I saw dozens more before I was through. I saw dead Americans. I saw Eisenhower there reviewing the victory scene, and I thought he looked sick too. In a town called Grosshau past Belgium at the German border near another town, called Hürtgen, I was standing no more than two feet away from Hammer, who was telling me the Germans had pulled out and the place was clear, when he was hit by a sniper in the back of the head. He was still reporting it was safe when he fell forward into my arms and sank down into the snow. It didn't surprise me that it was him, not me. I took for granted I would always be lucky. It turned out I was right. Even in the prison camp I was lucky and not really afraid. The day we finally got there after that miserable train trip and were put on line to be registered in, I saw this cold-looking skinny officer in a clean uniform staring at another Jewish prisoner, named Siegel, in a way I didn't like, and without even thinking I decided to speak up and do something. I was filthy like the rest, lousy, dead tired too, and stank of diarrhea also, but I moved to the officer, making myself look timid, and smiling very politely asked him:

"*Bist Du auch Jude?*"

His mouth opened and he gaped at me like I was mad. I've never seen anyone look more surprised. I have to laugh again when I think of it. I don't think he'd been asked very often in his German army if he also was Jewish.

"*Sag das noch einmal,*" he ordered sharply. He couldn't believe it.

I did what he told me and said it again. Shaking his head, he began to chuckle to himself, and he tossed me a hard biscuit from a small pack he was holding.

"No, I'm afraid not," he answered in English, with a laugh. "Why do you wish to know if I am Jewish?"

Because I was, I told him in German, and showed him that letter J on my dog tags. My name was Rabinowitz, Lewis Rabinowitz, I went on, and then added something I wanted him to think about. "And I can speak German a little."

He snickered again with a look like he couldn't believe me and then drifted away and left us alone.

"Hey, buddy, are you crazy?" said a tall guy behind me with curly, rusty hair, whose name was Vonnegut and who later wrote books. He couldn't believe it either.

They would have found out anyway at the front of the line, I figured.

I was still not afraid.

I was in love with my gun from the first day I had one, and nobody ever had to remind me to keep it clean. After all that junk in the old man's junkshop, it was something like heaven to find myself with a machine like new that worked and could be put to good use. I had great faith in all my guns. When I came into the squad overseas as a new guy and a replacement, I was happy to take the BAR, that Browning automatic rifle, even after I noticed the guys who knew better shying away from it and soon found out why. The man with the firepower was the one who would draw it. It was best never to fire at all unless we had to. I learned that one fast too. The man who gave our position away when there was nothing more important to shoot at than just another German soldier risked being battered around by the rest of us. I had faith in my guns, but I can't remember that I had to fire them much. As a corporal first and then a squad leader, I mostly told the rest of the twelve where to put themselves and what to go for. We were pushing forward into France toward Germany, and it's a fact that we did not often see the human figures we were shooting at until they were dead and we passed them lying stiff on the ground. That part was eerie. We saw empty space, we spotted gun bursts and directed fire there, we shrank from tanks and armored cars, and hugged ground from artillery shells; but in our own platoon we almost never laid eyes on the people we were warring with, and when they weren't charging or bombarding us, it was almost like being back in a Coney Island shooting gallery or a penny arcade.

Except it wasn't always much fun. We were wet, we were cold, we were dirty. The others had a tendency to huddle up together under barrages, and I had to keep bellowing at them to spread out and get away from me and each other, like they were supposed to. I didn't want anybody too close fouling up my own bright destiny.

I came as a replacement into a platoon already filled with replacements, and it didn't take long to figure out what that meant. No one lasted long. The only one I met who had lasted from D day was Buchanan, my sergeant, and he was losing his grip by the time I got there and was cut down later by machine gun fire in a dash from cover to some hedges across the road in this town of Grosshau in the Hürtgen forest that was supposed to be clear. Then there was David Craig, who had landed in Normandy on D day plus nine and took out the Tiger tank, and he was soon in a hospital with a leg wound from artillery outside a place called Luneville.

By the time of the tank, Buchanan did not know what to do when he got the order and he looked at me. I could see the poor guy was shaking. We had no guns with us that would pierce a Tiger. The tank had pinned down the rest of our platoon.

I made the call. "Who's got the bazooka?" I asked, and looked around. "David? Craig? You'll go. Slip through the street through the houses and come up on the back or side."

"Aw, shit, Lew!" By then he'd had enough too.

Aw, shit, I thought, and said, "I'll go with you. I'll handle the shells. Find out where to hit." A rocket from a bazooka would not go through a Tiger's armor plate either.

The instructions were good. Put a shell in the seam of the turret of the cannon. Put another in the tracks if we could, from no more than a hundred feet away. I carried four shells. Once past the houses and outside the village, we followed a gully with a thin stream of green water until we came to a bend, and then it was there, straddling the ditch, no more than thirty feet in front of us. All sixty tons of that big thing right up above us, with a soldier with binoculars in the open hatch, wearing a smile I couldn't stand that made that nerve in the side of my jaw turn tight and start to tick. We made not a sound. I put a finger to my lips anyway, slipped in a shell and wired it up. Craig had hunted in Indiana. He landed right on target. The binoculars flew when the rocket shell exploded, and the German dropped down out of sight with his head limp. The tank started backing. The second shot hit the tracks and the wheels stopped turning. We watched long enough to see the guys from the rest of the platoon drop grenades down inside as they went charging past, and soon that whole thing was on fire.

Craig and I were put in for a Bronze Star for that one. He was wounded in the thigh from a tree burst outside that place called Luneville before he could get his, and I was a prisoner of war before I got mine. On the ground on the other side of me about five yards away when Craig got hit was a dead kid with his head opened by that same shell, and I wasn't touched. The tree burst got eight of our twelve.

That German soldier in the tank was the one German soldier I ever saw who wasn't dead or a prisoner, except for the ones who captured me, and those looked good as new.

Snow fell in December in the Hürtgen forest, and we knew we would not be home for Christmas. David Craig might be, but not us.

In the middle of the month we were packed up in a hurry in a convoy of troop trucks to be shipped south as reinforcements to a regiment outside a different forest, near a town called Ardennes. When we got there and dismounted, a captain was waiting in the clearing to greet us, and as soon as we were assembled to hear him, he announced:

"Men, we're surrounded."

We had a funny guy named Brooks then, and he started yelling: "Surrounded? How can we be surrounded? We just got here. How could we get here if we're all surrounded?"

It was true, it turned out. The Germans had broken through that forest, and it wasn't so funny.

And the next day we found out, only by being told, that we'd surrendered, all of us, the whole regiment.

How could that be? We were armed, we were there, we were equipped. But someone in back had surrendered us all. We were to lay down our arms in a pile on the ground and just wait to be taken in as prisoners. That made no sense.

"Captain, can we try to get back?" someone called out nervously.

"When I turn my back, I'm no longer in command."

"Which way should we go?"

No one knew the answer to that.

Ten of us piled into a light-duty truck with the two drivers who'd brought us there and we took off. We gassed up at the motor pool, that's how calm things were there. We took extra woolen shawls for the face and the neck, dry socks. We had rifles, carbines, and grenades. Inside my shirt against my heavy army underwear I had cartons of food rations, cigarettes, packets of Nescafé, sugar, matches, my good old reliable Zippo lighter to help start fires, a couple of candles.

We didn't get far.

We didn't even know where we were going. We headed away on the road we'd come in on and turned left onto a wider road when we hit an intersection, thinking we were heading back west toward our own lines. But then the road veered around and we saw we were going north again. We followed other cars. The snowfall turned thick. We began passing jeeps, staff cars, and trucks that had skidded off into drifts and been left there. Then we came to others that had been battered and burned. Some were still smoking. Windows had been shattered. We saw some with bodies. We heard rifle fire, mortars, machine guns, horns, strange whistles. When our own truck fishtailed off into an embankment, we left it and split up into smaller groups to try to go for it separately on foot.

I sloshed off to one side of the road, over the grade and down into the cover of the other side, slipping and sliding as I trudged along as fast as I could move. Two others came with me. Soon we heard cars, dogs, then voices calling orders in German. We moved apart and hid on the ground. They had no trouble finding us. They came right up to us from out of the whirl of snowflakes and had us at gunpoint before we could even make them out. They were dressed in white uniforms that merged into the background, and everything they carried looked brand-new. While we looked like dog shit, as this guy Vonnegut said when I met up with him in the train station and then later put into a book he wrote, Claire told me, and so did the kids.

They caught all of us, all twelve, and had a few hundred more we joined up with as they moved us along. They herded us onto trucks that drove across a river I later found out was the Rhine and dropped us off at a large railroad terminal, where we sat inside moping until a long troop train of boxcars pulled up to the siding. German soldiers hurried out and swarmed into the trucks and staff cars that were waiting. We saw whole detachments wearing American uniforms with MP bands and white helmets, and we had to wonder what the hell was happening. It was the Battle of the Bulge and they were kicking the shit out of us, but we didn't find that out until half a year later.

We spent three nights and three whole days locked inside the cars of that train. We slept standing up, sitting, squatting, and lying down too when we found the room. We had no toilet paper. They didn't care how we did it. We used helmets. When our handkerchiefs were gone, so was our modesty. It took that long to deliver us to that big prisoner of war camp all the way into Germany, almost to the other side. They had a compound there for British soldiers. We recognized the emblem on the gates of the barbed-wire fence. There was another for the Russians. There was one for other Europeans, from which this old guy named Schweik I met later came from. And now there was one for Americans. Some of the Englishmen I spoke to had been prisoners for over four years. I didn't think I could take that. Then I thought that if they could do it, I could too.

About a week and a half after I got there, that officer I spoke to the first day sent for me by name. He began in German.

"You know German, you say?"

"*Jawohl, Herr Kommandant.*"

"Let me hear," he continued in English. "Speak only in German."

I spoke a little bit of German, I told him. Not well, I knew, but I understood more.

"How does it happen you know it?"

"*Ich lernte es in der Schule.*"

"Why did you study German?"

"*Man musste in der Schule eine andere Sprache lernen.*"

"Did you all pick German?"

"*Nein, Herr Kommandant.*"

"The others?"

"*Fast alle studierten Französisch oder Spanisch.*"

"Your accent is atrocious."

"*Ich weiss. Ich hatte keine Gelegenheit zu üben.*"

"Why did you choose German?"

I gambled a smile when I told him I thought I would have a chance to speak it someday.

"You were right, you see," he answered dryly. "I am speaking English to you now because I don't want to waste time. Do you like it here, in the camp?"

"*Nein, Herr Kommandant.*"

"Why don't you?"

I did not know the word for boring, but I knew how to tell him I had nothing to do. "*Ich habe nicht genug zu tun hier. Hier sind zu viele Männer die nicht genug Arbeit haben.*"

"I can propose something better. A work detail in the city of Dresden, which is not very far. Do you think you would prefer that?"

"I think I—"

"In German."

"*Jawohl, Herr Kommandant. Entschuldigen Sie.*"

"You will be safe in Dresden, as safe as here. There is no war industry there and no troops stationed, and it will not be bombed. You will eat a bit better and have work to keep you busy. We are sending a hundred or so. We are permitted to do that. Yes?"

I was nodding. "*Ich würde auch gerne gehen.*"

"You would be useful to interpret. The guards there are not educated. They are old or very young, as you will see. The work is correct too. You will be making a food preparation, mainly for pregnant women. Does it still suit you?"

"*Ja, das gefällt mir sehr, Herr Kommandant, wenn es nicht verboten ist.*"

"It is allowed. But," he said, with a pause and a shrug, to let me know there was some kind of catch, "we can put only privates to work. That is all that is allowed by the rules of the Geneva Convention. We are not permitted to send officers, not even noncommissioned officers. And you are a sergeant. Not even when they volunteer."

"*Was kann ich tun?*" I asked. "*Ich glaube Sie würden nicht mit mir reden, wenn Sie wüssten dass ich nicht gehen kann.*" Why else would he send for me if he didn't know a way around it?

"*Herr Kommandant*," he reminded.

"*Herr Kommandant.*"

He uncupped a palm on the top of his table and pushed toward me a single-edge razor blade. "If you cut off your sergeant's patch we could deal with you like a common soldier. You will lose nothing, no privileges anywhere, not here, not home. Leave the razor blade there when you go, the sergeant's stripes too, if you do decide to take them off."

Dresden was just about the nicest-looking city I'd ever seen. Of course I hadn't seen many then I'd call real cities. Just Manhattan, and then a few thin slices of London, mainly gin mills and bedrooms. There was a river through the middle, and more churches everywhere than I'd seen in my whole life, with spires and domes and crosses on top. There was an opera house in a big square, and around a statue in another place of a man on a horse with a big rump, rows of tents had been put up to house the refugees who were flooding into the city to get away from the Russians who were pushing ahead in the east. The city was working. Trolley cars ran regularly. Kids went to school. People went to jobs, women and old men. The only guy our age we laid eyes on had the stump of a missing arm pinned up in a sleeve. There were plays in the theaters. A big metal sign advertised Yenidze cigarettes. And after a couple of weeks the posters went up, and I saw that a circus was coming to town.

We were put in a building that had been a slaughterhouse when they still had cattle to kill. Underneath was a meat storage basement that was hollowed out of solid rock, and that's where we went when the sirens sounded and the planes came near to bomb somewhere else. They always went to places nearby that had more military value than we did. In the daytime they were American. At night they were English. We could hear the bombs going off very far away and felt good when we did. Often we could see the planes, very high up and in big formations.

Our guards were kids under fifteen or wheezing old men over sixty, except for one tough-looking supervisor they said was Ukrainian who looked into the factory or our billet every few days to make sure we were still there and to see that our uniforms were being preserved. Whenever one of us fell very sick, they took away the uniform and folded it carefully. The Russians were coming close from one side and they hoped, especially the Ukrainian, to escape to us as Americans. The women and girls in the factory were all slave laborers. Most were Polish and some of the old ones looked like my aunts and grandmother did, and even my mother, but thinner, much thinner. I joked a lot to pep things up and made flirting signs. When some joked back or gave those deep looks of longing, I began to think, Oh, boy, wouldn't that be something to talk about. I kidded with the guards about it too, to set me up with a place for a *Fräulein* and me to use for our *Geschmuse*.

"Rabinowitz, you're crazy," this guy Vonnegut said to me, more than once. "You do that once with a German woman and they'll shoot you dead."

I was glad he warned me. He must have spotted me eyeing the girls outside as they marched us back and forth.

"Let's have a dance," I decided one time. "I bet I really could get a dance going here if we could talk them into giving us some music."

"Not me," said Schweik, in his heavy accent, and told me again that he wanted only to be a good soldier.

Vonnegut shook his head too.

I decided to try it alone. The planes droned overhead almost every night, and the guards looked more worried every day.

"*Herr Reichsmarschall,*" I said to the oldest.

"*Mein lieber Herr Rabinowitz,*" he answered in kind.

"*Ich möchte ein Fest haben und tanzen. Können wir Musik haben, zum Singen und Tanzen? Wir werden mehr arbeiten.*"

"*Mein lieber Herr Rabinowitz.*" They had fun with me too. "*Es ist verboten. Das ist nicht erlaubt.*"

"*Fragen Sie doch, bitte. Würden Sie das nicht auch gerne haben?*"

"*Es ist nicht erlaubt.*"

They were too scared to ask anybody. Then came the circus posters, and I decided to make a real try for that one, with Vonnegut and the good soldier Schweik, the three of us. They wanted no part of it. I could see nothing to lose.

"Why not? Shit, wouldn't we all want to? We'll go ask him together. We need a rest. We'll all die here of boredom if we just have to keep waiting."

"Not me," said Schweik, in his very slow English. "Humbly begging your pardon, Rabinowitz, I find I can get myself in enough trouble just doing what I'm told. I've been through this before, longer than you think, more times than you know about. Humbly begging your pardon—"

"Okay, okay." I cut him off. "I'll do it myself."

That night the bombers came for us. In the daytime American planes flew in low, far apart, and shattered buildings in different parts of the city, and we thought it strange that the bombs should drop so far from each other and be aimed at nothing but houses. We wondered why. They were making splintered wreckage for the fires to come, but we didn't know that. When the sirens sounded again in the evening we went down as usual to our meat storage locker underneath our slaughterhouse. This time we stayed. There was no all clear. Through our rock walls and cement ceiling we heard strange strong, dull thumps and thuds that did not sound to us like bomb explosions. They were the charges of incendiaries. In a little while the bulbs hanging from the ceiling went out and the hum of the ventilation fans stopped. The power plant was out. Air blew into the vents anyway, and we could breathe. An unusual roar arose, came closer, grew louder, stayed for hours. It was like the noise of a train going suddenly into a tunnel with a blast of wind, except it just stayed, or a roller-coaster at the top accelerating down. But it did not weaken. The roar was air, it was the draft miles wide sucked into the whole city by the flames outside, and it was as powerful as a cyclone. When it finally lessened, near dawn, two guards climbed timidly back up the stairs to try a look outside. They came back like ghosts.

"*Es brennt. Alles brennt. Die ganze Stadt. Alles ist zerstört.*"

"Everything's on fire," I translated, in the same hushed voice. "The city is gone."

We could not imagine what that meant.

In the morning when they led us up outside into the rain, everyone else was dead. They were dead in the street, burned black into stubs and turned brown by the ash still dropping from the layers of smoke going up everywhere. They were dead in the blackened houses in which the wood had all burned and dead in the cellars. The churches were gone and the opera house had tilted over and fallen into the square. A trolley car had blown over onto its side and burned also. A column of smoke sailed up through the roof of the blackened skeleton of the railroad station, and the raindrops were blotched with soot and ashes and reminded me of the dingy water from the hose in the junkshop we cleaned up with when the day's work was finished. At the far side of the park, we could see that the trees, all the trees, were burning singly like torches, like a civic display, and I thought of blazing pinwheels, of the fireworks in Coney Island off the Steeplechase pier I'd enjoyed every Tuesday night in the summer for as long as I'd lived, of the million dazzling lights of Luna Park. Our building was gone, the slaughterhouse we'd lived in, and every one of the other buildings in our section of the city. We stood without moving for more than an hour before someone drove up in a car to tell us what to do, and these people in uniform were as dazed as we were. It took more than another hour before they could decide, before they pointed off and told us to walk out of the city toward the hills and the mountains. All around us, as far as we could see, everyone was dead, men, women, and children, every parrot, cat, dog, and canary. I felt sorry for them all. I felt sorry for the Polish slave laborers. I felt sorry for the Germans.

I felt sorry for myself. I didn't count. For a second I almost cried. Didn't they care that we might be there? I still don't know why we were spared.

I saw I made no difference. It all would have taken place without me and come out just the same. I would make no difference anywhere, except at home with my family and maybe with a few friends. And after that, I knew I would never even want to vote. I did for Truman, because he was good for Israel, but after that I never have. After FDR there hasn't been a single one I thought enough about to look up to, and I don't want to give any of those bragging bastards in both parties the satisfaction of thinking for a minute I'm in favor of seeing them succeed in their ambitions.

"They don't know that, Lew," Sammy said to me way back, with that superior, college-educated smile he used to wear. He was trying to get me interested in Adlai Stevenson, and then later in John Kennedy. "They don't know that you aren't giving them the satisfaction."

"But *I* do," I answered. "And that's what I mean. We don't count, and our votes won't count either. About how long do you think it will take you to get sick of Kennedy?"

It took him less than a week, I think, before those inauguration balls were even half over, and I don't think Sammy has voted again either since maybe Lyndon Johnson.

I don't spend much time keeping track of the world and can't see that it would change anything if I did. I mind my own business. What's important I hear about. What I learned I remembered, and it turned out to be true. It didn't mean a thing, me being in the army, it didn't count at all. It would have happened the same way without me—the ashes, the smoke, the dead, the outcome. I had nothing to do with Hitler and nothing to do with the state of Israel. I don't want the blame and I don't want the credit. The only place I've counted is at home, with Claire and the kids. Somewhere for whoever wants them later on, maybe the grandchildren, I've put away my Bronze Star, my combat infantryman's badge, my unit citation, the sergeant's stripes I had when I got out of the army, and the shoulder patch with the red number 1 of the First Division, the Big Red 1, which went through hell before I joined them and went through more hell after I was gone. We've got four grandchildren now. I love everyone in my family and feel I would demolish, maybe really kill, anyone who threatened to hurt any one of them.

"You would break his back?" Sammy said this with a smile the last time he visited.

"I will break his back." I smiled too. "Even now."

Even now.

When it starts popping up again in one spot, the radiation sharpshooters at the hospital can take aim and burn away what they like to call another new growth and I know is another tumor. If it pops up again in what they call the diaphragm and I call the belly, I am nauseous before and nauseous afterward, with that nausea I can't stand the thought of that I really think might finally put me away someday if I have to keep living with it. Unless I'm with Sammy, and then I am "nauseated," because he likes to play at what he calls a pedagogue and I call a smartass.

"Lew, tell me," he asked. He laughed softly. "How many backs have you broken in your lifetime?"

"Counting that guy on the car who grabbed that purse?"

"That wasn't a fight, Lew. And you didn't break his back. How many?"

I thought a minute. "None. I never had to. Saying I would was always enough."

"How many fights have you had?"

"In my life?" I thought hard again. "Only one, Sammy," I remembered, and this time I laughed. "With you. Remember that time you tried to teach me how to box?"

BOOK
EIGHT

22

Rhine Journey: Melissa

Like the hero Siegfried in *Götterdämmerung*, he supposed, Yossarian himself began what he was later to look back on as his own Rhine Journey with a rapid clutch of daylight lovemaking: Siegfried at dawn in his mountain aerie, Yossarian around noon in his M & M office in Rockefeller Center. But he ended his pleasurably in the hospital four weeks later with another clean bill of health after his aura and hallucinatory TIA attack, and with five hundred thousand dollars and the sale of a shoe.

Siegfried had Brünnhilde, now mortal, and the rocky haunt they shared.

Yossarian had his nurse, Melissa MacIntosh, most human also, and a desktop, the carpeted floor, the leather armchair, and the broader windowsill of olden times in his office in the newly renamed M & M Building, formerly the old Time-Life Building, with a pane of glass looking down on the rink of ice on which Sammy and Glenda had gone skating more times than Sammy could remember now, and who subsequently had become man and wife, until death did them part.

Yossarian, nodding as he groped, did indeed agree that the door to the office was not locked, when he knew that it was, and that somebody might indeed walk in on them while they were thus lustfully teamed, when he knew that no one would or could. He was titillated by her apprehension; her tremors, doubts, and indecisions electrified him fiendishly with mounting passion and affection. Melissa was flustered in her ladylike terror of being come upon uncovered in those disarraying exertions of vigorous sexual informalities and, blushing, wished him, for a change, to finish fast; but she laughed when he did and disclosed the ruse as she was checking his baggage for his medicines and preparing to ride with him to the airport before his flight to Kenosha at the start of his journey. Along with basic toilet articles, he wanted Valium for insomnia, Tylenol or Advil for back pain, Maalox for his hiatus hernia. Much to his wonder, there were direct jumbo-jet flights now to Kenosha, Wisconsin.

The phone rang as he zipped closed his carry-on bag.

"Gaffney, what do *you* want?"

"Aren't you going to congratulate me?" Gaffney spoke merrily, ignoring Yossarian's evident tone of rancor.

"Have you been listening in again?" asked Yossarian, looking furtively at Melissa.

"To what?" asked Gaffney.

"Why'd you call?"

"You just won't give me credit, will you, John?"

"For what? I got a bill from you finally. You didn't charge much."

"I haven't done much. Besides, I'm grateful for your music. You don't know happy I am to play back the tapes we record. I love the Bruckner symphonies at this darkening time of year, and the *Boris Godunov*."

"Would you like the *Ring?*"

"Mainly the *Siegfried*. I don't hear that one often."

"I'll let you know when I schedule the *Siegfried*," said Yossarian, acidly.

"Yo-Yo, I'll be so obliged. But that's not what I'm talking about."

"*Mr.* Gaffney," said Yossarian, and paused to allow his point to sink in. "What *are* you talking about?"

"We're back to Mr. Gaffney, are we, John?"

"We never passed John, Jerry. What do you want?"

"Praise," answered Gaffney. "Everybody likes to be appreciated when he's done something well. Even Señor Gaffney."

"Praise for what, Señor Gaffney?"

Gaffney laughed. Melissa, reposing upon the arm of the leather sofa, was rasping away at her fingernails with an emery board. Yossarian gave her a menacing scowl.

"For my gifts," Gaffney was saying. "I predicted you'd be going to Wisconsin to see Mrs. Tappman. Didn't I say you'd be changing in Chicago, for your trip to Washington to Milo and Wintergreen? You didn't ask me how I knew."

"Am I going to Washington?" Yossarian was amazed.

"You'll be getting Milo's fax. M2 will phone to the airport to remind you. There, that's the fax coming in now, isn't it? I'm on target again."

"You *have* been listening, haven't you, you bastard?"

"To what?"

"And maybe watching too. And why would M2 be phoning me when he's right down the hall?"

"He's back at the PABT building with your son Michael, trying to decide if he's willing to be married there."

"To the Maxon girl?"

"He'll have to say yes. I have another good joke that might amuse you, John."

"I'll miss my plane."

"You've plenty of time. There'll be a delay in departure of almost one hour."

Yossarian burst out with a laugh. "Gaffney, you're finally mistaken," he crowed. "I had my secretary call. It's leaving on schedule."

Gaffney laughed too. "Yo-Yo, you have no secretary, and the airline was lying. It will be late taking off by fifty-five minutes. It was your nurse you had call."

"I have no nurse."

"That warms my heart. Please tell Miss MacIntosh the kidney is working again. She will be happy to hear that."

"What kidney?"

"Oh, Yossarian, shame. You don't always listen when she telephones. The kidney of the Belgian patient. And as long as you're going to Washington, why don't you invite Melissa—"

"Melissa, Mr. Gaffney?"

"Miss MacIntosh, Mr. Yossarian. But why don't you invite her to join you there? I bet she'll say she'd really love to go. She's probably never been. She can go to the National Gallery when you're busy with Milo and Noodles Cook, and to the National Air and Space Museum of the Smithsonian Institution."

Yossarian covered the telephone. "Melissa, I'm going to stop in Washington on the way back. How about taking time off to meet me there?"

"I'd really love to go," Melissa replied. "I've never been. I can go to the National Gallery when you're busy, and to that aeronautical museum of the Smithsonian Institution."

"What did she say?" asked Jerry Gaffney.

Yossarian replied respectfully. "I think you know what she said. You really are a man of mystery, aren't you? I haven't figured you out yet."

"I've answered your questions."

"I must think of new ones. When can we meet?"

"Don't you remember? In Chicago, when your connecting flight is delayed."

"It will be delayed?"

"For more than an hour. By unpredictable blizzards in Iowa and Kansas."

"You predict them already?"

"I hear things and see things, John. It's how I earn my living. May I try out my joke now?"

"I'll bet you do. And you have been listening, haven't you? Maybe watching too."

"Listening to what?"

"You think I'm simpleminded, Gaffney? Would you like to hear *my* joke? Jerry, go fuck yourself."

"That's not a bad one, Yo-Yo," said Gaffney, sociably, "although I've heard it before."

The opera *Siegfried* brought to mind, Yossarian was recalling in the pearl-gray limousine, that the *heldentenor* in that one, after a mere touch to his lips of the blood of the slain dragon, illustriously began to understand the language of birds. They told him to take the gold, kill the dwarf, and dash to the mountain through the circle of fire to find Brünnhilde lying there in charmed sleep, this message in bird notes to a youth who had never laid eyes on a woman before and needed more than one look at the buxom Brünnhilde to make the startling discovery that *this was not a man!*

Siegfried had his birds, but Yossarian had his Gaffney, who could report, when Yossarian phoned him from the car, that the chaplain was passing tritium in his flatulence.

Nurse Melissa MacIntosh had not heard of an intestinal condition like that one before but promised to ask a number of gastro-enterologists she was friendly with.

Yossarian was not certain he wanted her to.

He was wounded and abashed by the question that leaped to mind, and too shamed to voice it: to ask if she'd dated these doctors and slept with them too, even with only four or five. It told him again, to his inconceivable delectation, that he indeed thought himself in love. Such pangs of jealousy for him were extremely few. Even far back in his torrid affair with Frances Beach, though almost monogamous himself, he had indifferently assumed that she, in the vernacular of the age, was at that time also "boffing" others who were potentially supportive of her aspirations as actress. Now he reveled like an epicure in the euphoria of impressions of love that were again rejuvenating him. He was not embarrassed or afraid, except that Michael or the other children might find out, while it was still in the outlandish character of a rapture.

In the car she held his hand, pressed his thigh, ran fingers through the curls at the back of his head.

Whereas Siegfried from the start was in the evil hands of a wicked dwarf greedy for dragon's gold and drooling to liquidate him as soon as he had collared it.

Melissa was preferable.

She and her roommate, Angela Moore, or Moorecock, as he now called her, disapproved righteously of married men in quest of secret girlfriends, except for the married men who had quested specifically for *them,* and Yossarian was glad his newest divorce was final. He thought best not to divulge to her that, even with ravishing women, the seduction over, there was only the infatuation and sex, and that often in men of his years, caprice and fetishism were more arousing than Spanish fly. He was already scheming to take the last shuttle plane back with her from Washington and in the semidarkness of the interior attempt, while she sat near the window, to succeed in removing her underpants in the fifty or so minutes they had. Unless, of course, she wore jeans.

Unlike Angela, she herself never verbally tendered evidence of the versatile range of amatory experiences her roommate and best friend had bawdily claimed for them both. Her vocabulary tended toward the pristine. But she seemed a stranger to nothing and evinced no need for guidance or definitions. In fact, she knew a trick or two he had not imagined. And she so stubbornly resisted conversing about her sexual history that he soon left off searching for it.

"Who is Boris Godunov?" she asked in the car.

"The opera I was listening to the other night when you came in from work and then had me turn it off because you wanted to hear the fucking television news."

"When you get back," she next wanted to know, "can we listen to the *Ring* together?"

Here again, he considered, they both enjoyed another large advantage over the Wagnerian prototypes.

For good Brünnhilde had savored little delight once Siegfried set out on his mission of heroic deeds and had experienced only betrayal, misery, and jealous fury after he returned to' seize and deliver her to another man. It did not once cross her mind while conspiring in his death that he might have been slipped a potion that caused him to forget who she was.

Whereas Yossarian was making Melissa happy.

This was a thing he had not been able to do for long with any other woman. He was hearing bird notes too.

Melissa found him expert and benevolent when he concluded she could indeed give up her staff job and have more money and time as a private-duty nurse, *if*—and it was a big *if*—she was willing to forgo her paid vacations and an eventual pension. But for her future security she *must* make up her mind that she *must* soon marry a man, handsome or not, even a boor, a dolt, forget charm, who *did* have a pension plan and *would* have a retirement income to bequeath when he died. Melissa listened blissfully, as though he were caressing and celebrating her.

"Do you have a pension plan?"

"Forget about me. It must be someone else."

She thought his brain immense.

A simple discharged promise made shortly after they'd met in the hospital affecting outdated silver fillings in two upper teeth meant more than he would have guessed; they were exposed when she laughed; and he'd pledged to have them replaced by porcelain crowns if she kept her eyes out for oversights and he came out of the hospital alive. And this, when done, went farther with her than all the long-stemmed red roses and lingerie from Saks Fifth Avenue, Victoria's Secret, and Frederick's of Hollywood, and suffused her with an exhilarated gratitude he had never witnessed before. Not even Frances Beach, who had so much from Patrick, knew how to feel grateful.

John Yossarian lay awake some nights in a tremulous agitation that this woman with whom he was entertaining himself might already be somewhat in love with him. He was not that positive he wanted what he wished for.

Since the shock in the shower, the course of this true love had run so smoothly as to beguile him into a presumption of the notional, fictitious, and surreal. On the memorable evening following his talk with Michael, in the movie house down from the lobby level of his apartment building, she showed no surprise when he put a hand on her shoulder to fondle her neck awhile, then another on the inside of her knee to see what good he could do for himself there. *He* was the one surprised when her resistance this time was perfunctory. With the coming of spring she wore no panty hose. Her jacket lay folded in her lap for tasteful concealment. When he moved upward to arrive at the silken touch of the panties and the feel of the lacework of curls underneath, he had come as far as he had aspired to and was content to stop. But she then said:

"We don't have to do that here." She spoke with the solemnity of a surgeon rendering a verdict that was inevitable. "We can go upstairs to your apartment."

He found he preferred to see the rest of the movie. "It's okay here. We can just keep watching."

She glanced about at others. "I'm not comfortable here. I'll feel better upstairs."

They never did find out how that movie ended.

"You can't do it like that," she said in his apartment, when they had been there a very little while. "Don't you put something on?"

"I've had a vasectomy. Don't you take the pill?"

"I've had my tubes tied. But what about AIDS?"

"You can see my certificate of blood work. I have it framed on the wall."

"Don't you want to see mine?"

"I'll take my chances." He put a hand on her mouth. "For God sakes, Melissa, please stop talking so much."

She bent up her legs and he pressed himself down between them, and after that they both knew what to do.

Counting back late the next morning, when he had to believe they finally were through, he found himself convinced he had never in his life been more virile and prodigious, or more desirous, amorous, considerate, and romantic.

It was wonderful, he whistled through his teeth while washing up after the last time, then switched in a syncopated, swinging beat to the foreplay and orgasmic love music from *Tristan*. It was more marvelous than anything in all his libidinous experience, and he knew in his heart that never, never, not once, would he ever want to have to go through anything like all *that* again! He presumed she understood that there would be a rather sheer falling off: he might not, in fact, find the wish, the will, the actual desire, and the elemental physical resources ever to want to make love to her again, or to any other woman!

He recalled Mark Twain in one of his better writings employing the simile of the candlestick and the candleholder to emphasize that between men and women sexually it was not close to an equivalent competition. The candleholder was always there.

And then he heard her on the telephone.

"And that one made it five!" she was confiding exuberantly to Angela, her face flushed with prosperity. "No," she continued, after an impatient pause to listen. "But my knees sure hurt."

He himself would have fixed the tally subjectively at five and three eighths, but he felt a bit better about the near future to hear that her bones were aching also.

"He knows so much about everything," she went on. "He knows about interest rates, and books, and operas. Ange, I've never been happier."

That one gave him pause, for he was not sure he wanted again the accountability of a woman who had never been happier. But the fillip to his vanity sure felt good.

And then came the shock in the shower. When he turned it off he heard men murmuring in wily discussion outside the closed bathroom door. He heard a woman in the obvious cadence of assent. It was some kind of setup. He knotted the bath towel around his waist and moved out to confront whatever danger awaited. It was worse than he could have foreseen.

She had turned on the television set and was listening to the news!

There was no war, no national election, no race riot, no big fire, storm, earthquake, or airplane crash—there *was* no news, and she was listening to it on television.

But then, while dressing, he caught the savory aromas of eggs scrambling and bacon frying and bread warming into slices of toast. The year he'd lived alone had been the loneliest in his life, and he was living alone still.

But then he saw her putting ketchup on her eggs and had to look at something else. He looked at the television screen.

"Melissa dear," he found himself preparing her two weeks later. He had his arm atop a shoulder again and absently was stroking her neck with his finger. "Let me tell you now what is going to happen. It will have nothing to do with you. These are changes I know will occur with a man like me, even with a woman he cares about very much: a man who likes to be alone much of the time, thinks and daydreams a lot, doesn't really enjoy the give-and-take of companionship of anyone all that much, falls silent much of the time and broods and is indifferent to everything someone else might be talking about, and will not be affected much by anything the woman does, as long as she doesn't talk to him about it and annoy him. It has happened before, it happens to me always."

She was nodding intently at each point, either in agreement or in worldly perception.

"I'm exactly the same way," she began in earnest response, with eyes sparkling and lips shining. "I can't stand people who talk a lot, or speak to me when I'm trying to read, even a newspaper, or call me on the telephone when they've nothing to say, or tell me things I already know, or repeat themselves and interrupt."

"Excuse me," interrupted Yossarian, as she seemed equipped to say more. He killed some time in the bathroom. "I really think," he said, upon returning, "I'm too old, and you're really too young."

"You're not too old."

"I'm older than I look."

"So am I. I've seen your age on the hospital charts."

Oh, shit, he thought. "I have to tell you also that I won't have children and will never have a dog, and I won't buy a vacation house in East Hampton or anywhere else."

Off the entrance to his apartment in each direction was a good-sized bedroom with a bathroom and space for a personal television set, and perhaps they could start that way and meet for meals. But there again was the television, turned back on, and voices were at work to which she was not listening. She never could tell when there might come something interesting. Although television was the one vice in a woman he could not abide, he believed that with this woman it was worth a try.

"No, I won't tell you her name," said Yossarian to Frances Beach, after the next, tumultuous meeting of ACACAMMA, at which Patrick Beach had spoken out dynamically to second the anonymous proposal by Yossarian that the Metropolitan Museum of Art settle financial problems by getting rid of the artwork and selling the building and real estate there on Fifth Avenue to a developer. "It's not a woman you know."

"Is it the friend of the succulent Australian woman you keep talking about, the one named Moore?"

"Moorecock."

"What?"

"Her name is Moorecock, Patrick, not Moore."

Patrick squinted in puzzlement. "I could swear you'd corrected me and said it was Moore."

"He did, Patrick. Pay no attention to him now. Is it that nurse you mentioned? I'd be saddened to think you sank so low as to marry one of my friends."

"Who's talking about marriage?" protested Yossarian.

"You are." Frances laughed. "You're like that elephant who always forgets."

Was he really going to have to marry again?

No one had to remind a doubtful Yossarian of a few of the blessings of living alone. He would not have to listen to someone else talking on the telephone. On his new CD player with automatic changer, he could put a complete *Lohengrin, Boris Godunov,* or *Die Meistersinger,* or four whole symphonies by Bruckner, and play them all through in an elysian milieu of music without hearing someone feminine intruding to say, "What music is that?" or "Do you really like that?" or "Isn't that kind of heavy for the morning?" or "Will you please make it lower? I'm trying to watch the television news," or "I'm talking to my sister on the telephone." He could read a newspaper without having someone pick up the section he wanted next.

He could stand another marriage, he imagined, but did not have time for another divorce.

23

Kenosha

Such portentous food for equivocal thought weighed heavily on Yossarian's mind as he flew west on his journey for his rendezvous with the chaplain's wife, the sole purpose of which visit now was commiseration and a mutual confession of ignominious defeat. Her face fell with a disappointment she was not able to suppress when she picked him out at the airport.

They each had hoped for somebody younger.

The hero Siegfried, he afterward remembered, had cruised into action like a galley slave, rowing Brünnhilde's horse in a boat, and was soon tête-à-tête with another woman, to whom he was swiftly affianced.

Yossarian had his first-class seat on a jet and no such demented daydream in mind.

Siegfried had to climb a mountain and walk through fire to claim the woman Brünnhilde.

Yossarian had Melissa fly to Washington.

Looking back when it was over and he was thinking of a parody for *The New Yorker* magazine, he considered he had fared pretty well in comparison with the Wagnerian hero.

Half a million dollars richer, he was on the horns of a dilemma but alive to deal with it.

Siegfried was dead at the end; Brünnhilde was dead, even the horse was dead; Valhalla had collapsed, the gods were gone with it; and the composer was elated while his voluptuous music subsided in triumph like a delicate dream, for such is the calculating nature of art and the artist.

Whereas Yossarian could look forward to getting laid again

soon. He had his doctor's okay. All his life he had loved women, and in much of that life he had been in love with more than one.

The small port city of Kenosha on Lake Michigan in Wisconsin, just twenty-five miles south of the much larger small city of Milwaukee, now had a jet airport and was experiencing an upturn in economic activity that the town fathers were at a loss to explain. Local social engineers were attributing the middling boom, perhaps waggishly, to benign climate. Several small new businesses of somewhat technical nature had opened and an agency of the federal government had established laboratories rumored to be CIA fronts in an abandoned factory that had long lain idle.

In the lounge in New York, Yossarian had taken note of the other travelers in first class, all men younger than himself and in very good spirits. Only scientists were so happy in their vocations these days. They held pencils at the ready as they talked, and what they talked about most—he was startled to hear—was tritium and deuterium, of which he now knew a little, and lithium deuteride, which, he learned when he asked, was a compound of lithium and heavy water and, more significantly, was the explosive substance of preference in the best hydrogen devices.

"Does everyone know all this?" He was amazed they talked so openly.

Oh, sure. He could find it all written in *The Nuclear Almanac* and Hogerton's *The Atomic Energy Handbook*, both perhaps on sale in the paperback rack.

Boarding, he'd recognized in business class several prostitutes and two call girls from the sex clubs in his high-rise building and as streetwalking attractions near the cocktail lounges and cash machines just outside. The call girls were fellow tenants. In economy class he spotted small clumps of the homeless who had somehow acquired the airplane fare to leave the mean streets of New York to be homeless in Wisconsin. They had washed themselves up for the pilgrimage, probably in the lavatories of the PABT building, where posters Michael had once designed still warned sternly that smoking, loitering, bathing, shaving, laundering, fucking, and sucking were all forbidden in the washbasins and toilet stalls, that alcohol could be harmful to pregnant women, and that anal intercourse could lead to HIV and hepatitis infections. Michael's posters had won art prizes. Their carry-on luggage consisted of shopping carts and paper bags. Yossarian was sure he saw sitting far back the large black woman with the gnarled melanoma moles he had come upon swabbing herself clean in only a sleeveless pink chemise on the emergency staircase the one time he had gone there with McBride. He looked for but did not find the addled woman with one leg who, as a matter of common practice, was raped by one derelict man or another perhaps three or four times daily, or the pasty blonde woman he also remembered from the stairwell who was sewing a seam in a white blouse listlessly.

From the physicists on the plane, Yossarian also thought he heard, without understanding any of it, that in the world of science, time continuously ran backward or forward, and forward *and* backward, and that particles of matter could travel backward and forward through time without undergoing change. Why, then, couldn't he? He also heard that subatomic particles had always to be simultaneously in every place they could be, and from this he began to consider that in his nonscientific world of humans and groups, everything that could happen did happen, and that anything that did not happen could not happen. Whatever *can* change, will; and anything that doesn't change, can't.

Mrs. Karen Tappman proved a slight, shy, and uneasy elderly woman, with a vacillating attitude on many aspects of the plight that had brought them into communication. But of the meaning of one thing there could soon be no doubt: the understanding they shared that he was sorry he had come and she regretted having asked him to. They would soon not have much to say to each other. They could think of nothing new to try. He had recognized her, he stated honestly, from the snapshots he remembered the chaplain had carried.

She smiled. "I was just past thirty. I recognize you now too from the photograph in our study."

Yossarian had not guessed the chaplain would possess a picture of him.

"Oh, yes, I'll show you." Mrs. Tappman led the way into the back of the two-story house. "He tells people often you just about saved his life overseas when things were most horrible."

"I think he helped save mine. He backed me up in a decision to refuse to continue fighting. I don't know how much he told you."

"I think he's always told me everything."

"I would have gone ahead anyway, but he gave me the feeling I was right. There's a blowup of that picture of you and the children he used to carry in his wallet."

One wall of the study was filled with photographs spanning

almost seventy years, some showing the chaplain as a tiny boy with a fishing pole and a smile with missing teeth, and some of Karen Tappman as a tiny girl in party dress. The photograph he remembered displayed the Karen Tappman of thirty sitting in a group with her three small children, all four of them facing the camera gamely and looking sadly isolated and forsaken, as though in fear of a looming loss. On a separate wall were his war pictures.

Yossarian halted to stare at a very old fading brown photograph of the chaplain's father in World War I, a small figure petrified by the camera, wearing a helmet too massive for the child's face inside it, holding clumsily a rifle with the bayonet fixed, with a canteen in canvas hooked to his belt on one side and a gas mask in a canvas case on the other.

"We used to have the gas mask as a souvenir," said Mrs. Tappman, "and the children would play with it. I don't know what's become of it. He was gassed slightly in one of the battles and was in the veterans hospital awhile, but he took care of himself and lived a long time. He died of lung cancer right here in the house. Now they say he smoked too much. Here is the one he has of you."

Yossarian stifled a smile. "I wouldn't call that a picture of me."

"Well, he does," she answered contentiously, showing a streak he had not thought existed. "He would point it out to everyone. 'And that's my friend Yossarian,' he would say. 'He helped pull me through when things were rough.' He would say that to everyone. He repeats himself too, I'm afraid."

Yossarian was touched by her candor. The photograph was of a kind taken routinely by the squadron public relations officer, showing members of a crew waiting at a plane before takeoff. In this one he saw himself standing off in the background between the figures in focus and the B-25 bomber. In the foreground were the three enlisted men for that day, seated without evidence of concern on unfused thousand-pound bombs on the ground as they waited to board and start up. And Yossarian, looking as slender and boyish as the others, in parachute harness and his billed, rakish officer's cap, had merely turned to look on. The chaplain had lettered the names of each man there. The name Yossarian was largest. Here again were Samuel Singer, William Knight, and Howard Snowden, all sergeants.

"One of these young men was killed later on," said Mrs. Tappman. "I believe it was this one. Samuel Singer."

"No, Mrs. Tappman. It was Howard Snowden."

"Are you sure?"

"I was with him again on that one too."

"You all look so young. I thought you might still look the same when I was waiting for you at the airport."

"We were young, Mrs. Tappman."

"Too young to be killed."

"I thought so too."

"Albert spoke at his funeral."

"I was there."

"It was very hard for him, he said. He didn't know why. And he almost ran out of words. Do you think they will set him free soon and let him come back home?" Karen Tappman watched Yossarian shrug. "He hasn't done anything wrong. It must be hard for him now. For me too. The woman across the street is a widow and we play bridge together evenings. I suppose I might have to learn to live like a widow sooner or later. But I don't see why I should have to do it now."

"There really is some concern for his health."

"Mr. Yossarian," she answered disapprovingly, in an abrupt change of mood. "My husband is now past seventy. If he's going to be ill, can't he be ill here?"

"I have to agree."

"But I suppose they know what they're doing."

"I never, never could agree with that one. But they're also afraid he might explode."

She missed the point. "Albert doesn't have a temper. He never did."

Neither could think of any new effort to make, what with a local police force recording him as a missing person, a department of the federal government that professed no knowledge of him, another department that brought cash and regards every fifteen days, and a third department that insisted he had been called back into the army reserves.

"They're all rather fishy, aren't they?" he observed.

"Why is that?" she asked.

The newspapers, two senators, a congressman, and the White House were all not impressed. In the latest version of the chaplain's Freedom of Information file, Yossarian had witnessed changes: everything on him now had been blacked out but the words *a, an,* and *the.* There was no Social Security number and there remained in the file only a copy of a scrawled personal letter from a serviceman dating back to August 1944, in which all but the salutation "Dear Mary" had been blacked out and, at the bottom, the message from the censor, who'd been Chaplain Tappman: "I yearn for you tragically. A. T. Tappman, Chaplain, U.S. Army." Yossarian thought the handwriting was his own, but could not remember having written it. He said nothing to Karen Tappman, for he did not want to risk upsetting her about a woman in the chaplain's past with the name Mary.

In the psychological profile constructed by the FBI, the chaplain fit the model of that kind of preacher who runs off with another woman, and the empirical evidence was preponderant that the woman he had run off with was the organist in his church.

Mrs. Tappman was not convinced, for there had been no church organist and her husband had been without church or congregation since his retirement.

Yossarian waited almost until they had finished eating before he gave her the new piece of information he had gained from Gaffney in a telephone call from the plane over Lake Michigan. They dined early at her request and were able to save three dollars on the early bird specials. This was new to Yossarian. They enjoyed an additional discount as senior citizens and did not have to show ID cards. This was new too. He ordered dessert only because she did first.

"I don't want to alarm you, Mrs. Tappman," he said, when they were finishing, "but they are also speculating it might be"— the word did not come easily to him—"a miracle."

"A miracle? Why should it alarm me?"

"It would alarm some people."

"Then maybe it should. Who will decide?"

"We will never know."

"But they must know what they're doing."

"I would not go that far."

"They have a right to keep him, don't they?"

"No, they don't have the right."

"Then why can't we do anything?"

"We don't have the right."

"I don't understand."

"Mrs. Tappman, people with force have a right to do anything we can't stop them from doing. That's the catch Albert and I found out about in the army. It's what's happening now."

"Then there's not much hope, is there?"

"We can hope for the miracle that they do decide it's a miracle. Then they might have to let him go. There's also the chance they might call it"—he was hesitant again—"a natural evolutionary mutation."

"For making heavy water? My Albert?"

"The problem with the miracle theory is another psychological profile. It's almost always a woman now, in a warm climate. A woman, if you'll pardon me, with full breasts. Your husband just doesn't fit the mold."

"Is that so?" The words were a blunt retort delivered with cold dignity. "Mr. Yossarian," she continued, with a look of belligerent assurance on her sharp face, "I am now going to tell you something we have never disclosed to anybody, not even our children. My husband has already been witness to a miracle. A vision. Yes. It came to him in the army, this vision, to restore his faith at the very moment when he was about to declare as a public confession that he had given it up, that he no longer could believe. So there."

After a moment during which he feared he had angered her, Yossarian took heart from this show of fighting spirit. "Why would he not want to tell anybody?"

"It was given just to him, and not for notoriety."

"May I pass that information on?"

"It was at that funeral in Pianosa," she related, "at the burial of that young Samuel Singer we spoke of before."

"It was not Singer, Mrs. Tappman. It was Snowden."

"I'm sure he said Singer."

"It makes no difference, but I gave him first aid. Please go on."

"Yes, he was conducting this Singer's funeral service and felt himself running out of words. That's just how he describes it. And then he looked up toward the heavens to confess and resign his office, to renounce right there any belief in God, or religion, or justice, or morality, or mercy, and then, as he was about to do it, with those other officers and enlisted men looking on, he was granted his sign. It was a vision, the image of a man. And he was sitting in a tree. Just outside the cemetery, with a grieving face, watching the funeral with very sad eyes, and he had those eyes fixed on my husband."

"Mrs. Tappman," said Yossarian, with a long sigh, and his heart was heavy. "That was me."

"In the tree?" She arched her brows in ridicule. He had seen such looks before on true believers, true believers in anything, but never a self-assurance more rooted. "It could not be," she informed him, with a certitude almost brutal. "Mr. Yossarian, the figure was unclothed."

With delicacy, he asked, "Your husband never told you how that might have come about?"

"How else could it come about, Mr. Yossarian? It was obviously an angel."

"With wings?"

"You're being sacrilegious now. He did not need wings, for a miracle. Why should an angel ever need wings? Mr. Yossarian, I want my husband back. I don't care about anyone else." She was beginning to cry.

"Mrs. Tappman, you have opened my eyes," said Yossarian, with pity and renewed fervor. He had learned from a lifetime of skepticism that a conviction, even a naive conviction, was in the last analysis more nourishing than the wasteland of none. "I will try my best. In Washington I have a last resort, a man at the White House who owes me some favors."

"Please ask him. I want to know you're still trying."

"I will beg him, implore him. At least one time a day he has access to the President."

"To the little prick?"

It was still early when she dropped him at his motel.

Coming back from the bar after three double Scotches, he saw a red Toyota from New York in the lot, and a woman inside eating, and when he stopped to stare, she turned on the headlights and sped away, and he knew with a half-inebriated sniffle of laughter that he had to have been imagining the Toyota and her.

Lying in bed ingesting candy bars and peanuts and a canned Coca-Cola from the vending machine outside, he felt too wakeful for sleep and too sluggish for the meaningful work of fiction he had carried with him hopefully still one more time. The book was a paperback titled *Death in Venice and Seven Other Stories* and was by Thomas Mann. Lighter fiction was even heavier for him these days. Even his revered *New Yorker* seldom had power to rivet his attention. Celebrity gossip now was largely about people who were strangers, the Academy Awards were likely to go to films he did not know and to performers he had not seen or even heard of.

He missed Melissa but was glad he was there alone; or, as he tickled himself in elusive modification, he was glad he was alone, although he missed Melissa. He found a classical music station and was horrified to hear a German Bach choir begin the score from the American musical comedy *Carousel*. He jammed his middle finger hurling himself at the tuning dial. With the second station he was luckier: he came into a medley that brought him the children's chorus from *La Bohème* and next the children's chorus from *Carmen*. And after that, to the accompaniment of rising static from distant sheet lightning, there came the chorus of anvils he recognized from the German *Das Rheingold*, attending the descent of the gods into the bowels of the earth to steal gold from the dwarfs to pay to the giants who had built their glorious new home, Valhalla, under a contract from whose original terms they were already backing away. The giants had been promised the goddess conferring eternal youth; they had to settle for money. In doing business with the gods, Yossarian judged again, with eyes growing heavier, it was always smarter to collect up front.

As that chorus of anvils diminished into static, he heard faintly in the static an illogical musical pandemonium of primitive wild laughter ascend through the scales in tune and in key and then, nebulously, beneath a hissing layer of electrical interference, a very different, lonely, lovely, angelic wail of a children's chorus in striking polyphonic lament he believed he recognized and could not place. He remembered the novel by Thomas Mann about which he had once thought of writing and wondered in his fuzziness if he was losing his bearings and dreaming he was listening to the Leverkühn *Apocalypse* of which he had read. And in several more seconds that failing broadcast signal faded out too until there survived only in a primeval void of human silence the insistent sibilance of that simmering and irrepressible electrical interference.

He did dream that night in disjointed sleep that he was back in his high-rise apartment in New York and that the familiar red Toyota with the woman inside eating sugar buns was pulling back into the same spot in the parking area outside his motel room in Kenosha, on whose far border a paunchy, stocky, bearded middle-aged Jew who was a G-man trudged back and forth with moving lips and his head bowed. A lanky, conspicuous, orange-haired man in a seersucker suit looked on inoffensively from a corner, with twinkling flames in his eyes, holding an orange drink with a straw in a large plastic cup, while a darker man with a peculiarly

Oriental cast to his features was observing all of them cannily, dressed fastidiously in a blue shirt, rust-colored tie, and a single-breasted fawn-colored herringbone jacket with a thin purple cross-pattern. Hiding slyly in the shadows was a shady man wearing a dark beret who smoked a cigarette without using his hands, which were deep in the pockets of a soiled raincoat that was unbuttoned and ready to be flashed open instantly for the man inside it to expose his hairy self in a lewd invitation to stare at the repellent sight of his underwear and his groin. Yossarian at the end of his dream had satisfying sex briefly with his second wife. Or was it his first? Or both? He came awake thinking of Melissa guiltily.

When he stepped outside for breakfast, the red Toyota with the New York license plates and the woman inside chewing food was parked there again. It pulled away when he stopped to stare, and he knew he had to be fantasizing. She could not be there.

24

Apocalypse

"And why not?" asked Jerry Gaffney, in the airport in Chicago. "With Milo's bomber and the chaplain's heavy water, and your two divorces, and Nurse Melissa MacIntosh and that Belgian patient, and that fling with that woman with a husband, you must know you're of interest to other people."

"From New York to Kenosha for just one day? She couldn't drive that fast, could she?"

"Sometimes we work in mysterious ways, John."

"She was in my dream, Jerry. And so were you."

"You can't blame us for that. Your dreams are still your own. Are you sure you were not imagining that?"

"My dream?"

"Yes."

"It's how I was able to recognize you, Gaffney. I knew I'd seen you before."

"I keep telling you that."

"When I was in the hospital last year. You were one of the guys looking in on me too, weren't you?"

"Not you, John. I was checking on employees who phoned in · sick. One had a staphylococcus infection and the other salmonella food poisoning picked up—"

"From an egg sandwich in the cafeteria there, right?"

Arriving at an airport in turbulent disorder because of flights canceled by unpredictable blizzards in Iowa and Kansas, Yossarian had quickly spotted a dark, tidy, dapper man of average height and slightly Oriental cast waving aloft a plane ticket in a signal to attract him.

"Mr. Gaffney?" he'd inquired.

"It's not the Messiah," said Gaffney, chuckling. "Let's sit down for coffee. We'll have an hour." Gaffney had booked him on the next flight to Washington and gave him the ticket and boarding pass. "You will be happy to know," he seemed pleased to reveal, "that you'll be all the richer for this whole experiençe. About half a million dollars richer, I'd guess. For your work with Noodles Cook."

"I've done no work with Noodles Cook."

"Milo will want you to. I'm beginning to think of your trip as something of a Rhine Journey."

"I am too."

"It can't be coincidence. But with a happier ending."

Gaffney was dark, stylish, urbane, and good-looking—of Turkish descent, he disclosed, though from Bensonhurst in Brooklyn, New York. His complexion was smooth. He was bald on top, with a shiny pate, and had black hair trimmed close at the sides and black brows. His eyes were brown and narrow and, with the raised mounds of his fine cheekbones, gave to his face the intriguing look of someone cosmopolitan from the east. He was dressed faultlessly, spotlessly, in a fawn-colored single-breasted herringbone jacket with a thin purple cross-pattern, brown trousers, a pale-blue shirt, and a tie of solid rust.

"In the dream," said Yossarian, "you were dressed the same way. Were you in Kenosha yesterday?"

"No, no, Yo-Yo."

"Those clothes were in the dream."

"Your dream is impossible, Yo-Yo, because I never dress the same on consecutive days. Yesterday," Gaffney continued, consulting his appointment diary and licking his lips in obvious awareness of the effect, "I wore a Harris tweed of darker color with an orange interior design, trousers of chocolate brown, a quiet-pink shirt with thin vertical stripes, and a paisley tie of auburn, cobalt blue, and amber. You may not know this, John, but I believe in neatness. Neatness counts. Every day I dress for an occasion so that I am dressed for the occasion when an occasion arises. Tomorrow, I see by my calendar, I'll be wearing oatmeal Irish linen with green, if I go south, or a double-breasted blue blazer with horn buttons and gray trousers if I stay up north. The pants will be flannel. John, only you can say. Did you have sex in your dream?"

"That's not your business, Jerry."

"You seem to be doing it everywhere else."

"That's not your business either."

"I always dream of sex my first night out when I travel alone. It's a reason I don't mind going out of town."

"Mr. Gaffney, that's lovely. But it's none of my business."

"When I go with Mrs. Gaffney, there's no need to dream. Fortunately, she too likes to perform the sex act immediately in every new setting."

"That's lovely too, but I don't want to hear it, and I don't want you to hear about mine."

"You should be more guarded."

"It's the reason I hired you, damn it. I'm followed by you and followed by others I don't know a fucking thing about, and I want it to stop. I want my privacy back."

"Then give up the chaplain."

"I don't have the chaplain."

"I know that, Yo-Yo, but they don't."

"I'm too old for Yo-Yo."

"Your friends call you Yo-Yo."

"Name one, you jackass."

"I will check. But you came to the right man when you came to the Gaff. I can tell you the ways they keep you under surveillance, and I can teach you to avoid surveillance, and then I can give you the measures they employ to thwart someone like you who has learned to thwart their surveillance."

"Aren't you contradicting yourself?"

"Yes. But meanwhile I've spotted four following you who've disguised themselves cleverly. Look, there goes the gentleman we know as our Jewish G-man, trying to get on a plane to New York. He was in Kenosha yesterday."

"I saw him somewhere but wasn't sure."

"Possibly in your dream. Pacing in the motel parking lot and saying his evening prayers. How many do you recognize?"

"At least one," said Yossarian, warming to the counterintelligence business in which they now seemed to be conspiring. "And I don't even have to look. A tall man in seersucker with freckles and orange hair. It's almost winter and he's still wearing seersucker. Right? I'll bet he's there, against a wall or column, drinking soda from a paper cup."

"It's an Orange Julius. He wants to be spotted."

"By whom?"

"I'll check."

"No, let me do it!" Yossarian declared. "I'm going to talk to that bastard, once and for all. You keep watch."

"I have a gun in my ankle holster."

"You too?"

"Who else?"

"McBride, a friend of mine."

"At PABT?"

"You know him?"

"I've been there," said Gaffney. "You'll be going again soon now that the wedding has been set."

"It has?" This was news to Yossarian.

Gaffney again looked pleased. "Even Milo doesn't know that yet, but I do. You can order the caviar. Please let me tell him. The SEC has to approve. Do you find that one funny?"

"I've heard it before."

"Don't say much to that agent. He might be CIA."

Yossarian was displeased with himself because he felt no real anger as he strode up to his quarry.

"Hi," said the man, curiously. "What's up?"

Yossarian spoke gruffly. "Didn't I see you following me in New York yesterday?"

"No."

And that was going to be all.

"Were you in New York?" Yossarian was now much less peremptory.

"I was in Florida." His mannerly bearing seemed an immutable mask. "I have a brother in New York."

"Does he look like you?"

"We're twins."

"Is he a federal agent?"

"I don't have to answer that one."

"Are you?"

"I don't know who you are."

"I'm Yossarian. John Yossarian."

"Let me see your credentials."

"You've both been following me, haven't you?"

"Why would we follow you?"

"That's what I want to find out."

"I don't have to tell you. You've got no credentials."

"I don't have credentials," Yossarian, crestfallen, reported back to Gaffney.

"I've got credentials. Let me go try."

And in less than a minute, Jerry Gaffney and the man in the seersucker suit were chatting away in untroubled affinity like very old friends. Gaffney showed a billfold and gave him what looked to Yossarian like a business card, and when a policeman and four or five other people in plain clothes who might have been policemen also drew close briskly, Gaffney distributed a similar card to each, and then to everyone in the small crowd of bystanders who had paused to watch, and finally to the two young black women behind the food counter serving hot dogs, prepackaged sandwiches, soft pretzels with large grains of kosher salt, and soft drinks like Orange Julius. Gaffney returned eventually, immensely satisfied with himself. He spoke softly, but only Yossarian would know, for his demeanor appeared as serene as before.

"He isn't following you, John," he said, and could have been talking about the weather as far as anyone watching could tell. "He's following someone else who's following you. He wants to find out how much they find out about you."

"Who?" demanded Yossarian. "Which one?"

"He hasn't found out yet," answered Gaffney. "It might be me. That would be funny to somebody else, but I see you're not laughing. John, he thinks you might be CIA."

"That's libelous. I hope you told him I'm not."

"I don't know yet that you're not. But I won't tell him anything until he becomes a client. I only told him this much." Gaffney pushed another one of his business cards across the table. "You should have one too."

Yossarian scanned the card with knitted brow, for the words identified the donor as the proprietor of a Gaffney Real Estate Agency, with offices in the city and on the New York and Connecticut seashores and in the coastal municipalities of Santa Monica and San Diego in lower California.

"I'm not sure I get it," said Yossarian.

"It's a front," said Gaffney. "A come-on."

"Now I do." Yossarian grinned. "It's a screen for your detective agency. Right?"

"You've got it backwards. The agency is a front for my real estate business. There's more money in real estate."

"I'm not sure I can believe you."

"Am I trying to be funny?"

"It's impossible to tell."

"I'm luring him on," Jerry Gaffney explained. "Right into one of my offices pretending he's a prospect looking for a house, while he tries to find out who I really am."

"To find out what he's up to?"

"To sell him a house, John. That's where my real income is. This should interest you. We have choice rentals in East Hampton for next summer, for the season, the year, and the short term. And some excellent waterfront properties too, if you're thinking of buying."

"Mr. Gaffney," said Yossarian.

"Are we back to that?"

"I know less about you now than I did before. You said I'd be making this trip, and here I am making it. You predicted there'd be blizzards, and now there are blizzards."

"Meteorology is easy."

"You seem to know all that's happening on the face of the earth. You know enough to be God."

"There's more money in real estate," answered Gaffney. "That's how I know we have no God. He'd be active in real estate too. That's not a bad one, is it?"

"I've heard worse."

"I have one that may be better. I also know much that goes on under the earth. I've been beneath PABT too, you know."

"You've heard the dogs?"

"Oh, sure," said Gaffney. "And seen the Kilroy material. I have connections in MASSPOB too, electronic connections," he appended, and his thin, sensual lips, which were almost liverish in a rich tinge, spread wide again in that smile of his that was cryptic and somehow incomplete. "I've even," he continued, with some pride, "met Mr. Tilyou."

"Mr. Tilyou?" echoed Yossarian. "Which Mr. Tilyou?"

"Mr. George C. Tilyou," Gaffney explained. "The man who built the old Steeplechase amusement park in Coney Island."

"I thought he was dead."

"He is."

"Is that your joke?"

"Does it give you a laugh?"

"Only a smile."

"You can't say I'm not trying," said Gaffney. "Let's go now.

Look back if you wish. That will keep them coming. They won't know whether to stick with Yossarian or follow me. You'll have a smooth trip. Think of this episode as an entr'acte, an intermezzo between Kenosha and your business with Milo and Noodles Cook. Like Wagner's music for Siegfried's Rhine Journey and the Funeral Music in the *Götterdämmerung,* or that interlude of clinking anvils in *Das Rheingold.*"

"I heard that one last night, in my room in Kenosha."

"I know."

"And I learned something new that might help the chaplain. His wife thinks he's already had one miracle."

"That's already old, John," belittled Gaffney. "Everything in Kenosha is bugged. But here is something that might be good. To Milo, you might suggest a shoe."

"What kind of shoe?"

"A military shoe. Perhaps an official U.S. Government shoe. He was too late for cigarettes. But the military will always need shoes. For ladies too. And perhaps brassieres. Please give my best to your fiancée."

"What fiancée?" Yossarian shot back.

"Miss MacIntosh?" Gaffney arched his black eyebrows almost into marks of punctuation.

"Miss MacIntosh is not my fiancée," Yossarian remonstrated. "She's only my nurse."

Gaffney tossed his head in a gesture of laughter. "You have no nurse, Yo-Yo," he insisted almost prankishly. "You've told me that a dozen times. Should I check back and count?"

"Gaffney, go north with your Irish linen or south with your blazer and flannel pants. And take those shadows with you."

"In time. You like the German composers, don't you?"

"Who else is there?" answered Yossarian. "Unless you want to count Italian opera."

"Chopin?"

"You'll find him in Schubert," said Yossarian. "And both in Beethoven."

"Not entirely. And how about the Germans themselves?" asked Gaffney.

"They don't much like each other, do they?" replied Yossarian. "I can't think of another people with such vengeful animosities toward each other."

"Except our own?" suggested Gaffney.

"Gaffney, you know too much."

"I've always been interested in learning things." Gaffney confessed this with an air of restraint. "It's proved useful in my work. Tell me, John," he continued, and fixed his eyes on Yossarian significantly. "Have you ever heard of a German composer named Adrian Leverkühn?"

Yossarian looked back at Gaffney with tense consternation. "Yes, I have, Jerry," he answered, searching the bland, impenetrable dark countenance before him for some glimmer of clarification. "I've heard of Adrian Leverkühn. He did an oratorio called *Apocalypse*."

"I know him for a cantata, *The Lamentations of Faust*."

"I didn't think that one had ever been performed."

"Oh, yes. It has that very touching children's chorus, and that hellish section in glissandos of adult voices laughing ferociously. The laughter and sad chorus always remind me of photos of Nazi soldiers during the war, your war, herding to death those Jewish children in the ghettos."

"That's the *Apocalypse*, Jerry."

"Are you sure?"

"I'm positive."

"I'll have to check. And don't forget your shoe."

"What shoe?"

25

Washington

"A fucking shoe?" Wintergreen ridiculed Yossarian on the next leg of his Rhine Journey. "What's so great about a fucking shoe?"

"It's only a fucking thought," said Yossarian, in one of the hotel suites constituting the Washington offices of M & M E & A. For himself with Melissa he had favored a newer hotel of comparable prestige and livelier clientele that boasted, he recalled with a kind of blissful vanity as he lay in the hospital with his condition stable and the danger of brain damage and paralysis past, a more various choice of superior-grade XXX-rated films in all the languages of UN member nations. "You've been saying you wanted a consumer product."

"But a shoe? By now there must be fifty fucking shoe companies turning out shoes for fucking feet for fucks like us."

"But none with an exclusive franchise for an official U.S. Government shoe."

"Men's shoes or women's shoes?" pondered Milo.

"Both, now that women get killed in combat too." Yossarian was sorry he had started. "Forget it. There's much about business I don't understand. I still can't see how you guys bought eggs for seven cents apiece, sold them for five cents, and made a profit."

"We still do," bragged Wintergreen.

"Eggs spoil," Milo ruminated pitifully. "And break. I'd rather have a shoe. Eugene, look it up."

"I'd rather have the plane," Wintergreen grumbled.

"But after the plane? Suppose there's no more danger of war?"

"I'll look it up."

"I'm not happy with the plane," said Yossarian.

"Are you thinking of leaving us again?" Wintergreen jeered. "You've been objecting for years."

Yossarian was stung by the gibe but ignored it. "Your Shhhhh! could destroy the world, couldn't it?"

"You've been peeking," answered Wintergreen.

"And it can't," said Milo, with heartache. "We conceded that much at the meeting."

"But maybe Strangelove's can?" Wintergreen needled.

"And that's why," said Milo, "we want the meeting with Noodles Cook."

Yossarian again was shaking his head. "And I'm not happy with the atom bomb. I don't like it anymore."

"Who would you like to see get the contract?" Wintergreen argued. "Fucking Strangelove?"

"And we don't have the bomb," conciliated Milo. "We only have plans for a plane that will deliver it."

"And our plane won't work."

"We'll guarantee that, Yossarian. Even in writing. Our planes won't fly, our missiles won't fire. If they take off, they'll crash; if they fire, they'll miss. We never fail. It's the company motto."

"You can find it on our fucking letterhead," Wintergreen added, and continued deliberately with a sneer. "But let me ask you this, Mr. Yo-Yo. What country would you rather see be strongest if not us? That's the fucking catch, isn't it?"

"That's the catch, all right," Yossarian had to agree.

"And if we don't sell our fucking war products to everyone who wants to buy, our friendly fucking allies and competitors will. There's nothing you can do about it. Time's run out for your fucking ideals. Tell me, if you're so smart, what the fuck would you do if you were running the country?"

"I wouldn't know what to do either," Yossarian admitted, and was enraged with himself for being bested in argument. It never used to happen that way. "But I know I'd want my conscience to be clear."

"Our conscience is clear," responded both.

"I don't want the guilt."

"That's horseshit, Yossarian."

"And I wouldn't be responsible."

"And that's more horseshit," countered Wintergreen. "There's nothing you can do about it, and you *will* be responsible. If the world's going to blow up anyway, what the fuck difference does it make who does it?"

"At least my hands will be clean."

Wintergreen laughed coarsely. "They'll be blown off at the wrists, your fucking clean hands. No one will even know they're yours. You won't even be found."

"Go fuck yourself, Wintergreen!" Yossarian answered irately, with raised voice. "Go straight to hell, with *your* clear conscience!" He turned away, sulking. "I wish you were dead already, so I could finally in this lifetime get at least a little bit of pleasure out of you."

"Yossarian, Yossarian," chided Milo. "Be reasonable. One thing you do know about me—I never lie."

"Unless he has to," appended Wintergreen.

"I think he knows that, Eugene. I'm as moral as the next man. Right, Eugene?"

"Absolutely, Mr. Minderbinder."

"Milo, have you ever," asked Yossarian, "in your life done anything dishonest?"

"Oh, no," Milo responded like a shot. "That would be dishonest. And there's never been need to."

"And that's why," said Wintergreen, "we want this secret meeting with Noodles Cook, to get him to speak secretly to the President. We want everything out in the open."

"Yossarian," said Milo, "aren't you safer with us? Our planes can't work. We have the technology. Please call Noodles Cook."

"Set up the meeting and stop fucking around. And we want to be there."

"You don't trust me?"

"You say you don't fucking understand business."

"You say it puzzles you."

"Yes, and what does fucking puzzle me," said Yossarian, giving in, "is how guys like you do understand it."

Noodles Cook grasped quickly what was wanted of him.

"I know, I know," he began, after the introductions had been effected, speaking directly to Yossarian. "You think I'm a shit, don't you?"

"Hardly ever," answered Yossarian, without surprise, while the other two watched. "Noodles, when people think of the dauphin, they don't always think of you."

"Touché," laughed Noodles. "But I do enjoy being here. Please don't ask me why." What they wanted, he went on, was clearly improper, unsuitable, indefensible, and perhaps illegal. "Normally, gentlemen, I could lobby with the best of them. But we have ethics in government now."

"Who's in charge of our Department of Ethics?"

"They're holding it open until Porter Lovejoy gets out of jail."

"I have a thought," said Yossarian, feeling it was a good one. "You're permitted to give speeches, aren't you?"

"I give them regularly."

"And to receive an honorarium for them?"

"I would not do it without one."

"Noodles," said Yossarian, "I believe these gentlemen want you to make a speech. To an audience of one. To the President alone, recommending that the government buy their plane. Could you deliver a successful speech like that one?"

"I could give a very successful speech like that one."

"And in return, they would give you an honorarium."

"Yes," said Milo. "We would give you an honorarium."

"And how much would that honorarium be?" inquired Noodles.

"Milo?" Yossarian stepped back, for there was much about business he still did not understand.

"Four hundred million dollars," said Milo.

"That sounds fair," responded Noodles, in a manner equally innocuous, as though he too were hearing nothing rare, and it was then, Yossarian recalled with amusement as he killed time later in his hospital bed, that Noodles offered to give him a peek into the Presidential Game Room, after the others had dashed away to the urgent financial meeting they'd mentioned for which they were already anxious to depart, for Gaffney's joke about antitrust approval for the M2 marriage to Christina Maxon turned out, after all, not to be a joke.

"And for you, Yossarian . . . ," began Milo, when the three were parting.

"For that wonderful idea you came up with . . . ," Wintergreen joined in, expansively.

"That's why we need him, Eugene. To you, Yossarian, we're giving, in gratitude, five hundred thousand dollars."

Yossarian, who had expected nothing, responded levelly, learning fast. "That sounds fair," he said with disappointment.

Milo looked embarrassed. "It's a little bit more than one percent," he insisted sensitively.

"And a little bit less than the one and a half percent of our standard finder's fee, isn't it?" said Yossarian. "But it still sounds fair."

"Yossarian," Wintergreen cajoled, "you're almost seventy and pretty well off. Look into your heart. Does it really matter if you make another hundred thousand dollars, or even if the world does come to an end in a nuclear explosion after you're gone?"

Yossarian took a good look into his heart and answered honestly.

"No. But you two are just as old. Do you really care if you make millions more or not?"

"Yes," said Milo emphatically.

"And that's the big difference between us."

"Well, we're alone now," said Noodles. "You do think I'm a shit, don't you?"

"No more than me," said Yossarian.

"Are you crazy?" cried Noodles Cook. "You can't compare! Look what I just agreed to do!"

"I proposed it."

"I accepted!" argued Noodles. "Yossarian, there are nine other tutors here who are much bigger shits than you'll ever amount to, and they don't come close to me."

"I give in," said Yossarian. "You're a bigger shit than I am, Noodles Cook."

"I'm glad you see it my way. Now let me show you our playroom. I'm getting good at video games, better than all the others. He's very proud of me."

The renovated Oval Office of the country's chief executive had been reduced in size drastically to make room for the spacious game room into which it now led. In the shrunken quarters, which now could comfortably hold no more than three or four others, presidential meetings were fewer and quicker, conspiracies simpler, cover-ups instantaneous. The President had more time free for his video games, and these he found more true to life than life itself, he'd said once publicly.

The physical compensations for the change lay in the larger, more imposing second room, which, with extension, was spacious enough for the straight-backed chairs and game tables for the multitudinous video screens, controls, and other attachments that now stood waiting like robotic stewards along the encircling periphery of the walls. The section nearest the entrance was designated THE WAR DEPARTMENT and contained individual games identified singly as *The Napoleonic War, The Battle of Gettysburg, The Battle of Bull Run, The Battle of Antietam, Victory in Grenada, Victory in Vietnam, Victory in Panama City, Victory at Pearl Harbor,* and *The Gulf War Refought.* A cheerful poster showed a gleaming apple-cheeked marine above the sentences:

> STEP RIGHT UP AND TRY.
> ANYONE CAN PLAY.
> ANY SIDE CAN WIN.

Yossarian moved by games named *Indianapolis Speedway, Bombs Away, Beat the Draft,* and *Die Laughing.* The place of prominence in the Presidential Game Room contained a video screen grander than the others and, waist-high, on a surface with the proportions and foundations of a billiard table, a transparent contour map of the country, vivid with different hues of green, black, blue, and desert pinks and tans. On the colorful replica were sets of electric trains on labyrinths of tracks that crossed the continent on different planes and went belowground through tunnels. When Noodles, with an enigmatic smile, pressed the buttons that turned on bright internal lights and set the trains running, Yossarian perceived a model of a whole new miniature world of vast and hermetic complexity functioning beneath the surface of the continent on different plateaus, extending from border to border, through boundaries northward into Canada to Alaska, and eastward and westward to the oceans. The name for this game read:

TRIAGE

On the map, he spotted first, in the peninsula state of Florida, a tiny cabin-shaped marker labeled Federal Citrus Reservoir. Large numbers of the railroad cars traveling underground were mounted with missiles, and many others carried cannons and transported armored vehicles. He saw several medical trains marked with a red cross. His eyes found a Federal Wisconsin Cheese Depository on the banks of Lake Michigan not far from Kenosha. He noted another Citrus Fruit Reservoir in California and a nationwide subterranean dispersion of pizza parlors and meat lockers. There was the nuclear reactor at the Savannah River, about which he now knew. Star-shaped Washington, D.C. was enlarged in blue within a white circle; he read markers there for the White House, the Burning Tree Country Club, MASSPOB, the new National Military Cemetery, the newest war memorial, and Walter Reed Hospital. And underground beneath every one of these, if he comprehended what he was looking at, was a perfect reconstruction of each concealed on a lower tier. Traveling out from the capital city were directional arrows paralleling the train tracks leading by subterranean route to destinations including the Greenbrier Country Club in West Virginia, the Livermore Laboratories in California, the Centers for Disease Control in Atlanta, the Burn Treatment Center at New York Hospital, and also in New York City, he noted with tremendous surprise, PABT, the bus terminal so close to the building that was presently his home.

He was stunned to find PABT joined to MASSPOB and incorporated in a local network with an underground tentacle that slithered through the buried canal under Canal Street and a wall walling off Wall Street. In Brooklyn, he saw Coney Island symbolized on the surface by an iron-red miniature of a phallic tower he recognized as the defunct parachute jump of the old Steeplechase Park. And underground, on what appeared to be a facsimile of an amusement park, Steeplechase Park, was a sketch of a grinning face with flat hair and lots of teeth, which he also knew.

"But ours work," Noodles told him with pride. "Or they wouldn't be on our map. He had this whole model built to make sure it's as good as the one in the game. If there's one word he lives by, it's be prepared."

"That's two words, isn't it?" corrected Yossarian.

"I used to think that way too," said Noodles, "but now I see it his way. I'm getting better at golf also."

"Is that why those country clubs are there?"

"He's putting them into the video game so they'll both match. See up there in Vermont?" Yossarian saw a Ben & Jerry Federal Ice Cream Depository. "He found that one in the video game only a little while ago, and now he wants one too. We'll also have Häagen-Dazs. We may be underneath a long time when it ever comes to that, and he wants to be sure of his ice cream and his golf. This is confidential, but we already have a nine-hole course finished underneath Burning Tree, and it's identical to the one up here. He's down there now, practicing the course so he'll have an advantage over others when the time comes."

"Who would those others be?" asked Yossarian.

"Those of us who've been chosen to survive," answered Noodles, "and to keep the country running underground when there's not much left above."

"I see. When would that be?"

"When he unlocks the box and presses the button. You see that second unit beside the game? That's the Football."

"What football?"

"Newspapermen like to call it the Football. It's the unit that will launch all our planes and defensive-offensive weapons as soon as there's word of the big attack or we decide to launch our own war. That will have to happen, sooner or later."

"I know that. What happens then?"

"We go down below, the little prick and I, until the embers cool and the radiation blows away. Along with the rest who've been picked to survive."

"Who does the picking?"

"The National Bipartisan Triage Committee. They've picked themselves, of course, and their best friends."

"Who's on it?"

"Nobody's sure."

"What happens to me and my best friends?"

"You're all disposable, of course."

"That sounds fair," said Yossarian.

"It's a pity we don't have time for a game now," said Noodles. "It's something to watch when we're fighting each other for purified water. Would you like to begin one?"

"I'm meeting a lady friend in the aeronautical museum of the Smithsonian."

"And I have a history lesson to give when he gets back from his golf. That part isn't easy."

"Do you learn a lot?" Yossarian teased.

"We both learn a lot," said Noodles, offended. "Well, Yossarian, it will soon be Thanksgiving, and we ought to talk turkey. How much will you want?"

"For what?"

"For getting me that speaking engagement. You're in for a piece, naturally. Name your price."

"Noodles," said Yossarian in censure, "I couldn't take anything. That would be a kickback. I don't want a penny."

"That sounds fair," said Noodles, and grinned. "You see what a bigger shit I am? That's one more I owe you."

"There's that one I do want," Yossarian remembered later he had requested earnestly. "I want the chaplain set free."

And at that point Noodles had turned grave. "I've tried. There are complications. They don't know what to do with him and are sorry now they ever found him. If they could dispose of him safely as radioactive waste, I think they would do it."

After the tritium, they had to see what came out of the chaplain next. Plutonium would be dreadful. And worse, lithium, that medication of choice he'd been receiving for his depression, bonded with heavy water into the lithium deuteride of the hydrogen bomb, and that could be a catastrophe.

26

Yossarian

Noodles Cook had his history lesson to prepare and Yossarian had his date at the museum. Yossarian was remembering Noodles a week later when he drew near PABT and heard the tiny steam whistles of the nearby vendors of hot peanuts. These brought back to mind the tuneful phrases of the "Forest Murmurs" in *Siegfried*, and the struggle for that magic ring of stolen gold that supposedly conferred world power on anyone who owned it—and brought doleful misery and ruin to all those who did. As he pushed through the doors to enter the bus terminal, he envisioned that Germanic hero, who was only Icelandic, at the lair of the dormant dragon that was lying there minding its own business. "Let me sleep," was the growling thanks to wretched king-god Wotan, who, in mournful, frustrated hopes of getting back that ring in gratitude, had come sneaking up to warn him of the fearless hero approaching.

Young Siegfried had his dragon to face, and Yossarian had those savage dogs below at the entrance to that mysterious underworld of basements that McBride now had license to inspect.

Yossarian, looking back, could recall no intimations then of what he came to know later in the hospital when contemplating his Rhine Journey as narrative jest, that he would start seeing double that same day and end in the hospital with his predicament with Melissa and his half-million dollars, and with the sale of a shoe.

With Germany unified and bristling with neo-Nazi violence again, he thought *The New Yorker* might jump at this mordant spoof of a Rhine Journey by a contemporary American middle-class Assyrian Siegfried of ambiguous Semitic extraction, surely a contradiction. But, inevitably, distracting visitors and doctors soon depleted him of time and that optimistic verve essential for the renewal and consummation of serious literary ambition.

Yossarian was forced to admire the veteran poise with which Melissa and even Angela could turn nondescript in the presence of his children or Frances and Patrick Beach, blending innocuously into the background or slipping noiselessly from the room. And then popping up out of nowhere entirely by coincidence, even old Sam Singer the tail gunner was there too, as a visitor to his big-boned friend with cancer, and their curious, fey friend from California, with the plump face and pinched eyes, who came seeking Yossarian out for his access to Milo. There was even a phantasmagorical brush with a gruesome war casualty in plaster and bandages called the Soldier in White, in mystical flashback to another warped delusion.

Siegfried, he contrived in analogy, had gone zipping off on foot to awaken Brünnhilde with a kiss after lifting the ring the slain dragon had earned by working like a giant to build eternal Valhalla for the immortal gods, who already knew it was twilight time for them too.

Whereas Yossarian went by taxi and had more than a kiss in mind for Melissa when he came upon her practically alone in the semidarkness of the cinema in the museum with the continuously running film of the record of aviation. But so swiftly was he swept up by the flickering ancient movies of the first aviators that he forgot entirely to interfere with her. The Lindbergh airplane on view was more astonishing to him than any space capsule. Melissa was reverent too. The Lindbergh kid of twenty-four had flown by periscope, his view in front obstructed by an auxiliary fuel tank.

At night after dinner he felt dead from his trip and already too well acquainted with their agendas of eros to be avid for sex. If she was offended, she gave no sign. To his mild disbelief, she was asleep before he was.

Meditating in solitude on his back, he made spontaneously the gratifying decision to surprise her with a fifth of the half-million-dollar gold hoard he had picked up that day, absorbing taxes himself. He thought a gift of a hundred thousand dollars to be conserved for the future by a hardworking woman with a net worth of less than six thousand might affect her as favorably as the replacement of the two silver fillings, the eight dozen roses in a two-day period, and the silken, frilly upper-body lingerie from Saks Fifth Avenue, Victoria's Secret, and Frederick's of Hollywood. To someone like her, a windfall of a hundred thousand dollars might seem a lot.

She wore a skirt on the plane, but he had lost his desire to fool with her there. He talked more about the wedding at the bus terminal. She wanted to go, although he had not yet asked her. What he had most in mind was a few evenings apart.

For Yossarian, the prurient anticipation of unexpected lascivious treats and discoveries with Melissa was already beginning to lessen with the likelihood of their occurrence. They had grown familiar with each other too quickly—that had happened before: it happened every time—and he'd decided already they ought to start seeing less of each other. When not getting ready for bed or planning what to eat, they often had not much to do. That had happened before also; it happened every time. And doing nothing was often more bracing when done alone. He would not for anything ever take her dancing again, and he would sooner die than go to the theater. After the hundred grand, it might be wiser to separate as friends. He'd said nothing to her yet about that altruistic impulse. He'd had quixotic notions before.

And then he was stricken.

Here again was a Rhine Journey contrast.

Siegfried went out hunting and was stabbed in the back.

Yossarian set out for the bus terminal and was saved in the hospital.

He'd had his aura and his TIA, and for the next ten days he and his nurse Melissa, whom he'd thought he might see less of, were together every morning and most of every afternoon, and much of all evenings too until she left for the sleep she needed to report for work the next morning and help keep him alive by making sure that none on the medical staff did anything wrong. Not till the next-to-last day did she find out she was with child. He did not doubt the child was his.

BOOK
NINE

27

PABT

The dogs were a recording, of course. McBride skipped down to the steps that set them stirring and charging, then to the next, that closed them back into silence. The fierce charge came from three, said the official audiologists. Or from one—Yossarian reasoned—with three heads.

"Michael not here?" McBride asked at the beginning.

"Joan not coming?"

Joan, a lawyer with the Port Authority, was McBride's new lady friend. It would be funny, Yossarian had already conjectured, if *their* wedding too took place in the bus terminal. He could picture the *Lohengrin* "Wedding March" in the police station and the nuptial procession past the wall chains to the makeshift altar in a prison cell in back modified to a chapel. McBride's obstetrical cell was now a resting place for McMahon. The play cell for children was a recreation room utilized by officers on their breaks and as a hangout for those in no hurry to go home. There were checkerboards and jigsaw puzzles too, girlie magazines, a television set, and a video player on which to rerun the XXX-rated movies confiscated from pornographers, while smoking dope extorted from drug dealers, whom they also despised. McMahon had to look the other way. McBride was disillusioned again.

"Where's your friend?" timidly asked McBride.

"She has to work, Larry. She's still a nurse."

"Aren't you jealous," McBride wished to know, "of men patients and doctors?"

"All the time," admitted Yossarian, remembering adventurers

like himself, and his fingers on the lace of her slip. "What do you know about those agents?"

"They're downstairs. They think I'm CIA. I'm not sure I trust them. I guess that other noise is phony too."

"What other noise? The carousel?"

"What carousel? I mean the roller-coaster."

"What roller-coaster? Larry, that train is not a roller-coaster. Are we waiting for Tommy?"

"He says it's none of his business, because it's not on his chart. He's resting again."

Yossarian found McMahon where he expected to find him, in bed in the cell in back, the television on. Captain Thomas McMahon had more or less moved all his office work and his telephone into the cell with the bed and now spent much of each working day resting. He came in on days off too. His wife had died of emphysema that year, and living alone, he would relate while smoking cigarettes, with a glass ashtray on the arm of the rocker he had found, was not much fun. He had found the rocker in a thrift shop that raised money for cancer relief. His eyes had grown sizable in his narrow face, and the bones seemed gaunt and crude, for he had been losing weight. A year or so earlier, he had lost his breath chasing a youth who had murdered someone in another part of the terminal, and he had not yet got it all back. McMahon now disliked his work but would not retire, for keeping this occupation he loathed, now that he was a widower, was all the fun he had.

"There are more of them now than there are of us," McMahon would reiterate moodily about his criminals. "And that's something you educated wise guys never thought of with that Constitution of yours. What's out there now?" he asked wearily, folding away a tabloid newspaper. He enjoyed following grotesque new crimes. He was bored working on them.

"A drunk on the floor, three druggies in chairs. Two brown, one white."

"I guess I'll have to go look." McMahon uncoiled himself and rose, panting in the effort from what could have been lassitude. He seemed now to Yossarian another good candidate for late-life depression. "You know, we don't arrest every crook we can catch," he repeated, in a repetitious lament. "We don't have the men to process them, we don't have the cells to put them in, we don't have the courts to find them guilty, and we don't have the prisons to keep them in. And that's something a lot of you people complaining all the time about cops and courts don't want to understand, not even that man from *Time* magazine who had his pocket picked and raised such a racket." McMahon paused for a chuckle. "We had to lock him up, while those thieves who'd robbed him looked on at all of us with smiles."

McMahon smiled too and told about the retired advertising executive from *Time, The Weekly Newsmagazine* who'd been left without a penny because he had given his change to some panhandlers and had then had his wallet stolen. He had his Social Security number but could not prove it was his. He went out of control when the policemen made no move to arrest any in the slick band of pickpockets. The wallet was already miles away; there would be no evidence. "We're stuck with this lousy legal system of yours that says a person is innocent until we can prove him guilty," said McMahon. "Since when, is what *we* would like to know! That's what drove him crazy, I think. There were the crooks. Here were the cops. And here was the cold fact that he couldn't do a thing about it. And he had no identification. He couldn't even prove he was him. That's when he panicked and made such a fuss we had to chain him in a wall cuff before he showed some sense and shut up. He saw what we had waiting for him in the cells, where he wouldn't have a chance of competing. Neither would we, or you. Then he could not establish his identity. That's always fun to watch. That always terrifies them. Nobody we telephoned was home. He couldn't even prove his own name. Finally"—McMahon was chuckling now—"he had to give us the name of this friend up in Orange Valley somewhere who turned out to be a big war hero in World War II. A big shot now in the army reserves. A big man in the construction industry too, he told us, and a big contributor to the Patrolmen's Benevolent Association. He had a name like Berkowitz or Rabinowitz, and he talked strong on the telephone, the way you did the first time you called, Yossarian, except this guy was telling the truth and wasn't sort of full of shit, the way you were. Then this guy Singer had no money to get home. So Larry here gave him a twenty-dollar bill for a taxi, remember? And guess what. The guy paid him back. Right, Larry?"

"He mailed it. Tommy, I think you ought to come."

"I don't want to find out any more about anything. And I don't like those guys. I think they're CIA."

"They think you're CIA."

"I'm going back to your delivery room." McMahon was running out of energy again. "To rest awhile until one of your pregnant kids shows up and gives us one of your babies she wants to throw away. We haven't got any so far."

"You won't let me announce it. We hear about plenty."

"They'd lock us both up. Now, Larry, do this for me—find something down there to cancel that crazy wedding he's scheduled. I'm too old for that kind of stuff."

"They already have something they can't figure out," McBride reported to Yossarian. "An elevator that's down there and won't move, and we can't find out where it comes from."

From the front of the station house there came abruptly the explosive noise of a brawl.

"Oh, shit," groaned McMahon. "How I've grown to hate them all. Even my cops. Your pregnant mothers too."

Two burly young men who were cronies had broken each other's noses and split each other's mouths in an altercation over money robbed from a drug-addicted young black prostitute, a close friend of theirs, with white skin, yellow hair, and AIDS, syphilis, tuberculosis, and new strains of gonorrhea.

"There's another weird thing about these federal intelligence guys," McBride confided, when the two were out of the station. "They don't see anything funny about those signs. It's like they've seen them before."

They cut across the main concourse below the Operations Control Center, and Yossarian remembered he was now on view on one of the five dozen video monitors there, traveling with McBride through the encasing structure. Perhaps Michael was up there again, watching with M2. If he picked his nose someone would see. On another screen, he supposed, might be the redheaded man in the seersucker suit, drinking an Orange Julius, and maybe the scruffy man in the sullied raincoat and blue beret, observed upstairs while observing him.

"They don't seem surprised by anything," grumbled McBride. "All they want to talk about when we plan the wedding is to get themselves invited, their wives too."

The stairwell was practically empty, the floor almost tidy. But the odors were strong, the air fetid with the rancid, mammalian vapors of unwashed bodies and their fecund wastes.

McBride went ahead and tiptoed carefully around the one-legged woman being raped again not far from the large, brown-skinned woman with thickened moles that looked like melanomas, who had taken off her bloomers and her skirt again and was swabbing her backside and armpits with a few damp towels, and Yossarian knew again he had not one thing to talk to her about, except, perhaps, to know if she had ridden to Kenosha on the same plane with him, which was out of the question and entirely possible.

On the last flight of steps sat the skinny blonde woman with a tattered red sweater, still dreamily engaged in sewing a rip in a dirty white blouse. At the bottom, there was already a fresh human shit on the floor in the corner. McBride said nothing about it. They turned underneath the staircase and proceeded to the battered metal closet with the false back and hidden door. In single file they came again into the tiny vestibule, facing the fire door of military green with the warning that read:

EMERGENCY ENTRANCE
KEEP OUT
VIOLATORS WILL BE SHOT

"They don't see anything funny in that," sulked McBride. Yossarian opened the massive door with just his fingertip and was once more on the tiny landing near the roof of the tunnel, at the top of the staircase that fell steeply. The thoroughfare below was empty again.

McBride did a little jig step on the activating steps that roused the sleeping dogs and sent them back with hardly a peep of protest into the unstirring limbo in which they made their noiseless abode and spent their dateless hours. Showing off, he grinned at Yossarian.

"Where are the loudspeakers?"

"We haven't found them. We aren't authorized to look far yet. We're only checking security for the President."

"What's that water?"

"What water?"

"Oh, shit, Larry, I'm the one who's supposed to be hard of hearing. I hear water, a fucking stream, a babbling brook."

McBride shrugged impartially. "I'll check. We're looking into both ends today. We can't even find out if it's supposed to be secret. That's secret too."

Approaching the bottom of the lopsided ellipse of this staircase,

Yossarian caught glimpses below of shoulders and trouser cuffs and shabby shoes, one pair a dingy black, one pair an orange brown. Yossarian was beyond surprise when he reached the last flight and saw the two men waiting: a lanky, pleasant redheaded man with a seersucker jacket and a swarthy, seamy, chunky man in a scruffy raincoat, with ill-shaven cheeks and a blue beret. The latter wore a surly look and compressed a limp cigarette between wet lips. Both hands were deep in the pockets of his raincoat.

They were Bob and Raul. Bob was different from the agent in Chicago. But Raul was the spitting image of the man outside his building and in his dream in Kenosha. Raul badgered his moist cigarette about his mouth, as though in moody exception to some restriction against lighting it.

"Were you in Wisconsin last week?" Yossarian could not help asking, with a guise of affable innocence. "Around the motel near the airport in a place called Kenosha?"

The man shrugged neutrally, with a look at McBride.

"We were together every day last week," McBride answered for him, "going over the floor plans of that catering company you brought in."

"And I was in Chicago," offered the redheaded man named Bob. He folded a stick of chewing gum into his mouth and tossed the crumpled green wrapper aside to the floor.

"Did I meet you in Chicago?" Yossarian faced him doubtfully, positive he had never laid eyes on him. "At the airport there?"

Bob answered leniently. "Wouldn't you know that?"

Yossarian had heard that voice before. "Would you?"

"Of course," said the man. "It's a joke, isn't it? But I don't catch on."

"Yo-Yo, that guy in charge of the wedding wants *six* dance floors and *six* bandstands, with one as a backup in case the other five all don't work, and I don't see where they can find the room, and I don't even know what the hell that means."

"Me *aussi*," said Raul, as though he hardly cared.

"I'll talk to him," said Yossarian.

"And something like thirty-five hundred guests! That's three hundred and fifty round tables. And two tons of caviar. Yo-Yo, that's four thousand pounds!"

"My wife wants to come," said Bob. "I'll have a gun in my ankle holster, but I'd like to pretend I'm a guest."

"I'll take care of it," said Yossarian.

"*Moi* also," said Raul, and threw away his cigarette.

"I'll take care of that too," said Yossarian. "But tell me what's happening here. What is this place?"

"We're here to find out," said Bob. "We'll talk to the sentries."

"Yo-Yo, wait while we check."

"Yo-Yo." Raul sniggered. "My *Dieux.*"

All three looked left into the tunnel. And then Yossarian saw sitting inside on a bentwood chair a soldier in a red combat uniform with an assault rifle across his lap, and behind him near the wall stood a second armed soldier, with a larger weapon. On the other side, in the amber haze telescoping backward into the narrowing horizon of a beaming vanishing point, he made out two other motionless soldiers, in exactly that grouping. They could have been reflections.

"What's over there?" Yossarian pointed across toward the passageway to SUB-BASEMENTS A–Z.

"Nothing we found yet," said McBride. "You take a look, but don't go far."

"There's something else *très* funny," said Raul, and finally smiled. He stamped his foot a few times and then began jumping and landing on both heels heavily. "Notice anything, my *ami*? No noise down here, *nous* can't make noise."

All shuffled, stamped, jumped in place to demonstrate, Yossarian too. They made no dent in the silence. Bob rapped his knuckles on the banister of the staircase, and the thud was as expected. When he rapped them on the ground there was nothing.

"That's pretty weird, isn't it?" said Bob, smiling. "It's as though we're not even here."

"What's in your pockets?" Yossarian questioned Raul abruptly. "You don't take your hands out. Not in my dream or in the street across from my building."

"My cock and my balls," said Raul at once.

McBride was embarrassed. "His gun and his badge."

"That's *mon* cock and *mes* balls," joked Raul, but did not laugh.

"I've got one more question, if you want to come to the wedding," said Yossarian. "Why have you got your sentries there—to keep people in or keep people out?"

All three shot him a look of surprise.

"They aren't ours," said Bob.

"It's what we want to find out," explained McBride.

"Let's *allons.*"

They moved away, with no fall of footsteps.

Yossarian made no sound either when he started across.

He noted next another strange thing. They cast no shadows. He cast none either as he crossed the sterile thoroughfare like a specter or soundless sleepwalker to the catwalk of white tile. The steps going up were also white, and the handrails of an albumescent porcelain that shimmered almost into invisibility against the like background of pure white, and they also were without shadows. And there was no dirt, and not one beaming reflection from one mote in the air. He felt himself nowhere. He remembered the gum wrapper and the wet cigarette. He glanced down backward to make sure he was right. He was.

The crumpled green wrapper balled up by Bob was nowhere to be seen. The unlit cigarette had vanished too. Before his eyes as he searched, the green gum wrapper materialized through the surface of the compound underfoot and was again on the ground. Then it dwindled away rearward and was altogether gone. The unlit cigarette came back next. And then that went away also. They had come out of nowhere and gone away someplace, and he had the unearthly sense that he had only to think of an object to bring it into an unreal reality before him—if he mused of a half-undressed Melissa in ivory underwear, she would be lying there obligingly; he did and she was—and to turn his sensibility away to something else and it would dwindle from existence. She disappeared. Next he was sure he heard faintly the distinctive puffing music of the band organ of a carousel. McBride was nowhere near to verify the sound. Possibly, McBride would hear it as a roller-coaster. And then Yossarian was no longer sure, for the calliope was producing gaily in waltz time the somber, forceful Siegfried Funeral Music from the culminating *Götterdämmerung*, which precedes by less than one hour the immolation of Brünnhilde and her horse, the destruction of Valhalla, and the death knell of those great gods, who were always unhappy, always in anguish.

Yossarian went up to the catwalk and moved into the archway past the memorial affirming that Kilroy had been there. He sensed with a twinge that Kilroy, immortal, was dead too, had died in Korea if not Vietnam.

"Halt!"

The order rang through the archway with an echo. In front on another bentwood chair, slightly forward of a turnstile with rotating bars of steel, sat another armed sentry.

This one too was uniformed in a battle jacket that was crimson and a visored green hat that looked like a jockey cap. Yossarian advanced at his signal, feeling weightless, insubstantial, contingent. The guard was young, had light hair in a crew cut, sharp eyes, and a thin mouth, and Yossarian discerned as he drew close enough to see freckles that he looked exactly like the young gunner Arthur Schroeder, with whom he had flown overseas almost fifty years before.

"Who goes there?"

"Major John Yossarian, retired," said Yossarian.

"Can I be of help to you, Major?"

"I want to go in."

"You'll have to pay."

"I'm with them."

"You'll still have to pay."

"How much?"

"Fifty cents."

Yossarian handed him two quarters and was given a round blue ticket with numbers in sequence wheeling around the rim of the disk of flimsy cardboard on a loop of white string. In helpful pantomime, the guard directed him to slip the loop over his head to hang the ticket around his neck and down over his breast. The name above the piping of his pocket read A. SCHROEDER.

"There's an elevator, sir, if you want to go directly."

"What's down there?"

"You're supposed to know, sir."

"Your name is Schroeder?"

"Yes, sir. Arthur Schroeder."

"That's fucking funny." The soldier said nothing as Yossarian studied him. "Were you ever in the air corps?"

"No, sir."

"How old are you, Schroeder?"

"I'm a hundred and seven."

"That's a good number. How long have you been here?"

"Since 1900."

"Hmmmmm. You were about seventeen when you enrolled?"

"Yes, sir. I came in with the Spanish-American War."

"These are all lies, aren't they?"

"Yes, sir. They are."

"Thank you for telling me the truth."

"I always tell the truth, sir."

"Is that another lie?"

"Yes, sir. I always lie."

"That can't be true then, can it? Are you from Crete?"

"No, sir. I'm from Athens, Georgia. I went to school in Ithaca, New York. My home is now in Carthage, Illinois."

"Is that so?"

"Yes, sir. I cannot tell a lie."

"You are from Crete, aren't you? You know the paradox of the Cretan who tells you Cretans always lie? It's impossible to believe him, isn't it? I want to go inside."

"You have your ticket." The guard punched a hole in the center and another in a number. The number was for the Human Pool Table.

"I can't go on that ride?"

"You've already been, sir," advised the guard named Schroeder. "Those are aluminized metal detectors just inside that arcade. Don't bring drugs or explosives. Be prepared for noise and the bright lights."

Yossarian pushed through the turnstile and walked into the framework of silver metal detectors at the entrance to the hallway. The moment he did, the lighting blinked off. And next, harsh white lights flashed on with a blaze that almost staggered him. He discovered himself inside a brilliantly illuminated hallway of magic mirrors. A roaring noise all but deafened him. It seemed like the blasts of an MRI machine. And he saw that the mirrors glittering grotesquely on all sides and overhead were deforming his reflections dissimilarly, as though he were liquefied into highlighted mercury and melting distinctly into something different from every point of view. Discrete parts of him were enlarged and elongated as though for extracting examination; his images were billowing into quantities of swells. In one mirror, he witnessed his head and neck misshapen into a slender block of Yossarian, while his torso and legs were stunted and bloated. In the mirror beside that one his body was monstrously inflated and his face reduced to a grape, a pimple with hair and a minuscule face with crushed features and a grin. He perceived that he was close to laughing, and the novelty of that surprise tickled him more. In no two mirrors were the deformities alike, in no one lens were the anomalies consistent. His authentic appearance, his objective structure, was no longer absolute. He had to wonder what he truly looked like. And then the ground beneath his feet began to move.

The floor jerked back and forth. He adjusted smoothly, recalling the jolly tricks of George C. Tilyou in his old Steeplechase Park. This was one. The deafening noise had ceased. The heat from the lights was searing. Most piercing was a scorching dazzle of pure white that burned above his right eye and another, just as hot, that gleamed like a flare off his left. He could not find them. When he turned to try, they moved with his vision and remained in place, and then he felt the ground beneath his feet shift again, to a different prank, in which the right half jerked in one backward or forward thrust while the other went opposite, the two reversing themselves rapidly to the regulated pace of an undeviating heartbeat. He bore himself forward easily on this one too. The lights turned indigo blue, and much of him looked black. The lights turned red, and areas of him were drained of color again. Back in normal light, he almost swooned at a hideous glimpse of himself as homeless, abominable, filthy, and depraved. In a different mirror he ballooned into a nauseating metamorphosis of a swollen insect inside a fragile brown carapace; then he was Raul, and Bob, and then with another revolting fright he saw himself reflected as the frowsy, squat, untidy, middle-aged woman with the pudgy chin and crude face dogging him in the red Toyota, and then he changed again to look the way he always thought he did. He walked onward, hurrying away, and found himself challenged at the end by a last mirror in front, which blocked him in like a massive barrier of glass. In this one, he was still himself, but the features on the face in the head on his shoulders were those of a smiling young man with a hopeful, innocent, naive, and defiant demeanor. He saw himself under thirty with a blooming outlook, an optimistic figure no less comely and immortal than the lordliest divinity that ever was, but no more. His hair was short, black, and wavy, and he was at a time in his life when he still smugly fostered audacious expectations that all was possible.

With no hesitation he made use of momentum to take a giant step forward directly into the looking glass, smack into that illusion of himself as a hale youth with something of a middle-aged spread, and he came out the other side a white-haired adult near seventy into the commodious landscape of an amusement park unfurling before him on a level semicircle. He heard a carousel. He heard a roller-coaster.

He heard the high-pitched squeals of gaiety and simulated panic from a far-off group of men and women in a flat-bottomed boat rumbling down a high watery incline to a splashing stop in a pool.

Rotating clockwise slowly in front of him now was the perfect circle of a magic barrel, the Barrel of Fun, number one on his blue-and-white ticket. The ridged outer edges of the turning tubular chamber facing him were the raspberry red of candies and the sweetened syrup at soda fountains, and the sky blue of the rim was marked with yellow comets amid strewn white stars and a sprinkling of apricot crescent moons wearing smiles. He walked through casually simply by guiding himself on a line contrary to the direction of rotation and came out the other end into a conversation the late author Truman Capote was having with a man whose name gave him pause.

"Faust," repeated the stranger.

"Dr. Faust?" inquired Yossarian eagerly.

"No, Irvin Faust," said the man, who wrote novels also. "Good reviews, but never a big best-seller. This is William Saroyan. I bet you never even heard of him."

"Sure I did." Yossarian was miffed. "I saw *The Time of Your Life*. I read 'The Daring Young Man on the Flying Trapeze' and 'Forty Thousand Assyrians.' I remember *that* one."

"They're not in print anymore," mourned William Saroyan. "You can't find them in libraries."

"I used to try to write like you," Yossarian confessed. "I couldn't get far."

"You didn't have my imagination."

"They try to write like me," said Ernest Hemingway. Both wore mustaches. "But don't get far either. Want to fight?"

"I never want to fight."

"They try to write like him too," said Ernest Hemingway, and pointed off to William Faulkner, sitting in profound silence in a packed area populated by heavy drinkers. Faulkner wore a mustache too. So did Eugene O'Neill, Tennessee Williams, and James Joyce, not far from the area of those with late-life personality disorders embodying depression and nervous breakdowns, in which Henry James sat silent with Joseph Conrad staring at Charles Dickens blending into the populous zone of the suicides where Jerzy Kosinski was chatting up Virginia Woolf near Arthur Koestler and Sylvia Plath. In a cone of brown sunlight on violet sand he spied Gustav Aschenbach on a beach chair and recognized the book in his lap as the same paperback edition as his own copy of *Death in Venice and Seven Other Stories*. Aschenbach beckoned.

And Yossarian responded inwardly with a "Fuck you!" and mentally gave him the finger and the obscene Italian gesture of rejection as he hastened past the Whip, the Pretzel, and the Whirlpool. He caught Kafka spying on him with a bloody cough from a shadowy recess below the shut pane of the window from which Marcel Proust watched him above a hooded alleyway with the street sign DESOLATION ROW. He came to a mountain in a framework of iron with tracks rising high and saw the name DRAGON'S GORGE.

"Holy shit!" exulted McBride, who was nowhere about. "There really is a roller-coaster!"

He came next to the carousel, ornate, elaborate, mirrored, spinning, with panel paintings in antique white molding alternating between the upright oval frames with reflecting glass on the main rounding board and inner cornice. The lively waltz from the calliope was indeed the Siegfried Funeral Music, and situated grandly on one of the gaudy gondolas drawn by swans was an elderly German official with domed helmet and encyclopedic insignia and a bearing majestic enough for an emperor or a kaiser.

Yossarian caught sight of the rowboat before he saw the canal, a wooden craft with riders sitting upright two, three, and four abreast, floating into view without power in the man-made channel barely wide enough to accommodate one craft at a time, and he was outside the Tunnel of Love, where a watchman in a red jacket and green jockey cap stood guard at the entrance with a portable telephone and a hand-held ticket punch. He had orange hair and a milky complexion and wore a green rucksack on his back. Garish billboards and lavender-and-ginger illustrations gave alluring notice of a fabulous wax museum inside the Tunnel of Love that headlined life-size wax statues of the executed Lindbergh-baby kidnapper, Bruno Hauptmann, and a nude Marilyn Monroe lying on a bed, restored in every detail to lifelike death. The fabulous wax museum was called ISLE OF THE DEAD. In the first seat of the flat-bottomed boat coasting out of one murky opening of the tunnel to continue gliding onward into the inky opening of the other, he saw Abraham Lincoln in a stiff stovepipe hat sitting motionless beside the faceless Angel of Death, and they seemed to be holding hands. He saw his wounded gunner Howard Snowden on the same bench. Side by side in the boat, on the bench immediately behind them, he saw Mayor Fiorello H. La Guardia and President Franklin Delano Roosevelt. The mayor was wearing a dashing wide hat with a rolled brim something like a cowboy's, and FDR sported a creased homburg and was flaunting his cigarette holder, and both were grinning as though alive in a front-page photograph in a bygone newspaper. And on the seat in back of La Guardia and Roosevelt's he saw his mother and his father, and then his Uncle Sam and Aunt Ida, his Uncle Max and Aunt Hannah, and then his brother Lee, and he knew that he too was going to die. It struck him all of a sudden that overnight everyone he'd known a long time was old—not getting old, not middle-aged, but *old!* The great entertainment stars of his time were no longer stars, and the celebrated novelists and poets in his day were of piddling significance in the new generation. Like RCA and *Time* magazine, even IBM and General Motors were of meager stature, and Western Union had passed away. The gods were growing old again, and it was time for another shake-up. Everyone has got to go, Teemer had propounded the last time they'd talked, and, in an uncharacteristic display of emotional emphasis, had added: "Everyone!"

Yossarian rushed past that Tunnel of Love with its true-to-life wax figures on the Isle of the Dead. Crossing a white footbridge with rococo balustrades, he found himself back in Naples, Italy, in 1945, on a line behind the imperturbable old soldier Schweik and the young one named Krautheimer who had changed his name to Joseph Kaye, waiting to go home by steamship outside the vanished old L. A. Thompson Scenic Railway on Surf Avenue past vanished old Steeplechase Park.

"Still here?"

"What happened to you?"

"I'm back here too. What happened to you?"

"I am Schweik."

"I know. The good soldier?"

"I don't know about good."

"I thought I'd be the oldest now," said Yossarian.

"I'm older."

"I know. I'm Yossarian."

"I know. You ran away once to Sweden, didn't you?"

"I didn't get far. I couldn't even get to Rome."

"You didn't escape there? In a little yellow raft?"

"That happens only in the movies. What's your name?"

"Joseph Kaye. I told you before. Why are you asking?"

"I have trouble with names now. Why are you asking?"

"Because somebody has been telling lies about me."

"Maybe that's why we're still on line," said Schweik.

"Why don't you go back to Czechoslovakia?"

"Why should I," said Schweik, "when I can go to America? Why don't you go to Czechoslovakia?"

"What will you do in America?"

"Raise dogs. Anything easy. People live forever in America, don't they?"

"Not really," said Yossarian.

"Will I like it in America?"

"If you make money and think you're well-off."

"Are the people friendly?"

"If you make money and they think you're well-off."

"Where the fuck is that boat?" griped Kaye. "We can't wait here forever."

"Yes, you can," said Schweik.

"It's coming!" cried Kaye.

They heard the rattling noise of outdated wheels on outdated iron rails, and then a chain of roller-coaster carriages painted red and pale gold rode into view at the decelerating end of the ride on the L. A. Thompson Scenic Railway. But instead of stopping as expected, these cars continued onward past them to start around all over again, and, while Kaye shook in frustration, Yossarian stared at the riders. Again he recognized Abraham Lincoln in front. He saw La Guardia and FDR, his mother and his father, his uncles and his aunts, and his brother too. And he saw each of them double, the Angel of Death double and the gunner Snowden too, and he was seeing them twice.

He whirled around, staggering, and hastened back, escaping, and searched in baffled terror for help from the soldier Schroeder who now claimed to be a hundred and seven years old, but found only McBride, both of him, near Bob and Raul, who combined made four. McBride thought Yossarian looked funny and was walking with a falter and a list, a seesawing hand held out for stability.

"Yeah, I do feel funny," Yossarian admitted. "Let me hold your arm."

"How many fingers do you see?"

"Two."

"Now?"

"Ten."

"Now?"

"Twenty."

"You're seeing double."

"I'm beginning to see everything twice again."

"You want some help?"

"Yes."

"Hey, guys, give me a hand with him. From them too?"

"Sure."

28

Hospital

"Cut," said the brain surgeon, in this last stage of his Rhine Journey.

"You cut," said his apprentice.

"No cuts," said Yossarian.

"Now look who's butting in."

"Should we go ahead?"

"Why not?"

"I've never done this before."

"That's what my girlfriend used to say. Where's the hammer?"

"No hammers," said Yossarian.

"Is he going to keep talking that way while we try to concentrate?"

"Give me that hammer."

"Put down that hammer," directed Patrick Beach.

"How many fingers do you see?" demanded Leon Shumacher.

"One."

"How many now?" asked Dennis Teemer.

"Still one. The same."

"He's fooling around, gentlemen," said former stage actress Frances Rolphe, born Frances Rosenbaum, who'd grown up to become mellow Frances Beach, with a face that again looked its age. "Can't you see?"

"We made him all better!"

"Gimme eat," said Yossarian.

"I would cut that dosage in half, Doctor," instructed Melissa MacIntosh. "Halcion wakes him up and Xanax makes him anxious. Prozac depresses him."

"She knows you that well, does she?" clucked Leon Shumacher, after Yossarian had been given more eat.

"We've seen each other."

"Who's her busty blonde friend?"

"Her name is Angela Moorecock."

"Heh, heh. I was hoping for something like that. What time will she get here?"

"After work and before dinner, and she may come again with a house-building boyfriend. My children may be here. Now that I'm out of danger, they may want to bid me farewell."

"That son of yours," began Leon Shumacher.

"The one on Wall Street?"

"All he wanted to hear was the bottom line. Now he won't want to invest more time here if you're not going to die. I told him you wouldn't."

"And I told him you would, naturally," said Dennis Teemer, in bathrobe and pajamas, livelier as a patient than as a doctor. His embarrassed wife told friends he was experimenting. " 'For how much?' he wanted to bet me."

"You still think it's natural?" objected Yossarian.

"For us to die?"

"For me to die."

Teemer glanced aside. "I think it's natural."

"For you?"

"I think that's natural too. I believe in life."

"You lost me."

"Everything that's alive lives on things that are living, Yossarian. You and I take a lot. We have to give back."

"I met a particle physicist on a plane to Kenosha who says that everything living is made up of things that are not."

"I know that too."

"It doesn't make you laugh? It doesn't make you cry? It doesn't make you wonder?"

"In the beginning was the word," said Teemer. "And the word was *gene*. Now the word is *quark*. I'm a biologist, not a physicist, and I can't say 'quark.' That belongs to an invisible world of the lifeless. So I stick with the gene."

"So where is the difference between a living gene and a dead quark?"

"A gene isn't living and a quark isn't dead."

"I can't say 'quark' either without wanting to laugh."

"Quark."

"Quark."

"Quark, quark."

"You win," said Yossarian. "But is there a difference between us and that?"

"Nothing in a living cell is alive. Yet the heart pumps and the tongue talks. We both know that."

"Does a microbe? A mushroom?"

"They have no soul?" guessed the surgeon in training.

"There is no soul," said the surgeon training him. "That's all in the head."

"Someone ought to tell the cardinal that."

"The cardinal knows it."

"Even a thought, even this thought, is just an electrical action between molecules."

"But there are good thoughts and bad thoughts," snapped Leon Shumacher, "so let's go on working. Were you ever in the navy with a man named Richard Nixon? He thinks he knows you."

"No, I wasn't."

"He wants to come check you out."

"I was not in the navy. Please keep him away."

"Did you ever play alto saxophone in a jazz band?"

"No."

"Were you ever in the army with the Soldier in White?"

"Twice. Why?"

"He's on a floor downstairs. He wants you to drop by to say hello."

"If he could tell you all that, he's not the same one."

"Were you ever in the army with a guy named Rabinowitz?" asked Dennis Teemer. "Lewis Rabinowitz?"

Yossarian shook his head. "Not that I remember."

"Then I may have it wrong. How about a man named Sammy Singer, his friend? He says he was from Coney Island. He thinks you may remember him from the war."

"Sam Singer?" Yossarian sat up. "Sure, the tail gunner. A short guy, small, skinny, with wavy black hair."

Teemer smiled. "He's almost seventy now."

"Is he sick too?"

"He's friends with this patient I'm looking at."

"Tell him to drop by."

"Hiya, Captain." Singer shook the hand Yossarian put out.

Yossarian appraised a man delighted to see him, on the smallish side, with hazel eyes projecting slightly in a face that was kindly. Singer was chortling. "It's good to see you again. I've wondered about you. The doctor says you're okay."

"You've grown portly, Sam," said Yossarian, with good humor, "and a little bit wrinkled, and maybe a little taller. You used to be skinny. And you've gotten very gray, with thinning hair. And so have I. Fill me in, Sam. What's been happening the last fifty years? Anything new?"

"Call me Sammy."

"Call me Yo-Yo."

"I'm pretty good, I guess. I lost my wife. Ovarian cancer. I'm kind of floundering around."

"I've been divorced, twice. I flounder too. I suppose I'll have to marry again. It's what I'm used to. Children?"

"One daughter in Atlanta," said Sammy Singer, "and another in Houston. Grandchildren too, already in college. I don't like to throw myself on them. I have an extra bedroom for when they come to visit. I worked for *Time* magazine a long time—but not as a reporter," Singer added pointedly. "I did well enough, made a good living, and then they retired me to bring in young blood to keep the magazine alive."

"And now it's practically dead," said Yossarian. "I work now in that old Time-Life Building in Rockefeller Center. Looking out on the skating rink. Were you ever in that one?"

"I sure was," said Singer, with recalled affection. "I remember that skating rink. I had some good times there."

"It's now the new M & M Building, with M & M Enterprises and Milo Minderbinder. Remember old Milo?"

"I sure do." Sammy Singer laughed. "He gave us good food, that Milo Minderbinder."

"He did do that. A better standard of living than I had before."

"Me too. They were saying afterward that he was the one who bombed our squadron that time."

"He did that too. That's another one of the contradictions of capitalism. It's funny, Singer. The last time I was in the hospital, the chaplain popped in out of nowhere to see me."

"What chaplain?"

"Our chaplain. Chaplain Tappman."

"Sure. I know that chaplain. Very quiet, right? Almost went to pieces after those two planes collided over La Spezia, with Dobbs in one plane and Huple in the other and Nately and all the rest of them killed. Remember those names?"

"I remember them all. Remember Orr? He was in my tent."

"I remember Orr. They say he made it to Sweden in a raft after he ditched after Avignon, right before we went home."

"I went down to Kentucky once and saw him there," said Yossarian. "He was a handyman in a supermarket, and we didn't have much to say to each other anymore."

"I was in the plane when we ditched after the first mission to Avignon. He took care of everything. Remember that time? I was down in the raft with that top turret gunner Sergeant Knight."

"I remember Bill Knight. He told me all about it."

"That was the time none of our Mae Wests would inflate because Milo had taken out the carbon dioxide cylinders to make ice cream sodas for all you guys at the officers' club. He left a note instead. That was some Milo then." Singer chuckled.

"You guys had sodas too every Sunday, didn't you?"

"Yes, we did. And then he took the morphine from the first-aid kit on that second mission to Avignon, you said. Was that really true?"

"He did that too. He left a note there also."

"Was he dealing in drugs then?"

"I had no way to know. But he sure was dealing in eggs, fresh eggs. Remember?"

"I remember those eggs. I still can't believe eggs can taste so good. I eat them often."

"I'm going to start," Yossarian resolved. "You just convinced me, Sammy Singer. It makes no sense to worry about cholesterol now, does it?"

"You remember Snowden then, Howard Snowden? On that mission to Avignon?"

"Sam, could I ever forget? I would have used up all the morphine in the first-aid kit when I saw him in such pain. That fucking Milo. I cursed him a lot. Now I work with him."

"Did I really black out that much?"

"It looked that way to me."

"That seems funny now. You were covered with so much blood. And then all that other stuff. He just kept moaning. He was cold, wasn't he?"

"Yes, he said he was cold. And dying. I was covered with everything, Sammy, and then with my own vomit too."

"And then you took off your clothes and wouldn't put them on again for a while."

"I was sick of uniforms."

"I saw you sitting in a tree at the funeral, naked."

"I had sneakers."

"I saw Milo climb up to you too, with his chocolate-covered cotton. We all kind of always looked up to you then, Yossarian. I still do, you know."

"Why is that, Sam?" asked Yossarian, and hesitated. "I'm only a pseudo Assyrian."

Singer understood. "No, that's not why. Not since the army. I made good friends with Gentiles there. You were one, when that guy started beating me up in South Carolina. And not since those years at *Time*, where I had fun and hung around with Protestants and my first heavy drinkers."

"We're assimilated. It's another nice thing about this country. If we behave like they do, they might let us in."

"I met my wife there. You know something, Yossarian?"

"Yo-Yo?"

Sam Singer shook his head. "After I was married, I never once cheated on my wife, and never wanted to, and that seemed funny to people everywhere, to other girls too. It didn't to her. They might have thought I was gay. Her first husband was the other way. A ladies' man, the kind I always thought I wanted to be. She preferred me, by the time I met her."

"You miss her."

"I miss her."

"I miss marriage. I'm not used to living alone."

"I can't get used to it either. I can't cook much."

"I don't cook either."

Sam Singer reflected. "No, I think I looked up to you first because you were an officer, and back then I had the kid's idea that all officers had something more on the ball than the rest of us. Or we would be officers too. You always seemed to know what you were doing, except when you were getting lost and taking us out across the Atlantic Ocean. Even when you were going around doing crazy things, it seemed to make more sense than a lot of the rest. Standing in formation naked to get that medal. We all got a big kick out of seeing you do that."

"I wasn't showing off, Sam. I was in panic most of the time. I'd wake up some mornings and try to guess where I was, and then try to figure out what the hell I was doing there. I sometimes wake up that way now."

"Baloney," said Singer, and grinned. "And you always seemed to be getting laid a lot, when the rest of us weren't."

"Not as much as you think," said Yossarian, laughing. "There was a lot more of just rubbing it around."

"But, Yossarian, when you said you wouldn't fly anymore, we kept our fingers crossed. We'd finished our seventy missions and were in the same boat."

"Why didn't you come out and walk with me?"

"We weren't that brave. They sent us home right after they caught you, so it worked out fine for us. I said no too, but by then they gave me a choice. What happened to you?"

"They sent me home too. They threatened to kill me, to put me in prison, they said they would ruin me. They promoted me to major and sent me home. They wanted no fuss."

"Most of us admired you. And you seem to know what you're doing now."

"Who says that? I'm not sure of anything anymore."

"Come on, Yo-Yo. On our floor, they're saying you've even got a good thing going with one of the nurses."

Yossarian came close to a blush of pride. "It's traveled that far?"

"We even hear it from my friend's doctor," Singer went on, in a merry way. "Back in Pianosa, I remember, you were pretty friendly with a nurse too, weren't you?"

"For a little while. She dumped me as a poor risk. The problem with sweeping a girl off her feet, Sammy, is that you have to keep on sweeping. Love doesn't work that way."

"I know that too," said Singer. "But you and a couple of others were with her up the beach with your suits on that day Kid Sampson was killed by an airplane. You remember Kid Sampson, don't you?"

"Oh, shit, sure," said Yossarian. "Do you think I could ever forget Kid Sampson? Or McWatt, who was in the plane that smashed him apart. McWatt was my favorite pilot."

"Mine too. He was the pilot on the mission to Ferrara when we had to go around on a second bomb run, and Kraft was killed, and a bombardier named Pinkard too."

"Were you in the plane with me on that one too?"

"I sure was. I was also in the plane with Hungry Joe when he forgot to use the emergency handle to put down his landing gear. And they gave him a medal."

"They gave me my medal for that mission to Ferrara."

"It's hard to believe it all really happened."

"I know that feeling," said Yossarian. "It's hard to believe I let myself be put through so much."

"I know *that* feeling. It's funny about Snowden." Singer hesitated. "I didn't know him that well."

"I'd never noticed him."

"But now I feel he was one of my closest friends."

"I have that feeling too."

"And I also feel," Sammy persevered, "he was one of the best things that ever happened to me. I almost hate to put it that way. It sounds immoral. But it gave me an episode, something dramatic to talk about, and something to make me remember that the war was really real. People won't believe much of it; my children and grandchildren aren't much interested in anything so old."

"Bring your friend around and I'll tell him it's true. What's he in here for?"

"Some kind of checkup."

"By Teemer?" Yossarian was shaking his head.

"They know each other," said Singer, "a long time."

"Yeah," said Yossarian, with a sarcastic doubt that left Singer knowing he was unconvinced. "Well, Sammy, where do we go from here? I never could navigate, but I seem to have more direction. I know many women. I may want to marry again."

"I know some too, but mostly old friends."

"Don't get married unless you feel you have to. Unless you need to, you won't be good at it."

"I may travel more," said Singer. "Friends tell me to take a trip around the world. I know people from my days in *Time*. I've got a good friend in Australia who was hit with a disease called Guillain-Barré a long time ago. He's not young either and doesn't get around too easily on his crutches anymore. I'd like to see him again. There's another in England, who's retired, and one in Hong Kong."

"I think I'd go if I were you. It's something to do. What about the one that's here? Teemer's patient."

"He'll probably be going home soon. He was a prisoner in Dresden with Kurt Vonnegut and another one named Schweik. Can you imagine?"

"I stood on line in Naples once with a soldier named Schweik and met a guy named Joseph Kaye. I never even heard about Dresden until I read about it in Vonnegut's novel. Send your friend up. I'd like to hear about Vonnegut."

"He doesn't know him."

"Ask him to drop by anyway if he wants to. I'll be here through the weekend. Well, Sammy, want to gamble? Do you think we might see each other again outside the hospital?"

Singer was taken by surprise. "Yossarian, that's up to you. I've got the time."

"I'll take your number if you're willing to give it. It may be worth a try. I'd like to talk to you again about William Saroyan. You used to try to write stories like his."

"So did you. What happened?"

"I stopped, after a while."

"I gave up too. Ever try *The New Yorker?*"

"I struck out there every time."

"So did I."

"Sammy tells me you saved his life," said the big-boned man in a dressing gown and his own pajamas, introducing himself as Rabinowitz in a lusty, lighthearted manner, with a hoarse, unfaltering voice. "Tell me how you did it."

"Let him give you the details. You were in Dresden?"

"He'll give you those details." Rabinowitz let his eyes linger again on Angela. "Young lady, you look like someone I met once and can't remember where. She was a knockout too. Did we ever meet? I used to look younger."

"I'm not sure I know. This is my friend Anthony."

"Hello, Anthony. Listen to me good, Anthony. I'm not joshing. Treat her real fine tonight, because if you don't treat her good I will find out about it, and I will start sending her flowers and you will be out in the cold. Right, darling? Good night, my dear. You'll have a good time. Anthony, my name is Lew. Go have some fun."

"I will, Lew," said Anthony.

"I'm retired now, do a little real estate, some building with my son-in-law. What about you?"

"I'm retired too," said Yossarian.

"You're with Milo Minderbinder."

"Part time."

"I've got a friend who'd like to meet him. I'll bring him around.

I'm in here with a weight problem. I have to keep it low because of a minor heart condition, and sometimes I take off too much. I like to check that out."

"With Dennis Teemer?"

"I know Teemer long. That lovely blonde lady looks like something special. I know I've seen her."

"I think you'd remember."

"That's why I know."

"Hodgkin's disease," confided Dennis Teemer.

"Shit," said Yossarian. "He doesn't want me to know."

"He doesn't want anybody to know. Not even me. And I know him almost thirty years. He sets records."

"Was he always that way? He likes to flirt."

"So do you. With everybody. You want everybody here to be crazy about you. He's just more open. You're sly."

"You're cunning and know too much."

In Rabinowitz, Yossarian saw a tall, direct man with a large frame who had lost heavy amounts of flesh. He was almost bald on top and wore a gold and graying brush mustache, and he was aggressively attentive to Angela, with an indestructible sexual self-confidence that overrode and reduced her own. Yossarian was amused to see her bend herself forward to take down her bosom, lay her hands in her lap to hold down her skirt, tuck back her legs primly. She was faced with an excess of overbearing friskiness, of a kind she did not take to but could not defeat.

"And he's not even Italian," Yossarian chided.

"You're not Italian, and I don't mind you. The trouble is I do know him from somewhere."

"Aha, Miss Moore, I think I may have it," said Rabinowitz with a probing smile, when he sauntered in and saw her again. "You remind me of a lovely little lady with good personality I met one time with a builder I was doing business with out in Brooklyn, near Sheepshead Bay. An Italian named Benny Salmeri, I think. You liked to dance."

"Really?" answered Angela, looking at him with eye-shadowed eyelids half lowered. "I used to know a builder named Salmeri. I'm not sure it's the same."

"Did you ever have a roommate who was a nurse?"

"I still do," answered Angela, now more flippant. "The one on duty here before. That's my partner, Melissa."

"That nice-looking thing with that good personality?"

"She takes care of our friend here. That's why he's in. She fucks old men and gives them strokes."

"I wish you wouldn't say that to people," Yossarian reproved her mildly, after Rabinowitz had gone. "You'll destroy her prospects. And it wasn't a stroke. You'll ruin mine too."

"And I wish," said Angela, "you wouldn't tell people my name is Moorecock."

They studied each other. "Who've I told?"

"Michael. That doctor Shumacher." Angela Moore hesitated, for intentional effect. "Patrick."

"Patrick?" Surprised, Yossarian sensed the reply before he put the question. "Which Patrick? Patrick Beach?"

"Patrick Beach."

"Oh, shit," he said, after his jolt of surprise. "You're seeing Patrick?"

"He's called."

"You'll have to go sailing. You'll probably hate it."

"I've already been. I didn't mind."

"Doesn't he have trouble with his prostate?"

"Not right now. It's why he isn't coming by here anymore. You were close with his wife. Do you think she'll know?"

"Frances Beach knows everything, Angela."

"I'm not the first."

"She knows that already. She'll be able to guess."

"There really is something going on between you and that nurse, isn't there?" guessed Frances Beach. "I can almost smell coitus in this rancid air."

"Am I letting it show?"

"No, darling, she is. She watches over you more protectively than she should. And she's much too correct when others are here. Advise her not to be so tense."

"That will make her more tense."

"And you still have that vulgar compulsion I never could abide. You look down at a woman's bottom whenever she turns around, at all women, and with so much pride at hers. It's that pride of possession. You eye mine too, don't you?"

"I know I always do that. It doesn't make me proud. You still look pretty good."

"You would not think that if you didn't have memories."

"I've got another bad habit you'll find even worse."

"I'll bet I can guess. Because I do it too."

"Then tell me."

"Have you also arrived at that wretched stage when you can't look seriously into a human face without already picturing what it will look like when old?"

"I can't see how you knew."

"We've been too much alike."

"I do it only with women. It helps me lose interest."

"I do it with every face already giving clues. It's evil and morbid. This one will wear well."

"Her name is Melissa."

"Let her know it's safe to trust me. Even though I'm rich and fashionable and used to have some bitchy fame as an actress. I'm glad you're not marrying for money."

"Who's thinking of marriage?"

"By my time with Patrick it was much more than the money. I think I approve. Although I don't like her girlfriend. Patrick has taken to sailing again. I think he may be flying as well. What more can you tell me?"

"I can't tell you a thing."

"And I don't want to know, not this time either. I would feel so guilty if he thought I suspected. I would not want to step on anybody's happiness, especially his. I wish I could have more too, but you know my age. Our friend Olivia may be my exception. She won't visit often but fills the room with this glut of flowers. And she signs each card 'Olivia Maxon,' as though it were a British title and you knew a thousand Olivias. I adore your catering company."

"It's Milo Minderbinder's."

"Two tons of caviar is divine."

"We could have got by with one, but it's safe to have a little more. This wedding in the terminal is just about the biggest piece of fun I see in my future."

"It's just about my only fun. Oh, John, Johnny, it's a terrible thing you just did to me," said Frances Beach. "When I learned you were sick, I finally felt old for the first time. You will recover, and I never will. There's somebody here. Please come in. Your name is Melissa?"

"Yes, it is. There's someone else here to see him."

"And my name is Rabinowitz, madam, Lewis Rabinowitz, but friends call me Lew. Here's someone else—Mr. Marvin Winkler, just in from California to pay his respects. Where's our lovely friend Angela? Marvin, this is Mr. Yossarian. He's the man who

will set it up for you. Winkler wants to meet with Milo Minderbinder about a terrific new product he's got. I told him we'd
arrange it."

"What's the product?"

"Lew, let me talk to him alone."

"Well, Winkler?"

"Look down at my foot." Winkler was a man of middle height
with conspicuous girth. "Don't you notice anything?"

"What am I looking at?"

"My shoe."

"What about it?"

"It's state-of-the-art."

Yossarian studied him. "You aren't joking?"

"I don't joke about business," answered Winkler, issuing words
with strain as though emitting sighs of affliction. His voice was
low and guttural, almost inaudible. "I've been in it too long. I
manufactured and sold surplus army film after the war. I was in
baked goods too and was known for the best honey-glazed doughnuts in New York, Connecticut, and New Jersey. Everything I did
was state-of-the-art. I still make chocolate Easter bunnies."

"Have you ever hit it big?"

"I've had trouble with my timing. I was in the food-service
business too once and offered home-delivered breakfasts Sunday
mornings so that people could sleep late. My firm was Greenacre
Farms in Coney Island, and I was the sole proprietor."

"And I was a customer. You never delivered."

"It was not cost-effective."

"Winkler, I will get you your meeting. I can't resist. But I will
want you to tell me about it."

"I won't leave out a word."

"We've been thinking of a shoe," Milo admitted, "to sell to the
government."

"Then you certainly want mine. It's state-of-the-art."

"Just what does that mean?"

"There's none better, Mr. Minderbinder, and no good reason
for the government to choose any other. Look down at my foot
again. See the flexibility? The shoe looks new when you first start
to wear it; when it's older it looks used as soon as you break it in.
If it's dull you can polish it, or you can leave it the way it is or
wear it scuffed, if that's what you want. You can make it lighter
or darker and even change its color."

"But what does it do?"

"It fits over the foot and keeps the sock dry and clean. It helps protect the skin on the sole of the foot against cuts and scratches and other painful inconveniences of walking on the ground. You can walk in it, run in it, or even just sit and talk in it, as I'm doing with you now."

"And it changes color. How did you say it does that?"

"You just put this magic plastic insert into the slot of the heel and then take them to the shoemaker and tell him to dye it to whatever color you want."

"It seems like a miracle."

"I would say that it is."

"Can you make them for women too?"

"A foot is a foot, Mr. Minderbinder."

"One thing escapes me, Mr. Winkler. What does your shoe do that the ones I'm wearing will not?"

"Make money for both of us, Mr. Minderbinder. Mine is state-of-the-art. Look down at the difference."

"I'm beginning to see. Are you very rich?"

"I've had trouble with my timing. But believe me, Mr. Minderbinder, I'm not without experience. You are doing business with the man who devised and still manufactures the state-of-the-art chocolate Easter bunny."

"What was so different about yours?"

"It was made of chocolate. It could be packaged, shipped, displayed, and, best of all, eaten, like candy."

"Isn't that true of other Easter bunnies?"

"But mine was state-of-the-art. We print that on every package. The public did not want a second-rate chocolate Easter bunny, and our government does not want a second-rate shoe."

"I see, I see," said Milo, brightening. "You know about chocolate?"

"All that there is to know."

"Tell me something. Please try one of these."

"Of course," said Winkler, taking the bonbon and relishing the prospect of eating it. "What is it?"

"Chocolate-covered cotton. What do you think of it?"

Delicately, as though handling something rare, fragile, and repulsive, Winkler lifted the mass from his tongue, while maintaining a smile. "I've never tasted better chocolate-covered cotton. It's state-of-the-art."

"Unfortunately, I seem unable to move it."

"I can't see why. Have you very much?"

"Warehouses full. Have you any ideas?"

"That's where I'm best. I will think of one while you bring my shoe to your procurer in Washington."

"That will definitely be done."

"Then consider this: Remove the chocolate from the cotton. Weave the cotton into fine fabric for shirts and bedsheets. We build today by breaking up. You've been putting together. We get bigger today by getting smaller. You can sell the chocolate to me for my business at a wonderful price for the money I receive from you for my shoe."

"How many shoes do you have now?"

"At the moment, just the pair I'm wearing, and another one at home in my closet. I can gear up for millions as soon as we have a contract and I receive in front all the money I'll need to cover my costs of production. I like money in front, Mr. Minderbinder. That's the only way I do business."

"That sounds fair," said Milo Minderbinder. "I work that way too. Unfortunately, we have a Department of Ethics now in Washington. But our lawyer will be in charge there once he gets out of prison. Meanwhile, we have our private procurers. You will have your contract, Mr. Winkler, for a deal is a deal."

"Thank you, Mr. Minderbinder. Can I send you a bunny for Easter? I can put you on our complimentary list."

"Yes, please do that. Send me a thousand dozen."

"And whom shall I bill?"

"Someone will pay. We both understand that there is no such thing as a free lunch."

"Thank you for the lunch, Mr. Minderbinder. I go away with good news."

"I come with good news," called Angela buoyantly, and swept into the hospital room in an ecstasy of jubilation. "But Melissa thinks you might be angry."

"She's found a new fellow."

"No, not yet."

"She's gone back to the old one."

"There's no chance of that. She's late."

"For what?"

"With her period. She thinks she's pregnant."

Defiantly, Melissa said she wanted the child, and the time left to have a child was not unlimited for either one of them.

"But how can it be?" complained Yossarian, at this end to his Rhine Journey. "You said you had your tubes tied."

"You said you had a vasectomy."

"I was kidding when I said that."

"I didn't know. So I was kidding too."

"Ahem, ahem, excuse me," said Winkler, when he could endure no more. "We have business to finish. Yossarian, I owe everything to you. How much money will you want?"

"For what?"

"For setting up that meeting. I am in your debt. Name what you want."

"I don't want any of it."

"That sounds fair."

29
Mr. Tilyou

Securely ensconced in his afterlife in a world of his own, Mr.
George C. Tilyou, dead now just about eighty years, took pleasure
in contemplating his possessions and watching the time go by,
because time didn't. Purely for adornment, he wore in his waist-
coat a gold watch on a gold chain with a snaggletooth pendant of
green bloodstone, but it remained unwound.

There were intervals between occurrences, naturally, but no
point in measuring them. The rides on both roller-coasters, his
Dragon's Gorge and Tornado, and on his Steeplechase Horses, all
governed by the constants of gravity and friction, never varied
noticeably from beginning to end, and neither did the water journey by boat through his Tunnel of Love. He could, of course, alter
the duration on his El Dorado carousel and enlarge or decrease
the circlings on the Whip, Caterpillar, Whirlpool, and Pretzel.
There was no added cost. Here nothing went to waste. The iron
wouldn't rust, paint didn't peel. There was no dust or refuse anywhere. His wing-collared shirt was always clean. His yellow house
looked as fresh as the day fifty years before on which he had
finally brought it down. Wood did not warp or rot, windows did
not stick, glass did not break, plumbing would not even drip. His
boats did not leak. It was not that time stood still. There was no
time. Mr. Tilyou exulted in the permanence, the eternal stability.
Here was a place where the people would not grow older. There
would always be new ones, and their number would never grow
less. It was a concessionaire's dream.

Once he had back his house, there was nothing on earth he
wanted that he did not have. He kept abreast of conditions outside

through the felicitous fellowship of General Leslie Groves, who came by periodically to chat and make enjoyable use of the amusements offered, arriving at his railroad siding in his private train. General Groves brought newspapers and weekly newsmagazines that simply vanished into thin air, like all other trash, after Mr. Tilyou had finished skimming only those rare stories peculiar enough to merit his perusal. Punctually too, every three months to the day, a Mr. Gaffney, a pleasant acquaintance of a different order who worked as a private investigator, dropped in from above to find out all he could about anything new. Mr. Tilyou did not tell him everything. Mr. Gaffney was remarkable for his civility and dress, and Mr. Tilyou looked forward to his alighting there for good. Sometimes General Groves arrived with a guest he thought fitting for Mr. Tilyou to know beforehand. Mr. Tilyou had men and women in abundance and no express need for ministers, and he felt far from slighted upon hearing that the chaplain General Groves had spoken of had declined to be introduced to him. In the larger den in one of the two railroad coaches encompassing the elegant living quarters of General Groves, Mr. Tilyou could entertain himself in singular fashion by peering at the glass pane in any of the windows and, once acquainted with the controls, looking out at just about any place in the world. Usually, he wanted only New York City, and mostly those parts of Brooklyn he thought of as his stamping grounds and his burial ground: the carnival area of Coney Island, and Green-Wood Cemetery in the Sunset Park section of Brooklyn, in which, in 1914, he had been laid, temporarily, he could now complacently certify, to rest.

The site on which his house had stood remained a vacant space, a parking lot for visitors in high season who now had automobiles. Where his spangled wonderland had flourished famously now functioned objects of lesser reputation. Nowhere he looked was there any new thing under the sun he envied. His gilded age had passed. He saw decline and corrosion at the end of an era. If Paris was France, as he'd been wont to repeat, Coney Island in summer certainly was no longer the world, and he congratulated himself on having gotten out in time.

He could play with the color of things in the windows of General Groves's railroad car, could see the sun go black and the moon turn to blood. The modern skylines of large metropolises did not appeal to his sense of the appropriate and proportionate. He beheld soaring buildings and gigantic commercial enterprises that were not owned by anybody, and this impressed him with a negative dismay. People bought shares of stock which they might not ever see, and these shares had not one thing to do with ownership or control. He himself, as a matter of scale and responsible moral behavior, had always put effort and capital into only such projects as would in entirety be his, and to own only such things as he could see and watch and wish personally to make use of with a satisfaction and pleasure enjoyed by others.

He was better off now than poor Mr. Rockefeller and autocratic Mr. Morgan, who had put their wealth in bequests and their faith in a sympathetic Supreme Being overseeing a mannerly universe, and now lived to regret it.

Mr. Tilyou could have told them, he did indeed keep telling them.

Mr. Tilyou always kept at hand a shiny new dime to give to Mr. Rockefeller, who, though there were no days, came begging almost daily in his repentant struggle to collect back all those shiny new dimes he had handed away in a misguided effort to buy public affection, which he now understood he never had needed.

Mr. Morgan, gimlet-eyed and eternally furious, was firmly convinced that a mistake had been made of which he was the diabolical and undeserving victim. Like clockwork, although there were no working clocks, he demanded to be told if the mandates correcting his situation had come down from on high yet. He was not used to being treated that way, he crossly reminded with sullen astonishment and obstinate stupidity when told they had not. He had no doubt he belonged in heaven. He had gone to the Devil and to Satan too.

"Could God possibly make a mistake?" Mr. Tilyou was finally compelled to point out.

Although there were no weeks, almost a full one passed before Mr. Morgan could answer.

"If God can do anything, he can make a mistake."

Mr. Morgan seethed openly too over his unlit cigar, for Mr. Tilyou would no longer permit anyone to smoke. Mr. Morgan owned a deck of playing cards that he would not share, and although there were no hours, he spent a great many of them alone playing solitaire on one of the gondolas on the sparkling El Dorado carousel created originally for Emperor William II of Germany. One of the more flamboyant chariots on that wheel of fortune that never went anywhere was still embellished pompously with the imperial crest. With the emperor aboard, the carousel always played Wagner.

Mr. Tilyou had warmer sentiments for two airmen from the Second World War, one of them Kid Sampson by name, the other McWatt—sailors and soldiers on leave had always been prevalent in Coney Island and welcome at Steeplechase. Mr. Tilyou always was gladdened by any new arrival from the old Coney Island, like the big newcomer Lewis Rabinowitz, who learned his way around in record time and recognized the George C. Tilyou name.

Mr. Tilyou enjoyed the company of good-natured souls like these, and he joined them frequently on their speedy plunges on the Tornado and the Dragon's Gorge. For relaxation, and in persistent inspection, he cruised back often into his Tunnel of Love, flowing into darkness beneath the lurid billboard images of the Lindbergh kidnapper in the electric chair and Marilyn Monroe dead on her bed, into his wax museum on the Isle of the Dead, to find his future by floating into the past. He had no visceral aversions, none at all, about taking his place alongside Abraham Lincoln and the Angel of Death, where he was likely to find himself in front of a New York City mayor named Fiorello H. La Guardia and the earlier president Franklin Delano Roosevelt, mortals from the past who lay ahead in his future. They had come along after his time, as had the Lindbergh kidnapper and Marilyn Monroe. Mr. Tilyou could not yet bring himself to say that the man now in the White House was another little prick, but that was only because neither he nor the Devil used bad language.

Mr. Tilyou had room to grow. Below him was a lake of ice and a desert of burning sand, some meadows of mud, a river of boiling blood, and another of boiling pitch. There were dark woods he could have if he could think what to do with them, with trees with black leaves, and some leopards, a lion, a dog with three heads, and a she-wolf, but these were never to be caged, which ruled out a zoo. But his imagination was not as supple as formerly; he had fears he might be getting old. He had triumphed with symbols, was used to illusions. His Steeplechase ride was not really a steeplechase, his park was not a park. His gifts were in collaborative pretense. His product was pleasure. His Tornado was not a tornado, his Dragon's Gorge was not a gorge. No one thought they were, and he could not imagine what he would have done with a true tornado or a genuine gorge and a real dragon. He was not positive he could hit upon sources of hilarity in a desert with burning sand, a rain of fire, or a river of boiling blood.

The recapture of his house filled him still with pride in his patient tenacity. It had taken thirty years, but where there is no time, one always has plenty.

The house was of yellow wood, with three floors and gabled attic. No one seemed to comment when, shortly after his death, the lowest floor had disappeared and the house of three stories had become a house with two. Neighborhood pedestrians did sometimes remark that the letters on the front of the lowest step appeared to be sinking, as indeed they were. By the time of the war, the name was almost half gone. During the war, young men went into military service, families moved, and Mr. Tilyou spied again his chance to act. Soon after the war, no one found curious the empty space, soon a parking lot, that was where the house had been. When shortly afterward his Steeplechase amusement park disappeared too, and then the Tilyou movie theater closed, his name was gone from the island and out of mind.

Now, in possession of everything he wanted and safe at home, he was the envy of his Morgans and Rockefellers. His engaging magic mirrors never had any deforming effect upon him or his ticket takers.

Returning to his office after work near the end of a day, although there were no days and he had no work, he found Mr. Rockefeller. He gave him another dime and chased him off. It was hard to associate the poor figure even remotely with that complex of business buildings in Rockefeller Center and with that oval pearl of an ice-skating rink. He saw from an imperious note on his rolltop desk that Mr. Morgan would be back to have it out with him once more over Mr. Tilyou's new no-smoking policy. Rather than face him again so soon, Mr. Tilyou took back his dust-free bowler from the peg on his coatrack. He fluffed up the petals of the flower in his lapel, which was always fresh and always would be. With energetic gait, he hurried from the office to his home, humming quietly the delightful Siegfried Funeral Music that resonated from his carousel.

Bounding up his stoop of three steps, he stumbled very slightly on the top one, and this had not happened to him before. On the shelf above the pair of sinks at his kitchen window, he spied something strange. The Waterford crystal vase with the white lilies looked perfectly normal, but, mysteriously, the water inside seemed to lie on an angle. In a minute he found a carpenter's level and set it down on the sill of the window. He shivered with a chilling surprise. The house was out of plumb. He strode back outside with wonder, his brow furrowing. At the stoop with the vertical face bearing his name, he had no need for the carpenter's level to tell him the steps were awry, as was his walkway. The right side was dipping. The baseline of the letters spelling TILYOU was tilting downward and the oval bottoms of the letters at the end were already out of sight. He went rigid with alarm. Without his knowledge or intent, his house was beginning to sink again. He had no idea why.

BOOK
TEN

30

SAMMY

For reasons she did not know, her father had not seemed to like her as a child or exhibit anything closer to acceptance when she was older and married. He was friendlier to her sister and brother, but not by much.

She was the oldest of three children. Her mother was more of a comfort but could effect no alleviating refinements in the household atmosphere dominated by the restrained and aloof male parent. They were Lutherans in Wisconsin, not far from the state capital in Madison, where, in winter, the days are short, the nights black and long, and the biting winds frigid. "It was just the way he always was," explained her mother, defending him. "We knew each other from church and school." They were the same age and both were virgins when they married. "Our families picked us out for each other. That's the way we did things then. I don't think he has ever been really happy."

He ran a small retail agricultural supply business he had inherited and enlarged, and he bantered more freely with his employees and suppliers, who were fond of him, than he was likely to do at home. He was commonly more at ease with others. It was nothing against her personally, her mother kept insisting, for as a child she had always been good. But at her father's death, from lung cancer too, they found out he had made no provision for her in his will, although he bequeathed to her three children portions that in total equaled that left her brother and her sister, and he awarded her discretionary power as trustee. She was not altogether surprised.

"What else would I expect?" Glenda said, when she spoke of it. "Don't think it still doesn't hurt."

As a youth, the Lutheran father, who had no taste for music and no feel for dancing or any other kind of the festive foolery the mother savored—she made masks for Halloween and loved costume parties—had revealed a native talent for drawing and an excited curiosity in the structures of buildings and elaborate architecture. But these latent aptitudes were ignored in the severe circumstances of a rural environment regulated by a father sterner than he turned out to be, with parents leading lives of restriction more spare than his own. No thought was given to college or art studies, and the suppression of these propensities could have been crucial in the forging of his dour personality and the inexpressible anguish in which his character was rooted. Only later could she define him that way and pity him sporadically. A frugal man of cautious extravagances, he nevertheless made known early his aspiration to provide a higher education for each of the children and the sentiment that he would be pleased if they availed themselves of the opportunity. Glenda alone made use of this singular generosity; and he did not ever let abate his disappointment with the others, as though rebuffed and mortified intentionally. He was pleased with her performance in her primary schools but gave voice to his praise critically, in a vein of reproach that provided little ground for rejoicing. If she brought home a test paper of ninety in algebra or geometry, perhaps the sole person with a grade so high, he wished to know, after a reluctant compliment, why she had missed the one problem in ten she had failed to solve. An A – would evoke questions about the minus, an A would impel him to sulk about the absence of the plus. There was no drollery in his seriousness; there was a wry kind in her retelling.

It is a miracle of sorts that she grew up to be lighthearted, with little self-doubt, and was competent and decisive, which was much what I needed.

In her secondary school, with some support from her mother and much encouragement from her younger sister, she succeeded in winning a place on the cheerleading squad. However, still somewhat shy and not then by nature gregarious, she was never inducted wholeheartedly into the buoyant social life the other girls enjoyed among themselves and with the school athletes and their gross acolytes. There were many parties and social rallies she did not attend. She was shorter by an inch or two than most her age, with dimples, brown eyes, and honey-colored hair; thin when young but with a noticeable bosom. She did not date much, mainly because she was not always comfortable when she did, and in this too lay the occasion for mixed signals from her father. He was vexed when she went out unchaperoned, as though she were guilty of indecency merely by going; and on the other hand, he spoke in self-referential humiliation, as though himself shunned, when she was home evenings on weekends. He prophesied in dire admonition of the lifelong, bleak pitfalls inherent in becoming a "wallflower" early, as he was inclined to feel he himself had been, and of the misuse he had made of his chances when young. *Wallflower* was a word he spoke often. *Personality* was another; it was his grim conclusion that a person always ought to have more. Neither she, her brother, nor her sister could recall ever being held by him in a hug.

She was not sexually active. One time in the front seat of the automobile of an older football player she allowed her panties to be slid down before she could realize what was happening and was stricken with terror. She pulled his penis; she would not kiss it. That was her first sight of semen, about which she had heard girls in school titter and talk with grave understanding, she remembered uneasily, when I asked. I would assume a blasé objectivity in these explorations into her past, but my dilemma was ambivalently both prurient and painful. After the football player, she dated more warily and schemed to avoid being taken off somewhere alone by any boy older who was self-assured and experienced. Until she met Richard in college. She enjoyed petting and of course was aroused, but detested being forced and mauled, and throughout almost all the rest of her teens, as far as I could find out, rather strong erotic surges and powerful romantic yearnings were unfulfilled and, with clean, religious rectitude, repressed.

In her first year at college, it was her very good fortune to fall in as friends with two Jewish girls from New York and one beautiful blonde music major from Topanga Canyon in California. She was astonished and enthralled by what she took to be their savoir faire, their knowledge and experience, their loud voices and brash self-assurance, by their unconstrained humor and bold and unabashed disclosures. They took pleasure in coaching her. She could never adapt without diffidence to their heedless sexual vocabulary, which seemed the university norm. But she was their equal in wit and intelligence, and in the integrity and fealty of friendship too. By her second year the four were living in rather carefree circumstances in a large house they united to rent. They remained in touch thereafter, and all three came to see her in that final month. All had more money from home than she did but shared it bountifully.

Richard was the first man she slept with and both were gratified, because he competently and proudly did the needed work well. He was two years older, already a senior, and by then had been to bed at least one time with all three of the others, but no one back then thought anything about that. They saw each other some more in Chicago, where she went to work summers, because he was already employed there and could introduce her to other people in an interconnecting cluster of social circles. He was in the regional office of a large Hartford insurance firm, where he was doing very well and quickly establishing himself as an outstanding personality and go-getter. Both liked to drink evenings after work, and often lunchtimes too, and they usually had good times together. She knew he had other girlfriends there but found she did not mind. She dated others too, as she had been doing in college, and more than once went out with men from the office she knew were married.

Soon after graduating, she moved to New York, where he had joined another company in a significant promotion, and found herself in her own small apartment with an exciting job as a researcher with *Time* magazine. And soon after that, they decided to try marriage.

She was ready to change and he would not. He remained charming to her mother, much more than he had reason to be, and produced chuckles from her father, and she began to find his habitual outgoing friendliness irritating and unworthy. He traveled a lot and was out late often even when back home, and when the third child, Ruth, was born with conjunctivitis that stemmed from an infection of trichomonads, she knew enough about medicine and the techniques of medical research to verify it was a venereal disease and enough about him to know where the affliction had come from. With no word to him, she went one day to her gynecologist and had her tubes tied, and only afterward did she tell him she wanted no more babies from him. Largely because the infant was new, it took another two years for them to part. She was too principled then to take alimony, and this soon proved an awful misjudgment, for he was incorrigibly tardy with the child support agreed to, and deficient in amount, and soon was in arrears entirely when involved with new girlfriends.

They could not talk long without quarreling. After I was on the scene, it grew easier for both to allow me to speak to each on behalf of the other. Her mother came east to help in the large, rent-controlled apartment on West End Avenue with the many large rooms, and she was able to go back to work with good income in the advertising-merchandising department of *Time, The Weekly Newsmagazine*, and that was where I met her. She sat facing a low partition, and I would lean on it and gossip when neither of us had anything important to get done. She was smarter than the man she worked for and more responsible and particular, but that never made a difference for a woman back then at that company—no female could be an editor or a writer in any of the publications or the head of any department. Without me she would not have been able to manage expenses and possibly would have had to retreat from the city with her mother and three children. Naomi and Ruth would not have had time or money to go through college. There would have been no funds for the private schools in Manhattan or, later, despite the excellent Time Incorporated medical plan, the expensive personal psychotherapy for Michael, which in the end did no good.

I do miss her, as Yossarian observed in our talks in the hospital, and make no attempt to hide it.

I miss her very much, and the few women I spend time with now—my widowed friend with some money and a good vacation home in Florida, two others I know from work who were never successful in resolving their own domestic lives, none of us young anymore—know I will continue to miss her, and that now I am pretty much only marking time. I enjoy myself a lot, playing bridge, taking adult education courses and subscribing to concerts at Lincoln Center and the YMHA, making short trips, seeing old friends when they come to town, doing my direct-mail consulting work for cancer relief. But I am only marking time. Unlike Yossarian, I expect nothing much new and good to happen to me again, and I enjoy myself less since Lew finally, as Claire chose to phrase it, "let himself" pass away. His family is strong and there was no weeping at the funeral services, except by an older brother of his and a sister. But I cried some tears myself back home after Claire gave me her account of his final few days and told me his last words, which were about me and my trip around the world.

I find myself looking forward to the trip I've started planning, to see sights everywhere of course, but mainly to see people I know in Australia, Singapore, and England, and in California too, where I still have Marvin and his wife, a nephew with a family, and some other acquaintances left from the days in Coney Island. I will begin, it's been decided, with short stops in Atlanta and Houston, to visit Naomi and Ruth, with their husbands and my grandchildren. The two girls have long since come to think of me as their natural father. Richard raised no objection to my adopting them legally. From the start I found myself dealing with them psychologically as my biological children, and I've felt no regrets about not siring my own. But we are no closer than that. As in most families I see, we find only desultory entertainment in each other's company and are soon all of us mutually on edge. Richard never showed jealousy because we grew close so quickly, and he eased himself away from all pretense of family life as soon as he decently could. In just a couple of years he had some new wives of his own and with the last one a child.

I am also looking forward to finding out more about that grotesque wedding in the bus terminal, the Wedding of the Close of the Century, as Yossarian and others now name it, to which, while I snorted humorously, he said I would be invited.

"I was robbed once in that bus terminal," I told him.

"My son was arrested there."

"I was too," I told him.

"For being robbed?"

"For raising a fuss, a hysterical fuss, when I saw the police doing nothing."

"He was put in a wall chain."

"So was I," I informed him, "and I still don't think I'll ever want to go there again."

"Not even for a wedding? A wedding like this one? With four thousand pounds of the best beluga caviar on order?"

I won't want to go. There are some compromises left I just don't want to make. Although Esther, the widowed lady I see most often, "would die" to attend, just to be on the scene and gape at others.

By the time I met Glenda, her loose days were behind her. I occasionally felt at least a little bit cheated because I had not been there in her bohemian heyday to enjoy her sexually then too, as more others had done than she wished comfortably to recall, and enjoy her roommates and other female friends too. The thought of the freedom with which those four had lived continued to titillate, and torment, me. I'd had my own good promiscuous years too, with girls from student days at New York University and Greenwich Village and then from the company, and with others I'd met through people in the company, and even on a lark or two each semester while I was teaching at my college in Pennsylvania for two years. Nevertheless, for a little while about the time of our marriage, I could still find myself temperamental, privately jealous and petulant, over her entire erotic past, and resentful of all the males, the youths, that high school football player, and then of all the men who had played their fornicating roles as partners with her. I hated especially the ones I imagined who could bring her always and simply to dizzying climaxes. Virile performances did not seem to matter to her. They mattered to me, and among those rogues of whom I had some knowledge, or was otherwise motivated to invent, I had to put her husband Richard. I saw him in these demeaning dramas as a conquering cavalier and irresistible adversary, and this was true even after I'd grown to discount him as a bothersome, vain man, shallow and empty-headed, always brimming with energetic plans of narrow ambition, and one whom Glenda also now considered only boring and exasperating. That she had harbored a long passion for the likes of him was a shameful recollection almost too distressing for either one of us to bear.

I still don't know how a guy with melanoma was able to keep working and get raises and new girlfriends and even a couple of wives. But Richard did. Lew could have told me, I'd always thought; but I did not want Lew to guess what I had come to understand about myself, that I had never fully grown up, not even with Glenda, when it came to that matter of a man's way with a woman.

Richard's first new girlfriend that we laid eyes on was the nurse in the office of his oncologist. She was perky and knew everything about his physical state; yet she was soon sleeping with him anyway and answering the phone in his apartment as though the place were her own. His next was her closest friend, to whom she gave him up in good spirit, who also knew about his malignancies but married him anyway. While that marriage was breaking up, there were girls in succession and concurrently, and then came the willowy, intelligent woman from good family he married next, a successful lawyer with a large firm in Los Angeles, to which city he packed himself up and migrated, into an even better job than the one he resigned from, to set up house with her there and move farther away from any familial claims upon him here. And these were only the ones he went to extremes to make sure we learned about, the attractive ones he had call for him in our apartment when he showed up on his visitation rights while he still chose to exercise them, or to haggle once more over money for maintenance or the problems with Michael, which grew more marked as he grew older. Richard had already gone west before we heard that horrifying word *schizophrenia* ventured and learned from the *Time* library and research files what a borderline case was then presumed to be. Glenda disdained my awe of Richard.

"He's a salesman, for God sakes, and a show-off," she would exclaim in condemnation, when she heard me speculating enviously. "If he pitches a hundred women, he's bound to find a few who would find him better than nothing, or than the dopes they're already tied up with. He can talk, we know that."

We knew he had a certain persevering charm, though none for us. At times when she was moping, I would clarify things for her, in the argument we'd first used with each other over the morning newspaper about whichever man was then in the White House: he was base, self-centered, conceited, bogus, and untruthful, so why expect him to behave any other way? I still can't tell whether the little prick we have there now is a bigger little prick than the two little pricks before him, but he certainly seems big enough, what with Noodles Cook as a confidant and that gluttonous, silver-haired parasite C. Porter Lovejoy, just out of prison on another one of those presidential pardons, his moral supervisor.

I always managed the mediation with Richard craftily. With me too he was driven to come across as likable and worldly, and I never let him feel positive he was succeeding.

"Set up a lunch," I volunteered, not long after Glenda and I started telling each other things and singling each other out to talk to at parties. "Let me speak to him for you."

"To who?" she asked.

"To whom," came out of me spontaneously.

"Oh, Lord!" she cried, her dark mood lifting. "You're a pedant, you know. Singer, you're a nice bright man, but what a pedant you are!"

It was the first time I'd heard that word *pedant* spoken. It was then, I believe, maybe at just that moment, that I consciously began to put to sleep my resistance against ever allowing myself to feel much lasting connection to any woman, even to those with whom I'd been feverishly enthralled for a while. My fear was not of commitment but of entrapment. But any woman who could use that word *pedant*, I reasoned, call her ex-husband "duplicitous" and a "narcissist," and describe an assistant manager we both worked for as a "troglodyte" was a woman I felt I could spend time talking to and perhaps even want to live with, despite the three kids, a first husband, and her extra year in age. And a Christian too. Guys from Coney Island thought I was going crazy when they heard who Sammy Singer was finally marrying, a girl with three children, a Gentile, one year older than he was. And not even rich!

Glenda had another trait I never mentioned to anyone until after she was gone, and then I told only Lew, one time when both of us were drinking, me with my Scotch on ice, he still with his Carstairs and Coke: she was amorous and daring when drinking and out for a good time, full of mischievous fun, and all the more so after we were married, and there was no end to her spontaneity and my exhilarating surprises right up until the time she fell sick and slowed down. More than once in the back of a car coming home from a party with people we hardly knew, she would begin to neck and grope and rub, and she would go farther and farther, and it was up to me to strain to continue a level conversation with the couple in front, making inordinately loud jokes to supply an explanation for my laughing and talking loudly and brokenly, for she would bob up with remarks and answer questions also before ducking down again to work on me some more, and it was something to keep more than the catch out of my voice when she finally made sure I came. I had stupefying orgasms, she knew, and I still do. They are slower in starting but last much longer. Lew told Claire I had tears in my eyes when I reminisced about that part, she let me know the last time we saw each other, at lunch in a restaurant, not long after Lew died, when she was flying off to Israel the first time on the chance she might buy a seashore house there for vacations for herself and any of her children who might want to come.

Glenda and I never courted each other, and that's one of the reasons our marriage happened the way it did. She took me ice-skating downstairs one afternoon in the rink in Rockefeller Center. I'd been a whiz on metal roller skates as a kid, playing our kind of hockey in the street, and I mastered the ice skates so adeptly she was tempted to believe I'd been hoaxing. I rented a car one Sunday in spring and took her and the children to Coney Island, where they'd never been. I guided them through Steeple-chase. They all of them rolled around in the Barrel of Fun and hooted at their deformed reflections in the magic mirrors, and afterward I led them across the avenue to show them the two-story Tilyou house of the founder. I showed them the chiseled name on the stone face of the bottom step that was continuing to bury itself in the sidewalk and was already all but submerged. They were skeptical of my impression that the house was sinking too and had earlier been a level higher. A week later I rented a larger car and took her mother along too when we went back and then had early Sunday dinner at a big seafood restaurant in Sheepshead Bay called Lundy's. When Glenda and I kissed good-bye that time, there was a second kiss in which we pressed into each other, and we knew it had started. I felt a powerful sentimen-tal affection toward her mother. I missed my own. I lived down-town and Glenda lived uptown, and one late evening when she did not feel like journeying home, following birthday cocktails after work for a different girl that stretched into a long dinner with about twelve of us and after that into a club with jazz and a dance floor in Greenwich Village, I said she could sleep at my place. She said sure. I had a platform bed and a long sofa too.

"We don't have to do anything," I promised reassuringly, when we were there. "I really mean it."

"Yes, we do," she decided, with laughing determination. "And don't try that bashful-little-boy act on me. I've seen you work."

And after that we seldom went out without fitting into our schedule the chance to be alone unobserved. We went to movies, we went to plays, we went off for weekends. One time she wanted to take the girls to see *The King and I*.

I said, "You mean the king and me, don't you?"

After a second of surprise, she saw I was joking and let out a hoot. "Oh, God!" she cried, with disbelieving praise. "You still really are a pedant, aren't you! Even just to think of a crack like that one. But I'd rather be married to a pedant than a prick, especially to a pedant who can make me laugh. Sam, it's time. Move in with me. You're practically living there now, and I've got room. You don't mind my kids, you spend more time with them than Richard ever did. You take them to Coney Island, and to see the king and me, and you get along better with Michael than the rest of us. Naomi and Ruth look up to you, even though Naomi is already taller. And you get along better with my mother than I can when I'm having my periods. Don't argue. Just move in and give it a try. You don't have to marry me."

"You know that's not true. You know it's a lie."

"Not right away."

I was not sure I wanted to see her every day.

"You see me at work every day now. We're together every weekend."

"You know that's different."

"And when I quit and you're supporting me, you'll have more time away from me, in the office, than you have now."

She was not as good a housekeeper as my mother had been and only ordinary as a cook. Even her own mother made better food, and she was not good either. I told her staunchly I would not consider it.

But as we continued going off weekends, I began leaving spare clothes in her apartment, and when we had a late night, it was easier to sleep over, and when I slept over, it soon became easier and then easy to sleep with her. She had her clothes in mine, and a cosmetic bag too, with a diaphragm inside. No one in her family seemed to find my being there novel. Only Michael was occasionally curious and might murmur something cryptic, or droll, but Michael could turn spontaneously curious about almost anything and not sustain that curiosity long. Sometimes Michael could lose interest in what he was saying even as he was saying it and change subject in midsentence. The rest of them thought it was his special way of teasing. He pretended it was, but I took him seriously and began to feel it was something more.

The household collaborated to simplify our trysts: soon the living room too was privileged space when the hour was late and we had closed the door. And it was just as well, for if we were both still animated by drink, we might start in there with a casual embrace and then finish there too, and it was anybody's guess where our clothing might fly. And in the beginning, and for a good many years afterward, there was rarely a night we were alone together, even those that were late, or hardly a morning or afternoon on a trip away, that we did not make love at least once, even during menstrual periods. We slowed down later and skipped chances, too often because she might turn miserably depressed and brood with the worries and troubles we had with Michael. By then we'd written Richard out of our lives as useless. She would talk solemnly and weep quietly in my arms until we kissed to console each other, and even then, when she'd feel I had gotten hard, we would make love with a different spirit, in a way that was solicitous and tender. I would delay long enough to gauge her responses and then yield myself into release, and she might or might not have hers, but she would be pleased I was contented, and grateful I had helped divert her again somewhat from the oppressive weight of our problems with Michael, as much mine now as hers. It is still my conviction that I have not in my lifetime met a person less selfish, more kindhearted, and less self-centered than she was, or less demanding or troubling, and I cannot even conceive of a woman who would have been better for me as a wife and a friend than she had been. And that was true for all the years we were married, even through Michael's flip-outs and eventual, inevitable suicide, right up until the time she began feeling sick too often in her stomach and intestines and the doctors, after tests, agreed she had cancer of the ovary, and only then was the honeymoon over.

And those were the best, and I mean best, years of my life, with not one minute of regret. It was better than the war. Yossarian would know what I meant by that.

She died in thirty days, as Teemer determined she would, fading weakly away into illness, with little acute pain, as he had all but guaranteed, and I still felt indebted when I met him again in the hospital taking care of Lew and learned with bemusement that he had put himself into the psychiatric ward there for help with the relentless stress of the idiosyncratic "theology of biology" he was formulating, which was proving too difficult for him to cope with unaided. He continued working daytimes, but slept there evenings, alone. His wife could reside there with him, but she preferred not to.

Teemer, intent, industrious, melancholic, was older too and, as Yossarian described him, a disabled casualty in his war against cancer. His was now a view of the world that decoded living cancer cells and expiring societies as representations of the same condition. He saw cancers everywhere. What he saw in a cell he saw enlarged in the organism, and what went on in the human he found re-created in groups. He shouldered a bewildering conviction, a conviction, he maintained, as healthy and vigorous in growth as a typical malignancy of the kind in which he specialized: the conviction that all the baleful excesses he spied multiplying unstoppably everywhere were as normal and inevitable to our way of life as the replications of malignant cells he knew of in animal life and vegetation.

Dennis Teemer could look at civilization, he liked to joke in pessimistic paradox, and see the world as just a microcosm of a cell.

"There are two more things about these cancer cells you might like to know. They live forever in the laboratory. And they lack self-control."

"Hmmmmm," said Yossarian. "Tell me, Teemer, does a cancer cell live as long as a healthy cell?"

"A cancer cell *is* a healthy cell," was the reply that came back and displeased us all, "if strength, growth, mobility, and expansion are the standards."

"Does it live as long as a normal cell?"

"A cancer cell *is* normal," was the frustrating answer, "for what it is. Biologically, why would you expect it to behave any differently? They can live forever—"

"Forever?"

"In the laboratory, unlike our others. They multiply irresistibly. Doesn't that sound healthy? They migrate and colonize and expand. Biologically, in the world of living things, why would you expect there would not be cells more aggressive than the rest?"

"Hmmmmm."

"And biology always does what it has to do. It doesn't know why and it doesn't care. It doesn't have choices. But unlike us, it doesn't seek reasons."

"Those are very large thoughts you are working with," I said to him, ambiguously.

"I wish he would stop," said his wife.

"It's my pleasure," said Teemer, with what passed for a smile. "Radiation, surgery, and chemotherapy are my work. But it's not the work that depresses me. It's the depression that depresses me."

"I wish he'd come home," said Mrs. Teemer.

He was honored to be taken seriously by his medical colleagues in psychiatry: they thought he was crazy but found that irrelevant.

Meeting Yossarian again brought back a flood of treasured war memories, even of gruesome events that were perilous and revolting, like those of wounded Snowden dying of cold and Yossarian throwing up numbly into his own lap. And of me blacking out dizzily each time I recovered and saw something else taking place I could not force myself to watch: Yossarian folding flesh back into a wound on the thigh, cutting bandages, retching, using the pearly cloth of Snowden's parachute as a blanket to warm him, and then as a shroud. There was that ditching with Orr, and the missing carbon dioxide cylinders for the ice cream sodas from Milo that the officers could have every day and we enlisted men got only on Sundays. At the investigation, it turned out logistically that there could be life vests or sodas, not both. They voted for sodas, because there were more of us to enjoy sodas than would ever need life jackets. I had that crash-landing with Hungry Joe. They gave him a medal for bringing the plane back and wrecking it needlessly. And there was a medal to Yossarian for going around over the bridge at Ferrara a second time, with McWatt at the controls caroling: "Oh, well, what the hell." Yossarian, seeing the crosshairs drifting and knowing he would miss, had not wasted his bombs. We were the only planes left with a chance at the target, and now all the antiaircraft fire would be aimed just at us.

"I guess we have to go back in again, don't we?" I heard McWatt on the intercom, when the bridge was undamaged.

"I guess we do," Yossarian answered.

"Do we?" said McWatt.

"Yeah."

"Oh, well," sang McWatt, "what the hell."

And back we went and hit the bridge, and saw Kraft, our copilot in the States, get killed in the plane alongside. And then Kid Sampson too, of course, cut apart at the beach by McWatt in a plane while capering on the raft anchored in the water. And "Oh, well, what the hell," McWatt had caroled to the control tower, before banking around lazily to fly himself into a mountain. And, of course, always Howie Snowden, cold and bleeding just a few feet away, crying out suddenly as he bled:

"It's starting to hurt me!"

And then I saw he was in pain. Until then I didn't know there could be pain. And I saw death. And from that mission on, I prayed to God at the start of every one, although I did not believe in God and had no faith in prayer.

At home, there was never much interest in that war, my war, except by Michael, whose attention span was short. To the girls it was merely a tall tale and a travelogue. Michael would listen hard a minute or two before whirling off on tangents more personal. As a tail gunner, I faced backward and crouched on my knees or sat on a rest like a bike seat. And Michael could picture it perfectly, he contended swiftly, because he had a bike with a seat and would ride it to the beach to stare at the waves and the bathers and could I look straight ahead while facing backward? Michael, that wasn't funny, the girls scolded. He grinned as though joking. No, I answered, I could look only straight back, but a top turret gunner like Bill Knight could spin his guns around in all directions. "Well, I can also," said Michael, "still spin. I can still spin a top, I betcha. Do you know how come we all put away our bathing suits at the same time of year, and . . . begin spinning our tops?" The girls threw up their hands. Glenda too. Michael did not seem to me always to be trying to be funny, although he obligingly assumed that character when charged. We called him Sherlock Holmes because he paid attention to details and sounds the rest of us ignored, and he played that role too with the same exaggerated comic theatricality. He had difficulty with proverbs, such as I had not imagined could exist. He could understand that a stitch in time might save nine, but he could not see how that applied to anything but sewing. He appeared absolutely dumbfounded one time when Glenda, advising him about something else, remarked that it was always better to look before you leaped, for he had not been thinking about leaping. Like his mother when a child, he was obedient to everyone. He helped with dishes when asked to. And when classmates told him to take drugs, he took drugs. When we demanded he stop, he did. He started again when urged to. He had no close friends and seemed pathetically to want them. By the time he was fifteen, we knew he would not be able to go through college. We speculated privately about work for him that would not involve close relationships with others: forest ranger, night watchman, lighthouse keeper, those were among our darkest jokes and far-fetched outlooks. By the time he was nineteen, we were wondering what we could do with him. Michael made the decision for us. Glenda found him first when she stepped out the back with a basket of wash from the washing machine. In the backyard of the house we had rented on Fire Island there was just one small tree, a stubby Scotch pine, they told us, and he had hanged himself from that.

The photographs we had of Michael could break your heart. Glenda said nothing when I put them away in the cabinet in which she had stored the photographs of herself as a cheerleader and her father as a vendor of agricultural supplies. Into the same cabinet with my Air Medal and gunner's wings, my patch of sergeant's stripes, that old picture of me with Snowden and Bill Knight sitting on a row of bombs, with Yossarian looking on from the background, and that older picture of my father with a gas mask and a helmet in World War I.

Not long after, Glenda, who had always been healthy, began suffering often with symptoms of vague character that eluded verification: Reiter's syndrome, Epstein-Barr virus, fluctuations in blood chemistry, Lyme disease, chronic fatigue syndrome, numbness and tinglings in the extremities, and, finally, digestive upsets and the ailment that was all too specific.

I'd met Teemer through Lew, who suggested we at least consult with the oncologist who'd been managing his Hodgkin's disease. Teemer reviewed the data and did not disagree. The primary growth in the ovary was no longer the main problem. The ones in other areas could prove tougher.

"It will depend," he counseled evasively, the first time he talked to us, "on the individual biology of the tumors. Unfortunately, those in the ovary do not reveal themselves until they've already spread. What I feel we—"

"Do I have one year?" Glenda broke in curtly.

"One year?" faltered Teemer, who looked taken aback.

"I mean a good one, Doctor. Can you promise me that?"

"I can't promise you that," said Teemer, with a regretful gloom we soon learned was typical.

Glenda, who had asked her question with false, blithe confidence, was shocked by his answer. "Can you promise six months?" Her voice was weaker. "Good ones?"

"No, I can't promise you that."

She forced a smile. "Three?"

"It's not up to me."

"I won't ask you for less."

"I can guarantee one, and it won't be all good. But there won't be much pain. We will have to see."

"Sam." Glenda heaved a great sigh. "Bring home the girls. I think we'd better start planning."

She died all at once in the hospital just thirty days later, from a coronary embolism while a new medication was being administered experimentally, and I've always suspected a humanitarian covenant about which I was told nothing. Yossarian, who knew Teemer well, thought the possibility credible.

Yossarian, paunchy, large, with hair turning white, was not

how I would have pictured him. I had not turned out the way he would have guessed either. He would have pictured a lawyer or professor. I was surprised to find him associated with Milo Minderbinder; he awarded me no honors for my promotion work at *Time*. Yet we agreed it was marvelous that, by luck and natural selection, we had managed to survive prosperously.

It seemed logical that the two of us should have taught school awhile and then moved into advertising and public relations, for the higher salaries and livelier milieu, and that we both had aspired to write fiction that would elevate us into that elite of the famous and opulent, and distinguished plays and film scripts too.

"By now we like luxury and call it security," he observed with a cursory rue. "As we grow older, Samuel, we're always in danger of turning into the kind of person we used to say we despised when young. What did you imagine I *would* look like now?"

"An air force captain, still in his twenties, who looked a little bit crazy, and always knew what he was doing."

"And unemployed?" he answered with a laugh. "We don't have much choice, do we?"

"I walked into a room once in Rome," I revealed to him, "a room I was sharing with Snowden on one of our rest leaves, and saw you on top of that chubby maid who was always putting out for any of us who asked her to and had those lime-colored panties she always wore."

"I remember that maid. I remember them all. She was nice. Do you ever stop to wonder what she looks like now? I have no trouble doing that, I do that all the time. I'm never wrong. I can't work backwards, though. I can't look at a woman now and see what she looked like when young. I find it much easier to predict the future than to predict the past. Don't you? Am I talking too much?"

"I think you sound like Teemer with that last one."

I also thought he was talking with a spark of the old Yossarian, and he liked hearing that.

He and Lew did not really take to each other. I could sense each wondering what I saw in the other. There was space in those hospital colloquies for only one life of the party, and it was hard for Lew to triumph as an extrovert when he was six feet tall and his weight had dropped down below a hundred and fifty. Lew toned down tactfully with Yossarian and his more sedate visitors like Patrick Beach and the socialite Olivia Maxon, with all her ludicrous delight in her two tons of caviar, and even with the sprightly blonde woman and the pretty nurse.

Often we would congregate evenings in Teemer's room in the psychiatric ward to talk about sanity, democracy, neo-Darwinism, and immortality amid the other patients there, all of them heavily medicated and staring impassively at us with no interest, as though waiting like cows with dropped jaws while we struggled to our conclusions, and that seemed a little bit crazy too. To live or not to live was still the question for Yossarian, and he was not mollified to hear that he had already been living much longer than he thought he had, perhaps even since the origin of the species, and, through the DNA transmitted into his children, would go on living long after he died, genetically speaking.

"Genetically speaking is not what I mean, Dennis, and you know that. Put a gene in me that will disable the ones that are aging me. I want to remain forever the way I am now."

Teemer socializing was crazily obsessed with the laboratory knowledge that metastatic cancer cells were genetic advances on the original malignancy, vastly more hardy, adroit, and destructive. He had to think of them, therefore, as evolutionary improvements and to wonder if all his medical interventions on behalf of patients were crimes against nature, trespassing intrusions upon the balancing currents of biological life he saw germinating in harmonious synchronization everywhere things lived. After all, he'd had to ask, what was so noble about mankind, or essential?

"We've had nothing to do with our own evolution and are having everything to do with our own decline. I know it sounds revolutionary, but I have to consider that possibility. I'm a neo-Darwinist and a man of science."

"I'm a man of junk," said Lew, who'd by then had enough of the hospital. "It's how I began."

"No, Lew, you began in a sperm cell as a strand of DNA that still doesn't know who you are."

"Balls!" Lew told him.

"Exactly," said Teemer. "And that's all we ever are."

"Sure, Dennis, if that's what you like to think," said Lew, who'd had enough of such intellectualizing too and went home the next day to wait things out there.

For that matter, Yossarian and I were not all that compatible either. I'd not heard of his movie scripts. And he seemed a bit miffed when I reacted to his idea of a play about the Dickens

family with only a smile and with nothing at all to his thought of
a comic novel about Thomas Mann and a composer in one of his
novels who'd made a Faustian bargain.

What I did not like about Yossarian was that he seemed somewhat conscious of himself as a special being and more than a trifle
smug in the range of his friendships.

And what I did not like about myself was that I still felt disposed
to accept him as someone superior. I was amazed to find among
his visitors the man McBride from the bus terminal, with a pleasant, bright-eyed woman he introduced as his fiancée. A man
named Gaffney dropped by to shake his head reproachfully at
Yossarian in his sickbed. He expressed the idea he had of a primeval Faustian bargain between God, or maybe it was the Devil, and
the first man, who perhaps was a woman.

"I will give you intelligence," submitted the Creator, "enough
knowledge to destroy everything on earth, but you will have to
use it."

"Done!" said our ancestor, and that was our Genesis.

"How do you like it?" asked Gaffney.

"Let me think about that one," said Teemer. "It may be the key
to my unified theory."

"Come home," said his wife.

"Are you crazy?" cried Teemer. "Not till I'm done."

McBride was the man at PABT who'd given me the money to
get home after I was arrested there. It was fascinating to see him
friendly with Yossarian and both working together on that wedding at the bus terminal, to which the President might come by
underground railway, and at which the cardinal would be among
the several prelates officiating.

"If you get the chance," I schemed subtly with Yossarian, "ask
the cardinal whose genes Jesus had."

"Teemer wants to know that too."

I want to take that trip around the world while there still is a
world. In Hawaii, there's a woman who used to work with me
and also the former wife of a friend from whom I used to buy
artwork when I was still doing slide shows for the space salesmen
at *Time*. She's been married to someone else a long time now. I'd
like to see both these acquaintances once more. Yossarian advises
me not to miss New Zealand as long as I'm going to Australia,
and especially the south island for its high mountains and glacier.
I might even try trout fishing with waders while there. That is

something else I've never done. In Sydney I have my old office buddy and his wife in a house facing the bay, with a swimming pool for the exercises he's been doing since the age of twenty-nine to keep the muscles in his upper body strong, and they've already decreed I stay with them at least two weeks. He lost the use of both legs when paralyzed by the disease called Guillain-Barré after preventive antitoxin inoculations for a sales meeting in Mexico. Yossarian knows unmarried women in Sydney and Melbourne and has offered to telephone with introductions. He suggests I send a dozen red roses to each beforehand. He says red roses always appeal. After that I want to go to Singapore, where a girl who used to be an assistant now lives with her husband, a lawyer there for an American firm, and then to Hong Kong, where I still also know people. From there I will fly to Italy, just to Rome. I want to try to find the building at the top of the Via Veneto in which we had those apartments on two whole floors. I think I might enjoy Rome more than last time, when I went as a fill-in to a speedy business conference, but not nearly as much as I did the first time as a young soldier in wartime with a ravenous appetite for Italian cooking and a youthful libido that was highly combustible and mystically and inexhaustibly renewable. After that, I'll go to England, where I know a couple of others I used to work with too. It seems a shame to skip Paris, but I don't know anyone in France anymore, and I don't think I'd know what to do with myself if I went there alone. And then back again to my high-rise apartment after seven weeks or eight, to a house and life without the person who'd meant more to me than any other.

I've picked safe countries and neutral airlines. But I'll probably be hijacked by terrorists anyway, Esther jokes, and then shot to death because of my American passport and Jewish origin. Esther probably would marry me if I could bring myself to ask, but only if she could safeguard all her widow's assets. She's officious and opinionated. We would not get along.

Yossarian is better off than I am because he still has big decisions to make. Or so says Winkler, who was there in the hospital room reporting on his business agreement with Milo Minderbinder for his new state-of-the-art shoe—I still laugh when I remember those days as kids when Winkler was starting up his new state-of-the-art breakfast-sandwiches-for-home-delivery business and I was writing the copy, headlined SLEEP LATE SUNDAY MORNING! for his advertising leaflets—when the flashy blonde woman came bursting into the hospital room with the news for Yossarian that had to be a shocker. Approaching age seventy, he was faced with the daunting prospect of becoming a father again, or not, and marrying a third time, or not.

"Holy shit," were the words Winkler remembered emerging from him.

The woman thus fertilized was the dark-haired nurse. It was obvious to everyone they'd been close for some time. If ever she was going to have a child, she wanted it to be his. And if she didn't have this one now, they both might soon be too old.

"Doesn't she realize," exhorted Yossarian, "that when he asks me to run out for a pass, I'll be eighty-four years old?"

"She doesn't care about that."

"She'll want me to marry her?"

"Of course. I do too."

"Listen—you too, Winkler!—not a word about this," commanded Yossarian. "I don't want anyone else to know."

"Who would I tell?" asked Winkler, and immediately told me. "I know what I would do," he offered, with the pompous demeanor he likes to affect as a businessman.

"What would you do?" I asked.

"I don't know what I would do," he answered, and we both laughed again.

Finding Yossarian there in the hospital and seeing all that he's up to, with that enthusiastic blonde for a friend and that pregnant nurse who wants him to marry her, with Patrick Beach and his wife there, and with something secret going on between Beach and that blonde, as well as between Yossarian and the woman married to Patrick Beach, and with McBride with his fiancée dropping in regularly too, and their talk about the bus terminal and the crazy wedding scheduled there, and with those two tons of caviar on order—all that and more leave me with the sheepish remorse that I've missed out on much, and that now that I no longer have it, mere happiness was not enough.

31
Claire

When it reached his stomach again, he decided to give up and let himself pass away. There was nothing he could think of anymore that was worse than the nausea. He could take losing his hair, he said, trying to raise a laugh, but he wasn't sure anymore about the other. There was so much around him now he was sick of. He was nauseous from the cancer, he was nauseous from the cure, and then there was something new they called lymphoma. He just didn't want to fight it anymore. He'd had pain of every kind. He said the nausea beat them all. I'd had the feeling right off there was something different about him this time. As soon as we were home, he started in with the arithmetic. He wouldn't let up.

"Which is more—eight percent or ten percent?"

"Of what?" I answered him back. "Ten percent. What did you expect me to say?"

"Yeah? Then which weighs more—a pound of feathers or a pound of lead?"

"I'm not an idiot, you know. You don't have to start all over from the beginning again."

"Which is worth more—a pound of copper or a pound of newspapers?"

We both smiled at that memory.

"I know the answer to that one too now."

"Yeah, big-tits? Let's see and make sure. How many three-cent stamps in a dozen?"

"Lew!"

"Okay, then, which is more—ten percent of eighty dollars or eight percent of a hundred dollars?"

"Let me get you something to eat."

"This time they're the same. Can't you see that?"

"Lew, leave me alone. The next thing you'll want to hear is seven times eight. It's fifty-six, Lew, right?"

"That's wonderful. Is seven times eight more than six times nine? Come on, baby. Try. How do they measure?"

"For Christ sakes, Lew, ask me things I know! Should your omelet be runny or well cooked, or do you want your eggs turned over today?"

He wasn't hungry. But the smell of cheese always brought him a smile. He might not eat much, but his face sure turned bright, and it was a way to get him to let up. It was like he thought that if I couldn't remember those multiplication tables of his, I wouldn't be able to hold on to a penny he left me. There was no more Scrabble or backgammon or rummy or casino, and he couldn't sit through a movie on the VCR without losing interest and falling asleep. He liked getting letters; he got a kick out of those letters of Sammy's. That's why I asked him to keep writing them. He didn't want visitors. They tired him. He had to entertain them. And he knew he made them sick too. Emil came to the house to treat him for anything else whenever we felt we needed him, unless he was out playing golf. He wouldn't give that up for hardly anyone now, that family doctor of ours, not even for his own family. I really let him have it once. But he's tired too. By then we were all sick of Teemer, and I think Teemer had given up on us as well. That going crazy stuff is just a dodge he's using. He just can't stand his patients anymore; he just about said as much to Lew. He thinks we've come to blame *him* for everything. So we decided to use the hospital near home, since Teemer couldn't think of anything different anymore. Lew would go in whenever he had to and come back home whenever he felt like it. He always felt more at home in our own house, but he didn't want to end there. And I knew why. He didn't want to lay that extra misery on me. So he went back in when he knew it was time. The nurses there were all still crazy about him, the young ones and the old married ones. With them he could still find the mood to joke. With them he could still find things to laugh about. Nobody might believe it —he would believe it, because I always let him know when I was angry about it—but I was always proud that women always found him so attractive, although I could get pretty worked up when some of the other wives at the club came on to him too openly and I'd see him leading them on and begin wondering where it was going to stop. What I liked to do was go out and buy the most expensive dress I could find and have them all in for a great big party just to let them see I was still the lady of the house. On vacations I always got a kick out of the joshing way he could start talking to other couples we thought we might want to hang around with. But this time there was really something different about him, and those lessons in arithmetic could drive me crazy. He was angry I couldn't learn things like he wanted me to—it was something to see what that face of his could turn into when his temper was starting to boil, and that nerve on the side of his jaw would begin to tick like a time bomb, and then I would get angry too.

"I think he's getting ready to die, Mom," my daughter Linda told me when I said I couldn't stand it anymore, and our Michael was right there with her and agreed. "That's why there's all that accounting now, and all that stuff about banking."

I had missed that part of it, and I'd always been able to read him like a book. Oh, no, I told them, Lew would never stop fighting. But he did, and he didn't deny it.

"You want to know what Linda thinks?" I said to him, fishing. "She says she thinks you've made up your mind to get ready to die. I told her she's crazy. People just don't decide like that, not normal people, and not you. You'd be the last person for something like that."

"Oh, baby, that's my good girl," he said with relief, and for a minute he looked happy. I think he actually smiled. "Claire, I'm tired of fighting it," he said right out, and then I swear I thought he was going to cry. "What's the use?" I remember his blue eyes, how pale they were, and I remember they were suddenly misty. He wouldn't let himself, not while I was there to see, but now I'll bet he did, at least a little, when no one was around to see, maybe more than a little, maybe all the time. What he did tell me was this: "It's been a lot of years now, Claire, hasn't it? I've made it to almost seventy, haven't I? Even Teemer thinks that's pretty good. I can't stand feeling nauseous so much, feeling weak now all the time. Sammy would like to hear I was saying nauseated instead of nauseous, but what does he know about this? It wasn't all that long ago I grabbed that guy stealing a purse and lifted him up onto the hood of the car. What could I do with him now? I can't stand looking so skinny. That's why I want to go back into the hospital so often. I can't stand having you see me this way, or the kids too."

"Lew, don't talk to me that way."

"Claire, listen good. Always keep lots of cash in a safe-deposit box in case you have to do something real quick. You'll find plenty in two of these. They'll seal the safe-deposit boxes when I go, so rent a couple now in just your own name in two different places and move some money into them. You know I always like to plan ahead. Give the children a set of keys so they'll have them, but don't tell them where they are until it's time. Let them find that out from the lawyers, and don't let the lawyers know everything. Never trust a lawyer. That's why I always have two. When they start trusting each other, get rid of both. There's a big piece of beachfront land we have on one of the islands I never told you about, and it's now all in your name, and there's another very good hunk of land out in California that you also didn't know about. Sell that one soon to help you with the inheritance taxes. You can trust the partner you'll find on that one. You can trust Sammy Singer too on things like advice when you aren't sure about the kids. And Marvin Winkler too. But hold on to the apartment house if you can. Don't give a thought to what we used to say about landlords. The coins from the laundry machines—those alone make that one worth keeping."

"I know that much, Lew. I saw that before you did."

"Sure. But tell me this if you're really so smart. Claire, if you have a million dollars invested in triple-tax-free bonds at six percent, how much income will that give you?"

"Annually?"

"That's my baby. You've got a head on your shoulders."

"With capped teeth. And a little face work too."

"So why can't you learn numbers?"

"Sixty thousand dollars a year, with no taxes to pay."

"Great. That's my sweetheart. And that's where the beauty of being really rich comes in. If a Rockefeller or anyone else has a hundred million in those same bonds, he'll make—"

"Six hundred thousand? That's some bundle!"

"No, a bigger bundle! Six *million* a year in interest for doing nothing, and no taxes, and that's better than you or I will ever do. Isn't finance wonderful? Now then, if instead of a million tax-free you have only nine hundred thousand invested at that same six percent—"

"Oh, Lew, for God sakes, give me a rest!"

"Think. Work on it."

"That's six times nine all over again, isn't it?"

"Yes, right, that's the only difference. So how much money will you earn at six times nine?"

"The kids will know."

"Forget the kids! I don't want you to have to depend on them and I don't want them to have to depend on you. People change, people turn crazy. Look at Teemer. Look at all the fuss and fighting that went on with Glenda and her sister over that farmhouse after her mother died. You remember what happened to my father with the ten thousand I borrowed, and you saw what happened to my mother's head before she even got old."

When his father loaned him the ten thousand dollars to start up the secondhand-plumbing business that then became our lumberyard too, the money he produced was all in cash, and none of us knew where it came from or where he kept it before he set the terms and had the papers drawn up, all official and very legal, so it would go to Minnie and then to all of the others if anything happened to him first. There had to be papers, and there had to be interest. The old man, old Morris, who was never afraid of anyone in his life, was afraid of being poor in his old age, and he was already over eighty.

God, how I remember that junkshop like it was only yesterday. It was small, small quarters, about the width of a truck garage, about the size of the restaurant in the city Sam Singer and I had lunch in, although the truck was always parked outside because there was always so much junk inside, and out in back. Heaps of metal, sorted into brass, iron, and copper, and a big scale large enough to hold a bale of newspapers, and so much dirt, filth. The clean newspapers were hauled from the cellars of the janitors all over the houses in Coney Island, who saved them, for a price, and these were put on the outside of the big bales. Inside them could be anything. At the end of the day, all of them—Lew, his father, the brothers, the brothers-in-law, and even Smokey Rubin and the black guy—they scrubbed their bodies and fingernails with cold water from the hose, a big industrial scrub brush, and lye soap. And I'd be waiting there all dressed up, ready to go out with him on a date.

His one fear was rats, not just the rats themselves, but the thought of them, in the army too when he was overseas, and then in the prison camp. In the slaughterhouse in Dresden it was all very clean, he said.

All of that, all of those people and all of that work, was as foreign to me as I'm going to find the Israelis if I do buy a house and ever start living there. Lew would have liked the idea of me in Israel, although I never could get him to go—I hardly ever could get him to go anywhere abroad where he didn't know the language and they didn't know who he was. It's just about the farthest part of the world I think I can find to live in and relax and maybe enjoy some memories while I try to experience some new kind of adventures in a place of old lore for me with people with a morale that has some kind of hope and meaning. I want to enjoy it.

I was brought up Jewish too, but my home life in a small family upstate was nothing like that one. My father was a bookkeeper. And then he was a bookmaker like Marvin's, and he gambled a lot, but he always wore a suit and shirt and tie and liked those panama hats and fancy black-and-white shoes they used to wear, I remember, with those large perforated holes. This big, loud, hardworking family of Lew's, with their Yiddish and Brooklyn accents, confused me and appealed to me. And so did that whole open, noisy, fast bunch of guys in Coney Island. I met him on a blind double date with my cousin, who lived there, and I was supposed to be with someone else, but once he made his play for me and let me know he'd kind of like to go on, no other fellow I ever met anywhere else ever had a chance. We were just the right type for each other. We never brought the subject up, but I guessed I would want to marry again, whether he would have liked the idea or not, and I think I do. We married young, and I've always been married, and I don't know if I can ever get used to living alone, but where am I ever going to find a guy who will fill his shoes?

"Don't count on me," said Sammy, when I poured all this out to him.

"You didn't have to tell me," I snapped. I have that habit: it sounded ruder than I'd meant. "Sam, no offense, but I could never share a bedroom with you."

"I don't think so either," Sam said, with his soft smile, and I was pleased to see his feelings weren't hurt. "He's going to be a tough man to replace."

"Don't I know it? But he used to envy you, envy you a lot, for your life in the city. Or for what he thought was your life. Even after you married Glenda he had this picture of you drinking it up every night and scoring with all those fancy girls in the office and those others you kept meeting in advertising."

Sam looked very pleased. "I never did," he said, looking a little proud, and a little ashamed. "Not once after I married Glenda. I stopped wanting to while she was alive. And hey, Claire, you know Glenda was right there in the office with me for a good couple of years too, so how did he think I was going to get away with that? Where do you think you're going to find someone, Claire? You may not know it, but you've got very strong standards."

I had no good ideas. I still owned most of that art school in Italy outside Florence Lew bought me as a surprise birthday present. How many other women ever got a birthday present like that one? But I don't trust Italian men on the whole or take to artists as anything but artists. I don't trust Israeli men, but they at least come right out and let you know they want your body for the night or half an hour and would like your money too. I've outgrown Coney Island men by now. They're all gone anyway. I'll have to lie about my age, and for how long can I get away with that?

"Sam, remember the junkshop on McDonald Avenue?"

He remembered the junkshop but only some in the family, because they weren't too cozy with outsiders, or even always with each other. There were always at least a couple of families living in close quarters in that small apartment building Morris bought and owned. They did not necessarily always like each other—his brother-in-law Phil went out of his way to be a pain in the ass to everybody, and even voted for Republicans like Dewey and Eisenhower and Nixon—but they were loyal in defense of each other, like no others, including in-laws, and then me, once I came there for dinner now and then and began sleeping over in the room of one of his sisters, even before we were married. God help anyone who ever hurt my feelings or said anything impolite, even when I was wrong. Except maybe Sammy and then Marvin, with their needling, and then a couple of those other wise guys with their cracks to Lew about my full bosom. I didn't enjoy hearing from him that they were kidding around about my breasts as big tits, but he could never figure out whether it might really be a compliment, as sly Sammy Singer kept arguing. The old man took a fancy to me, and set out to protect me because my father had died. He considered me an orphan. "Louie, listen to me, listen good," he told him, even when I was right there. "Either marry her or leave her alone." He did not want Lew to sleep over at my house, even when my mother was home. "Maybe her mother can't see, but I can."

And Lew did listen. He listened to him good until we were married, and then we started right in and hardly ever stopped, not even in the hospitals, almost until the last time. Lew was a rake and a big flirt, but he was a strict prude when it came to family. He was never really comfortable or forgiving with the girls with their bikinis and short skirts and their schoolgirl affairs. For that matter, I didn't like it either. And I didn't like the bad language. It was worse than boys used, and they didn't even seem to think it was dirty. But I could not let them know, because I did not want them to see I was as old-fashioned as their father while trying to talk some sense into them. That's how I got to him in Fort Dix finally when he was bullying that poor German orderly we called Herman the German and I was trying to make him stop. I finally stopped him by telling him I would strip off my clothes and straddle his hernia-operated-on body right there with Herman the German at attention and looking on. With no humor, without any laughter, did he finally let Herman leave. And that was after maybe close to half an hour of Herman standing there and reciting his past. He had a true mean streak when it came to Germans, and I swear I had to practically beg him to stop. But that's what finally got him, because Lew had seen me undressed but no other guy ever had, and I was still a virgin then. We got married in 1945, soon after he was back from the prison camp and had the hernia operation. And that was after three years of mailing him packages of kosher salamis and cans of halvah and other foods he liked that would keep, and even lipsticks and nylon stockings for the poor girls he said he was running into overseas. I was too smart to be jealous. Anyway, most of the packages never got to him, none after he was taken prisoner.

God, how they worked in that junkshop, worked their heads off with their thin rods of baling steel that sometimes snapped and were as dangerous as hell. The old man had the strength of three men and expected his sons and sons-in-law to have that much too, and that's why buying modern baling equipment for the old newspapers was always put off. They had baling claws and pliers for twisting the baling rods, and they had their pipe cutters for the plumbing junk they got hold of, but most of all they had their hands. And those big shoulders. And there was Lew, still just a kid, you know, stripped to the waist, with a baling hook in his right hand and a wink of encouragement to me while I helped with the paperwork or waited for him to finish so we could go out. A nasty thrust of the hook into the bale—a yank of arm, a twist of knee—and the bale was tumbled up and over, lying right on top of the one underneath and both of them quivering, and to us it was a reminder of sex.

Morris knew the value of money and did not want to waste any. Before he loaned us the ten thousand we needed to get started, he came up to inspect the building we wanted to lease, a condemned mousetrap factory, infested with mice, no less, poor Lew, at seventy-five dollars a month rent, our budget. He loaned us the money —we knew he would—but at ten percent interest, when banks were charging four. But he took the risk when the banks wouldn't touch it, and the money he wanted for his old age was also there for the rest of us too when we needed it. Shylocks asked less, we joked with him, but the old boy never stopped worrying about the money for his old age. Even after he got out of bed after his stroke, he would have someone drive him to the junkshop to do as much work as he could.

Lew was the sixth child, the second son of eight kids, but he was already making the decisions when I met him. After the war Morris expected Lew to keep working there and maybe someday take over to look after the place and everyone in the family. I, like a fool, thought I wanted him to stay in the army, but it was absolutely no go. He had a few thousand saved from his sergeant's salary, most of it banked—they paid him for all the time he was a prisoner of war—and the money he sent home from gambling. His father offered him a raise to keep him there—from his prewar thirty dollars a week or so to sixty-five a week. Lew's laugh was as kind as could be.

"Listen, Morris, listen good, because I will do better for you. I will give you a year, free, but then I will decide my salary. I will decide where, when, and how I will work."

"Accepted!" said Morris, with the soft grind of his dental plates. Everyone old had false teeth then.

Of course, Lew always had extra cash in his pockets for bargaining with janitors and with dealers of scrap. Sometimes you could remove a steam boiler from an apartment building intact.

Repair it somehow and then sell it to a different landlord as something used in good condition. The shortages made many such opportunities, along with kitchen sinks, pipes, radiators, toilet bowls, everything that goes into a house. Junkers did not think as far ahead as we did. Janitors—Lew always called them mister and spoke of them as managers or superintendents when he called on them to work something out—always liked the idea of making a little extra on the side. There was so much of that stuff around, and that's what gave us the idea of starting a business selling used building supplies in some place outside the city where there wasn't enough. I think the idea first came from me. It was a time to take chances. What we needed most was a sense of humor and a strong sense of self, and by then we both had plenty of that.

I have to laugh a lot again when I look back. We both knew so little, and with many things I knew more than he did. I knew what stemware was and Lew had never heard of it. But after I mentioned I wanted stemware, he made sure I had it for our first apartment. It came from a guy named Rocky, an Italian peddler of sorts he had made friends with somewhere, an "anything you need?" kind of entrepreneur. He was always dressed to kill, even when he dropped by the junkshop, a fashion plate with brilliantined hair. Our first car too came from Rocky, a used one. Rocky: "What do you need?" Lew: "A car." Rocky: "What make?" Lew: "A Chevy. Blue. Aqua, she wants." Rocky: "When?" Lew: "March of this year." In March it was there. That was 1947, and the car was a '45. Also the stemware, which Rocky had never heard of either, and I still have the image of the shy glance he gave me and the scratch of a head, with his fingers pushing back his generous mop of wavy hair. But no other sign that he did not know the product. Who did back then? But delivered the next week in partitioned paper leaf—each piece wrapped in a brownish tissue paper—came the two boxes, marked Woolworth's. No charge. A wedding gift from Rocky. Wow! I still have some pieces, I've kept them. And now it's almost fifty years later and Wow! once more, because Rocky pops back out of nowhere and turns out to be the partner on that piece of land in California who Lew said I could trust. They'd been in touch all those years, and Lew never said boo.

"Why didn't you ever tell me?" I had to ask.

"He's been in jail," said Lew.

Do people still make friendships that strong? Lew was hungry, always hungry, and filled with ambition, and always something of a foreigner in the world he saw around him that he wanted to be a part of, never stopped wanting to be in and own. He could have gone to college too, and he could have done as well as anyone else, because he learned fast, but he didn't want to take the time. His mother liked me too—they all did—because I was the only one who wrapped her presents in gift wrap and ribbons. I would sit and spend time with her, even though we could not talk much to each other. I didn't understand much Yiddish and that's about all she spoke, and soon she had what the doctors called hardening of the arteries of the head and was probably Alzheimer's disease, and she hardly ever made sense to anyone. Today it seems we'll all get Alzheimer's disease if we don't die of cancer first. There was Glenda, there was Lew.

"My father too," said Sam. "And don't forget about strokes."

"I don't forget. My mother had one."

"So did mine, finally," said Sam.

I would sit with Lew's mother anyway. My trick was to always answer yes. Every once in a while a no was required, and I could tell by shakes of the head and a kind of muttering that I had said the wrong thing, and when that didn't work and there was still no understanding, I smiled and said, "Maybe."

Lew learned fast enough, and when he struck out with the big oil company with his metered heating oil plan, he saw there were people he could not make headway with and places he would not be able to go, and we were smart enough to stick inside our limits. He never even tried joining the Gentile golf club, even when we had enough friends there to probably get in. He got a bigger kick out of inviting them as guests to ours. We both learned fast, and when we had money for two cars, we had two cars. And when the foreign cars came into fashion and were better than ours, we had two of those too.

No synthetic fibers for Lew, no imitations, ever. Cotton shirts made to order, as long as the cotton did not come from Egypt. Egypt was another pulse tingler for him after the wars with Israel. Custom-tailored suits from a shop named Sills even before anyone knew that John Kennedy was having his suits made there too. And most important: manicures, manicures! He never tired of manicures. I'm sure that came from the dirt from the junkshop, and then in the prison camp. We passed the time that way at the end, when he couldn't even watch television anymore. I gave him

pedicures too, and he'd just lie back and grin. We used to do that
a lot after we were married; it was something between us. I told
the nurses at the hospital to work on his fingernails when they
wanted to keep him happy, and they did, the staff nurses too.

"He died laughing, you know," I said to Sam.

"He did?"

"It's true. At least, that's what they told me." I'd said it on
purpose that way, and Sammy popped with surprise. "He died
laughing at you."

"What for?"

"Your letter," I said, and I laughed a little. "I'm glad you sent
us that long letter about your trip."

"You asked me to."

I'm glad I did. I read it to him in parts when it came to the
house and we both laughed about it a lot. Then he'd read it again
himself. He took it along into the hospital when he knew he was
going in for the last time, and he would read it aloud to the nurses.
At night he might have the night nurse read it aloud back to him.
The nurses adored him up there, I swear they did, not like those
cranky, snobby ones here in New York. He was always asking
them about themselves and telling them how good they looked,
the married ones with children and the old ones too. He knew
how to jolly them along and to say the right things when they had
problems. "Mary, tell your husband he'd better watch out, because as soon as I get just a little bit better, you're going to have
to start meeting me after work and on your days off too, and he'd
better start learning to make dinner for himself. And breakfast
too, because some mornings when he wakes up you won't be
there." "Agnes, here's what we'll do. Tomorrow, I'll check out.
You'll pick me up in your Honda at five, we'll go out for drinks
and dinner at the Motel on the Mountain. Bring enough along
with you in case you want to stay out all night." "Agnes, don't
laugh," I'd say too, because I'd be ʋitting right there. "He means
it. I've seen him work before, and he always gets his way. That's
how come I'm with him." It was really a nice, full trip Sam laid
out for us in his letter.

"New Zealand, Australia, Singapore . . ." I praised him. "And
with Hawaii, Fiji, Bali, and Tahiti thrown in? Did you really mean
all that?"

"Most of it. Not Fiji, Bali, or Tahiti. That was put in for you
two."

"Well, it worked. He got a big kick out of imagining you in those places. 'Poor Sammy,' is what he said to the night nurse, while she was reading it back to him again on that last night. He died at night, you know, and they phoned me in the morning, and those were just about his last words, Sam. 'Just when he needs me most, I have to be laid up in the hospital. Here the poor guy is going off without us on a trip around the world, and he still hasn't learned how to pick up a girl.' "

BOOK
ELEVEN

32

Wedding

The four thousand pounds of best-grade caviar were divided by automated machines into portions of one eighth of an ounce for the five hundred and twelve thousand canapés that, with flutes of imported champagne, were on hand for distribution by the twelve hundred waiters to the thirty-five hundred very close friends of Regina and Milo Minderbinder and Olivia and Christopher Maxon, as well as to a handful of acquaintances of the bride and the groom. The excess was premeditated for the attention of the media. Some of the surplus was reserved for the staff. The remainder was transported that same night by refrigerated trucks to the outlying shelters in the suburbs and New Jersey into which the homeless and other denizens of the bus terminal had been rounded up and concentrated temporarily for that day and night. The bedraggled beggars and prostitutes and drug dealers thus dislodged were replaced by trained performers representing them whose impersonations were judged more authentic and tolerable than the originals they were supplanting.

The caviar arrived at the workshops of the Commercial Catering division of Milo Minderbinder Enterprises & Associates in eighty designer-colored canisters of fifty pounds each. These were photographed for publication in vibrant high-style periodicals devoted to good taste and to majestic social occasions of the scope of the Minderbinder-Maxon wedding.

Sharpshooters in black tie from the Commercial Killings division of M & M were positioned discreetly behind draperies in the galleries and arcades on the various balconies of the bus terminal, watching most specially for illegal actions by the sharpshooters from the city police department and from the several federal agencies charged with the safety of the President and First Lady and other government officials.

Accompanying the caviar and champagne were tea sandwiches, chilled shrimp, clams, oysters, crudités with a mild curry dip, and foie gras.

There must be no vulgarity, Olivia Maxon had insisted from the beginning.

In this, her anxiety was allayed by the self-assured young man at the console of the computer model of the wedding to come, now taking place as having already occurred, on the monitors in the Communications Control Center of the PABT building, in which the equipment for the computer model had been installed for display and previewing. He flashed ahead to another of the sixty video screens there.

On that one, after the event that had not yet occurred was over, the socialite master of a media conglomerate was answering questions that had not yet been asked.

"There was nothing vulgar about it," he was asserting, before he even had attended. "I was at the wedding. I thought it was fantastic."

Olivia Maxon, her fears for the moment assuaged by this reassuring demonstration of what was projected as inevitable to occur, squeezed Yossarian's arm in a gesture of restored confidence and began fishing for another cigarette while extinguishing the butt of the one she'd been smoking. Olivia Maxon, a smallish, dark woman, wrinkled, smiling, and fashionably emaciated, had been anything but joyous at the unforeseen withdrawal from active cooperation by Frances Beach because of the serious stroke suffered by her husband, and by the need to rely more extensively than she wanted to on John Yossarian, with whom she had never felt altogether secure. Frances stayed much at home with Patrick, forbidding casual visitors.

The equipment in the command bubble in the South Wing of the terminal, between the main and second floors, was the property of the Gaffney Real Estate Agency, and the breezy young computer expert elucidating now for only Yossarian, Gaffney, and Olivia Maxon was an employee of Gaffney's. He had introduced himself as Warren Hacker. Gaffney's burgundy tie was in a Windsor knot. The shoulders of his worsted jacket today were tailored square.

Christopher Maxon was absent, having been told by his wife he

could be no use there. Milo, bored by this replay of the event
taking place in the future, had wandered outside to the surrounding balcony. Anything but at ease so near transvestites at the
railing above looking with shining iniquity on the figures below, of
which he understood he was one, he had coasted down the escalator to the main level below, to wait and go with Yossarian on the
tour of the terminal that now was authorized for all of them and
which some in his family thought he should make. With the income from his plane now assured, he had skyscrapers in mind. He
liked his M & M Building and wanted more. He was perplexed as
well by a nagging enigma: upstairs on a screen, he'd been disoriented to observe himself at the wedding in white tie and tails
delivering a short speech he had not yet seen, and then dancing
with that dark-haired woman Olivia Maxon, whom he'd only just
met, when he still did not know how to dance. He was not sure
where he was in time.

Before drifting down, he had taken Yossarian outside for a
word in private. "What is the fucking problem," he had wondered
absently, "with the fucking caviar?"

"It's not the money," Yossarian informed him. "It's the fucking
fish. But now they think they've caught enough."

"Thank God," said Olivia, hearing that news again.

In the social archives of the Metropolitan Museum of Art were
precedents with guidelines and milestones to be emulated and ex-
ceeded. The Minderbinder-Maxon affair would surpass them all.
Even in a recession, the country was awash in money. Even amid
poverty, there was room for much waste.

Although it was spring, the florist in charge had installed eighty
Christmas trees in the five banquet halls and had surrounded them
with thousands of pots of white narcissus. There were two sections
with dance floors and bandstands on the main and second floors
of the South Wing, and one on the main floor of the North Wing.
From midafternoon on, spotlights illuminated the entrances on
Eighth Avenue and Ninth Avenue and the lesser, more secluded
doorways along the side streets. The effect inside through the
smoked plate-glass windows of the major outside wall for two
whole city blocks was of lots of sunlight on stained glass. Rolling
buses seen through the panes were acclaimed as a clever approxi-
mation of the real world. Lauded equivalently as an impression of
reality was the occasional wafting scent of diesel fumes filtering in
through the natural clouds of perfumes from the women and emit-

ted by fragrances infused into the central ventilating system. All of the subcaterers, florists, and other workers contracting with M & M Commercial Catering, Inc. were required to sign confidentiality agreements with the Commercial Killings division of M & M E & A, and the secrecy of these confidentiality agreements was publicized widely.

The bottom floor of the North Wing, which was separated from the South Wing by a city street that the bride with her procession would have to cross, was converted into a chapel and select banquet area. Effecting this renovation had required the removal of massive staircases leading to the floor below, together with an information booth and the enormous activated sculpture of moving colored balls that normally occupied much of the floor space. The staircases, information booth, and work of sculpture were put on exhibition under a temporary canopy at the Metropolitan Museum of Art at the place where the Great Hall of the museum normally stood, and these attracted respectable attendance and decent reviews from art critics. The Great Hall of the museum had itself been transferred into the bus terminal, on loan for the occasion for a consideration of ten million dollars. Uprooting the staircases and sculpture from the North Wing made room for pews and rows of walnut benches, and, of more moment, for the installation there in the bus terminal of the Temple of Dendur from the same Metropolitan Museum of Art, which, through the peaceful application of much persuasive pressure and a fee of another ten million dollars, was also lent out temporarily by the museum for the evening. It was in the North Wing of PABT that those now watching in the Communications Control Center would soon observe the wedding ceremony enacted. There was space left as well in that area for a small head table for the principal participants in the ceremony and their two guests from the White House, and for six round tables, each with seats for ten people who were most closely connected with the proceedings and with those eminences at the oblong table in front of the columns of the Temple. The altar inside the Temple of Dendur was banked with flowers and blowing candelabra.

One million, one hundred and twenty-two thousand champagne tulips had been procured as door prizes and souvenirs. A massive variety of fabulous hanging chandeliers from different epochs was installed throughout all five banquet sections, and these were wrapped in curly willow branches. Wisps of raffia were added to the willow branches, and there were tiny twinkling lights in all of the leaves and in the boughs of all eighty Christmas trees. Ravishing tapestries for tablecloths, masses of staggered candles, antique cages full of live birds, and rare books and silver plate from different periods were in abundance everywhere. Thickets of summer asters in the twenty-two hundred Malaysian pots flanking all of the entrances into the principal terminal halls helped turn half the South Wing of the main floor of PABT into a miniature Versailles, with thousands of flickering lights in the terra-cotta pots simulating millions of candles. In one hundred and four vitrines along the sides of all banquet areas were living actors in poses and activities re-creating the hustlers, whores, drug dealers, child runaways, panhandlers, drug addicts, and other derelicts who regularly inhabited the terminal. Shops still surviving profitably in the terminal were paid to remain open all night, enhancing the novelty of the surroundings and setting, and many of the guests enjoyed spending time in the intervals buying things. Sixty-one sets of attractive female identical twins, all that could be found in the world for that work, posed as mermaids in the fifty or so artificial pools and fountains created, and thirty-eight pairs of male identical twins performed as heralds and banner wavers and offered humorous responses to questions.

Port Authority Patron Aides in red jackets were on duty everywhere to assist with instructions and directions. The AirTransCenter of the terminal was held open to transport to the city's three major airports those guests rushing directly from the lavish Minderbinder-Maxon affair to lavish parties in Morocco and Venice, music festivals in Salzburg or Bayreuth, and the Chelsea Flower Show or Wimbledon tennis matches in England.

Sophisticated managerial headhunters had ensured through intensive interview procedures that only well-bred models and thespians from good families, with degrees from good colleges, were hired for the parts of the male and female whores and other penurious, degenerate inhabitants of the premises who normally made their residences and livelihoods there, and they threw themselves into these roles with a wholesome waggery and an endearing enthusiasm for good, clean sport that won the hearts of all in the several audiences. Toward party's end, as those observing on the video screens could see, these mingled with the guests in their costumes and feigned vocations, and this was another innovation contributing much to the general hilarity.

Other actors and actresses and male and female models outfitted to resemble figures in famous paintings and motion pictures strolled through the several galleries, striking the characteristic poses of the characters they were aping. There were a number of Marilyn Monroes, a couple of Marlon Brandos playing Stanley Kowalski, a Humphrey Bogart here and there, a pair of dying Dantons, and at least two Mona Lisas, whom everyone recognized. Waiters wore flowing white blouses and embroidered tunics of different periods. The Off-Track Betting parlor and Arby's restaurant on the second floor and the Lindy's Restaurant and Bar below were reconstructed to resemble seventeenth-century Flemish eating-drinking houses, with bric-a-brac and artifacts of that time filling the taverns appropriately. In one of these tableaux, smoking a cigarette rather than a pipe and scrutinizing everything shrewdly, was a lean man with milky skin, pink eyes, and copper hair. He wore Bavarian lederhosen and had a hiking staff and green rucksack, and Yossarian, who was vaguely sure he had seen him somewhere else, could not tell whether he was there at work or as an outfitted element in the decor. There were several Rembrandt self-portrait look-alikes and one Jane Avril. There were no Jesus Christs.

After dinner, the guests would find themselves free to dance or drift past Greek and Roman antiques to buy Zaro's bread at Zaro's Bread Basket, Fanny Farmer candy, or New York State Lottery tickets, or peer into a Drago shoe repair shop or one of the Tropica Juice Bars, where the pyramids of oranges were decorated in French Directoire, with swags, rosettes, and tassels. Many had never laid eyes on pyramids of oranges before. The centerpieces of their dining tables were of gilded magnolia leaves and spring branches, and the upright columns supporting the Communications Control Center were majestic in silver floodlights, with fountains tumbling whitely around them, and with the multitude of hoisted sail-like corporate banners and pennants luffing and snapping in the artificial breezes. One hall leading to gates outside to long-distance buses heading west to Kenosha, Wisconsin, and north to the Pole was decorated in the Greek Renaissance style and furnished with Italian tapestries, Japanese lanterns, medieval armors, and carved-walnut wainscoting from a French château. Opposite this was another passageway for departures; this one featured Regency furniture, overstuffed chintz cushions, and mahogany woodwork, all just inside the wrought-iron gates of a medieval court. The Charles Engelhard Court, also on loan from the Metropolitan Museum of Art, was ablaze with pink and gold light and featured fifty thousand French roses, with almost as many gold-dipped magnolia leaves, and a dance floor hand-painted for just that evening in harlequin blocks of green, yellow, red, and black.

Forty-seven chiefs of protocol from the Foreign Service had assisted with the sensitive matter of seating arrangements, making sure the thirty-five hundred guests were properly, though not always contentedly, placed. The basic seating attack ultimately agreed to left many of the thirty-five hundred unfulfilled and displeased, but propitiated to an extent by the disappointment evident in others.

There was no head table anywhere other than the privileged small one facing outward from the Temple of Dendur in the North Wing for the principals and, of course, the President and his First Lady, with Noodles Cook sitting in already for the chief executive until he made his entrance.

The First Lady had arrived early to collect autographs from celebrities.

"I wonder where the President is," said Olivia Maxon, watching with impatient expectation. "I wish he'd come."

He would journey, some knew, by speedy special train to PABT directly from the secret MASSPOB underground terminal in Washington. And he would, of course, be among the last to appear, materializing only in time to wave with a broad smile and shake but few hands before giving the bride away while simultaneously taking his stand beside the groom as M2's best man. This was another first in matrimonial procedure and promised to set a standard for wedding ceremonies, perhaps even for royal families with traditions centuries old.

All of the other tables were round, in order that no one person be in a dominant place, and the chairs, ostensibly, were democratically equal. And each of the remaining three hundred and forty-four round tables outside the North Wing featured an important public figure and a multimillionaire, or a woman married to one. The multimillionaires were not entirely happy, for all would have preferred the President himself, or failing that, one of the eight billionaires invited, who well understood their metaphorical dimensions as deities, trophies, inspirations, and ornaments. A few of the billionaires had bought hotels in Manhattan that same week merely to possess facilities for private parties for friends.

The cardinal had requested the President or, if not him, the governor and the mayor, one owner of a major metropolitan newspaper, at least two of the eight billionaires, and one Nobel physicist to convert. Yossarian gave him Dennis Teemer instead, to teach him the facts of biological life, one newspaper publisher, and one dejected multimillionaire who had hoped for tête-à-tête access to a billionaire. He set them at a table with a good view of the bride on the Ninth Avenue side of the South Wing, not far from the police station and the table with Larry McBride and his new wife, and Michael Yossarian and his old girlfriend Marlene, between the Sport Spot Lingerie Shop outside the doors of the police station and Jo-Ann's Nut House. McMahon was there too, emerging from his cell to honor McBride and his new missus, on duty in his police captain's dress uniform instead of a dinner jacket.

McBride was in line for a presidential commendation for his masterful achievement in finding space for the three hundred and fifty-one tables for the thirty-five hundred closest friends of Regina and Milo Minderbinder and Olivia and Christopher Maxon, who had no close friends and did not want any, and for the Temple of Dendur and other monumental structures in the five refulgent halls, along with sites for the bandstands and dance floors. He was responsible as well for the coordination of activities by others in disciplines with which he had no previous experience.

Of crucial priority in the planning was the need for a clear passage for the bridal procession to move from the Ninth Avenue side of the South Wing almost all the way through to the Eighth Avenue side as far as the Walgreen's drugstore, around which corner the party then turned uptown through exits to cross Forty-first Street beneath an overhead shelter and advance into the chapel and dining hall in the North Wing to the altar set up just inside the Temple of Dendur. The Temple of Dendur, the Blumenthal Patio, the Engelhard Court, and the Great Hall of the famed Metropolitan Museum of Art, the four hallowed areas of the museum consecrated to parties and other social and promotional events, had all been relocated to the bus terminal for the evening and allocated in a way that afforded all guests their own celebrated monument with a history of glorious catering.

As laid out by McBride, all guests could obtain at least a partial view of the bride and her retinue as they rose to the top of the escalators from the Subway Level on the Ninth Avenue side of the terminal and made their dignified way toward Eighth Avenue and eventually into the North Wing. This route of some duration allowed for an unusual program of music to aggrandize the occasion as unique. Yossarian listened with amazement to the first familiar notes.

The opening piece for the matrimonial celebration was the prelude to the opera *Die Meistersinger.*

And it was to the first, blaring, jubilant chords of this that Yossarian watched the bride come levitating up into sight, as though over a horizon, at the head of an escalator. The music, which was of adequate span for the long walk, was handclapping perfect in bouncy spirit. The flower girls and ring bearers were especially stimulated by the quickening and changing tempos and came into their own when the "Dance of the Apprentices" was added for the two minutes and six seconds needed for the last in the bridal party to turn into the passageway to the side exit to the North Wing. There, after the bride had completed her turn outside and crossed the street into the North Wing, the music changed to a ceremonious orchestral rendition of the "Prize Song" from that same Wagnerian opera, which ended on a soft, palpitating note when the bride was in the chapel and came at last to a stop where the cardinal, a Reform rabbi, and six other prelates from different faiths stood waiting with the groom and their primary attendants. Here, while the recitations were made, the music diminished to underlying refrains of the Liebesnacht duet from *Tristan,* while the cardinal tried to ignore that the music was both heavenly and carnal, and the rabbi tried to forget that it was composed by Wagner. In that part of the ceremony, the lucky couple was pronounced man and wife nine times, by the eight clergymen and Noodles Cook, who was still standing in for the overdue President. When they turned from the altar to kiss chastely before moving to the dance floor, the soaring melodies chosen, Hacker announced before they began, were those of the closing measures of *Götterdämmerung,* with their soulful, soaring strains of the "Redemption Through Love" theme.

"Do you know it?" asked Hacker.

"I know it," said Yossarian, in surprised appreciation, and was tempted to whistle along with the peaceful violins and somnolent brass now rising and softening into so holy a conclusion. "I was about to suggest it."

"Was he really?" the kid asked Gaffney, and with a button put a pause to the activities.

"No, I wasn't," recanted Yossarian before Gaffney could answer. "But I think it's perfect. It's peaceful, sweet, melodic, erotic, and certainly climactic and final." He gave no voice to his shifty and vindictive presentiment that he was seeing on the video monitors another *Götterdämmerung,* that it was almost closing time for all of the people he was watching in oblivious revelry on the video screens, including himself and Frances Beach as he watched himself dance with her, maybe for Melissa too and McBride and his new wife, for the bride and M2. "Your guests will love it, Olivia. They'll walk out to the dance floor humming that *Götterdämmerung* tune."

"No, sir," corrected smugly the patronizing young man. "No, sirree. Because we come up with something better as they break away. Wait till you hear it."

Gaffney nodded. "I think you said you already have."

"It's a children's chorus," said the computer technician. "As the Wagner fades, softly underneath it and rising steadily we introduce a chorus of children that most people have never heard. It's angelic. And just when it's most moving, we blast in comedy, a chorus of musical laughter, to set the new mood we want for the rest of the evening. It's a chorus of laughing men that overpowers and drowns out the kids, and we're off. They're both by a German composer named Adrian Leverkühn. Do you know him?"

"I've heard of him," said Yossarian, wary, feeling strangely as though he were wobbling about in time again. "He's a character in a work of fiction," he added nastily.

"I didn't know that," said the young man Hacker. "Then you know how great he was. Both these choruses are from his cantata called *The Lamentations of Faust,* but we don't have to tell people that."

"Good," snapped Yossarian. "Because they're not. They're from his oratorio called *Apocalypse.*"

The computer whiz smiled up at Yossarian pityingly. "Mr. Gaffney?"

"He's wrong, Hacker," Jerry Gaffney said, shrugging at Yossarian with a shade of courteous apology. "Yo-Yo, you keep making that mistake. It's not the *Apocalypse.* It's from his *Lamentations of Faust.*"

"God damn it, Gaffney, you're wrong again. And I ought to know. I've been thinking of writing a novel about that work for something like fifteen years."

"How quaint, Yo-Yo. But not thinking seriously, and not a serious novel."

"Cut the Yo-Yo, Gaffney. We're in an argument again. I did the research."

"You were going to have Thomas Mann and Leverkühn in scenes together, weren't you? And put that Gustav Aschenbach in with Leverkühn as one of his contemporaries. You call that research?"

"Who's Gustav Aschenbach?" said Hacker.

"A dead man in Venice, Warren."

"Gentlemen, I can settle it easily for both of you, right here on my computer. Hold on three ten-thousandths of a second. Ah-ha, come see. There, Mr. Yossarian, *Lamentations of Faust*. You are mistaken."

"Your computer is wrong."

"Yo-Yo," said Gaffney, "this is a model. It can't be wrong. Go ahead with the wedding. Let them see how it went."

On the largest screens the sun turned black, the moon turned the color of blood, and the ships in the rivers and the harbor were overturned.

"Warren, stop kidding." Gaffney was displeased.

"It's not me, Jerry. I swear. I keep deleting that. And it keeps coming back. Here we go."

The Leverkühn music, Yossarian saw, went over well. As the dying harmonies ending *Götterdämmerung* neared conclusion, a tender children's chorus Yossarian could not remember having heard before came stealing in ethereally, at first a breath, a hint, then rose gradually into an essence of its own, into a celestial premonition of pathetic heartbreak. And next, when the sweet, painful, and saddening foreshadowing was almost unbearable, there smashed in, with no warning, the shattering, unfamiliar, toneless scales of unrelenting masculine voices in crashing choirs of ruthless laughter, of laughter, laughter, laughter, and this produced in the listeners a reaction of amazed relief and tremendous, mounting jollity. The audience quickly joined in with laughter of its own to the barbaric cacophonous ensemble of rollicking jubilation that rebounded from speakers everywhere, and the festal mood for the gala evening was ready to commence gleefully, with food, and drink, and music, and with more ingenious displays and aesthetic delicacies.

Yossarian was there and laughing too, he saw with a shock. He frowned at himself in reproach, while Olivia Maxon, at his side there in the Communications Control Center of the terminal, saw herself laughing with him in the chapel of the North Wing and said it was divine. Yossarian now looked contrite in both places. He was scowling, in this place and that place, in peevish detachment. Staring into this future, Yossarian was mesmerized to find himself in white tie and tails: he had never in his life worn white tie and tails, the costume prescribed for all males in that elite group of insiders in the North Wing. Soon he was dancing a restrained two-step with Frances Beach, then in succession with Melissa, the bride, and Olivia. What displeased Yossarian often about himself, he remembered now, seeing these pictures of himself looking silent, acquiescent, and accommodating at that wedding awaiting him, was that he did not truly dislike Milo Minderbinder and never had, that he thought Christopher Maxon congenial and unselfish, and found Olivia Maxon, though unoriginal and unchanging, grating only when expressing strong opinions. He had an abstract belief that he ought to be ashamed, and another abstract idea he should be more ashamed he was not.

He was seated with Melissa and Frances Beach at a table close enough to communicate with the Minderbinders and Maxons, near Noodles Cook and the First Lady, awaiting the arrival of the President. The chair reserved for Noodles at the table adjacent to Yossarian's was vacant. Angela, who wanted desperately to come, was not there, because Frances Beach would not allow her to be.

"I don't like myself for feeling that way," Frances confessed to him. "I just can't help it. God knows, I did that same thing myself, more than once. I did it with Patrick too."

Dancing with Frances, for whom he preserved that special shared friendship some might call love, he felt only bone, rib cage, elbow, and shoulder blade, no fleshly thrill, and was uncomfortable holding her. Dancing equally inexpertly with pregnant Melissa, whose plight, stubbornness, and irresolution were agitating him at present into an almost ceaseless fury, he was aroused by the first contact with her belly in her sea-green gown and lusting to lead her away into a bedroom once more. Yossarian peered now at that belly to ascertain if the plumpness was fuller or whether the corrective measures restoring her to normal had already been taken. Gaffney regarded him with humor, as though again reading his mind. Frances Beach at the wedding spied his difference in response and ruminated dolefully on her sad facts of life.

"We're unhappy with ourselves when we're young, and unhappy with ourselves when we're old, and those of us who refuse to be are abominably overbearing."

"That's pretty good dialogue you give her," Yossarian challenged Hacker, with belligerence.

"I like that too. I got it from Mr. Gaffney here. It sounds pretty real."

"It should sound real." Yossarian glowered at Gaffney. "She and I already had that conversation."

"I know," said Gaffney.

"I thought so, you fuck," Yossarian said without anger. "Excuse me, Olivia. We say things like that. Gaffney, you still keep monitoring me. Why?"

"I can't help doing it, Yossarian. It's my business, you know. I don't make information. I just collect it. It's not really my fault that I seem to know everything."

"What's going to happen to Patrick Beach? He isn't getting better."

"Oh, dear," said Olivia, shuddering.

"I'd say," answered Gaffney, "he's going to die."

"Before my wedding?"

"After, Mrs. Maxon. But, Yo-Yo, I would say that about you also. I would say that about everyone."

"About yourself too?"

"Sure. Why not?"

"You aren't God?"

"I'm in real estate. Isn't God dead? Do I look dead? By the way, Yossarian, I've been thinking of writing a book too."

"About real estate?"

"No, a novel. Maybe you can help. It begins on the sixth day of creation. I'll tell you about it later."

"I'm busy later."

"You'll have time. You're not meeting your fiancée until two."

"Are you getting married again?" Olivia looked pleased.

"No," said Yossarian. "And I have no fiancée."

"Yes, he is," answered Gaffney.

"Don't listen to him."

"He doesn't know yet what he's doing. But I do. On with this wedding, Warren."

"He still hasn't come," reported Hacker, puzzled, "and no one knows why."

Thus far there had been no hitch, except for the absence of the President.

McBride, dutifully, tirelessly, had seen to parking space for the automobiles and coordinated their comings with the arrivals and departures of the commercial buses, routing many in both groups to the ramps and gates on the third and fourth floors. The one thousand and eighty parking places in the garages overhead provided room for most of the nearly seventeen hundred and seventy-five limousines expected. Most were black and the rest were pearl gray. Other cars were diverted to the parking lot across the avenue, where the sidewalk was lined with shish kebob and peanut vendors and clusters of shoeshine stands with convivial old black and brown men who sometimes spent the balmy nights sleeping at their stands beneath beach umbrellas. They made use of the basins and toilets of the terminal, ignoring the enduring artwork of Michael Yossarian explicitly banning "Smoking, Loitering, Shaving, Bathing, Laundering, Begging, Soliciting," oral sex, and copulation. The shabby street scenes were amusing to many crossing the avenue to enter beneath the block-long metal-and-smoked-glass canopy, who assumed they had been staged expressly for them.

Photographers covered every access on all streets of the landmark, as though the structure were under siege, and journalists had come from foreign countries. A total of seventy-two hundred and three press passes had been issued to accredited newsmen. This was a record for an American wedding. Forty-six owners of foreign publications had come as guests.

Invitations to the gala occasion had been delivered in envelopes that were stiff and square, for they were on platinum, and only Sammy Singer on the primary list of thirty-five hundred invited declined to come, courteously pleading prior commitment to a trip to Australia. Yossarian thought better of Sam Singer than ever before. The secret agents Raul and carrot-topped Bob and their wives were on hand as guards as well as guests. Yossarian had exiled them deliberately to distant tables far apart from each other; now he saw with indignant surprise at the wedding ahead taking place just then that both were nevertheless seated right there with him at his own table in the inner sanctum of the North Wing, close enough to keep watch while taking in the epic spectacle of which they themselves were a part, and that Jerry Gaffney, who'd not been invited, was there with his wife at his table too!

Someone somewhere had countermanded orders without letting him know.

As expected, the limousine crush began to form *earlier* than expected. By 6:00 P.M. many arrived who did not wish to waste an opportunity to be photographed before the thicker crush of people more important began. And many of those coming soonest, the First Lady among them, were eager to be there to ogle everything.

It was a feast for fashion editors.

Women were aided beforehand by a proclamation from Olivia Maxon that "no dress would be too dressy." They were grateful as well for a tip sheet from leading fashion stylists of trends in their forthcoming collections. The result was a glorious extravaganza of up-to-the-minute dress designing recaptured on camera with exceptional brilliance, in which the ladies took part confidently as both spectators and spectacles. While numerous tastes in fashion were displayed by the nearly two thousand women there, none of the women were out of style.

They wore everything from cocktail dresses to ball gowns, arriving in a blissful and iridescent shimmering of unlined linen with gold pinstripes and with fringes of Indian beadwork, in palettes that were pale, ranging in the main from ivory to peach and sea green. Leopard spots were a favorite pattern in chiffon skirts, or in organdy dresses with fringed hems, and on silk jackets. There were women in long evening dresses who were thrilled to see many other women there in long evening dresses, especially in dresses with fragile embroidery on crisp, pale silks. Short skirts were of prismatic chiffon too. Jackets were in pink, orange, and chartreuse satin decorated with rhinestones instead of nailheads, while sweeping black *point d'esprit* overskirts showed the knees in front and dripped to the floor in back, and those bold enough to have guessed right were especially proud of their sexy matte jersey evening clothes.

After champagne, caviar, and cocktails, and well before the bride and M2 had appeared, the lights in all wings of the bus terminal were lowered sacramentally and everyone took a seat around one of the five stages closest at hand to listen to a gifted violinist the age of a young Midori and four clones play Paganini caprices in each of the places. It was not possible to tell the original from the clones, and no prizes were awarded for correct guesses. Christopher and Olivia Maxon could be seen in the flesh and also larger than life on the closed-circuit television screens as huge as those in a cinema house. They were in the front row on the far right on the main floor of the North Wing, and all guests there and elsewhere suddenly noticed that a single spotlight seemed to have been positioned to shine directly down upon Olivia, who sat with her hands clasped together and a look of poised rapture on her illustrious face. As those in the Communications Control Center could see on the screens flashing to newsstands, she was already being described in a current future issue of *U.S. News & World Report* as "the queen of nouvelle society." And *Time, The Weekly Newsmagazine* would write, as they saw displayed at the newsstands inside the terminal kept open just for them, that "Olivia Maxon is a princess in the new social order, and the bus terminal is her palace."

The fantasy quintessence of the wedding joining two billionaire families was accentuated by a candlelight ceremony in stylish white-on-white, with all the dresses of the dozens of women and little girls in the bridal party designed by Arnold Scaasi. The bride herself wore an off-white taffeta dress, delicately embroidered in gold, with a twenty-seven-foot train. Her tulle veil was held in place by a diamond-and-pearl tiara. Her maid of honor was a former Miss Universe she had not met before. She had twenty auburn-haired and forty flaxen-haired attendants taller and more stunning than herself in her entourage of bridesmaids, and all were dressed in off-white moiré shot with gold. One hundred and twenty children under twelve recruited from friends and members of both families were done up as flower girls and ring bearers. The bridegroom's mother, Regina Minderbinder, was nervous in designer beige, while Olivia Maxon, in peach satin with overlapping ruffles beaded with tens of thousands of seed pearls, looked simply stunning with her huge, dark eyes and retroussé nose, and in the glistening cabochon emeralds that adorned her white throat.

The bridal congregation assembled in privacy below in the Greyhound Bus Company package express area on the subway level. There, the silent girl and her complete retinue, which consisted of her Miss Universe, sixty gorgeous bridesmaids, and one hundred and twenty flower girls and ring bearers, were bathed, groomed, and otherwise made ready for the grand event by personal couturiers and makeup artists. On time, they took their places in very long lines at the base of the matched escalators and, on musical cue timed to a fraction of a second, stepped aboard the rising staircase to be borne upward into the expectant assembly awaiting them. An exultant, heartwarming fanfare of imperious Wagnerian chords gave notice of their ascent onto the main floor of the South Wing, and the bride, on the arm of her stepuncle, Christopher Maxon, emerged and stepped forward to a ceremonious tribute of respectful applause from those seeing them first from the tables outside the police station near the Sport Spot Lingerie Shop and Jo-Ann's Nut House.

To the prelude to *Die Meistersinger* and the "Dance of the Apprentices," the bride and Christopher Maxon, to everyone's tremendous relief, led the one hundred and eighty-one others faultlessly down the center of the South Wing to the Walgreen's drugstore and the turn toward the exit to the street outside, on which motor and pedestrian traffic had been detoured—even the buses were rerouted—and then, to a sentimental orchestral rendition of the "Prize Song," into the North Wing and finally to the chapel and the Temple of Dendur.

The rites of ceremony discharged, and the Leverkühn interlude of children's lament and heinous laughter from the *Apocalypse* over—it *was* the *Apocalypse,* Gaffney's absurd insistence to the contrary—the multiple areas transformed into banquet halls filled gently with music. Much sedate dancing of a bygone day ensued while people found their places and prepared for their first dinner —the second dinner was planned as a dumbfounding surprise! The thirty-five hundred close friends of the Minderbinders and the Maxons twirled and dipped to ballads between courses of poached salmon with champagne aspic, trio of veal, lamb, and chicken, orzo with porcini, and spring vegetables. The wines for this main meal were Cordon Charlemagne Latour 1986 and Louis Roederer Cristal Champagne 1978.

Sets of music were timed to twenty minutes. In the ten-minute breaks between, there was the lively performance of the musicians in each group transferring to a different bandstand in the five different locations to play for a different audience. They moved singly up and down the escalators without missing a beat noticed by anyone but themselves. The waiters riding up and down behind them carrying trays kept time with their hips and their shoulders, and the busboys went flitting about like spirits of the wind to clear the tables noiselessly and rush the remains outside to the mammoth garbage trucks ready on the ramps, which tore away when fully loaded from their reserved parking spaces between the refrigerator vehicles discharging new edible treats at top speed. A number of old-timers in high fettle took to following the musicians up and down the escalators in a dance of their own, singing a tune of their own they called "The Hully-Gully." Soon all the bands were playing "The Hully-Gully" every time they rotated. Satellite video reruns of this part of the affair accelerated the tempos to simulate the effect in silent movies of people moving in jerky haste, and Milo Minderbinder, in tails, with his mustache and pained smile, looked to many who did not know him like Charlie Chaplin.

Immediately following the poached salmon with champagne aspic, trio of veal, lamb, and chicken, orzo with porcini, and spring vegetables, before the coffee and any dessert, there came to each table three frozen molds of mango-orange sorbet, each in the shape of the big sphinx in Egypt, except that one had the face of Milo Minderbinder and the other wore the face of Christopher Maxon, even to the unlit cigar. The third Egyptian sphinx—everyone jumped erroneously to the guess that it would be the President—wore the unknown face of a man later identified as someone named Mortimer Sackler. Not many knew who Mortimer Sackler was anymore, and this ruse was received as another of the zesty jokes of the evening. With no warning, the voice of a woman on the public-address system announced:

"Due to congestion on Route 3, all bus departures and arrivals are subject to delay."

The gathering roared with laughter and clapped again.

Hardly had the reveling crowds recovered from their titillation over this one when there commenced to their shocked delight the serving of the first course of another full meal: a second dinner, or surprise supper. This one consisted of lobster, followed by pheasant bouillon, followed by quail, followed by poached pear with spun sugar. And this meal, said the rousing voice of an anonymous, hooraying master of ceremonies on the speaker system, was "on the house." That is, it was provided at no cost to the Maxons by the parents of the groom, Regina and Milo Minderbinder, to express their love for their new daughter-in-law, their undying friendship for her stepuncle and stepaunt, Christopher and Olivia Maxon, and their deep gratitude to every single person present who had taken the trouble to come. After the poached pear and spun sugar, when the time was at hand for Milo's brief speech that had not yet been written for him at the time those in the

Communications Control Center watched him deliver it, he recited, stiffly, this tribute to his wife:

"I have a wonderful woman and we're very much in love. I've never done this into a microphone before, but there is only one way to say it. Yahoo."

He repeated this three more times for three more sets of video cameras and microphones and had difficulty each time with the word *Yahoo*. Christopher Maxon, his round face wreathed into a smile, was more to the point, orating:

"My mother always said, 'Don't tell people you love them, show them.' And this is my way of saying 'I love you' to my wife, Olivia, who tonight has done so much for the economy. Anyone who is talking about a recession—well, forget it."

At a distant table in the South Wing outside, the mayor of New York City rose to a smattering of applause to announce that Olivia and Christopher Maxon had just donated ten million dollars to the bus terminal to construct kitchen facilities for use for future events, and another ten million dollars to the Metropolitan Museum of Art for their generous cooperation in supplying for the occasion the Temple of Dendur, the Blumenthal Patio, the Engelhard Court, and the Great Hall.

Olivia Maxon sprang up to announce: "No wonder—after this! I've never seen my husband so excited about making a gift to any institution."

Then came the wedding cake, on which legions of master bakers and apprentices had toiled for months at the Cup Cake Café just down the block on Ninth Avenue at Thirty-ninth Street. The earlier applause was as nothing compared to the spontaneous effusion of shrieking veneration when the wedding cake was wheeled in on a hoist, lowered, and unveiled to an applauding audience in the large bandstand area in the South Wing in front of Au Bon Pain, where a bank had been formerly and the ceiling was high. The cake was a wondrous monument of whipped cream, spun sugar, innumerable icings, and airy platforms of layers of weightless, buttery angel food with ice cream and liqueur-flavored chocolate fillings on a scale no one had witnessed before. The wedding cake stood forty-four feet high, weighed fifteen hundred pounds, and had cost one million, one hundred and seventeen thousand dollars.

Everyone thought it a pity it could not be preserved in the Metropolitan Museum.

The bride herself could not cut this cake, for she was not tall enough.

In a spectacle befitting the occasion, the cake was sliced from the top down by teams of gymnasts and trapeze artists in white tights with pink bodices from the Ringling Bros. and Barnum & Bailey Circus, then at Madison Square Garden just several blocks downtown. It was served on thirty-five hundred plates, each decorated with a spun-sugar sprig of sweet peas. The china was Spode, and the pieces of Spode were thrown out with the garbage to save time and comply with the tight schedule of catering trucks and commercial buses speeding in and out without collision. There was more than enough cake for the thirty-five hundred guests, and the eight hundred pounds left over were carved into blocks and sped to the shelters for the evacuated reprobates to gorge on before the whipped cream and the ice cream fillings could melt and putrefy.

Limousines and delivery and refuse trucks were making use of half the terminal's four hundred and sixty-five numbered gates, synchronizing precisely with the arrival and departure schedules of the forty bus companies with their two thousand daily trips and two hundred thousand daily passengers. Travelers going out were allowed to ride free as an inducement to leave fast. Passengers coming in were steered directly away to their sidewalks, subways, taxis, and local buses, and they also seemed to be calculated particles of movement in a clever dumb show.

While it was predictable that the President would delay arriving to avoid exchanging pleasantries with all of the thirty-five hundred other guests, it was not expected that he would be so late as to miss the nuptial ceremony itself and the start and finish of the two meals. Unprepared and unrehearsed, Noodles Cook, reluctantly, stood up for the groom as best man and also took the bride from Christopher Maxon to give to M2. He got it done but did not look presidential.

Yossarian, in the Communications Control Center, could see himself lucidly in white tie and tails watching Noodles Cook glancing more and more nervously up toward him at his table and then down at his wristwatch. Yossarian, in both places simultaneously at different hours on different days, began to reel in both places with bewilderment too. In both locations he could overhear the First Lady complaining to Noodles Cook that it was often hard to know what was in the President's mind. At last he understood Noodles and rose alone.

In the main ticketing area of the South Wing was the work of art by the famed sculptor George Segal of three life-sized human figures symbolizing bus passengers, two men and one woman, walking in toward a doorframe. Yossarian knew that in dead of night the three statues had been replaced by three armed Secret Service agents noted for tenacity and cold-blooded passivity, impersonating the statues. They carried concealed walkie-talkies and without moving had stood listening all day for intelligence from Washington as to the whereabouts and estimated time of arrival of the most honored guest.

Yossarian now eased himself alongside one of these men posing as a statue and asked, *sotto voce:*

"Where the fuck is he?"

"How the fuck should I know?" the man shot back, hardly moving his lips. "Ask her."

"The cocksucker won't come out of his office," said the woman, without moving hers.

There was no information to account for the delay.

Meanwhile, the festivities progressed. Coordinating the multiple movements of equipment and supplies and the divisions of personnel was as exacting a procedure as a military invasion in the Arabian Gulf, with a lower margin for observable error. Experienced logistical experts from Washington were dispatched to work with McBride and executives on the Planning Committee of Milo Minderbinder's Commercial Catering, Inc.

Strategy was mapped out in the Operations Room of C.C. Inc. and put into action in the kitchens and shops there, as well as in the extensive food rooms of the Metropolitan Museum of Art and in the facilities of the numerous nearby food shops with storage room and processing machinery enlisted for the emergency. Because the designers of the PABT building had not anticipated a future in the catering business, they had failed to include kitchens, and it was necessary to effect alliances with numerous individual food establishments in the vicinity.

On the day of the event, the principal caterers would start, Yossarian saw, and did start, Yossarian also saw, arriving at the terminal hours before sunrise, and the inner areas of the floors to be utilized were occupied by armed men in civilian attire and sealed off to the public.

By 7:30 A.M. fifteen hundred workers were on station in assigned places and moving into action.

By 8:00 an assembly line constructed by a corps of engineers had been set up in C.C. Inc. to make the canapés and other small sandwiches, and for the trimming and slicing of the smoked salmon. Work there did not cease until four hundred dozen of these tea sandwiches had been completed and dispatched.

By 8:15 sixty cooks, seventy electricians, three hundred florists, and four hundred of the waiters and bartenders had reinforced the original landing parties in both places.

By 8:30 crews began scrubbing the fifty bushels of oysters and fifty bushels of clams, boiling two hundred pounds of shrimp, and making fifty-five gallons of cocktail sauce.

By 9:00 A.M. the tables, chairs, and furnishings were arriving at the terminal, and electricians and plumbers were on site for the extensive work required, while back at C.C. Inc. and the Metropolitan Museum of Art, the choppers were attacking and cutting up at record speed the vegetables for the crudités: a thousand bunches of celery, fifteen hundred pounds of carrots, one thousand and one heads of cauliflower, a hundred pounds of zucchini, and two hundred pounds of red peppers.

By 10:00 A.M. all one hundred and fifteen thousand red, white, and black balloons printed NEWLY WED were bobbing triumphantly over all the passageways of the bus ramps and the doorways of all the side and main entrances.

At noon the electricians had completed hanging the special chandeliers.

At 1:00 P.M. the portable toilets were delivered and set up unobtrusively in their designated places. There were over thirty-five hundred of these portable toilets, all in pastels of the season, more than one for each guest, behind the false fronts of millinery boutiques for women and haberdashery boutiques for men, and the guests took note with a frisson of enchanted awareness that no person would have contact with a toilet previously tainted through use by another. Each of the units was hurried away instantly and invisibly through egresses in the rear by stevedores, teamsters, and sanitary engineers to be trucked out, loaded on waiting barges in the Hudson River, and carried to sea with the ebbing tide to be thrown into the ocean, with no one any the wiser until a day or so later; the foresight with the individual Portosans was another hit of the genteel bacchanal, and many guests crept back twice, merely for the novelty of the experience, as though riding for a second time on a diversion at a germ-free amusement park. "Why didn't anybody else ever think of that?" was an expression repeated frequently.

Early in the afternoon, at 2:45 plus 10, five tons of ice were delivered as ordered, and as the clock struck 3:00, two hundred waiters, then two hundred more waiters, when the first contingent had advanced and cleared out of the way, then two hundred more when these latter two hundred had pushed into the area and fanned out, all began setting up tables, while the remaining six hundred held in reserve were icing down white wine, water, and champagne, and setting up supply posts of one hundred and twenty service bars on the main and second floors and on the spacious third floor too, where loud music and wild dancing were scheduled for the late hours.

At four the musicians were setting up at their bandstands and dance floors.

By five, fifty dessert buffets had been erected securely and the twelve hundred or more security guards from the city, federal government, and M & M Commercial Killings, Inc. had taken up positions on the high ground of the terminal. Outside, trucks with units from the National Guard were on watch for disturbances from protest groups that might be in dissonance with the celebratory mood of the gala.

After the hoisting, lowering, and cutting of the wedding cake, there was more dancing and congratulations. For the several finales, everyone mingled together in the Great Hall from the Metropolitan Museum of Art, where still more tables were heaped with dessert confections of spun sugar.

There, before the party dispersed into smaller, friendlier, almost conspiratorial groups, a number of toasts were offered to the Minderbinders and Maxons and short speeches made. Greed was good, proclaimed one Wall Streeter in risk arbitrage. There was nothing wrong with waste, boasted another. As long as they had it, why not flaunt it? There was nothing tasteless about bad taste, roared another, and was cheered for his wit.

"This was the kind of event," crowed a spokesman for the homeless, "that makes one proud to be homeless in New York."

But he turned out to be fake, a spokesman from a public relations firm.

The formal end of activities was signaled by a sentimental repeat of the "Redemption Through Love" music played by all five of the bands for the evening, the violinist and her four clones, and the earlier orchestral recordings, and many there locked arms shamelessly and hummed the melody boisterously, as though in a wordless rendition of the newest replacement of "Auld Lang

Syne" or that other immortal popular favorite, "Till We Meet
Again."

For those madcaps and hell-raisers who had chosen to linger on
to bowl in the alleys on the second floor or dance the night away
or otherwise avail themselves of the fascinating attractions and
facilities of the bus terminal, a third meal was provided at each of
the auxiliary serving stations remaining open all night, and this,
as displayed on all screens, was in store:

ALTERNATE MENU
Fricassee de Fruits de Mer
Les trois Rôti Primeurs
Tarte aux Pommes de Terre
Salade à Bleu de Bresse Gratinée
Friandises et Desserts
Espresso

Yossarian, still musing on the Alternate Menu, was next startled
to see himself speaking to the video cameras for a network television show in white tie and tails between Milo Minderbinder and
Christopher Maxon and saying:

"The wedding was the highlight of a lifetime. I don't think any
of us here will live to see anything like it again."

"Holy shit," he said in the flesh, and hoped his laconic irony
was obvious.

There was little doubt that Minderbinders and Maxons had that
night boosted the Port Authority Bus Terminal into the forefront
of great catering halls for the close of the century and the dawning
of the new one. Everyone leaving was given a colorful brochure
published jointly by PABT and the Metropolitan Museum of Art,
with which PABT now had so many interests in common. For as
little as $36,000, anyone in the world could engage space for a
party in either place.

It was anticipated that most guests would depart at 1:00 A.M.
They did, and the million, one hundred and twenty-two thousand
champagne tulips there as souvenirs and door prizes were quickly
depleted. A younger, livelier bunch stayed on to bowl, eat, and
dance madly to the recorded music provided by an all-night disc
jockey on the floors above. Eventually, those who still could not
tear themselves away went to sleep on sturdy clean cabana lounges
moved into the ticketing areas or bedded down in one of the

emergency stairwells, where new, unused mattresses had been laid out on the landings and stairs. When they awoke, there was fresh orange juice for them at the juice bars and pancake-and-egg breakfasts in the coffee shops. The stairwells had been emptied and scoured thoroughly; instead of disinfectant, the odors in the air were of aftershave lotion and designer perfumes. For the stairwells, a one-legged woman with a crutch was hired to go wandering about mumbling she'd been raped, but she was a minor actress with a pretty face that had modeled cosmetics, and a shapely leg that had modeled panty hose. A large, gracious, maternal black woman with moles that looked cancerous and a rich contralto voice hummed spirituals.

By 4:30 in the morning, the twenty-eight Cosa Nostra carting companies subcontracting through the Washington Cosa Loro with the Commercial Catering division of M & M E & A had removed the rest of the trash, and by 6:00 A.M., when the first of the customary bus travelers appeared, all was back to normal, except for the absence of the hustlers and the homeless, who would remain in forced exile until all was secure.

"That was sly of you," Gaffney said, in praise of Yossarian's little speech.

"I can't believe I said that," Yossarian repented.

"You haven't, yet. Well?" added Gaffney with a wish to know, as they watched on the monitor the crowds in the terminal that had not yet gathered there thinning out sort of wanly and drifting back in pale reflections to the places from which they had not yet come. "Mrs. Maxon seemed satisfied."

"Then her husband will be too. I love all that Wagner music. And I also have to laugh. Do you think the end of *Götterdämmerung* is a tactful choice for that occasion?"

"Yes. Would you prefer a requiem?" Gaffney's dark eyes twinkled.

"It's turning black again, that God-damned sun," said Hacker lightly, and laughed. "I can't seem to get it out."

"It can't turn black," snapped Yossarian, annoyed by him once more. "If the sun turned black, the sky would be black too, and you wouldn't be able to see it."

"Yeah?" The young man sniggered. "Take a look."

Yossarian took a look and saw that on the central screens, the sun indeed was black in a sky that was blue, the moon had turned red again, and all of the ships in the harbor and the neighboring waters, the tugs, barges, tankers, freighters, commercial fishing vessels, and different varieties of pleasure craft, were again upside down.

"It's a glitch," said Hacker. "We call it a glitch. I'll have to keep working on it."

"I saw another glitch," said Yossarian.

"You mean the President?"

"He never showed up, did he? I didn't see him."

"We can't get him to come out of his office. Here—look." Yossarian recognized the antechamber of the Oval Office in Washington. "He's supposed to walk out, be driven to the MASSPOB building, and take the new supertrain here. Instead, he keeps going off the other way. He walks into his playroom."

"You'll have to reprogram your model."

Hacker snickered again in affected despair and left the answer to Gaffney.

"We can't reprogram the model, Yo-Yo. It's the model. You'll have to reprogram the presidency."

"Me?"

"In fact, he's in there right now," said Hacker. "What the hell's he got in that playroom anyway?"

"Ask Yossarian," said Gaffney. "He's been there."

"He has a video game," said Yossarian. "It's called *Triage.*"

BOOK
TWELVE

BOOK TWELVE

33

Entr'acte

Milo lost interest quickly, flew off on business, and was out of the terminal when the alarm went off, not safely underneath it with Yossarian.

"Where is Mr. Minderbinder?" McBride was asking, as Yossarian came through alone to the landing on which he stood with Gaffney.

"Off to get more skyscrapers in Rockefeller Center," Yossarian reported with derision. "Or build his own. He wants them all." Someday, Yossarian thought as they descended the wrought-iron staircase, those monstrous hounds stirring now might really be there; and what a final tricky surprise *that* would be! They had found all the elevators, McBride told him, exulting. Michael and his girlfriend Marlene had wearied with waiting and had gone far down below with Bob and Raul. McBride had something else to show Yossarian.

"How far is far down?" asked Yossarian, humorously.

McBride tittered nervously, and, shiftily, answered over his shoulder. "Seven miles!"

"Seven miles?"

Gaffney was amused by these yelps of astonishment.

And those were *some* elevators, McBride went on. A mile a minute going up, a hundred miles an hour going down. "And they've got escalators too, going all the way. They say they go down forty-two miles!"

"Gaffney?" asked Yossarian, and Gaffney nodded slowly. "Gaffney, Milo's unhappy," Yossarian let him know, in a jocular vein. "I suppose you know."

"Milo's always unhappy."

"He fears."

"And what does he fear today? He's got the contract."

"He fears he did not ask enough and is not getting as much for the Shhhhh! as Strangelove is getting for his plane. And they won't even work."

Halting on the staircase so abruptly that the two men collided, Gaffney, to Yossarian's total astonishment, regarded Yossarian with a lapse in his aplomb.

"They won't? What makes you say that?"

"They will?"

Gaffney relaxed. "They do, Yo-Yo. For a second I thought you knew something I didn't. They're working already."

"They can't be. They won't. They gave me their word."

"They break their word."

"They made me a promise."

"They break their promises."

"I have a guarantee."

"It's no good."

"I have it in writing."

"Stick it in your Freedom of Information file."

"I don't understand. They've beaten Strangelove?"

Gaffney gave his silent laugh. "Yossarian, my friend, they *are* Strangelove. They've blended, of course. Except for the difference in names and companies, aren't they the same? They've had planes going for years."

"Why didn't you ever say so?"

"To whom? Nobody asked."

"You could have told me."

"You didn't ask. Often it's to my advantage to keep things to myself. Sometimes knowledge is power. Some say the ultimate weapon will be good for my business, some say it won't. That's why I'm down here today. To find out."

"What business?"

"Real estate, of course."

"Real estate!" scoffed Yossarian.

"You refuse to believe me," said Gaffney, smiling, "and yet you think you want the truth."

"The truth will make us free, won't it?"

"It doesn't," answered Gaffney. "And it won't. It never has." He pointed down to McBride. "Let's go, Yo-Yo. He has another truth to show you. Recognize that music?"

Yossarian was almost sure he was hearing the Leverkühn passages again on the speaker system, from the work that had never been written, in a mellow version for orchestra, played rubato, legato, vibrato, tremolo, glissando, and ritardando, sweetly disguised for popular absorption, with no quavering, jolting hint of fearful climax.

"Gaffney, you're wrong about that Leverkühn, you know. It's from the *Apocalypse.*"

"I know that now. I looked it up and saw I was mistaken. I can't tell you how it embarrasses me to say so. But I bet I do know what you're going to ask me next."

"Notice anything?" asked Yossarian anyway.

"Of course," said Gaffney. "We cast no shadows down here, our feet make no noise. Do *you* notice anything?" Gaffney asked, as they joined McBride. He was not referring to the guard in the archway on a chair at the elevator. "Do you?"

It was Kilroy.

He was gone.

The words on his plaque had been effaced.

Kilroy was dead, McBride revealed. "I felt I should tell you."

"I had a feeling he was," said Yossarian. "There are people my age who'll be sorry to hear that. Vietnam?"

"Oh, no, no," McBride answered with surprise. "It was cancer. Of the prostate, the bone, the lungs, and the brain. They have it down as a natural death."

"A natural death," repeated Yossarian in lament.

"It could be worse," said Gaffney, sympathizing. "At least Yossarian is alive."

"Sure," said McBride, like a hearty fellow. "Yossarian still lives."

"Yossarian lives?" repeated Yossarian.

"Sure, Yossarian lives," said McBride. "Maybe we can put that one up on the wall instead."

"Sure, and for how long?" Yossarian answered, and the alarm went off.

McBride gave an immediate start. "Hey, what the hell is that?" He looked frightened. "Isn't that the alert?"

Gaffney was nodding. "I think so too."

"You guys wait here!" McBride was already running toward the guard. "I'll go find out."

"Gaffney?" asked Yossarian, quivering.

"I don't know down here," Gaffney answered grimly. "It may be the war, triage time."

"Shouldn't we get the hell out? Let's jump outside."

"Don't go crazy, Yossarian. We're much safer here."

BOOK THIRTEEN

34

Finale

When he heard the alarm go off and saw the colored lamps on the mechanism blinking, the President was pleased with himself for having set something in motion and sat back beaming with self-satisfaction until it dawned on him that he did not know how to stop what he had started. He pressed one button after another to no avail. As he was about to call for help, help came crashing in: Noodles Cook, the stout man from the State Department whose name never came readily to mind, his slim aide from the National Security Council, Skinny, and that general from the air force newly promoted to the Joint Chiefs of Staff.

"What happened?" screamed General Bingam, with a horror-stricken countenance inflamed with confusion.

"It works," said the President, with a grin. "You see? Just like the game here."

"Who's attacking us?"

"When did it begin?"

"Is someone attacking us?" asked the President.

"You launched all our missiles!"

"You sent out our planes!"

"I did? Where?"

"Everywhere! With that red button you kept pressing."

"This one? I didn't know that."

"Don't touch it again!"

"How was I supposed to know? Call them all back. Say I'm sorry. I didn't do it on purpose."

"We can't call back the missiles."

"We can call back the bombers."

"We can't call back the bombers! Suppose someone retaliates? We have to take them out first."

"I didn't know that."

"And we'll have to send out our second-strike bombers too, in case they want to hit back after our first."

"Come on, sir. We have to hurry."

"Where to?"

"Underground. To the shelters. Triage—don't you remember?"

"Sure. I was playing that one before I switched to this one."

"Damn it, sir! What the hell are you smiling about?"

"There's nothing fucking funny about this!"

"How was I supposed to know?"

"Let's move! We are the ones who have to survive."

"Can I get my wife? My children?"

"You stay here too!"

They charged out like a mob and piled into the cylindrical escape elevator awaiting them. Fat was tripped by C. Porter Lovejoy, arriving desperately to get into the elevator too, and fell down inside, with Lovejoy clinging to his back like a crazed monkey in a clawing fury.

Removing from her dark hair hot rollers of fair blue that closely matched the color of her eyes and applying lipstick and other cosmetics as though for an evening out—she had reason to wish to look her best—nurse Melissa MacIntosh made up her mind again to try to make up her own mind at lunch with John Yossarian in the disagreement over whether to keep her appointment with the obstetrician to preserve her pregnancy or the one with her gynecologist to take steps to terminate it. She had no clue of anything dire happening elsewhere.

She understood his unwillingness to marry again so soon. She helped herself to another chocolate from the one-pound box so close at hand. The candy had come as a gift from the Belgian patient and his wife the day he left the hospital, alive, after nearly two years. She was relieved the Belgians were flying back to Europe, for she had a propensity for empathetic attachments and wanted her mind free to cope with this predicament of her own.

Yossarian could give very sound reasons against fatherhood again for him now.

They made no impression. He was better and quicker in argument, and therefore, to her mind, trickier. She could admit to herself, and to her apartment mate, Angela, that she did not always think things through clearly and was not unfailingly much good at looking ahead.

However, she would not see that as a weakness.

She had something Yossarian did not: confidence, a belief that everything must turn out all right in the end for people like herself, who were good. Even Angela now, since Peter's stroke, wearying of pornography and work, putting on fat and concerned about AIDS, was talking with longing of returning to Australia, where she still had friends and family, and a favorite aunt in a nursing home, whom she hoped to start visiting. If Angela had to start thinking about condoms now, she would just as soon give up sex and get married.

Yossarian made much of that matter of years and had almost neatly tricked her again—she congratulated herself on having thwarted him—just two evenings before.

"I'm just not afraid of anything like that," she let him know defiantly, with her backbone stiffened. "We would get along without you, if we had to."

"No, no," he corrected, almost maliciously. "Suppose *you* are the one who dies soon!"

She refused to consider talking further about that. That picture of her infant daughter with only a father past seventy was too complex a tangle for her to seek to unravel.

She knew she was right.

She had no doubt Yossarian would be adequate with financial help, even if she persisted despite him and they no longer continued as a couple. She knew in her gut she could trust him for that much. It was true he was less frequently fervidly amorous with her than he had been in the earliest stages. He no longer teased about shopping together for lingerie, and he had not yet taken her to Paris or Florence or Munich to buy any. He sent roses now only on birthdays. But she was less amorous too, she reflected now with some contrite misgivings, and occasionally had to remind herself, cerebrally, to strive more lasciviously to achieve the feats of gratifying sensuality that had sprung more normally between them in the beginning. She acknowledged, when Angela asked, that he never seemed jealous anymore and no longer showed interest in her sexual past. He rarely even wanted to take her to the movies. He had already mentioned with no anger and small discontent that, even into the present, he had never found himself with a woman who over a continuous liaison desired to make love as often as he did. She searched back to discern if this had been true with other men who had been her friends. For that matter, he was not working as hard as before to please her either and was not much concerned when he saw he'd failed to.

She did not feel any of that mattered.

Melissa MacIntosh knew she was right and could not see that there was anything wrong in what she wanted. She was a woman who spoke of "gut feelings," as she chose to describe her dogmatic intuitions, and her gut feeling now was that if she was patient, if she simply stuck to her guns and remained tolerantly inflexible, he would, as usual, ultimately consent to whatever she wanted. On this matter of her child, he had powerful arguments. She had one weak one, and that was enough: She wanted the baby.

The thought that he might not even appear at the restaurant to argue further did not cross her mind until she was checking the small flat before leaving. She shook it right off in an impulse of terror rather than even begin to contemplate what that defection might signify.

She'd put on high heels to look all the better and walked out rapidly with footsteps clicking seductively.

Outside the apartment, near the corner toward which she proceeded for a taxicab, she saw, as expected, maintenance trucks from the Consolidated Edison Company, with men tearing downward through the asphalt making improvements or repairs. They were always there, these men from the lighting company, almost since the beginning of time, it seemed to her, as she hurried past with her high heels clicking. She was engrossed in the specifics of the looming confrontation, and she scarcely noticed that the heavens were darker than natural for that time of day.

Out of the hospital finally after so long a time, the Belgian patient was flying back to Brussels and his executive position with the European Economic Community. He talked of himself humorously as "the sick man of Europe." He was in decent health, ebullient in nature but lesser in weight, and very much a weaker man, minus one vocal cord, a lung, and one kidney. Advised to give up spirits, he had been limiting his drinking to wine and beer during the two weeks of outpatient care since his discharge.

Through the dotlike circular opening in his neck, left permanent by a plastic implant for suctioning or intubation, and through which, when he wished to clown, he was able to speak, he inhaled cigarette smoke and wheezed contentedly. He was forbidden to smoke, but concluded that way didn't count. His playful, frolicsome wife, joyous to have him back alive, smoked for him also. With practiced skill and puckered mouth, she would inhale from a cigarette of her own and, kittenish, feed, in slim direct jets, cigarette smoke into him accurately through the surgical aperture with its plastic cylinder and removable cap. Then, if at home, they would cuddle, kiss, tickle, and try to make love. To their delight and their amazement, they succeeded more regularly than either of them would have thought likely not long before. He now was normally concealing the prosthetic fixture from outsiders with a high shirt collar and large knot in his necktie or with an ascot, scarf, or colorful neckerchief. He discovered in himself a weakness for polka dots. With his wife only, this sick man of Europe shared an additional secret, his absolute belief that nothing he, his colleagues, or any organization of experts could do would have any enduring corrective effect on the economic destiny of his continent or the Western world. Humans had little command over human events. History would follow its autonomous course independent of the people who made it.

On his leaving the hospital, the two had hosted a small celebration in his room and given to each of the nurses and other staff members a bottle of champagne, a one-pound box of Fanny Farmer chocolates, and a carton of cigarettes. They would have given cash too, a one-hundred-dollar bill to each, but the hospital frowned on gifts of money.

In planes, the Belgian patient and his wife ordinarily booked first class but enjoyed spending part of the time each trip in coach seats for the closer proximity of their persons and the intimacy that permitted them to press their thighs and arms against each other with risqué naughtiness while they smoked and, beneath the cover of blankets, to fondle and masturbate to climax each other's genitals.

Flying back over the Atlantic this time, they were complacently in their first-class seats watching the movie, a comedy, at that moment when the alarm they did not know about went off. Both thought hardly anything of the numerous spools of steamed white vapor they began to spot unwinding behind unseen flying bodies traveling faster than they were, higher and lower, which began to appear in the sky after the screen went black, the lights brightened back on with a ferocious glare, and the panels at the windows had been raised. Going east into nightfall, they were not disturbed to find the heavens darkening. Behind them the sun had turned as gray as lead. With the failure of the motion picture apparatus, the internal system of communications seemed affected too. There was no music or other entertainment in the headsets. When a stewardess stood up with a microphone at the front of the cabin to explain the inconveniences, her words were not transmitted. When passengers, in convivial mock annoyance, gestured to other cabin personnel to make their inquiries and the stewards and hostesses leaned downward to respond, their voices made no sound.

Dennis Teemer didn't hear it, and the cardinal, who'd previously had intimations of some designs for disaster, was not told about it. Many were called, but this man of science and this keeper of souls were not among them. Because it no longer was possible to shelter the public from attack, no public shelters were provided, and it was not thought politic to generate terror and despair with a warning that might prove unwarranted in the event the feared nuclear counterassault did not materialize.

When the alarm went off, only those happy, privileged few already chosen were summoned, rounded up, and allowed down. These were men of rare abilities deemed indispensable to the perpetuation of our way of life below earth. They were found and conducted speedily to the disguised entrances of heat-resistant elevators by special teams of dedicated MASSPOB policemen and policewomen, who had not stopped to consider, until the moment of truth arrived, that they themselves would be excluded as expendable too.

"This is Harold Strangelove, and you will be happy to hear that I and my key associates have made it down here safely and will be available to continue to provide you with our fine contacts and advice, and with our best-quality bombast too," said the voice over the public-address system, distinctly. "The President has been left behind, and I am the one who is now in charge, because I know more than everybody else. Our missiles have been launched and I guarantee we will achieve our objective successfully, once we are able to figure out what our objective in launching them was. We do not know yet if any of the territories we are attacking will retaliate. To reduce their capability, we now have all our first-strike bombers in the air. Soon we will break radio silence to let you listen. Meanwhile, I assure you that nothing has been overlooked. We have a viable community already functioning up to, or should I say down to, forty-two miles underground, and we will continue to operate smoothly and democratically as long as everyone here does exactly what I say. We are secure militarily. We have the personnel here needed to survive a nuclear counter-attack outside, should any eventuate. We have political leaders, career bureaucrats, medical men, intellectuals, engineers, and other technicians. What more could we want? The entrances to all our hiding places are now sealed off by our MASSPOB special forces. Anyone fortunate enough to be here now who grows dis-satisfied and wants to leave will be permitted to do so. This is a free country. But no one new will be allowed in without authoriza-tion, and none who survive will be admitted until I decide to let them in. We are well supplied with all the goods a reasonable man acting in good faith would require, and there is almost no foreseeable limit to the amount of time we can spend here com-fortably as long as you all do what I say. We have recreational facilities of wide variety. We have thought of everything. Now, to fill you in, here is the new chairman of my Joint Chiefs of Staff with a report of our military situation as it exists right now."

"My fellow Americans," said General Bernard Bingam. "Frankly, I don't know any more than you do about the reasons this war had to take place, but we do know that our reasons were good ones, our cause is just, and our military operation will be as completely successful as all those we have conducted in the past. Our antimissile-missile units are all on watch and probably are achieving unbelievable success against any enemy missiles that might be raining in on us in retaliation. Our strongest hand at this stage is our heavy bombers. We have hundreds of these for our first strike, and we are going to give them the go-ahead now, purely as a precautionary measure. You will be permitted to hear me communicate now with the commander of our aeronautical operations. Here we go. Hello, hello. This is Bingam, Bingam, Bigman Bernie Bingam, calling from underground headquarters in the Ben & Jerry's supply depot in Washington. Come in, come in, Commander, please come in."

"Häagen-Dazs."

"Thank you, Commander Whitehead. Where are you?"

"At fifty-two thousand feet, in our floating strategic command post over the geographic center of the country."

"Perfect. Instruct your units to proceed. Time is now of the essence. Then change your location."

"We have already changed our location, even as I was reporting it."

"So it's no longer accurate?"

"It was not accurate then."

"Perfect. Report all sightings of enemy missiles or aircraft. We will fill you in when you all come back."

"Good, sir. Where should we come back to?"

"Hmmmmm. There might not be a place. I don't think we thought of that. You might as well land in the territories you've destroyed. Proceed as planned."

"Absolutely, General Bingam?"

"Positively, Commander Whitehead."

"Häagen-Dazs."

"Ben & Jerry's. Dr. Strangelove?"

"That was splendid."

"Absolutely, Dr. Strangelove?"

"Positively, General Bingam. We have overlooked nothing. Now I must apologize to the rest of you, for there was one little thing we did forget." He continued with an intentional slurring of words in what was obviously a self-effacing and jocund apology. "We neglected to bring down any women. Oh, yes—I can picture all of you macho men clutching your heads and moaning with pretended unhappiness. But think of the dissension they would be causing here right now. It is not for me to recommend officially, but I am reminded by our chief of medicine here that abstinence has always proved a perfect replacement for the fairer sex. Other adequate substitutes for women are masturbation, fellatio, and sodomy. We recommend condoms, and you will find huge supplies at your drugstores and supermarkets. To maintain population, we may eventually have to let some women in, if there are any left. As to clergymen, we believe we have some of all our major faiths. Until we locate them, we have a man of no faith who is ready to minister to the spiritual needs of people of all faiths. As to the outcome, I beg you not to worry. We have overlooked nothing. After our first strike, we have secret defensive-offensive planes ready for a second-strike aerial attack to destroy any weapons withstanding our first strike that might come back at us. The only thing you have to fear is fear itself. We are almost absolutely sure we may have nearly not much to worry about, thanks to our new old versions of the old new Stealth bomber, my own Strangelove B-Ware and the Minderbinder Shhhhh! There will be no newspapers. Since all reports will come from official sources, there'll be no reason to believe them, and they will be kept to a minimum. Häagen-Dazs."

"The Shhhhh!?" Yossarian was dumbfounded.

"I told you they'd work."

"Gaffney, what's going to happen?"

"I'm cut off from my sources."

Speeding downward in the elevator to the seven-mile level at a hundred miles an hour had taken close to five minutes. The rest of the way to the forty-two-mile bottom would take some twenty minutes more, and the two had agreed to continue awhile on the escalators.

"Can't you guess? Where will it all end?"

Gaffney had an answer. "Where it began, say the physicists. That's what I have in mind for the novel I might want to write. It begins after both those stories of the creation of Adam and Eve. There are two, you know."

"I know," said Yossarian.

"You would be surprised how many people don't. My story begins at the end of the sixth day of creation."

"And then where does it go?"

"Backward," crowed Gaffney, unveiling that idea for his novel as though it were already a triumph. "It goes backward, to the fifth day, like a movie running in reverse. At the beginning of mine, God turns Eve back into a rib and puts the rib back into Adam, as we find in the second version. He simply uncreates Adam and Eve from his own image, as we find in the first, as though they'd never been made. He simply disappears them, along with the cattle and other beasts and creeping things brought forth on that sixth day. On my second day, his fifth, the birds and fish are taken back. Next, the sun and moon are gone, along with the other lights in the firmament. Then the fruit trees and vegetation from the third day are taken away and the waters come back together and the dry land called earth disappears. That was the third day, and on the one after that, he takes back the firmament called heaven that was put in the midst of the waters. And then on the first day, my sixth day, the light goes too and nothing remains to separate the day from the darkness, and the earth is again without form and void. We are back to the beginning, before there was anything. Then I steal from the New Testament for a very clever touch. In the beginning was the word and the word was God, remember? Now, of course, we take away the word, and without the word, there is no God. What do you think of it?"

Yossarian said caustically: "Children will love it."

"Will it make a good movie? Because for a sequel, the whole thing starts all over again in two or three billion years and is re-created exactly the same way, to the tiniest detail."

"Gaffney, I can't wait that long. I've got a pregnant girlfriend upstairs who'll be having a baby soon if I let her. Let's walk a few miles more. I don't trust that elevator."

Looking downward as he went, Yossarian suddenly could not believe his eyes. He had misplaced his eyeglasses. But even with spectacles on, he would not have believed at first glance what he saw walking up toward him.

When he heard the alarm, General Leslie R. Groves, who had died of heart disease in 1970, decided to run for his life, downward toward the molten center of the earth, where it was hot as Hades, he knew, but not so hot as the temperature of a fusion explosion or the heat the chaplain would produce if he continued to evolve successfully into a nuclear mixture of tritium and lithium deuteride and achieved a critical mass.

"Don't hit him! Don't grab him! Don't touch him!" he barked out orders as a duty to his country and a last kindness to the chaplain, who declined to go along and save himself too. "Don't let him get overheated! He might go off!"

When they saw the general bolt, all of his scientists, technicians, engineers, and housekeeping staff went running off too, and except for the armed men at battle positions at all of the entrances, the chaplain was alone.

. . .

When the train jolted to a stop, the chaplain saw the gleaming ice-skating rink in Rockefeller Center fall down out of his picture and the skyscrapers around it begin teetering on the video screen and come to rest with all of them erratically askew. Once before, the chaplain had sighted Yossarian crossing the street there beside a younger man who could have been his son, passing in back of a long pearl-gray limousine that seemed to be spilling tire tracks of blood from its wheels, with a sinister, angular figure with a walking stick and green rucksack eyeing both with an evil squint. He could not find Yossarian a second time either outside the Metropolitan Museum of Art each time he switched there to wait. He did not think of looking for him at the Port Authority Bus Terminal when he switched back there to gaze at those buildings wistfully. That was where he had come into the city the first time. Return trips home to Kenosha had by now grown painful. Three evenings a week he watched his wife walking slowly to meet the widow across the street to go in a car to the Presbyterian church for another session of bridge, in a group mainly of men and women who had lost their mates, watched with grief because he was no longer part of her life.

When the train stopped and the skating rink dropped, he heard outside a sudden racket of shouts and footsteps and guessed that something was amiss. He waited for someone to come tell him what to do. In fewer than ten minutes he was entirely on his own. General Groves was explicit.

"No, I want to go back out," he decided.

"There may be a war there."

"I want to go home."

"Albert, get mad. Don't you ever get mad?"

"I'm so mad now I can explode."

"That's a good one too! And I'll do what I can to clear the way." And that's when the chaplain heard him shouting his last commands before dashing away.

Cautiously, tentatively, the chaplain stepped down from the train. He had on his person some cash from the general, and his Social Security number had been returned to him too. He was last off the train. A distance away he saw a bank of escalators that looked brand-new. He was completely alone but for the guards in red field jackets, green trousers, and brown combat boots. These

were stationed with weapons at all the entrances and at the top
and the bottom of the down escalator. He was free to go up, free
to leave.

"You might have trouble coming back in, sir."

As soon as he stepped aboard the escalator, he began to walk,
anxious to get where he was going as quickly as he could. As he
climbed, he increased his pace. When he reached the top, he followed the arrow to a cylindrical elevator with transparent panels
that, after he pressed the topmost button, began rising with a
speed that robbed him of breath initially and made his viscera
sink. Through vertical transparent panels he saw himself passing
through a golf course and then an amusement park with a roller-
coaster and Ferris wheel, with attendants in jackets the same shade
of red as the special troops of soldiers. He passed roadways with
military vehicles and sedans with civilians. He passed a railway
with mobile missiles and another with refrigerated supply cars
marked WISCONSIN CHEESE and BEN & JERRY'S ICE CREAM. Where
the elevator stopped, after a ride of nearly twenty minutes, he
found another pair of brand-new escalators. Where these ended
he boarded another elevator and again pressed the highest button.
Then he was ascending on an escalator again. He felt he had been
trudging upward for miles. He did not tire. Gazing ahead upward
all the time, he suddenly, in jarring disbelief, came face-to-face
with Yossarian, who was walking down toward him rapidly on
the other escalator, and they gaped at each other in mutual recognition.

"What are you doing here?" they both exclaimed.

"Me? What are *you* doing here?" they both retorted.

They rode away in opposite directions.

"Chaplain, don't go out!" Yossarian shouted back up at him
through cupped hands. "There's danger outside. A war. Come
back down!"

"Fuck you!" cried the chaplain, and wondered where in the
world such words had come from.

Having passed his lips, they spurred him on with a spirit of
liberation he himself thought fanatic. Eventually, he stormed from
the last of the elevators and found himself facing a thoroughfare
cluttered with transport and rushing pedestrians, with a steep
staircase of wrought iron across the way that rose in short flights
to spiraling landings and had a platform at the top at an exit with
a large metal door. Mounting these, he paid no attention to an

outburst of barking wild dogs he heard behind him. At the top was a guard. On the door were the words:

EMERGENCY ENTRANCE
NO ADMITTANCE
THIS DOOR MUST BE LOCKED AND BOLTED WHEN IN USE

The guard made no move to stop him. Instead, obligingly, he turned the lock, shifted the bolt, and slid open the door. Two more guards were on duty at the other side. These did not interfere with him either. He found himself walking through a metal closet into a small service room of some kind and then outside into a corridor underneath a staircase slanting upward over his head, and then, out in front of him, he saw an exit door leading to the street. His heart leaped. He was beginning to see the light, he told himself, and pushed outside into a dark day, passing a small mound of shit in a corner, at which he glanced but briefly.

He was at the bus terminal, in a side street on a lower level from which buses set out. One, with engine warming, was about to leave for Kenosha, Wisconsin. He was one of three passengers. Once relaxed in his seat, he blew his nose, coughed to clear his throat, sighed heavily in relief. Each time they stopped for food he would try a phone call until he reached her. The boarding platform was beneath a sheltering overhang, and he was not surprised to see the light so dull. But when they were through the tunnel and out on the highway, the sky was no brighter. With hardly any curiosity, he looked upward out his window and saw that the sun itself was an ashy gray and darkened around its rim in a circle of black. In Wisconsin on drab days he had seen such feeble suns often behind masses of clouds. He didn't see that there were no clouds.

In the editorial meeting at the *New York Times* conducted daily to determine the makeup of the front page of the ensuing edition, they decided to predict, and the television newscasters would therefore decide to report, an unpredictable solar eclipse.

Frances Beach, devoting herself with priority to the care and comfort of an invalid husband, had long since passed the point where she cared what the *New York Times* or any other newspaper decided about anything but fashion. In her final years, she was not surprised to find herself deeply in love with Yossarian again. What had been lacking in their affection, she concluded benevolently with a remorseful smile, looking up from her book and lifting her reading glasses, was strife and drama. Neither had ever had real need for the other. What was wrong between them was that nothing between them had ever gone wrong.

Claire Rabinowitz felt herself in pugnacious opposition to all her fellow passengers on the El Al flight transporting her to Israel to see for herself the seaside summer house outside Tel Aviv on which she had made a down payment in the form of an option to buy. There had been not much eye contact with anyone in the first-class lounge or in the waiting area at the gate, to which, out of aggressive curiosity, she had also wandered to kill time. There was not a man aboard of any age, traveling with family or without, who came even close to what she considered with pride her standards. There wasn't one who could hold a candle to her Lew. Sammy Singer, in California or on his way to Hawaii or Australia, had predicted that might happen, and she had taken his warning as a compliment. When she spoke of Lew to anyone, to her children or Sammy, she never spoke of him as hers. When she thought of him, he was still her Lew. She was conquering slowly her reluctance to concede that it would forever be impossible for her to re-create what had been. She took for granted that all of the others on the flight were Jewish too, even those, like herself, who looked American and agnostic.

Crossing the Mediterranean while the day was breaking, there was no signal of any new disaster portending. There was a sketchy news report that an oil tanker had collided with a cruise ship somewhere below. Her mood was surly, and she did not care that her expression might show it. Another dimension to her latent disappointments was that she did not feel yet as she had hoped she might, that in going to Israel, she was going home.

Shortly after the alarm went off, Mr. George C. Tilyou felt his world shudder. In his Steeplechase Park, he saw the power fail on his El Dorado carousel and the elegant rotating platforms coast to a standstill with the emperor on board. He saw, strangely, that his two World War II airplane pilots were gone, as though called away. His Coney Island acquaintance Mr. Rabinowitz was staring at the mechanism from a distance, as though analyzing a malfunction he might have it in his means to correct. Frowning, Mr. Tilyou walked back into his office. He dusted his derby with his sleeve while restoring it to its peg on the coatrack. He felt his anger melt away. His depression returned.

His appointment with the higher authorities, with Lucifer and perhaps Satan himself, to demand an explanation for the peculiar behavior of his house, would be postponed again. There was no longer doubt it was sinking gradually, without his blessing and beyond his control. Careful measurements betrayed subversive disappearance. As he glanced at it now from his rolltop desk, it went down suddenly before his eyes. Almost before he could understand what was happening, the entire bottom floor was gone. His house of three stories was now one of two stories. From overhead, while he was still staring, widening showers of dirt came spilling down, and then great rough clumps of earth, stones, and other debris began to fall in too. Something new he had not planned on was coming through from outside with a crunching roar. He saw torn electrical connections dangling. He saw ducts of bolted sheet metal. He saw tubes. He recognized a bulky underside with a dense configuration of ponderous dripping refrigeration pipes encased in a crystalline jacket of melting frost.

His mood of depression lifted.

He saw in a red jacket a Japanese man with ice skates holding on to a corner of the floor for dear life.

It was the skating rink from Rockefeller Center!

He had to smile. He saw Mr. Rockefeller turn pale, quiver, and flee in panic. Mr. Morgan slumped naked to the ground with bowed head, weeping, and began to pray. The emperor had no clothes either.

Mr. Tilyou had to laugh. There was nothing new under the sun? He was seeing something new, learning a lesson he had never dreamed possible. Even hell was not forever.

Yossarian could not believe his ears. Where in the world had the chaplain learned to say "Fuck you!" so well? By the time Yossarian reached bottom, the chaplain was over the top and gone from view. Gaffney had started to tell him they had better return to the elevators to get down to McBride and the others when the Strangelove voice returned to announce that they had nothing to fear but a shortage of tailors.

"That is something else we forgot, and some of us at headquarters look sloppy. We have irons but nobody who knows how to use them. We have cloth and thread and sewing machines. But we need someone who sews. Does anyone hear me? Come in if you sew."

"Häagen-Dazs. I can do laundry and iron. My weapons officer is the son of a tailor."

"Turn back immediately and join us here."

"Right, sir. How can we get there?"

"We forgot that too!"

"Gaffney," said Yossarian, when they had ten miles more to go. "How long will we be here?"

"My future may lie here," replied Gaffney. "When we're down and have time, there's something I want to show you. It's on an acre and a half on a lake under Vermont, near an underground golf course and good skiing in Ben & Jerry territory, in case you're planning to buy."

"Now? You think I'm planning to buy now?"

"One must always look ahead, says the good Señor Gaffney. It's waterfront property, Yo-Yo. You can triple your money in a couple of months. You have to see it."

"I won't have time. I have an appointment for lunch."

"Your appointment might be canceled."

"I might want to keep it."

"All plans are off if it's really a war."

"The wedding too?"

"With bombs coming in? We don't really need the wedding anymore, now that we have it on tape."

"Are there bombs coming in?"

Gaffney shrugged. McBride didn't know either, they found out, when they rode the long escalator down to the bottom from the final stop on the elevator. Neither did the disparate pair of intelligence agents, who had no idea what to do with themselves next.

Strangelove had an answer when he came back on. "No, no bombs are sighted yet coming this way. This has us confused. But those of us here have nothing to fear. Only one air force in the world has bombs that can penetrate this deeply before exploding, and they all belong to us. We have overlooked nothing, except some barbers. While we wait to see if anyone strikes back, we need some barbers, even one. Any barber who hears this, respond at once. We have overlooked nothing. All our facilities will be operational in two or three weeks if you abide by my rules. If any of you anticipate trouble following my instructions, please follow this instruction and leave today. General Bingam will now send all our B-Wares and Shhhhh!s out on a second-strike attack, after we confirm there are no tailors or barbers on board."

Raul scowled and said, *"Merde."* Gangly, orange-haired, freckle-faced Bob looked much less happy than usual. Both had families they worried about.

McBride worried too. "If there's a war outside, I'm not sure I want to be down here."

Michael did want to be, with Marlene agreeing, and Yossarian did not blame him.

There was need, said Strangelove, for a shoemaker.

"Merde," said Raul. "That man is so full of *merde.*"

"Yes, we have overlooked nothing, but we forgot that too," Dr. Strangelove continued, with an affected snigger. "We have warehouses full of these lovely new state-of-the-art shoes, but sooner or later they are going to need shines and repairs. Apart from that too, we have overlooked nothing. We can live here forever, if you do what I tell you."

They were near the platform of a train station overlooking narrow-gauge railroad tracks of a type Yossarian felt certain he had seen before. The reduced span of the tunnels ensured a train of small size, something on the scale of a miniature amusement ride.

"Here comes another one," called out McBride. "Let's see what's there this time."

He moved closer to observe more quickly as a bright-red small locomotive pulled into sight at moderate speed with a signal bell clanging. It was running on electricity but flaunted a scarlet smokestack with designs in polished brass. Working the clapper of the bell with a piece of clothesline fixed to his control levers was a grinning engineer of middle age, uniformed in a red jacket with a circular MASSPOB shoulder patch. The little train went rolling on by, bringing smoothly in tow some open-topped, narrow passenger cars with people on board sitting two abreast. Again Yossarian could not believe his eyes. McBride pointed in frantic excitement at the two figures sitting in the first seat of the first car.

"Hey, I know those people! Who are they again?"

"Fiorello H. La Guardia and Franklin Delano Roosevelt," Yossarian answered, and said absolutely nothing about the two elderly couples who sat with his older brother in the seats in back of them.

In the next carriage he recognized John F. Kennedy with his wife alongside, behind the former governor of Texas and his wife who had been in the death car with him.

And by himself on a seat in the car that followed those immortals rode Noodles Cook, looking haggard, disoriented, and half dead in front of two government officials Yossarian remembered from news reports. One was fat and one was skinny, and seated side by side behind them in the last seat of this third of three cars were C. Porter Lovejoy and Milo Minderbinder. Lovejoy was talking, counting on his fingers. Both were alive, and Milo was smiling too.

"I could have sworn," said Yossarian, "that Milo had been left behind."

Gaffney formed with his mouth the one word "Never."

It was then that Yossarian decided to keep his date with Melissa. He did not want to remain down there with Strangelove and those others. Gaffney was shocked and thought he was mad. It was not in the cards.

"Oh, no, no, Yo-Yo." Gaffney was shaking his head. "You can't go out. It makes no sense now. You won't go."

"Gaffney, I am going. You're wrong again."

"But you won't get far. You won't last long."

"We'll see. I'll try."

"You'll have to be careful. There's danger outside."

"There's danger in here. Anyone coming?"

McBride, as though waiting, jumped forward and joined him. "You'd never find your way out without me." At Yossarian's side, he confessed, "I'm worried about Joan out there alone."

Gaffney would wait until he knew much more. "I know enough now not to take chances."

Michael too did not like taking chances, and Yossarian did not blame him for that one either.

Bob and Raul had too much intelligence to put themselves at risk when they did not have to, and could worry about their families just as well from down there.

As he saw Yossarian riding up away from him on the escalator
to the elevator to keep a lunch date with his pregnant girlfriend,
Michael, who'd been both proud and embarrassed by his father's
love affair, had the listless, desolate feeling that one of them was
dying, maybe both.

Yossarian, striding anxiously up the escalator to hurry back
outside as fast as he could get there, was stimulated joyously by a
resurrection of optimism more native to Melissa than himself,
the innate—and inane—conviction that nothing harmful could
happen to him, that nothing bad could happen to a just man. This
was nonsense, he knew; but he also knew, in his gut, he'd be as
safe as she was, and had no doubt then that all three of them, he,
Melissa, and the new baby, would survive, flourish, and live happily—forever after.

"Häagen-Dazs."

"What was that about?" the aviator Kid Sampson asked, from
the back compartment of the invisible and noiseless sub-supersonic attack bomber.

"Was your father a shoemaker?" answered the pilot McWatt.
"Are you the son of a barber?"

"I can't sew either."

"Then we have to go on. It's another mission for us."

"Where to?"

"I've forgotten. But inertia will guide us. Our inertial guidance
system will always take us."

"McWatt?"

"Sampson?"

"How long have we been together now? Two years, three?"

"It feels more like fifty. Sampson, you know what I regret? That
we never talked more to each other."

"We never got more to talk about, did we?"

"What's that down there? A missile?"

"Let me see on my radar." Crossing below them on a course
almost perpendicular were four parallel contrails gliding out from
jet engines as though extruded in chalk. "It's an airliner, McWatt.
A passenger plane on the way to Australia."

"I wonder how those passengers would feel if they knew we
were up here on this mission again . . . ghost riders in the sky."

"McWatt?"

"Sampson?"

"Do we really have to go in again?"

"I guess we have to, don't we?"

"Do we?"

"Yeah."

"Yeah. I think we have to."

"Oh, well. What the hell."

Sam Singer had no illusions. Unlike Yossarian, he had no hopes of finding romance and falling in love again with somebody new. Succumbing unresistingly to the harsh necessity of living alone, to which he had been presented with no agreeable alternative, he had not been shattered by the merciless deprivations. He had discussed this future with Glenda, who, despite her terminal condition, worried more about his solitary years ahead than he had been able to do.

He saw friends, read more, watched television news. He had New York. He went to plays and movies, occasionally to opera, used to always have engaging classical music on one of the FM radio stations, played bridge one or two evenings most weeks in neighborly communal groups of people largely like himself who were mostly even-tempered and congenial. Each time he listened to Gustav Mahler's Fifth Symphony he was filled with awe and amazed. He had his volunteer work with the cancer relief agency. He had his few female friends. He drank no more than before. He learned quickly to eat by himself, carry-out dishes at home, lunches and dinners in neighborhood coffee shops and small restaurants, meals that were not feasts, reading too at a table alone, his book or magazine or his second newspaper of the day. Occasionally, he played pinochle with others left over from Coney Island. He still was not good. He went out evenings about as often as he wished to.

He was greatly pleased so far on his trip around the world, greatly surprised by his feeling of well-being and his large amounts of satisfaction. It was good again to be out of his apartment. In Atlanta and Houston with his daughters and their husbands and children he had at last reached a stage at which he found himself sated with their company before any of them showed signs of growing restless with his. He must be feeling his age, he offered in apology early each evening, before departing for the night. He insisted always on staying in nearby hotels. In Los Angeles he was

still in lifelong harmony with Winkler and his wife. They all three
tired in perfect coordination. He had a few good dates with his
nephew and his family and was genuinely charmed by the preco-
cious brightness and beauty of the children. But between himself
and all the young adults with whom he found himself, he had to
concede that more than a generation gap divided them.

Once outside New York, he was thankful he had taken his
cassette player and tapes and some books of solid content that
demanded studious involvement.

In Hawaii he sunned himself in daytime and finished rereading
Middlemarch. Knowing better what to expect, he was able to
appreciate it richly. In his two evenings there he had dinner with
the former wife of his old friend and her present husband, and
with the woman, now single, he'd worked with at *Time* magazine,
with whom Glenda had been acquainted too. Had she invited
him home to spend the night with her, he would have certainly
consented. But she did not seem to know that. Lew or Yossarian
would have managed it better.

He looked forward keenly to the two weeks in Australia with
old good friends, also from his days back at *Time*. He had no
hesitation about staying in their house in Sydney. He and Glenda
had been there together one time before. The man walked with
metal canes. A long time had passed since they'd last come to New
York. In the narrow pool outdoors, on the harbor side of the
house, he would swim thirty or sixty laps before breakfast—Sam
was not sure he remembered which—and another thirty or sixty
soon after, keeping his torso hefty enough to continue moving
about on the canes and in the car with hand controls he'd been
using since the illness that had rendered him paraplegic forty years
back. From the hips up he probably would still have the brawny
body of a weight lifter. They had five grown children. Sam was
eager to see them again too. One was in agriculture in Tasmania,
and they planned to fly there for two days. Another ranched, a
third did work in genetics in a laboratory in the university in
Canberra. All five were married. None had been divorced.

Sam left Hawaii on an Australian airliner in dead of night and
was scheduled to arrive in Sydney after breakfast the next morning. He read, he drank, he ate, he slept and wakened. Daybreak
came stealing in with a dingy dawn, and the sun seemed slow in
rising. Clouds lay unbroken below. What light appeared remained
sunken on a low horizon and continued dim. To one side of him

the sky was navy blue, with a full yellow moon hanging low and distant like a hostile clock; on the other, the sky looked gray and black, almost the color of charcoal. High above, he saw snowy contrails cross the path of his own plane, in a ghostly formation traveling eastward at a speed more swift, and assumed they came from a military group on morning maneuvers. There was some consternation in the cabin crew when the radio system first went silent. But the other navigational systems remained operational, and there was no cause for alarm. Earlier there was a vague news report of an oil tanker colliding with a cargo ship somewhere below.

Sam Singer soon had going on his cassette player a tape of the Fifth Symphony of Gustav Mahler. Listening again, he discovered more new things he treasured. The remarkable symphony was infinite in its secrets and multiple satisfactions, ineffable in loveliness, sublime, and hauntingly mysterious in the secrets of its powers and genius to so touch the human soul. He could hardly wait for the closing notes of the finale to speed jubilantly to their triumphant end, in order to start right back at the beginning and revel again in all of the engrossing movements in which he was basking now. Although he knew it was coming and always prepared himself, he was expectantly bewitched each time by the mournful sweet melody filtering so gently into the foreboding horns opening the first movement, so sweetly mournful and Jewish. The small adagio movement later was as beautiful as beautiful melodic music ever could be. Mostly of late in music he preferred the melancholy to the heroic. His biggest fear now in the apartment in which he dwelt alone was a horror of decomposing there. The book he was holding in his lap when he settled back to read while listening was a paperback edition of eight stories by Thomas Mann. The yellow moon turned orange and soon was as red as a setting sun.

Acknowledgments

If I hadn't thought it better to present this novel without introductory statements, I would have dedicated it to Valerie, my wife, and again, as at first, to my daughter, Erica, and my son, Ted. I would have extended the dedication to Marvin and Evelyn Winkler, husband and wife, and to Marion Berkman and the memory of her husband, Lou—friends since childhood to whom I feel thankful for more than their encouragement, assistance, and cooperation.

Michael Korda proved a formidable and perfect editor for me, responsive, critical, blunt, appreciative.

One chapter of this novel, by droll coincidence the one titled "Dante," was prepared and written while I was a resident guest at Lake Como, Italy, at the Bellagio Study and Conference Center of the Rockefeller Foundation. The enjoyments and conveniences there were inimitable, and we, Valerie and I, remain grateful to all involved for the hospitality and work facilities and for the warm friendships we made with fellow residents that are still maintained.

Also available from the

"A long-overdue contribution to understanding and delighting in the mind and work of a writer who changed the language and the concept of inanity and war."
—*The Baltimore Sun*

CATCH AS CATCH CAN, 0-7432-5793-6

"Manic, knockdown, verbal comedy."
—*The Washington Post*

CLOSING TIME, 0-684-80450-6

"Heller has never been as entertaining."
—*People*

GOOD AS GOLD, 0-684-83974-1

"So inspired and funny.... It exceeds the achievement of Heller's *Catch-22*."
—*Chicago Tribune*

GOD KNOWS, 0-684-84125-8

"Richly amusing... positively cheering."
—*The New York Times*

NO LAUGHING MATTER, 0-7432-4717-5

author of *Catch-22*...